DRAGON

&

ISSOLA

STEVEN BRUST

DRAGON

&

ISSOLA

FANTASY

This is a work of fiction. All the characters and events portrayed in this novel are either fictitious or are used fictitiously.

DRAGON Copyright © 1998 by Steven Brust
    Originally published in hardcover by Tor Books, November 1998
ISSOLA Copyright © 2001 by Steven Brust
    Originally published in hardcover by Tor Books, July 2001

First SFBC Fantasy Printing: February 2001

Published by arrangement with:
Tom Doherty Associates, Inc.
175 Fifth Avenue
New York, NY 10010

Visit The SFBC online at *http://www.sfbc.com*
Visit Tor online at *http://www.tor.com*
Visit Steven Brust's website at *http://www.dreamcafe.com*

ISBN # 0-7394-2031-3

Printed in the United States of America

Contents

DRAGON

This book was written for my dear friend, Geri Sullivan, who rocked the whole album cover situation.

ACKNOWLEDGMENTS

Thanks to the following people who were of great help with research: Corwin Brust, Gail Catherine, Paul Knappenberger, Beki Oshiro, and Gypsy.

Thanks also to Emma Bull, Raphael Carter, Pamela Dean, and Will Shetterly for helpful suggestions and general Scribblification; to Fred A. Levy Haskell for last-minute proofing; to Liz, Beki, Cyndi, and Tesla for chocolate, first reactions, and Stuff; and to Patrick and Teresa for many things, but especially for the Staten Island Ferry.

It's high time I acknowledged and thanked Steve Bond, Reen Brust, John Robey, and John Stanley: You Know Who You Are.

Always and ever, my thanks to Adrian Morgan, whose fingerprints are on every page of every book I've written about Dragaera.

And special thanks to Stephen Jones of Wembly, England, who first suggested this one.

When all is in harmony the army can withstand natural attacks and those that appear to be supernatural.

Sun Tzu. *The Art of War*

1

MEMORY IS LIKE A WATCHACALLIT

No shit, there I was. . . .

We'd been cut up so many ways and so many times we hardly had a skirmish line, and the enemy kept getting reinforced. I, like the rest of the outfit, was exhausted and terrified from swords buzzing past my ear and various sorts of sorceries going "whoosh" over my head, or maybe it was the other way around; and there were dead people moaning and writhing on the ground, and wounded people lying still, and that was almost certainly the other way around, but I'm giving it to you as I remember it, though I know my memory sometimes plays tricks on me.

More on that in a second.

First, I have to ask you to excuse me for starting in the middle, but that's more or less where it starts.

So there I was, in a full-scale battle; that is, in a place where no self-respecting assassin ought to be. Worse, in a full-scale battle with the keen sense that I was on the losing side, at least in this part of the engagement. I stood on Dorian's Hill, with the Wall about two hundred yards behind me, and the Tomb (which is not a tomb, and never was, and ought not to be called that) about a quarter of a mile to my left. I wanted to teleport out, or at least run, but I couldn't because, well, I just couldn't. I had a sword, and I carried enough other weaponry to outfit half of Cropper Company (my unit, hurrah hurrah). In front of us was The Enemy, getting closer with each step, and looking like this time they meant to stay. There were so many of them, and all I could think of was, "If they want this damned hill so badly, let them have it," but I knew that was wrong, and certainly my messmates would have argued with the sentiment; we'd worked hard enough to take it away from them the first time. (And we had failed. So why did we now occupy the hill? I don't know; they don't explain these things to foot soldiers.)

Then, as if that wasn't bad enough, I heard the rip of the juice-drum playing "Time To Be Alive," which meant to form up for a charge. I guessed the Captain had decided we weren't strong enough to defend, or else he wanted to go out in a blaze of glory. I don't know: it seemed to me that if you already had the high ground, why waste it by charging? I wanted to call him an idiot but I knew he wasn't.

I relaxed my grip on my sword and took the requisite Three Deep Breaths as he positioned himself in front of us. I found myself right next to Dunn, the alternate bannerman, which put my life expectancy at just marginally above his, and his was just about the same as the bannerman, and *hers* was mathematically almost indistinguishable from zero. Well, they had both wanted the job; now they had it.

The Captain gave no speeches this time; I guess he'd said everything he had to say over the last couple of days. He gave the signal that started us moving forward.

As before, I discovered that I was moving, although I don't remember ever deciding to; I wondered, as I had several times before, if there was some sort of subtle magic involved, but I don't think so. I recall that I really, really, *really* wanted to bolt, but I still couldn't, so of course I did the only thing I could: I started praying. It was far too late for that, however, and nothing happened.

Or maybe something did; I'm not sure.

Oh yeah, I was going to talk about memory. Maybe memory is where it starts. I don't know where it starts; that's part of why I'm doing this, hoping to put it together and make some kind of sense out of the whole thing. Of course, the gold ingots are a bigger part of why I'm doing this. Where was I? Right, memory.

I woke up one morning remembering something I'd forgotten the day before. I'd been having a one-sided conversation with a metal box, much as I'm doing now, in exchange for a good sum of raw gold and various useful oddities and trinkets, and I'd felt like I'd fulfilled my part of the bargain, but then, the morning after I finished, I realized what I'd forgotten, and my first thought was that someone had been playing with my memories. My second thought was that, if this were true, I was going to hurt someone. My third thought was to consider, if someone *was* repressing my memories, who that someone had to be. This was chilling, and it brought me fully awake, which led to one of those irritating sessions of "How much was a dream?" After several minutes I had it sorted out in my head so I got up.

Loiosh, my familiar, was just stirring. He gave his bat-like wings one lazy flap, hissed at me sleepily, and said, *"How 'bout something to eat?"* into my mind.

I said, *"Do you remember Deathgate Falls?"*

"No. I'm senile. Of course I remember—"

"As you approach the Falls, do you remember there being a large statue?"

"Sure, Boss. Where Morrolan performed that embarrassing ritual. What about it?"

"Nothing." Right. The ritual. I had forgotten that, too. I hate having disturbing thoughts before breakfast. I hate having thoughts before breakfast.

"Is it important, Boss?"

"Let it go, Loiosh."

That was then, and it illustrates what a tricky thing memory is: I had forgotten something important that had happened just days before, yet now, more than three years later, I remember waking up and talking to Loiosh about it. Interesting, isn't it?

But here, I've left you, you odd, shiny contraption with presumed ears at both ends, confused about who and what I am, and generally what I'm on about. Okay. I'll let you stay confused a little longer, and if you don't trust me to clear everything up, then you can go hang. I've been paid.

I whipped up a quick omelet, ate it, and washed up, considering whether to ask someone about my odd memory lapse. I'd made two acquaintances recently who might know, but I felt loath to ask them; something about expressing weakness, I suppose. But it bothered me. I was still thinking about it when I finished donning my Jhereg colors (grey and black, if you're taking notes) and making sure my various weapons were in place; after which I stepped out onto the street I all but owned.

I don't usually travel with a bodyguard. For one thing, it would be hard to find anyone who could give me more warning of danger than Loiosh; for another, I'm not important enough to be a real threat to anyone; and for yet another, it's humiliating. I know that to some in the Organization the number of bodyguards is a status symbol, but to me they are only an irritation.

But I'm different. I wasn't born into the Organization. I wasn't even born into House Jhereg. In fact, I wasn't born a citizen; I'm human. They aren't. This is enough of a difference that it can explain all others.

So you can look around as I did. See the Teckla running around like the small rodents they are named for, doing things they think are important, selecting fruits at the fruit stands or pieces of fabric from the weavers, laying a bet with the local bookmaker, rushing to work in a garden or at a weaver's, and, directly or indirectly, feeding me. See the Chreotha or the Jhegaala, with titles of the nobility but lives of the bourgeois selling the fabric or the fruit or buying brain-drugs or trying to get a bargain from the local fence and, directly or indirectly, feeding me. And, rarest of all, see the nobles themselves, strutting about like Issola in spring, scattering pennies to the paupers, having servants buy select wines and the more exotic brain-drugs, and, directly or indirectly, feeding me.

It's surprising that I stay so thin.

None of them gave me any special regard as I strolled by for another day of extracting from them everything I could. I like it that way.

The walk from flat to office was short, yet it was enough time for me to get a feel for what was going on in the neighborhood; on that day there was nothing worth noting—not the least clue, as it were, of the events that had already been set in motion. I arrived, as I recall, early that day. The Jhereg operates all day, but the real action is mostly at night, so things get started correspondingly late; I rarely see my office before noon. That day I arrived before my secretary, hung my cloak on the cloak-rack, set my rapier against the wall, and sat down at my desk to see what, if any, correspondence had arrived during the morning.

There was one item: a piece of expensive parchment sat in the middle of my desk; on it, in a neat, elegant hand, was written, "V. Taltos, Baronet." I picked it up and inspected the back, which showed a Dragonshead seal.

I set it down again and considered before opening it. I may have been a bit afraid of what it would say. No, I most certainly was afraid of what it would say. I picked it up and broke the seal before Loiosh could start on me.

> Baronet—
> It would give me great pleasure to see you again. It may also prove profitable for you. If you would like assistance in transportation, you may inquire of Baron Lokran e'Terics at the House of the Dragon. Arrive today between noon and the tenth hour, and I will take the time to see you at once.
> I Remain, my dear sir,
> Cordially
> Morrolan e'Drien
> P.S.: You expressed a preference for a formal invitation over our last method of asking for your help; I hope this meets with your approval—M.

I set the letter down again and thought about many things.

As always when dealing with Morrolan, I didn't quite know how to take him. He calls his home Castle Black, which is either pretentious to the point of being silly, or a just and reasonable statement of his power; take your pick. He was unusual—perhaps "unique" would be a better word—in that he was a Dragaeran, and a Dragonlord no less, who studied Eastern witchcraft, which either showed that he did not share his compatriots' attitude toward humans, or showed that he was so contemptuous of us that he could offhandedly learn our secret arts; take your pick. The "last method" he referred to had been offensive enough that we had almost killed each other over it, so this reference was either a nasty cut or a peace offering; take your pick.

However, it never occurred to me not to accept his invitation.

"We're going to Castle Black, Loiosh."

"I can hardly wait, Boss. When?"

I consulted the Imperial Orb through my psychic link. It was less than an hour before noon.

"Now," I told him.

I strapped my rapier back on, not terribly reassured by its weight hanging at my side and the scabbard's tapping against my leg. Melestav, my secretary, was just arriving. He seemed startled to see me. I said, "I have an errand. If you never see me again, blame Morrolan of the House of the Dragon. See you."

I stepped back out onto the street—the first steps, as it were, that began the journey that led me toward war and death. I hired a cabriolet to cut down on the number of actual steps involved. I gave the runner no particular attention, but I tipped him well. This is probably significant of something.

The House of the Dragon faces the Imperial Palace, just a bit west of north, and is marked by a forty-foot-high marble likeness of Kieron the Conqueror holding his greatsword in one hand, its point off to the East; seeing it makes my arm tired. There is no discernible expression on Kieron's face, at least from below. There are (surprise surprise) seventeen steps up to the doors, which were standing open when I arrived, a bit footsore, just about noon.

When you enter the House of the Dragon, you are in the Great Hall, a vast, huge, booming, echoing place with murals on the walls depicting violence, skinny windows that don't let much light in, a marble floor, a single, very wide stairway planted in the middle of the Hall and running up out of sight, and many tiny hanging lamps way, way up on the ceiling where they do no good at all and probably require levitation to service; yet there is sufficient light to see the murals, begging the question of how they actually illuminate the place.

I didn't much care for it.

I hadn't been surrounded by so many Dragonlords since I was arrested after the death of my previous boss, and I didn't like this a lot more than I liked that. They were standing in groups and were all of them armed. They were talking quietly, I suppose, but the place echoed horribly so it seemed awash with noise. There was grey bunting draped here and there, which meant that someone had died. I stood there like an idiot for a long, long time—say half a minute—with Loiosh on my shoulder, and then noticed a pair of sentries, on either of side the door—that is, either side of me—and observed that they were staring at me with decidedly unfriendly expressions. This made me feel much more comfortable, because I'd rather be hated than ignored.

I approached the man because the height of the woman would have put my eyes at breast-level and this didn't seem to be the right time for that. I put some jaunt into my step because Dragonlords, like many wild animals, can smell fear. He looked down at me (my eyes were level with his collar bone) and kept his eyes away from Loiosh; he probably thought I'd get too much satisfaction out of seeing him react to the Jhereg on my shoulder, and he was right. I said, "I seek Baron Lokran."

The Dragonlord swallowed, clenched his jaw, and said, "Who are you?"

I thought about making an issue of the question, but I didn't know the protocol and I didn't like the odds. "Vladimir Taltos of House Jhereg, on an errand for Lord Morrolan e'Drien." That should shut him up.

It did. "Up the stairs, straight back, last door on the left. Clap and enter."

I sketched a bow, resisting the temptation to make it over-elaborate.

"What are you afraid of, Boss?"

"Shut up, Loiosh."

The steps were set too high for my comfort, making it a challenge to climb casually with, I assumed, the eyes of the two Dragonlords on my back. I managed as best I could. My footsteps echoed, and the stairway went on for much too long. When I finally reached the top I walked straight back to the end of a hallway longer than the building that houses my entire operation. It ended in a large door which I ignored; instead stopping at the one to my left, as directed. One clap and I entered.

Lokran turned; he had, apparently, been staring out the window. He was young, with bright eyes, and had a faded white scar above his brows—the scar obviously had some sort of sentimental value for him or he'd have had it removed. His hair was dark, straight, and brushed back in almost a Jhereg-cut. He had rings on four fingers of each hand, and the rings all had jewels in them. The room held four stuffed chairs, a sofa, and no desk; a plain grey banner hung above the window. Three or four short, black staves were leaning against the far wall, and a heavy sword in a black sheath stood next to them.

His eyes narrowed briefly when I entered, then he said, "Taltos?" pronouncing it correctly.

I bowed and said, "Lokran?"

He nodded. "Come a little closer."

I did.

He gestured casually in my direction, as if he were brushing away an insect, and my bowels twisted, and I was in the courtyard of Castle Black, standing, as far as I could tell, on thin air that felt like a hard surface, say flagstones, but looked like nothing was holding me up. Just like that. He could have bloody warned me.

I've given a lot of thought to the question of why teleports upset my stomach; why they seem to have that effect on all Easterners, but not on Dragaerans. In between teleports, I've often decided it is all in the imagination of the Easterner, but right after a teleport I've found that answer unsatisfying. The explanation that sprang to mind as I stood before Morrolan's castle, surrounded by his walls, towers, and guards, is that teleports also upset the Dragaeran stomach, but Dragaerans just won't admit it; how can having your innards flop around so violently that you can *feel* them sloshing *not* make you queasy? Could natural selection account for it? I don't buy it; I just don't think that nature had it in mind for people to get from one place to another without passing through the intervening area.

These thoughts, I should explain, were one way I occupied my mind while I gave my stomach time to settle down. Another way was to observe that the sentries in the towers were watching me, although they didn't seem especially surprised. Okay, so I was expected. Over one tower floated a single banner, all of grey.

Eventually I risked a look down. There were trees below me that looked like miniature bushes, and the two roads and one stream were lines of brown and blue respectively, meeting and crossing and running almost parallel to form a design that, if I tried, I could convince myself was a mark in some runic alphabet. Maybe it was a symbol that told the castle, "Don't fall down." That was a comforting thought.

I adjusted my cloak, ran a hand through my hair, and approached the double doors of Castle Black. They swung open as I approached, which I should have been expecting, because they'd done the same thing last time. I cursed under my breath but kept a small smile on my lips and didn't break stride—there were Dragonlords watching.

I hadn't noticed it the last time, but one reason that it is so effective to see Lady Teldra appear when the doors open is that she is all you can see—the entryway is unlit, and except for her you might be entering the void that one imagines as the land of the dead. (The land of the dead, however, is not a void—it's worse. But never mind.)

"My Lord Taltos," said Teldra. "Thank you for gracing our home. The Lord awaits you. Please, enter and be welcome."

I felt welcome in spite of my more cynical side whispering, "Whatever."

I crossed the threshold. Lady Teldra did not offer to take my cloak this time. She guided me into the hall with all the paintings, through it, up the wide, curving stairway, and eventually to the library. It was big and full of stuffed chairs and thick books; three of the books, sitting just beyond the entrance, were massive jewel-encrusted objects each chained to a pedestal; I wondered but resolved not to ask. As I entered, Morrolan set a book down and stood up, giving me a small bow.

He opened his mouth, probably to make some sort of ironic courtesy, as a counterpoint to Teldra's sincere one, but I said, "Who died?" before he could get the words out. He shut his mouth, glanced at Loiosh, and nodded toward a chair next to his. I sat down.

He said, "Baritt."

I said, "Oh."

Morrolan seemed to want me to say something, so eventually I said, "You know, the first time I met him I had the feeling he wouldn't be—"

"Do not joke about it, Vlad."

"All right. What do you want me to say? I didn't get the impression he was a friend of yours."

"He wasn't."

"Well?"

Lady Teldra appeared with refreshment—a white wine that would have been too sweet except that it was served over chunks of ice. I sipped it to be polite the first time, and then discovered I liked it. The Issola glided from the room. There was no table on which to set the goblet down, but the chair had wide, flat arms. Very convenient.

"Well?" I repeated.

"In the second place," said Morrolan, "he was an important man. And in the first place—"

"He was a Dragon," I concluded. "Yeah, I know."

Morrolan nodded. I drank some more wine. The sensation of cold helps reduce the sensation of sweetness. I bet you didn't know that.

"So, what happened to the poor bastard?"

Morrolan started to answer, then paused, then said, "It is unimportant."

"All right," I agreed. "It is unimportant to me, in any case." I had met Baritt, or, more properly, his shade, in the Paths of the Dead. He had taken an instant dislike to Morrolan because Morrolan had the bad taste to be traveling with me, which should give you an idea of how Baritt and I had hit it off.

I continued, "I assume it isn't a request for sympathy that led to your invitation."

"You are correct."

"Well?"

He turned his head to the side and looked at me quizzically. "What is it you gave me, Vlad?"

I laughed. "Is that it? Is that what this is all about?"

"Actually, no. I'm just curious."

"Oh. Well, remain curious." I had, in fact, injected him with the blood of a goddess for reasons too complicated to explain now, and, at the time, I was in no condition to explain anything.

"As you wish. Baritt, as I say, died. In going through his possessions—"

"What? Already? He can't have been brought to Deathgate yet."

"And—?"

"Well, that seems awful quick for you long-lived types."

"There are reasons."

"You're just full of information, aren't you?"

"Were I to tell you matters pertaining to the internal politics of the House of the Dragon I should only weary you. And I should then have to kill you for knowing. So my thought was not to trouble you with such information."

"A good thought," I said.

Loiosh shifted on my shoulder, evidently getting restless. "As I was saying, in going through his possessions, certain items were discovered."

He stopped. I waited. He resumed.

"He had a large collection of Morganti weapons. A *large* collection. Hundreds of them."

I repressed a shiver. "I suppose the reason he had them is none of my business, too."

"That is correct. And, in any case, I don't know."

"Well then, what about them?"

"I spent a good portion of yesterday inspecting them. I have an interest in such things."

"Figures."

His eyes narrowed for a moment, then he evidently decided to ignore it. "Such weapons," he went on, "represent power. Some covet power, some are threatened by others coveting power."

"Which are you?"

"The former."

"I knew that," I said. "I didn't expect you to admit it."

"Why not?"

I couldn't answer that so I didn't. "Go on," I said. "Who's the enemy?"

"You are perspicacious."

"Yeah, but my physicker says it can be treated."

"*He means you're perceptive, Boss.*"

"*I know that, Loiosh.*"

"Yes," said Morrolan. "I believe that I am likely to come into conflict with someone over possession of these weapons."

"Who might that be?"

"I don't know. There are several possibilities. The likeliest is— well, it doesn't matter."

"That's helpful."

"For what I want from you, you don't need to know."

"That's fortunate. Well, what do you want then?"

"I want you to arrange for the stolen weapons to be traced."

"Some weapons have been stolen?"

"Not yet," he said.

"I see. How certain are you?"

"Reasonably."

"Why?"

"That, too, is unimportant. I will be protecting them, as will various others. Whoever wishes to steal one or more will have to hire an expert thief, and that means the Jhereg, and that means—"

"I might be able to find out what's become of it. I see."

"Boss, this could get you into trouble."

"I know."

I sat back and looked at Morrolan. He held my gaze. After a moment I said, "That isn't at all the sort of thing I'm any good at, Morrolan. And, to tell you the truth, if I did find out, I don't believe I could bring myself to tell you. It's a Jhereg thing, you know?"

"I believe I do, yes." He frowned and seemed to be considering. "On the other hand," he said, "if I understand how you—that is, how the Jhereg—work, whoever did the stealing would be unlikely to be more than a tool, hired by someone else, is that correct?"

"Yes," I said, not terribly happy about where this was going.

"Well then, could you find out—"

"Maybe," I admitted.

"What would it take?"

"Money. A lot of it."

"I have money."

"I still want to think about it. It could put me into a situation I'm not certain I'd like."

"I understand. Do think about it, though. I can offer you—"

"Don't tell me. I'd rather not be tempted. I'll let you know."

He nodded and didn't press the issue, which earned him some points with me.

"There's another matter," he said.

I bit back irony and waited.

"The circumstances of Baritt's death—"

"Which are none of my business."

"—have, among other things, made me aware of the vulnerability of Castle Black."

"I beg your pardon?"

"The circumstances of—"

"I heard you, I just don't understand. How is a castle floating half a mile or more in the air vulnerable? Other than to falling down, of course."

"That isn't likely."

"I'm glad to hear it. Which reminds me, why don't my ears pop when I teleport up?"

He looked smug but didn't tell me. "Obviously," he said, "the castle can be penetrated by anyone who can teleport and conceal himself from my guards."

"You don't have any security precautions?"

"Some, but not enough. It seems to me you could be of some assistance in telling me where to improve them."

I thought it over, and realized that I knew exactly how to go about it. "Yes, I can do that." I considered asking about payment, but on reflection calculated that it would be more profitable to do a good job and allow him to display his generosity.

He frowned for a moment, and seemed lost in thought.

"Psychic communication, Boss."

"I knew that, Loiosh."

"You're a liar, Boss."

"Well, yeah."

At about that time, a Dragonlord entered the room and bowed to Morrolan. He was short and rather stocky for a Dragaeran, with short, light-brown hair and pale eyes; he didn't strike me as a fighter, but he wore a blade, which meant he was on duty in some capacity.

Morrolan said, "Fentor, this is Baronet Vladimir Taltos. I know you are willing to work with Easterners, but are you willing to take orders from a Jhereg?"

Fentor said, "My lord?"

Loiosh said, *"What did he say?"*

I said, "Errgh?"

Morrolan said, "I've just hired Lord Taltos as a security consultant. That puts you in his charge, under certain circumstances."

I felt my mouth open and close. Morrolan had what? And when had he done this?

Fentor said, "That will not be a problem, my lord."

"Good," said Morrolan.

"Excuse me," I said.

"Yes?"

"I . . ."

"Yes?"

"Never mind. A pleasure, Fentor."

"The same, my lord."

"Boss, you've just been hired."

"Well, yeah. Recruited, actually."

"You should tell him to never use this power in the service of evil."

"I'll be sure to."

It occurred to me, also, that it was going to be harder, now that I was more or less working for him, to avoid trying to get the information he was after. Of course, maybe I'd get lucky, and no one would steal any of the weapons. Something made me doubt this.

Fentor bowed cordially to us both and made his exit.

I said, "Morrolan, what aren't you telling me?"

"Many things."

"In particular. I get the feeling that you aren't just generally worried about someone stealing some random Morganti weapon."

"You should trust your feelings; they seem to be reliable."

"Thank you so much."

He stood abruptly and said, "Come with me, Vlad. I'll show you around and introduce you to a few people."

"I can hardly wait," I said.

I got up and followed him.

2

CROSSING LINES

Do you know what a battlefield smells like? If so, you have my sympathy; if not, you still won't, because I have no intention of dwelling on it except to say that people don't smell so good on the inside.

We stepped over the piles of dirt (I can't call it a "bulwark" with a straight face) that we'd spent so much time and sweat creating, and moved forward at a steady pace; not too fast, not too slow. No, come to think of it, *much* too fast. A slow crawl would have been much too fast.

I adjusted my uniform sash, which was the only mark I carried to show which side I was on, since I'd lost my cute little cap somewhere during the last couple of attacks. About half of the company had lost their cute little caps, and many of the enemy had, too. But we all had sashes, which identified the side we were on, like the ribbons that identify sandball teams. I never played sandball. I'd seen Dragons playing sandball in West Side Park, alongside of Teckla, though never in the same game at the same time, and certainly not on the same team. Make of that what you will.

"*Have you thought about getting up in the air and away from this?*" I asked my familiar for the fifth time.

"*I've thought about it,*" he answered for the fourth (the first time he hadn't made any response at all, so I'd had to repeat the question; we'd only sustained three attacks hitherto). And, "*How did we get into this, anyway?*" I'd lost count of how many times he'd asked me that; not as many as I'd asked myself.

We moved forward.

How *did* we get ourselves into this?

I asked Sethra, not long ago, why she ordered us to hold that position, which never looked terribly important from where I sat— except to me, of course, for personal reasons that I'll go into later. She said, "For the same reason I had Gutrin's spear phalanx attack that little dale to your left. By holding that spot, you threatened an entire flank, and I needed to freeze a portion of the enemy's reserves. As long as you kept threatening that position, he had to either re- inforce it or remain ready to reinforce it. That way I could wait for the right time and place to commit *my* reserves, which I did when—"

"All right, all right," I said. "Never mind."

I hadn't wanted a technical answer, I'd wanted her to say "It was vital to the entire campaign." I wanted to have had a more important role. We were one piece on the board, and only as important as any other. All the pieces wish to be, if not a player, at least the piece the players are most concerned with.

Not being a player was one of the things that bothered me. I was, I suppose, only a piece and not a player when I would carry out the order of one of my Jhereg superiors, but I had been running my own territory for a short while at that point, and had already become used to it. That was part of the problem: In the Jhereg, I was, if not a commander-in-chief, at least a high ranking field officer. Here, I was, well, I guess I was a number of things, but put them all together and they still didn't amount to much.

But how *did* we get ourselves into this? There were no great prin- ciples involved. I mean, you judge a war according to who is in the right as long as you have no interest in the outcome; if you're one of the participants, or if the result is going to have a major effect on you, then you have to create the moral principles that put you in the right—that's nothing new, everyone knows it. But this one was so *raw*. No one could even come up with a good mask to put over it. It was over land, and power, and who got to expand where, without even the thinnest veneer of anything else.

Those veneers can be important when you're marching down toward rows of nasty pointy things.

Baritt died, that's what started it all. And Morrolan convinced me to set up a trap to find out who would be likely to steal what I preferred not to come anywhere near. Kragar, my lieutenant in the organization, looked worried when I told him about it, but I'm sure even he, who knew Dragons better than I ever would, had no clue how it would end up.

"What if someone does steal one, and you find out who," he said, "and it turns out to be someone you don't want to mess with?"

"That, of course, is the question. But it seems unlikely to be a Jhereg behind it."

"No, Vlad, it will be a Dragon. That's the problem."

Well, he was a Dragon; he should know. No, he wasn't a Dragon, he was a Jhereg, but he should still know. He had once been a Dragon, which meant—what?

I studied Kragar. I knew him better than I knew anyone I didn't know at all. We'd worked together as enforcers when I first entered the Jhereg, and we'd been working together ever since. He was the only Dragaeran I didn't hate, except maybe Kiera. Come to think of it, I didn't understand her, either.

Kragar was courageous, and timid, warmhearted, and vicious, and easygoing, and dedicated, and friendly, and utterly ruthless; as well as having the strange ability, or shortcoming, to blend into the wood-work so completely one could be staring right at him without realizing he was there.

I couldn't remember a single idea of mine that he hadn't thrown cold water on, nor a single one that he hadn't backed me on to the hilt—literally, in some cases.

"What is it?" he said.

"I was ruminating."

"Shouldn't you do that in private?"

"Oh, is someone here?"

"You're a riot, Vlad."

"In any case," I said, picking up the conversation from where it was lying in the middle of the floor, "there's a lot of money in it."

Kragar made a sound I won't attempt to describe. I could sense Loiosh holding back several remarks. It seems I surround myself with people who think I'm an idiot, which probably says something deep and profound about me.

"So," I said, "who do we put on it?"

"I don't know. We should probably go over there ourselves and look things over."

"I was afraid you'd say that."

He gave me a puzzled glance that went away quickly. There are matters on which Dragaerans and humans will never understand one another, and soul-killing weapons are, evidently, one of those. I mean, they hate them as much as or more than we do; but Dragaerans don't usually have the sort of overwhelming dread that such weapons inspire in a human. I don't know why that is.

"How do we get there?"

"I'll hire a coach."

Baritt had lived in a square, grey stone building on the outskirts of Adrilankha, in the hills to the west. He probably called it a castle. I could call my tunic a chair if I wanted to. It had three stories, a large front door, a couple of servants' entrances, a few glass windows, and a sharply sloped roof. His estate struck me as too rocky, and the soil too sandy, to be good for much. There was peasant activity, but not a great deal. There were a pair of guards in front of the main door, in the livery of the House of the Dragon. As Kragar and I approached, I saw one was wearing the same emblem that Morrolan's people sported; the other had a badge I didn't recognize.

I rehearsed the conversation I was about to have with them. I won't share it with you because the actual conversation disrupted my plans.

"Baronet Taltos?" said the one wearing Morrolan's badge.

I nodded.

"Please enter."

Trust me: The conversation I'd been prepared for would have been much more fun to relate. But there was compensation. The guard said, "Wait—who is he?" noticing Kragar for the first time.

"My associate," I said, keeping my chuckle on the inside.

"Very well," he said.

I glanced at the other guard, who was busy being expressionless. I wondered who he worked for.

Kragar and I passed within.

Rarely upon crossing a threshold have I been struck by such a sensation of entering a different world—I mean it felt as if between one step and another I had left Dragaera and entered a place at least as foreign as my Eastern ancestral homeland. The first surprise was that, after passing by the stone entryway of the stone house, you reached a foyer that was full of blown glass—vases, candelabra, empty decanters, and other glasswork were displayed on dark wooden pedestals or in cabinets. The walls were painted some color that managed to squeak in between white and yellow where no color ought to live, making everything seem bright and cheery and entirely at odds with any Dragonlord I'd ever met or heard of—and certainly with the Baritt I'd met in the Paths of the Dead.

My reverie was interrupted by Kragar saying, "Uh . . . Boss? Where are we going?"

"Good question." Most sorcerers would work either in a basement, where it's most reasonable to put any heavy objects they might need, or up in a tower, where there is less risk of wiping out the whole house if something goes wrong. In Baritt's case, probably some random room in a random place because it was convenient.

Loiosh moved nervously on my shoulder. We left the foyer and entered a sitting room of some sort, with more blown glass and decanters just like the others except full. On the wall to my left was a large oil of Baritt, looking imposing and dignified. There was a small door at the far end that should have led to the kitchen, and hallways heading off to the right and the left; one would presumably lead up a set of stairs to the bedchambers, the other to the rest of this floor. We took the one to the right and found a wide, straight stairway of polished white stone. We went back and tried the other hall, which looked more promising.

"Hey, Boss."

"Yeah, Loiosh?"

"There's something funny. I'm getting a feeling. It's like—"

"We're being watched, Vlad," said Kragar.

"Not really surprising," I said.

"I noticed first."

"Shut up."

"Ignore it, I think," I told Kragar. "It would be odd if no one had any surveillance spells. Should we try that door?"

"The big ironbound one with the rune carved on it, barred by a pair of Dragonlords with spears crossed in front of it? Why should it be that one?"

"You're funny, Kragar. Shut up, Kragar."

"Who are you, and what is your business?" said one of the guards, standing like a statue, her spear not moving from its position in front of the door.

"You know both answers," I told her.

She twitched a smile, which made me like her. "Yeah, but I have to ask. And you have to answer. Or you could leave. Or I could kill you."

"Baronet Taltos, House Jhereg, on an errand from Lord Morrolan, and for a minute there I liked you."

"I'm crushed," she said. Her spear snapped to her side; her companion's also moved, and the way was clear. She said, "Be informed that there is a teleport block in place around the house in general, and that it has been strengthened for that room."

"Is that a polite way of telling me not to try to steal anything?"

"I hadn't intended to be polite," she said.

I said, "Let's go."

"After you," said Kragar. Both guards twitched and then looked at him, as if they hadn't noticed him before, which they probably hadn't. Then they pretended they'd seen him all along, because to do anything else would have been undignified.

There didn't seem to be any way out of it, so I pulled back the bolt and opened the door.

There's a story, probably apocryphal but who cares, about Lishni, the inventor of the fire-ram. It seems he invented it out of desperation, having no other way for his flotilla of six cutters to escape a fleet of eight brigs and two ships of the line that had cut him off during what started as a minor action in one of the wars with Elde. As the story goes, after arming his cutters with his new invention, he went out, sank seven of the ten ships and damaged the other three, then, in another moment of inspiration, took his crews ashore, captured the Palace, and forced an unconditional surrender that ended the war right there. As he walked out of the Palace with the signed surrender in his hand, one of his subordinates supposedly asked him how he felt. "Fine," he said.

As I say, I very much doubt it happened like that, but it's a good story. I bring it up because, if someone had asked me how I felt when

I walked into a room full of more Morganti weapons than I had thought existed in the world, I'd have said, in the same way, "Poorly."

"Boss . . ."

"I know, Loiosh."

The weapons were piled everywhere. It was like stepping into a room full of yellowsnakes. I could feel the two Dragonlords behind me, and even the knowledge that I was showing fear in front of them couldn't propel me forward.

"This is pretty ugly, Vlad."

"Tell me about it, Kragar."

"I wonder what he wanted them for."

"I wonder why the Serioli invented them in the first place."

"You don't know, Vlad?"

"No. Do you?"

"Sure. Well, I know what they say, at least."

"What do they say?"

"Back before the beginning of the Empire they were invented by a Serioli smith in order to make war so horrible no one would fight anymore."

I snorted. "You're kidding. Do you believe they could be that stupid?"

"Oh, but it worked."

"Huh?"

"Among the Serioli."

"Oh."

"Shall we go in?"

"I don't think I can."

"That's a problem."

"Yes."

We stood there like idiots for a little longer.

"Should we leave, then?" he asked.

"No, dammit."

"All right."

Hours and hours went by. All right, maybe a minute. The worst part was knowing those Dragonlords were right behind me. Showing fear in front of a Jhereg is bad business; showing fear in front of a Dragon hurts my pride.

Kragar said, "I have an idea."

"Good," I said. "I accept. An excellent idea. Whatever it is."

"This will take a couple of minutes."

"Even better. You think I'm in a hurry?"

Kragar's brow wrinkled. I suspected psychic contact.

"All right," he said. "He'll be here."

"Who?"

"Someone who can help. I met him some years ago when I was—it doesn't matter."

He might as well have completed the sentence. Kragar wasn't born into the Jhereg—he'd once been a Dragonlord himself—and whatever reasons he had for not being one anymore were his own business.

"What's his name?"

"Daymar. He's a Hawklord."

"All right. How can he help?"

"Psychics."

"What about them?"

"He's very good. He can do things with the powers of his mind that skilled sorcerers can't do using the power of the Orb. He—just a minute." He stepped out of the room for a moment and spoke quietly with the guards. When he returned, there was a thin, sharp-featured Dragaeran with him, all in black, with a sort of dreamy, vague expression on his face that was quite at odds with his features and with other Hawklords I'd known.

"Hello, Kragar," he said in a low, quiet voice.

"Hello, Daymar. This is my boss, Vlad."

He bowed politely, which also set him apart from others of his House. "Pleased to meet you," he said.

"And you," I told him.

He studied the room. "Very impressive," he said. "I've never seen so many at once."

"I was thinking much the same thing," I said.

Kragar said, "Can you, uh, tone them down a little? Vlad is a bit sensitive to their aura."

He turned to me with a look of curiosity. "Really? That's interesting. I wonder why?"

I refrained from saying, "Because I'm an Easterner with a superstitious dread of the damned things"; instead I just shrugged.

"Mind if I find out what it is about you that—"

"Yes," I said.

"All right," he said, appearing to be a little hurt. Then he looked around the room again. "Well," he said, "it shouldn't be difficult," and, just like that, I felt better. Not *good*, mind you, but better—it was as if they were still out there, and still hungry, but much farther away.

"How did you do that?" I said.

Daymar frowned and pursed his lips. "Well," he said, "if we consider the aura emitted by each weapon as a spherical field of uni—"

"Psychics," said Kragar.

I walked into the room as if there was nothing to it, and began looking around. Kragar and Daymar stayed behind me.

The weapons were a bit more arranged than I'd first thought—they were stacked, rather than just lying around, and they were all in sheaths or scabbards—I tried not to think of how it would feel if they'd been naked. I couldn't, however, discern exactly what the order or arrangement was.

"The most powerful are at this end," said Daymar conversationally, "and the weakest are down there. That's a Jhereg on your shoulder, isn't it?"

"Psychics," I said. "And a keen eye for detail as well," I added.

"Excuse me? Oh, that was irony, wasn't it?"

"Sorry. I'm a bit jumpy."

"Oh? Why?"

I glanced at Kragar, who, it appeared, was gallantly attempting not to smile. I left the question hanging and tried to look like I was studying the weapons, while simultaneously not really looking at them. This isn't easy, and it didn't work—they kept assaulting my mind, Daymar's psychic ability notwithstanding.

"How do you link to it?"

"Excuse me?"

"The Jhereg. You must have some sort of psychic link to it. How—"

"Witchcraft," I said.

"I see. Does it involve—?"

"I don't care to discuss it."

"All right," said Daymar, looking puzzled and maybe a little hurt once more. I wasn't used to running into Dragaerans who had sensitive feelings.

"So," said Kragar. "Any ideas on how to go about this?"

I glanced at him again, and he flushed a little—whoever this Daymar was, I wasn't prepared to discuss my business in front of him, and Kragar ought to have known that.

"What are you trying to do?" said Daymar.

"It's hard to explain," I said.

"Oh, well then—" he said, and, as I was still looking at Kragar, I saw a startled look spread over his features.

I said, "What—"

"Mind probe, Boss. A really, really, good one. And fast. That guy—"

I picked up the weapon closest to me, a dagger, and pulled it from its sheath. I crossed the room, stopping in front of Daymar, about four feet away. I stared up at him, holding the weapon casually in front of me. I was no longer frightened of the thing; it was as if something had taken control of me, and that something was red and burning. I said, "Look, I appreciate your help, but if you ever mind-probe one of my people again, it'll be the last thing you ever do, in this life or any other. Is that clear?"

He seemed a little startled but not at all frightened. "Sorry," he said. "I won't do it again."

I turned away, took a deep breath, and sheathed the weapon. I never know what to say after I've intimidated someone; I ought to keep a list of tough-guy remarks.

"I do have a suggestion, however."

I turned around and stared at him, not quite sure what I was hearing.

"Boss, either you're losing your touch or this guy is really stupid."

"Well," continued Daymar, "since I know anyway . . ."

I gave Kragar a "What should I do about this?" look, and he returned a "Don't ask me" shrug.

I sighed. "All right, Daymar. Let's hear it."

"Well, Morrolan thinks someone is going to try to steal these weapons, right? And you—"

"Do you know Morrolan?" I said.

"Certainly. Why?"

"I just wondered. Go on."

"You want to trap whoever it is."

"Trap? Maybe. At least find the culprit, if there is one."

"I can set up a psychic trace that will let us identify anyone who steps in here."

"Sounds too easy," I said.

"No one guards against psychics."

"What about Kiera?"

"Who?"

"Never mind," I said. "If something is missing and we don't know how, Kiera took it."

"Then what?" put in Kragar.

"That's easy. We give up and report failure, which I should have done already."

"Sounds reasonable."

"Well?" said Daymar.

"All right," I said. "Do whatever you have to do."

"It's done," he said.

"I—"

"*I believe him, Boss. Something happened.*"

I graced Kragar with another look. In case I've failed to communicate it, I wasn't entirely comfortable with how things had worked themselves out, and Kragar presented an easy and not unreasonable target; he accepted the role with good grace.

Loiosh said, "*Don't worry, Boss; it'll all work perfectly. No, really.*"

I turned to Daymar. "How does it work?"

"If any of those weapons are moved from this room, I'll receive a psychic impression of whoever moved it."

"Then what?"

"Whatever you want. I can put you in touch with him, or get a location—"

"You can? *You* can?"

"Why, yes," he said, looking slightly startled. "Is something amiss?"

I don't know why I should have thought we'd be done with him. Wishful thinking, I suppose.

"All right," I said. "I think we can say we've done all we have to here. Let's go."

"Where are we going?" asked Daymar.

I started to answer, bit it off, gave Kragar a pleading look, and made my escape. Whatever Kragar said must have worked; at least Daymar didn't follow us back to the office.

That day, I was prepared to call even that a victory.

3

We had closed a good share of the distance between us before they broke into a run. I'd thought (insofar, that is, as I'd been thinking at all) that they were going to stop, take a defensive position, and wait for our attack, as we'd done when they'd charged us, and on reflection, they probably should have. They had spears, and if they'd just held steady and stuck them out, it would have been ugly for us. But that wasn't how they played it—they came right at us, maybe hoping we'd back down, turn, and run. Strategically a bad move, psychologically sound. Or, to put it another way, seeing them coming at us scared the shit out of me, a feeling mitigated only by the nasty pleasure of knowing how it felt to charge up a hill.

But there was no way we could stop, you see; the juice-drum was rattling around us, we were already moving, and we'd become a juggernaut, plowing forward, bristling with points, and at a certain stage I stopped feeling fear. I stopped feeling anything. I just went ahead and did it because there was nothing else to do. Even my own mission, my private plans and intentions, went out of my head, and the means became the end: I was advancing because my company was advancing, and when we met them we'd destroy them because that was what we did. It was never *my* job, but for a while, as I said, that didn't occur to me.

It was all different. I don't mean this battle in particular, but battle in general. I still wasn't used to it. Did anyone ever get used to it? If so, how? Except someone like Napper, and he was nuts.

I'd known battle would be different from assassination, and even different from the street brawls I'd been forced into from time to time, but knowing it and living it are not the same. I'm used to cold, but battle is hot; I'm used to precision, but war is chaos; I'm used to trying to kill, but this kind of fighting involved trying to stay alive.

The sound of footsteps, my own and my comrades', blended with the juice-drum, then overpowered it and became a rhythm that I picked up in my head to the echo of "Why? Why? Why? Why?" which was far too philosophical for the moment. We hardened soldiers, you see, are philosophical in camp, but very practical in the field. That was something else I learned. In camp, you have to be philosophical, or crazy, or funny, or nasty, or something, just to keep yourself from going out of your head while you're waiting for another chance to be a hero. It's a means of passing the time. That is one similarity between Dragons and Jhereg I can't deny: we know how to wait.

Another is that we don't like waiting. For my part, if something is going to happen, I'd just as soon that it happened quickly. With that in mind, I suppose you could say I got lucky way back at the beginning of all this, when I tried to carry out Morrolan's mission: I didn't have to wait. We heard from Daymar the very morning after we set the psychic trap.

I was just settling into my chair and enjoying the rare pleasure of an empty desk; if there's something on the desk, it usually means there is something I ought to be doing. I was about to have my secretary bring me some klava when Kragar, whom I had not noticed enter my office, said, "Someone stole one of the weapons, Vlad."

"Melestav!" I called. "Please bring me some klava."

"Right away, Boss," he answered from the next room.

Kragar began again, "Vlad—"

"I heard you. I'm going to pretend I didn't. I'm going to have some klava. Then you can tell me about it."

"If you want it directly, I could have Daymar—"

"No."

"Let me see if I understand. Do I take it you *don't* want Daymar to—"

"Kragar, shut up and let me drink my klava. Then you can be funny. If you try to be funny before I've had my klava, I will probably have to kill you, and then I'll be sad."

"Ah. Well. I wouldn't want you to be sad."

I squeezed my eyes tightly shut. When I opened them Kragar was gone. A little later Melestav tiptoed in, set a steaming cup in front of me, and tiptoed out again.

"Well, we're in some kind of mood today, aren't we, Boss?"

"I was fine when I got here."

I drank my klava slowly. There is a perfect way to position the lips on the cup to take in just the right amount of klava to avoid burning yourself. Everything comes with practice. I reflected on practice and on annoyance and I drank my klava and then I called for Kragar.

"Okay," I said. "Let's have it."

"I got word from Daymar this morning that his psychic alarm had been tripped sometime last night. He says it failed to wake him, for which he sends his apologies—"

"Apologies? I didn't think he did that."

"—and suggests that the thief must be quite accomplished."

"All right. We'd best head over and see what was taken."

"He knows what was taken: one greatsword, very large, not terribly potent. Plain cross-guard with brass knobs, leather grips, sharp on one edge and part of the other, enough of a point for stabbing."

I tried to call up a memory of that weapon, failed, but Loiosh managed—he put the picture into my mind. I saw it leaning against a wall along with several cousins. I hadn't noticed it; it had been utterly undistinctive and, for a Morganti blade, not even very well constructed.

"So, just as a guess, Kragar, I'd say it was a test, rather than that blade they were after. What do you think?"

"Possible. Or there's something about it we don't know. History, enchantments, something like that."

"Could be that, too. Any suggestions about what we do next?"

"You could always hire Kiera to steal it back."

"Letting whoever it is know that we know, for which we'd get a probably useless weapon. Any useful suggestions?"

"Whatever we do, we have to find whoever it was who took it. I presume Daymar will be able to find out."

"Right. See to it."

"Me?"

"Yes. I designate you Speaker to Daymar."

"Thank you so much."

"I pride myself on knowing my subordinates and matching tasks to their skills."

"Don't start, Vlad."

There was actually a bit of truth in that remark—though only a bit. Since I'd been in control of the area, one of the things I was learning was what I could delegate and what I had to do myself. In fact, a little later I ran into a situation where—but never mind. That's another story.

Kragar left; I stared off into space. Loiosh said, *"You worried, Boss?"*

"I'm a worrier, chum."

Unfortunately, there was nothing much to do that day, so I got to be pensive. I wanted to get up and pace, wander around the office, sit back down, and do all the things one does when one is nervous. But it's just no damn good letting your subordinates think you're easy to shake, so I sat at my desk, cooked some meals in my mind, remembered past lovers, and exchanged banter with Loiosh.

Lunchtime was a relief. I went to an Eastern place run by a woman named Tserchi and had roasted duckling in a sour cherry sauce garnished with celery root and served with a pan-fried garlic bread that wasn't as good as Noish-pa made but was perfectly edible. I tried to linger over the food, which of course made me eat faster. Tserchi joined me after the meal. I had a sorbet for dessert along with an orange liqueur and the pleasure of hearing her complain about how much she had to pay for ice. I was glad she was there, because I don't like eating alone. I made it back to the office and Kragar was waiting for me.

I noticed his cloak when I returned, so I knew he was there. I sat down at my desk and tried not to look like I was waiting for him.

If you're getting the impression that I'd built this thing up into something far more important than it probably was, well, I told myself the same thing. The fact that I turned out to be right might make me seem prescient. I don't know. I've been wrong about such things, too, but those occasions don't make for interesting stories.

"Okay, Vlad, I've got it," Kragar told me.

"Took you long enough," I said, just because I was irritated.

"Uh huh. And suppose I just walked in and gave you a name. What would you say?"

I'd have told him to go find out about the guy, of course, and probably have made some sarcastic remark about his failure to have already done so. Sometimes you have to admit defeat.

"Okay," I said. "Good work."

"Thanks."

"Sit down and let's hear it."

Melestav stuck his head in right then and said, "Kragar? I found that map."

"Thanks. Bring it in, please."

We're always polite to each other around the office.

I bit back any questions that Kragar would feel smug about answering, and waited. I shuffled paperweights and writing gear off to the side of my desk while Kragar unrolled a map that almost covered it. The map seemed fairly recent, and had the peculiar mix of sharp and fuzzy areas that denotes a psiprint; most of it, however, was very clean and distinct, indicating a skilled and careful artist. I recognized the region at once because Dzur Mountain was marked near the left-hand border, and I recognized the Barnsnake River two-thirds of the way toward the right, which meant the markings on the right border were the foothills of the Eastern Mountains.

Kragar pointed to an area a little above and to the right of Dzur Mountain. "Fornia County," he said, tracing an area that ran almost all the way to the edge of the map.

"Never heard of it."

"Oh, well, never mind, then."

"Get on with it."

"Melestav is looking for a more detailed map, just in case we need it. But that's where the weapon went."

"And what do you know of Fornia? Count or Countess?"

"Count. Fornia e'Lanya. Dragonlord, of course. And a neighbor of Sethra Lavode."

"I wonder who borrows sugar from whom?"

"Huh?"

"Never mind. Eastern custom."

"The name 'Fornia' comes from the old language of the House of the Dragon and means 'patience.' There's probably a story there but I don't know it. Fornia is old; over two thousand. A sorcerer of some repute. Battle magic, mostly. He also keeps a staff of sorcerers to assist him. No discoveries, but they have a good reputation in the House."

I grunted.

Kragar continued. "He did a fair bit of expanding before the Interregnum, and he's been at it again during the last hundred years or so. Maintains a standing army of about six hundred, but also hires as needed, including Easterners. He—"

"Easterners? I don't understand."

"He's been known to hire Eastern mercenaries for certain actions."

"Eastern mercenaries?"

"Yes."

"I didn't know—I've never heard of—"

"Neither did I and I haven't either."

"Are you sure about it?"

"Yes," said Kragar.

"From where in the East?"

"Not your part. Farther south, as I understand it. Some foot soldiers, but a lot of horsemen. He's known to keep a strong cavalry and to use it well."

"What do you mean, my part?"

"The part of the East your family came from."

"How do you know which part of the East my family came from?"

"Vlad—"

"Yes?"

"Did you think I would be willing to work for you without finding out anything about you?"

"Uh . . . what else did you find out?"

"You don't really want to know, do you?"

"Hmmm. All right. Go on."

"*That's very strange, Boss.*"

"*How much Kragar knows about me? Or the business with the Eastern mercenaries?*"

"*Well, both, but I was thinking about the Eastern mercenaries.*"

"*Yeah, it's strange.*"

"Did you find out why he'd have stolen the weapon?"

"No, but I have a theory: the same reason anyone else would have; they represent power. If you want things like that, they're the sorts of things you'd want."

I digested that and failed to find a suitable response. "You said he keeps trying to expand his area. What does the Empress have to say about it?"

"He's been going after other Dragonlords; the Empress has pretty much the same attitude about that as about Jhereg wars: Let them have at each other as long as it doesn't interfere with the workings of the Empire."

"Interesting parallel; I wonder what Morrolan would think about it?"

Kragar smiled. I think, as a one-time Dragonlord, he took special joy in remarks like that. Of course, it also made him a good source of information about matters military.

"All right," I said. "Let me summarize. What we have is a matter of Dragons acting like Dragons. This Fornia is after more land and power, so he steals a Morganti weapon, and Morrolan is after the same, so he doesn't want him to, and we can tell Morrolan who this guy is, and then we're done, and there's nothing more to it. Right? Heh. So, what haven't you told me?"

"The main thing is: Dragonlords don't steal."

"I see. And therefore?"

"One possibility is that he wanted it really, really badly. Another is that he intended to be outraged."

"Excuse me?"

Kragar paused and stared at the ceiling as if to formulate a complicated thought. "He steals the thing, Morrolan accuses him of stealing the thing, he gets outraged."

"Oh. Is he a Dragon or a Yendi?"

"They aren't all that different, Vlad." I started to speak, but Kragar quickly said, "I should qualify that. Yendi are like that all the time, but a Dragon on a campaign is capable of subtlety when necessary."

"Okay, I get it."

"So," said Kragar, "there's likely more going on than we know about."

"Well, okay, fine. How does it concern us?"

"I don't know. Maybe, if we're lucky, not at all."

I sighed. "Okay. I'll report what I've found out—"

"What *who* has found out?"

"—to Morrolan and see what he says. But I'm *not* going to go steal that thing back." Then I asked hopefully, "Is there anything that needs attention around here before I go put myself in the Dragon's maw?"

" 'Fraid not."

"All right. Thanks. Good work."

You don't, Sethra explained to me after it was all over, get to pick and choose your resources when you begin a campaign. In other words, the object is to make the best use of what you have and to find a way to pit your strengths against the enemy's weaknesses. She used a complicated example I didn't follow involving pitting cavalry against sorcery, and long, fast marches against an enemy entrenched in a long line. Her point being that the first thing you do when starting a campaign is assess your own strengths and weaknesses and your opponent's in light of your goals.

As I say, I didn't follow the analogy, but now, looking back on it, when I can, if I want, see everything I did in military terms, I suppose you could say that it was somewhere in there that I began to take stock of my own forces, as if this were a campaign I had decided to enter on. The fact is, it wasn't until a day or two later that I became committed to it, but even as I sat there in my office contemplating what Kragar had told me and preparing another visit to Castle Black, I was, even if I didn't know it, embarking on a campaign, and somewhere in the back of my head I was assessing the forces I had to work with and preparing myself for what was to come.

I just didn't think I was going to give my report to Morrolan and be finished with it, even though I couldn't have told you why I had that feeling.

But my campaign had no goal, at least at that point, which made the preparation a bit tricky. And it was all unconscious, which made it trickier. And the fact is, I still think I'd have been done with the whole thing if Fornia hadn't . . . but no, we'll leave that to its proper place.

This time I had one of my own sorcerers do the teleport: a guy named Temek who had been with me all along. He was competent as a sorcerer, though his main skill was, let's say, elsewhere. He did a good enough job.

When I reached Castle Black, I made a point of noting land-marks—most of them way below me—in case I had to teleport myself there one of these days. I achieved only limited success, but I'm never excited about performing a teleport; I'm not that good at it. The stream was very thin below me, and details were hard to pick out, but there was certainly some sort of footbridge over it, partially hidden by a pair of trees at one end. The trees themselves, and those nearby, seemed from above to be oddly shaped; perhaps shiptrees bred mil-lennia earlier for designs no longer used. Then again, perhaps my eyes and the altitude were conspiring to trick me.

When I felt ready, I moved toward the doors of Castle Black; I even managed a jaunty salute toward a pair of guards who watched me from the wall. They didn't appear to notice. Again the doors swung open and again Lady Teldra greeted me. She was tall and lithe and managed to achieve beauty without sexuality—that is, I enjoyed looking at her but felt no desire. This is unusual for me, and I won-dered if it was a calculated effect.

"The Lord Morrolan," she said, "will join you in the library di-rectly. Would you care for refreshment?"

"Please."

She escorted me up the long winding stairway to the library, left me for a moment, and returned with a glass of a red wine that had too much tannin for my taste and was too warm, but which was good anyway. I'd been in that library on several occasions; this time, while I waited, I looked at some of his books. Most of them seemed, pre-dictably, to be either history or sorcery. There were some books about the East that aroused my interest, in particular one called *Customs and Superstitions in the Eastern Mountains,* and another called *The Wars for Independence in the Mountain States,* both published in the East, and both written by someone called Fekete Szüszí, which I knew to be a Fenarian name. I wasn't sure what I thought about Morrolan having such books.

Loiosh informed me of his approach just before he said, "You may borrow them, if you wish," so I could avoid letting him startle me.

"I'd like that very much."

"I should warn you, however, that I have several volumes devoted to curses for people who don't return books."

"I'd like to borrow those, too."

"What brings you here?"

"I have the name you're after."

"Ah. So soon?"

"If you're going to employ Easterners, you'll have to adjust to things happening quickly."

"Boss, do you think he really has books full of curses for people who—"

"It wouldn't surprise me a bit, Loiosh."

"All right, then," said Morrolan. "Who is it?"

I gave him the name and watched his face. I might as well have been watching his rows of books.

"Very well," he said.

"Is that all?"

"No."

"Well, Boss, did you think—"

"Shut up."

"What else, then?"

"The weapon must be retrieved."

"Yeah. I know some thieves. If you want it stolen back I'll give you a name or two."

"They wouldn't work for me. Besides—"

"I know. Dragonlords don't steal. And that isn't what you want anyway."

Morrolan nodded, but his thoughts seemed elsewhere. "More important, however, is that the Count of Fornia be taught a lesson."

"A lesson? I hope you aren't going to ask me to kill him, because—"

Morrolan's nostrils flared and he started in on a glare which died on the vine. "You are jesting, I presume. Please do not make such jests in the future."

I shrugged. I hadn't been, but there was no reason to tell him that. I was relieved he wasn't going to ask me to put a shine on a Dragonlord anyway.

"No, I think I must go to war with him."

I looked at Morrolan and blinked. "Well, of course. Certainly.

That's obvious. What else can one do? But how does that concern me?"

"It doesn't, directly."

"Well, that's a relief, anyway."

"Too bad, Boss. I was hoping for a commission."

"Shut up, Loiosh."

"Lieutenant Loiosh . . . has a nice sound, don't you think?"

"Shut up, Loiosh."

"Attention, First Jhereg Lancers, forward at a march—"

"Shut the fuck up, Loiosh."

"Yes sir, Colonel. Aye aye. Shutting up, sir."

"I don't suppose you have any experience in military reconnaissance?"

"I assure you, in the small fishing village I come from it forms the sole topic of conversation."

"I hadn't thought so. Still, you may prove useful. In the meantime, I appreciate what you've done. I'll have payment sent over by messenger."

"Payment is always appreciated. But I'm not entirely happy with the 'you may prove useful' business. I don't suppose you could tell me what you have in mind?"

"If it were a Jhereg matter, would you tell me?"

"Of course. Openness and Honesty is my credo."

He twitched me a smile.

I said, "Just out of curiosity, how does this work? Are you going to declare war on him, or what?"

"A formal declaration of war isn't called for in an action of this type. I'll just send him a message demanding the return of the sword, or accusing him of stealing it, and that will accomplish the same thing. But there are preparations to be made first."

"Like gathering an army?"

"Yes, and planning a campaign, and, above all, hiring a general."

"Hiring a general?" That time I was actually startled. "You're not going to lead the army yourself?"

"Would you assassinate someone yourself if you could get Mario to do it?"

Actually, I probably would, but—"I see your point. And who is this military genius who is the moral equivalent of Mario? Wait, no, don't tell me. Sethra Lavode."

"Good guess."

"I've always been bright for my age." Then, "Wait a minute. How do you know about Mario?"

He looked smug again. I must stop giving him occasion to look smug.

I said, "You think Sethra will do it?"

"I know she will."

"Because she's a friend?"

"For that, yes, and other reasons."

"Hmmmph."

"Boss, there's a lot going on here that we don't know about."

"You think so? Really? Next you'll tell me that a Dzur in the wild can be dangerous."

"How 'bout if you do the killing and I do the irony?"

That, in any case, concluded the interview with Morrolan. I picked up the books I was borrowing and made my way down the stairs toward the front doors, where a sorcerer was prepared to make me sick again. I stopped at the landing and studied the painting there up close. It was ideally viewed from the floor below or above, but up close I could see the texturing that went into the detail work, and, though it strained my neck, I could study the head of the wounded Dragon. Even in a painting, there was something powerful and intriguing about the way those tentacle-like appendages around its neck seemed to wave and flutter—apparently at random, yet there was purpose in it. And the expression on the Dragon's face spoke of necessity, but of a certain joy as well. The wound in its side, which was closest to me, was skillfully rendered to evoke pity but not disgust, and even in the young Dragon there was a certain hint that, though requiring protection, it was still a Dragon and thus not to be trifled with either.

My eye kept returning to those tentacles, however, as if they were a puzzle that might be solved, revealing—what?

"Dragons are more complex than they seem, aren't they, Boss?"

"I was just thinking the same thing."

"Especially Morrolan."

"Yes."

"Did you notice what he didn't ask about?"

"Yes. He never asked about the weapon that was stolen."

"You're not as stupid as they say, Boss."

"Save it, Loiosh. Instead, tell me what it means."

"That he already knew about the theft. Which means when we were setting that trap, we weren't doing what we thought we were. Although what we were doing I couldn't guess."

"Yeah. Maybe. Or it might mean something else entirely."

"What else?"

I studied those tentacles again—random patterns that, somehow, made a kind of sense.

"That he knew there was a particular weapon that would be stolen, which means the theft wasn't just a test or trial, but accomplished what it was supposed to, and there's more to that weapon than we'd thought there was. Which would make sense, of course. Or Kragar's idea: It didn't matter what was stolen; the idea was to annoy Morrolan enough to start a war, just because he wanted a war. In fact, we were probably wrong about everything and, no doubt, still are. Whenever we come to a conclusion, we should just assume we're wrong and go from there."

Loiosh was silent for a moment. Then he said, "I like the artist."

"So do I," I said. "Come on. Let's go home."

I turned my back on the wounded Dragon and walked out of Castle Black.

4

Call to War

Sethra Lavode once gave me a brief history of battle-magic, but I don't remember a whole lot of it; it wasn't important at the time, and my acquaintance with her was new enough that I was thinking less about what she said than the fact that she was saying it. I do remember bits and pieces, however. Between what she said and what I subsequently learned from Morrolan and Aliera, I can give you a very rough overview. It goes something like this:

The earliest practical spells were reconnaissance and illusion; both very powerful, but easily countered. Later there were means developed of creating mass destruction, and all sorts of effort went into protecting one's army. Defense eventually outstripped offense to the point where a soldier could usually consider himself safe from any direct sorcerous attack as long as he wasn't carrying too much metal. It was somewhere in here that armor went by the board, except that some used (and still use) wooden armor, and wooden shields are still common, and warriors in the House of the Lyorn still wear copper or bronze vambraces to prove that they are fearless or stupid—two conditions I've never been able to tell apart.

Various methods were created for allowing the foot soldier to carry pre-prepared offensive spells into battle, and these, too, got stronger and more sophisticated, until some big battle, the name and date of which I didn't pay much attention to, where some sorcerer found a means of making every one of the enemy's "flashstones" blow up in his hand—which added a whole new level of spell and counterspell, and made the common foot soldier leery about having anything to do with sorcery.

Offensive spells, after that, got bigger, more powerful, more so-phisticated again, and often involved sorcerers working together to send huge, powerful spells capable of wreaking havoc on an entire force, and so, again, countermeasures were developed until battle be-came more a test of the skills of sorcerers than of soldiers and generals. This reached its peak just before the Interregnum with a Dragonlord named Adron, about whom the less said the better.

The Interregnum threw all of that out, and war returned to the proper mayhem of soldiers slaughtering each other like gentlemen, and since the end of the Interregnum the sciences of mass destruction have slowly been building up again, with the difference that, sorcery being now so much more powerful, it is hard to find a soldier inca-pable of some sort of sorcerous attack, and almost impossible to find one incapable of defending himself against sorcery. But the concen-tration required to cast a spell, or to defend against one, is concen-tration that isn't being used to avoid the sharp thing someone is likely swinging at you. All of which means that, for the most part, sorcery is beside the point. At least for now. Check back again in twenty or two hundred or two thousand years and you're likely to find a different answer.

To put it another way: In the early days of the Empire, when sorcery was simple and weak, it had little effect on battle; now, in the latter days of the Empire, when sorcery is powerful and sophisti-cated, it has little effect on battle.

Except, of course, against Easterners, who are helpless against it.

This, at any rate, was how Sethra had explained it before I began my brief military career. In the battle, her words seemed more im-portant and far less accurate; the enemy kept sending nasty spells at us, and sometimes they'd kill someone, and several times they almost killed me.

I hated that.

I would not have needed the lecture to understand what it all meant to the common foot soldier: It meant that, every once in a while one of your comrades would fall over, dead and twitching, with no visible sign of what had happened; that rather more frequently someone would go down, killed or wounded, after being hit by what looked like nothing more than a faint reddish light; and that, even while engaged in hand-to-hand fighting, you had to be aware that someone could be targeting you for something unhealthy.

At least, since the enemy was charging us, they couldn't throw javelins at us, and the spells became fewer as we clashed. The first few seconds after the lines meet is the most intense time of the battle; it is more intense, to the warrior, that is, than the inevitable crisis point where the battle is decided. The first few seconds are when you don't have to do any thinking; later the action gradually slows down, or seems to, until eventually you have time to let your fear catch up to you. As I said, I remember little of that first clash, but the thing I remember most is the sound of ten thousand steel swords thudding into ten thousand wooden shields, and the occasional clang and scrape of sword against spearhead. No, it wasn't really that many, it just sounded like it. Loiosh probably made some smart remarks. It is often a blessing to forget.

I remember noticing that Aelburr was somehow on his feet again, wounds notwithstanding, and swinging away with a will; and I caught a glimpse of Napper, being happy about the only time he ever was, which irony was lost on me because I'd grown used to it. It's amazing what you can grow used to with sufficient provocation, but irony, an old friend of mine, is just no good except at a distance. I wasn't catching any irony at the time, though now I can realize how ironic it is that, in spite of all my worry, and in spite of Kragar's comments, and in spite of Morrolan's hints, I almost certainly would have been done with the whole business when the messenger arrived with my payment the day after I made my report to Morrolan.

I would have been, if.

They showed up at my flat shortly after I returned from the office after speaking with Morrolan. I opened the door in answer to an imperious clap. There were three of them, all men, all Dragonlords, and two of them were armed. The third said, "Your name is Taltos." He pronounced it as if he'd seen it written but never heard it, from which I could draw conclusions that were, no doubt, useful for something.

"More or less," I told him. Loiosh flew over and landed on my shoulder. I was worried, and even a bit frightened. I don't worry much about opening my door, because the Jhereg considers one's home sacrosanct; but who knows what Dragons think?

"My name is Ori. My Lord the Count of Fornia requests and requires you not to interfere in any way in his concerns. This is the only warning you will receive. Is that understood?"

I took a moment to work that through. Fornia knew that I was involved. Okay. And he was warning me to stay out of the way. What did he imagine I was going to do? And why was he even bothering to threaten me?

It was puzzling as well as annoying, but the annoyance predominated. Three Dragonlords—*three*, for the love of Verra, and one of them clearly a sorcerer, come into my home and tell me what to do? Even the Jhereg doesn't do that. Even the Phoenix Guard, when they're harassing the Jhereg, doesn't do that. If a Jhereg or a representative of the Empire wanted to threaten or intimidate me, they'd have the courtesy to call on me in one of my workplaces—say the office, or a restaurant, or an alley. This business of having my home invaded set me off, but I resolved to be diplomatic about the whole thing. I said, "What if I request and require the Count of Fornia to kiss my ruddy bum?"

Both of the Dragonlords drew their swords as best they could in the confined space of my entryway; at the same time they moved forward. An instant later they fell backward; one because there was a Jhereg in his face, the other because I'd thrown a knife into his shoulder.

Ori raised his hand, but I knew very well what it means when a Dragonlord isn't carrying a sword. At the same time as I'd thrown the knife (a boot knife, one of only four knives I was still carrying after disarming myself when I'd gotten home), I let Spellbreaker, about eighteen inches of gold chain, fall into my left hand. I set it spinning to intercept whatever he was about to throw at me.

Ori turned out to be pretty fast; some part of his spell got past, and I felt weak, dizzy, and I couldn't move the right side of my body. I let myself fall over and started rolling away from the door.

The effects of the spell were short-lived; I was able to stand and come up with another knife—this one a stiletto, not well suited to throwing—and start Spellbreaker spinning again. If Ori threw something else at me, the chain got all of it, and Loiosh was keeping the one Dragon pretty busy, but the other one, my knife still sticking out of his shoulder, had picked up his sword with his left hand and was charging me.

This was cause for some concern.

There was no way to parry his sword with my stiletto, so I did the only thing I could, which was to move in at him and hope to get past his attack.

I felt my knife strike home, and, at the same time, something hit me in the side, and then I felt the floor against my face. I did some calculations as I was lying there: Loiosh could handle the one, and, with luck, I had disabled the other at the same time as he'd gotten me, but there was still the sorcerer to worry about. I tried to roll over, and noticed that Spellbreaker was no longer in my hand; this is where I got really worried. I tried again to roll over, and I figured I must have succeeded because I was looking at the ceiling; that was a start. Only the ceiling was wrong, somehow. I tried to get up, wondering when the pain was going to hit me. Someone said, "Lie still, Vlad."

A woman's voice. Whose? I knew it, but I couldn't place it. But I was like Hell going to lie still. I tried to sit up again.

"Lie still. It's all right."

All right? What—?

Aliera e'Kieron came into view overhead.

"You're at Castle Black, Boss."

"Castle Black? How did I get here?"

"Morrolan came and got you."

"How did he—?"

"I told him."

"How could you—?"

"I wasn't sure I could."

"Am I ever going to be able to complete a—"

"How do you feel?" asked Aliera.

"Angry," I said. "Very, very angry. I would badly like to kill someone. I—"

"I mean, how do you feel physically?"

That was a tougher question, so I took some time to consider it. "All right," I finally said. "My side is a little stiff. What happened?"

"Someone cut you."

"Bad?"

"Fairly deep," she said judiciously. "No organs were damaged. Two ribs were cracked."

"I see. Considering all of that, I feel great. Thanks."

"Any pain?"

"Some."

"It'll get worse."

"All right."

"Would you like something for the pain?"

"Pain doesn't bother me," I told Aliera.

She didn't choose to be impressed.

I'd first run into Aliera in a wizard's laboratory, trapped inside a piece of wood, which had hindered our ability to get to know one another. Later, when she was breathing and talking and such, we'd been too busy for much chatting. I'd picked up that she was related to Morrolan—which wasn't surprising, because I imagine most Dragons are related to most others, one way or another. As far as I knew then (I learned more later, but that doesn't come into this story), she was fairly typical for a Dragonlord, except shorter. Evidently she had some abilities as a physicker.

"Who was it?" she asked.

"A Dragon," I said.

She nodded. "So Morrolan informs me. I meant more specifically."

"Someone in the employ of Fornia. There was a sorcerer named Ori; I didn't get the names of the blademen."

"What did they want?"

"They wanted me to stay out of their business."

She nodded as if it made perfect sense that this request involved attempting to cut me in half crosswise. I suppose it makes sense to me, too. And it might even have seemed reasonable if they hadn't walked into my home to do it. Maybe that doesn't make sense to you, and maybe it is even irrational, but I'd been in the Jhereg for several years, and to us, well, you just don't do that.

"Will you?" she said.

"Stay out of his business? Not anymore," I told her.

She laughed a little. Her eyes were light brown. "You sound like a Dragon."

"I'd challenge you to a duel, but that would just confirm your opinion, so I'll pass."

"Good thinking," she said.

I kept my anger under a lid because it works better that way, because I can use it that way. It was a very cold anger, and I knew that it would sustain me for quite some time—for long enough, at least, to track down this Fornia and do unto him.

But not now. Now I had to stay cool and recover. I took a deep breath and let my vision wander. The ceiling was of some very dark hardwood; my own was a textured plaster of some kind and much lower—the trained eye picks up these details almost instantly. There were other subtle things that had made me feel I might be in the wrong place when I first became conscious—like, my entire flat would nearly have fit into the room, and every item of furniture—three chairs, a desk, a table, and a sofa—cost more than I made for killing a man.

I said, "What do you know of this weapon Fornia had stolen?"

"Why?"

"It seems to be the cause of all this unpleasantness; either the weapon, or the fact that he stole it, or . . ."

She waited. "Yes? Or?"

"Or something entirely different that I have no clue about. I always have to include that as one of the possibilities."

She looked at me. "Well, you seem to be out of danger, and I have better ways to spend my time than to be interrogated by a Jhereg, so you'll have to excuse me."

"Hugs and kisses to you, too."

She gave me a glance and floated out of the room. I carefully sat up, discovered that doing so hurt, and began looking around for my clothing.

"*On the little table at the foot of the bed, Boss. You're going to need a new shirt, and your trousers have some bloodstains.*"

"*All right. Feel like shopping?*"

"*Going to buy me something?*"

"*Like what?*"

"*Catnip.*"

"*Catnip? Does catnip affect you? When did you—?*"

"*Probably not. But I don't want to eat it myself.*"

"*Then why—?*"

"*Bait,*" said Loiosh.

"*Funny, Loiosh. No, but maybe I'll buy you a set of opposable thumbs.*"

"*Heh.*"

I was starting to lose count of the teleports to and from Castle Black over the last couple of days; but I had another done for me, and then went to South Adrilankha, the Easterners' quarter, where I replaced a few items of clothing and supped. I stopped by my grandfather's for a visit, but he was out. I returned to my own area, found a sorcery supply store that was still open, and started to buy a mild painkiller, but then changed my mind and bought a strong one. I also picked up an enchanted dagger because the spells on my own were wearing thin and you never know when you might need a spell in a hurry. The guy at the store explained that the enchantments on the blade were so powerful that three people I'd never heard of had been in awe of it, and so on until I shut him up and bought the thing for half of what he had first asked.

Then I went home, took the painkiller, and started cleaning up the damage to my flat. There were no bodies there, but there were some bloodstains. I resent bloodstains in my home, especially when some of the blood is mine. I became angry all over again. I got rid of the stains by covering them with a rug, then I picked up some furniture that I don't remember being overturned, and may have done a bit more before the painkillers hit and, apparently, I made it to the bed before falling asleep.

A day in the life.

I woke up sore, moody, and in need of klava. If I ever get really rich, I'm going to hire a servant just to bring me klava in the morning. I managed to rise, make the coffee, and brew a fairly effective pot of klava, into which I poured some cow's milk and the last of the honey. I made a note to order more ice, no matter how expensive it was. I should really learn to make my own; cooling and heating spells are supposed to be pretty simple.

I was dressed and working up the energy to leave when someone clapped outside my door. Twice in two days would be stretching the laws of probability, so I wasn't worried; or, at least, I told myself I wasn't worried as I picked up a dagger and opened the door.

I didn't recognize the visitor, but she wore the colors of the House of the Dragon. I might have struck immediately if I hadn't noticed that she wore Morrolan's emblem on her shoulder, and if I hadn't been too stiff to move quickly. She said, "You are—?"

"Baronet Vladimir Taltos, House of the Jhereg."

"Then this is for you," she said, handing me a small bag that jingled. "If you'd be so kind as to touch this ring."

I touched the ring, took the bag, and shut the door as she turned away. I'd forgotten that Morrolan owed me money. I counted it and was pleased.

I thought about treating myself to a cabriolet ride to the office, but I'd be seen, and people would wonder why, and some of them might guess right. I also thought about taking more painkillers, but even a little would make me woozy, and that just won't do in this business; I had to be as stoic as I'd pretended to be to Aliera the day before.

Bugger.

I took the walk to the office slowly, not noticing much going on around me; when you hurt, too much of your attention is focused in to have much to spare for the rest of the world. I made it to the office, and Melestav greeted me with the words "You okay, Boss?"

"Yeah," I said. "Anything new?"

"A couple of requests for credit extensions, a request for a meeting from someone named Koth, nothing else."

I grunted. "Any idea what Koth wants?"

"To hire you."

"Thank him and put him off. I'm busy for the next week, maybe two. I'll look at the requests later."

"All right."

"And tell Kragar I want to see him."

I hung up my cloak and eased myself into my chair. Then I leaned back and closed my eyes, and Kragar said, "You all right, Boss?"

"Fine," I said. "All things considered."

"All right. What things need consideration?"

"I got jumped."

I opened my eyes. I looked around the room for Kragar, then

found him sitting in the chair opposite me. He was staring at me intently, suspecting, I suppose, that we were about to be involved in some affair within the Jhereg—like someone trying to make a move on my territory. I said, "I got jumped by three Dragonlords."

"Phoenix Guards?"

"No. The business wasn't connected with the Organization in any way. They were Dragonlords doing business as Dragonlords, and their business was jumping me."

He leaned back, and his expression altered from worry to surprise.

"Really? My, my. Now, that isn't something every Jhereg can say. Where did it happen?"

"Right in my own Verra-be-damned flat."

"Hmmm," he said. "Want to tell me about it?"

I did. He said, "To a Dragon, it's different—"

"I know. I'm not a Dragon."

"Ah." He studied me. "So now you've decided to go after Fornia?"

"Yes."

"Has it occurred to you that you may have been attacked in order to get you to go after him?"

"Yes. It has occurred to me. It is even possible. But do you think it likely?"

"I have no idea. But when we were talking before, you were saying—"

"I know. But it's one thing to be aware of complex strategies and lies that might be going on around you. It's another to let yourself become so worried about deception that you become paralyzed."

"Profound, Boss."

"Shut up, Loiosh."

Kragar shrugged. "All right. If you write that down, I'll save it for your epitaph."

"In the meantime, what do we do about Fornia?"

Kragar caught my eye. "There's always the obvious."

"Yes. I'd been thinking about that."

"And?"

"What do you think?"

"It'll be tricky."

"I know. You can't just put down a Dragonlord as if he were a nine-copper hustler. It'll get ugly. People will talk. But I want to."

"I can start doing some checking."

"That would be good."

"But you should be aware that Morrolan will be, uh, pretty un-happy."

I said, "Not that I care all that much, but why?"

"People will think he had it done."

"Oh. That isn't my problem."

"Are you sure?"

I considered. "Just *how* unhappy is Morrolan likely to be?"

"Very," said Kragar. "From everything I know, he'll set out to make your life either miserable or short. You'll probably have to fight him."

"Great," I said. "Well, is there anything we can do to Fornia short of killing him that wouldn't set Morrolan on my ass?"

"Hmmmm. Maybe."

"Yeah?"

"Well, I know what would really get to him: losing."

"Losing? Like, in battle?"

"Yeah."

"Great. Well, Morrolan is going to attack him. I could always enlist in the army. But somehow I can't imagine myself in uniform, marching off to battle." I really said that. Funny, isn't it?

Kragar said, "There are other ways."

"Oh? Keep talking."

He studied his right thumb. "I'm not sure I have anything definite yet. We don't know enough. But if Morrolan is really going to attack him—"

"He is. He plans to sign Sethra Lavode on as his general-in-chief."

Kragar gave an I-am-impressed look and said, "Then you could probably do something nasty to him to help Morrolan. There are a number of possibilities. An army is a great deal more delicate than you'd think. Just destroy a list of supplies he needs and you've created enough confusion to give him headaches. Or sneak in and burn a map or two. Or have someone impersonate an officer and send a company marching the wrong way. Or—"

"I think I get the idea."

He nodded. "Once we know more we can be more specific."

I shook my head. "I'm trying to imagine myself as some sort of—I don't know—saboteur."

"I'm trying to imagine it, too. And I'm trying not to laugh."

"Thank you so much."

He shrugged. "Well, so he got you mad, and you want to get him back. You're stuck. If you can come up with something better, let me know."

"I can still kill him."

"Yeah, there's that."

I said, "If you come up with a way to turn a profit on this, let *me* know."

"Oh, that's easy. Morrolan will probably pay you for it."

"Do you think so?"

"Yep."

"Well, that's something."

He shook his head. "Hasn't anyone ever told you that revenge is wrong?"

"No, Kragar," I said. "That got left out of my education."

"Too late now," he said.

5

The next thing I remember doing is dodging around, trying to stay alert and not get killed. The first clash was over, and there were a lot of dead and wounded around, but things had broken up a bit. I didn't see Virt or Aelburr anymore, but I caught a glimpse of Napper about twenty yards to my left, flailing about in fine style; I was sure he, at any rate, was enjoying himself. Our colors were still waving, but I didn't recognize the woman holding them; Dunn was either dead or wounded. I hoped he was happy; he'd gotten what he wanted.

There was nothing like a line of battle, but there were clumps of fighting here and there, and many of us, on both sides, who were either looking for someone to fight or hoping not to find someone. This is, I suppose, where spirit of battle really matters: If we'd had more of it, I'd have been trying harder to kill someone. If they'd had more of it, I wouldn't have been able to hang around the fringes of the fighting. At some point in there, I noticed fresh blood on my sword, and I wondered how it got there.

The trouble was: My comrades were fighting for each other. In part, to keep each other alive, and in part because they knew each other, had trained together, and none wanted to be the only one to bug out. I'd been through enough with them to know that that was the thing that kept them going; but I *hadn't* trained with them, and I didn't know them, and even by then I wasn't quite sure why I hadn't bugged out. I still didn't know what had kept me there the first time the enemy had come at us over hastily thrown-up earthworks.

There was a short breathing space, and I relished it—hell, I gloried in it. Strange, huh? I was in as much danger, perhaps, as I'd ever been in, and I remember how delighted I was that there were spaces of time when no one was trying to kill me. Long spaces of time— seconds on end.

Then Loiosh said, *"Remember why we're here, Boss?"*

"Damn you anyway."

"Boss—"

"No, no. You're right. I have a job to do."

"But how—"

"Oh, I know how." There was a little hillock, really just a rise in the ground, before me—just down the hill and up another. *"I just have to get over that hill and spot their command post, which will be protected by the best warriors I've ever met and more sorcerous ability than you can find outside of Dzur Mountain. Then I have to finish up what I came here for. No problem."*

"I know that. I meant how. Too bad we don't know any invisibility spells that will stand up."

"Too bad I'm not Kragar."

Someone stumbled in front of me. An enemy. He looked at me, and I looked at him. He had lost his shield somewhere, but held most of a spear. I don't think he'd been coming after me, the force of battle had just placed him there. He probably would just as soon have run away, and I'd just as soon he did, but, of course, neither of us could trust the other to be sensible. He whipped the remains of his spear toward me. I moved in, knocked his weapon aside with the strong of my blade, and cut him in the neck. He went down and I moved on. I don't know if I killed him. I hope I didn't.

I looked around, and I was as alone as I could be, under the circumstances.

I started down the hill at a trot.

"Quick-march now, Boss."

"Oh, shut up."

I thought about how comfortable my office was. I thought about how pleasant it would be to be sitting there. I remember—now, I didn't think about it then—how Kragar left me alone in the office to think over the idea of working with Morrolan's army as some sort of spy or saboteur; I couldn't quite wrap my head around the idea,

but at the time, I was angry enough not to care. I needed to sort all
that out so I yelled out that I didn't want to be bothered for a while.

"Okay, Boss!" yelled Melestav. "Anyone wants to come in and
kill you, I tell them to wait, right?"

"Yeah," I yelled back. "Unless they're Dragons. Any Dragons who
want to kill me can come right in."

He didn't say anything. I had gotten in the last word on Melestav;
that had to be a good sign.

I closed my eyes and thought about Morrolan. I pictured him,
tall, thin, rather dark, a very slight hook in the nose, eyes deep and
rather close together, a bit of slant to his forehead, and I imagined
his voice, a smooth baritone, mellow, and forming words with an
assumed elegance—

"Who is it?"

"Vlad."

"Yes?"

"Am I reaching you at a bad time?"

"Not as bad as ten minutes later would have been. Which reminds
me: Do you prefer the blood of a reptile or a mammal when you want to
set up a room so you know if it's been violated?"

"Your own blood is best for anything of that type, because you want
it to come back to you. But you only need a drop; it's symbolic."

"Thank you. What is it you wish of me?"

"I want to know if I can be useful to you."

"You just were."

"Other than that."

"Exactly what do you mean?"

"Against Fornia. Could your army use someone able to sneak in and
out of the enemy camp, cause annoyance, disruption—"

"You're taking this rather personally, aren't you, Vlad?"

"Yes."

"Are you certain you want to do this?"

"Well, no. Not entirely. I'm just considering it."

"I see. We should talk."

"I suppose so."

"Are you busy later this afternoon? Say, in a few hours?"

"I could get free."

"Then meet me . . . no offense, Vlad, but are you able to receive a teleport position?"

"Yeah, just barely, if you give me a lot of time to fix it."

"Then I'll give you one. Are you ready?"

"Yeah, go ahead."

"Here."

Okay, I knew how to do this; I'd even done it once or twice before. I made an effort to drop those little controls we always keep on our thoughts. I mentally framed a picture—in my head, I always have big elegant gold frames—then thought of the space within as black. I held onto it and moved it around until it was mentally facing *out*, facing the imaginary direction of my psychic link with Morrolan. It gradually acquired color that I hadn't put into it, and details formed, until, in only a minute or two, I was seeing a place: the bottom of what appeared to be a cliff, a small stream before it, a few evergreens nearby. I couldn't tell how high the cliff was from what Morrolan was showing me, but it seemed to be large, and I certainly would have no desire to attempt to scale it: It seemed perfectly sheer, and grey, and, if you'll permit me, ominous. The ground was rocky and brown, with a few sparse bits of grass sticking up here and there; the stream, as far as I could tell, was little more than a trickle of water.

I concentrated; as I'd told Morrolan, I wasn't all that good at fixing locations for a teleport, but at last I felt reasonably certain I wasn't likely to send myself off to the middle of the ocean or forty feet under the ground. I said, "Got it."

"The seventh hour."

"Why there?"

"There will be an event taking place that you may wish to witness."

I thought about interrogating him some more, but decided it was pointless. "I'll be there," I told him.

"What do you suppose that was about, Boss?"

"I imagine I'll find out."

"Do you trust him?"

"Within limits. I doubt he wants to have me killed."

"Oh, good. Nothing to worry about, then."

I handled a few things around the office, then went down into what I called the "lab" and performed a very minor and easy ritual to help along the healing in my side—just a few instructions to the damaged parts suggesting they go ahead and heal; the indication of success was how hungry I was after, so I went over to the Garden House and had a big plate of egg noodles with squid and leeks to help the process along. Then I headed to Turningham's and looked for a book, found a historical romance by Munnis that I hadn't read, bought it, went home, read the first page, and set it aside for later. I discovered I was hungry again, and that my side was itching and feeling better, all of which meant my spell really was working. I've performed spells of that type, oh, I don't know, maybe a score of times, yet I still get a little thrill, almost of surprise, when I see evidence of it working; like I'm putting one over on nature.

I ate some bread and cheese, took a nap, and Loiosh woke me up a few minutes before the seventh hour.

I managed the teleport myself, without too much difficulty, and arrived right at the appointed hour. The spot at which Morrolan had me appear was a quarter of a mile away from a mass of humanity, all gathered together directly in front of the sheer cliff, which stretched up until its top was lost in the overcast. It was much bigger than I had guessed. I studied it until my neck hurt, then, as my gaze returned to what appeared to be a gathering of several hundred people, at which I could see new arrivals teleporting in at an alarming rate, Loiosh made a squeaking sound and dived into my cloak.

"What—?"

"Didn't you see them, Boss?"

"No, I was looking at—"

"Giant Jhereg, just like at Deathgate Falls."

"We can't be anywhere near there."

"Tell them that."

I looked up again, and, yeah, there were a few shapes that occasionally dipped out of the overcast, circled, and vanished again.

"They're very graceful, Loiosh. You should watch."

"You should drown in a chamberpot, Boss."

"Greetings, Vlad."

I jumped a little, then turned around and said, "Hello, Morrolan. What's the occasion?"

"A ceremony to honor Baritt's passing over Deathgate Falls."

"What? We're near there?"

"No. But his tomb will be here."

"His tomb? I don't . . . how can he have a tomb if his body is going over the Falls?"

"Well, it's not a tomb exactly. Call it a cenotaph. Or a monument. But this mountain has been selected as the place to be consecrated to his memory."

"He gets a whole mountain?"

"He earned it."

"What do I have to do to earn a mountain?"

Morrolan chose not to answer. He said, "I should appear at the ceremony. Would you like to come along?"

"Is that a joke? As what?"

"My retainer. I have the right to have anyone I choose in my suite."

"An Easterner? A Jhereg?"

"Certainly."

"You have something in mind, don't you?"

"Of course."

"Want to let me in on it, in my capacity as the device to be exploited?"

"I'd rather surprise you."

"I'm not all that fond of surprises."

"I understood that you wanted to exact payment from our friend Fornia for what he did to you."

"Yeah."

"Well then, come along and let's do so."

I sighed. "All right, lead on. But . . . skip it."

He led the way. As we approached, I spotted Aliera off to one side; she stood out as the shortest individual in the crowd. She spotted us and waved. A few others noticed us; I caught some double takes, and suspected I was now the object of a great deal of conversation among a few score Dragonlords. I had mixed feelings about this, but it wasn't all unpleasant. Morrolan, who had brought me, after all, was wearing the dexter half of a smile.

I said, "You enjoy being talked about, don't you?"

He smirked outright, but gave no other answer.

We reached Aliera, who nodded to me and looked a question at Morrolan, who said, "He is considering joining our cause."

"Against Fornia?" I nodded, and she said, "You're taking this a little personally, aren't you?"

"I think I will soon begin to take personally everyone telling me I'm taking things personally."

"Do that," she said. Then, to Morrolan, "But why bring him here?"

"I have reasons, my dear cousin. A little patience and you will know."

I could see Aliera deciding whether to take offense; eventually she gave a hint of a shrug and turned away. I was standing in quite a crowd of Dragons, many of whom were giving me looks; more of whom were glancing at Morrolan. He appeared to be enjoying the attention. I spotted a familiar figure: Ori. He was looking at me.

"Vlad!" said Morrolan sharply.

"What?"

"This isn't the place."

I almost asked "For what?" before I realized that my hand was on my sword hilt. It took a deliberate effort to drop my arm back to my side. Ori was standing next to a very old Dragonlord, who had dressed himself in the simplest military fashion: black everything with buttons and hems of silver. His face was wrinkled as a prune, and his slitted eyes were studying me.

I said, "Fornia?"

"Yes," said Morrolan.

I studied the man, then turned once more to Morrolan. "Well, here you both are."

"Yes?"

I shrugged. "Why don't you just kill him?"

He graced me with a scaled-down smile. "There are more reasons than I have time to expound upon."

"Name three."

"All right. One: We are at a ceremony where violence would be improper. Two: If I initiated violence at this ceremony, everyone would take his side and we'd be outnumbered about three hundred to one. Three: I want to see what happens if he's left alone."

I grunted. The second answer seemed convincing enough. And what happened was that Fornia and Ori approached us. Morrolan bowed deeply, Fornia acknowledged; I assume the difference in the bows had to do with respective age. Fornia looked me over and said to Morrolan, "What is *he* doing here?"

"Taking your measure, Lord Fornia. He seems to have developed a grudge against you, and I permitted him to accompany me so that he might get a good look at you. For later," he added. "I've just explained to him why he ought not to do anything improper just at the moment."

This seemed to be my cue, so I gave Fornia a big smile.

Fornia turned his head and spat.

I said, "In the desert culture of my people, to spit in a man's presence is to demonstrate loyalty. Am I to assume that you are my vassal?"

"You're making that up, aren't you, Boss?"

"What do you think, Loiosh?"

Ori said conversationally, "I should have killed you."

"Yes," I said promptly. "You should have. Your mistake. You won't be permitted another."

He took a step closer, so that he could look down on me. "Are you threatening me, Easterner?"

I grinned up at him. "Yes, but not as an Easterner; as a Jhereg. That's an entirely different matter, isn't it?" At that point Loiosh, who has always had a gift for theater, emerged from my cloak and climbed up to my shoulder.

Ori jumped, startled, in spite of himself, then he scowled. He said, "I will rip your soul from your body and bind it to an iron kettle so I can contemplate how your arse burns when I cook my stew."

"Good thinking," I said. "I know some excellent stew recipes if you need them. Adding a little fennel, for example, will—"

"That's enough, Vlad," said Morrolan.

"If you say so," I told him. "But I tell you, you Dragaerans don't know how to cook."

"Vlad—"

"Except for the occasional Lyorn, who seem—"

"Vlad!"

I shrugged and gave Fornia and Ori another big grin.

Fornia said, "I am not worried. You would not countenance assassination, Lord Morrolan."

"Of course not," said Morrolan. "And I assure your lordship I've been trying to talk my associate out of doing anything rash."

"Your veiled threats," said Fornia, "are as empty and absurd as your pet Easterner's coarse ones."

"Exactly," said Morrolan with a bow.

"If you want what is mine," said Fornia, "you may attempt to take it from me."

"Yours by right of theft, my lord?"

Fornia laughed. "You stand with a Jhereg at your heel and speak to me of theft?"

"You stand with a thug at your elbow and speak to me of Jhereg?"

"This is pointless," said Fornia, and turned away.

"So, as I understand it, is the weapon you've taken."

Fornia turned back, gave Morrolan a smile over his shoulder, then walked away, Ori trailing after him.

"And that, my dear Vlad," said Morrolan as soon as Fornia was out of earshot, "is what we came for."

"To bait him?"

"No, to see that smile."

"Oh. And what did you learn?"

"That whatever he was after, he got it."

"Excuse me?"

"The sword he took was what he was after, not a test, and not a failed effort at something else."

"But then, what is it?"

"I don't know."

"Morrolan, it was a very weak, very large, Morganti greatsword."

"No, it was more than that. Exactly what it is I still don't know, but more than that. I now know at least that much for certain."

"Because of that smile?"

"Because of that smile."

"If you say so. And, I take it, I was here to provide a basis for the sparring match?"

"That, yes, and to make him think. And maybe to worry him a little."

"If you worry him too much, he may decide you really do intend to have him assassinated, and he might beat you to the punch."

"He'd no more hire an assassin than I would."

"But Morrolan, you have."

"You know what I mean."

"Sure. But does he?"

"We've made our point here, Vlad. I must stay for the service, but you can return home if you wish. Or stay; it's up to you."

"What's going to happen?"

"Aliera will go forward and deliver a benediction, asking the Gods to receive Baritt's soul, and then his deeds will be related, and those who knew him will tell all manner of lies about what a fine fellow he was, and a bullock will be sacrificed to whoever his patron deity was—Barlen, if I'm not mistaken—and Aliera will perform another benediction, and then we'll all go home. It should take about ten hours."

"Ten hours?"

"More or less."

"Why Aliera?"

"It is her right and her duty."

"Why is that?"

"I assure you, Vlad, you don't need to know details of the internal politics of the House of the Dragon, nor would I be justified in telling you."

"All right. I guess I can skip the services."

"Very well. I'll be in touch."

"I imagine you will."

I walked away so I could perform my slow and clumsy teleport out of the sight of all those Dragonlords.

"Do you think he was telling the truth, Boss?"

"Who?"

"Morrolan."

"About what?"

"About why he brought you along."

"Oh. I imagine so. Why?"

"I think he was telling half the truth."

"All right. What's the other half?"

"He wanted you committed to helping him against Fornia."

I thought that over. "You're probably right," I said at length.

"It worked, didn't it, Boss?"

"Yeah, it worked."

Eventually we reached a large rock that I could step behind to perform the teleport. I never saw the services for Baritt. I hope they went well; I assume Aliera did a good job of whatever she was supposed to do. Actually, now that I think about it, I know why it is that it was Aliera's right and duty, but never mind; you don't need to know details of the internal politics of the House of the Dragon.

"What it comes down to, Loiosh, is that I just don't like the guy."

"Is that any reason to—"

"Of course it is. And if you say I'm taking this personally, I'll trade you in for a mockman and use its tail for a door-clapper."

"Heh."

I walked to the front of my flat, passed the bed, and opened the shutters on the window that looked down into the street. It was late evening, and as I watched the passersby I had the feeling that I was giving up the security of what I knew for a world in which I was ignorant and helpless as a newborn.

"Loiosh, no one's messed with my head, right?"

"I'm afraid not, Boss. This is all you."

"Just checking."

"You may want to visit your grandfather, Boss."

I felt a touch of annoyance, then sat on it. *"You're right, chum. I will, before I actually do anything. But—"*

"I know, Boss. You're committed."

"I hate being pushed around, that's all."

"But you don't mind being manipulated?"

"You talking about Morrolan?"

"Yes."

"Yeah, I mind. But he didn't have me beaten."

Loiosh fell silent, leaving me to think about it. I watched the people in the streets below me and thought about going out for a drink, then thought better of it. I touched my side, which was still a little sore, but getting better. In a day or two there would be nothing left of the beating I'd gotten except the memory.

"I'm going to take this guy down, Loiosh."

"I know you are, Boss."

I pulled the shutters closed.

6

Assault on Helpless Wood

There are, according to Sethra Lavode, in a brief conversation I got to listen to before I marched off to war, two basic schools of thought in terms of generalship: lead from the front, or lead from the rear. The former is better for morale but can have unfortunate consequences if your officer gets killed. The latter has many advantages in terms of communication and observation, but soldiers don't fight quite so well for a leader who is playing it safe. Sethra says that, really, it depends on circumstances, and a good general ought to be willing to lead either way when appropriate. In the case of our enemies, the officers in charge of brigades—a brigade being about three thousand strong, according to Sethra's intelligence reports—led from the front. The brigade size made sense, she explained, because that was about the largest number of soldiers who could hear the officer shouting orders. The other officers were in back, along with the chief of the sorcerers corps and whatever aides might be appropriate. The brigadier, as a compromise with safety considerations, tended to be surrounded by some elite group of warriors, dedicated to protecting him during the course of the battle. The higher ranking officers received similar protection, but they didn't need it as much—I suppose it was a status symbol the way having a lot of bodyguards is in the Jhereg.

The placing of sorcerers in battle also varies according to tastes of the general and needs of the situation, but, more often than not, sorcerers were attached to a brigade and hung around next to the brigadier. Thus, not only were the sorcerers able to receive orders quickly, but they could do a lot to protect the officer directing that part of the engagement.

Got all that?

I mention it because it flashed through my mind as I went over that hillock, behind the front line my company was engaged with, to seek out the command staff.

In other words, I was going to have to go up against an elite force of warriors as well as some number of sorcerers in order to accomplish my goal.

What was I doing here again? Oh yeah, I lost my temper and talked myself (I can't blame anyone else) into offering Morrolan my services, and he was rude enough to accept, that's what happened. And now—

And now things were moving, which is just what I'd wanted back then when everything came to a standstill. I got what I wanted; isn't that grand?

Still, as I said earlier, I don't enjoy waiting, and, especially after I've made a tough or questionable decision, I want things to be moving, and as usual when I want things to be moving, everything slowed down.

Nothing surprising there: Once you've determined to do something time is needed to make plans, gather materials, and put your plans into motion, all of which causes events to unfold too slowly; it's when you are forced into action before making a decision that things happen too quickly. Watching Morrolan and Sethra taught me that this is true in military matters, and I've always known it was true in my own life.

Or else it's just the universe being perverse; that's the other possibility.

Whichever, I spent several days having fruitless and aimless conversations with Morrolan, who agreed that I could be useful but was infuriatingly vague on the specifics. He seemed to understand without my saying it that I had become committed to helping him. This, in turn, increased my suspicion that the beating had been a setup on Morrolan's part to recruit me, and I retained that suspicion for some time, but I won't keep you in suspense: I eventually learned that Morrolan had nothing to do with it; the attack was just what it seemed.

Every once in a while, a Dragon will do something obvious and direct that is no more than it appears to be. I think they do it to throw you off.

I met with Morrolan, Sethra, Aliera, and a pale Dragonlord I didn't recognize. Morrolan didn't perform any introductions. I didn't say anything, because I didn't know what to say and because I was still a bit intimidated to be in the presence of Sethra Lavode.

She spread out a map, pointed to a spot, and said, "We strike here, wait for a counterattack, and retreat this way, toward the Eastern Mountains."

There were nods around the table. I'd been there for about half a minute and I was already confused.

She went on, "Of course, if there is no counterattack, we continue this way, hit here, and here, and here, until there is one, then retreat as planned. If he should allow us all the way to here, we can lay a siege, but I can't imagine it playing out that way."

"What will be the organization?" said Morrolan.

"Divisions. Three of them. I want each self-contained, with its own infantry, cavalry, sorcerers, and engineers. The First Division will be mine, and will make the attack. The others will guard our flank and cover the retreat."

"Marching in column, then?" said Aliera.

"There are plenty of good roads leading into and out of the place; once we near the mountains we'll come back together to bivouac. Here." She pointed to another spot. "We can arrange for provender from the area along this route; we'll need to make arrangements if we're west of the Flatstone River, or north of Turtle. Who's doing logistics?"

"I will take personal charge," said Morrolan.

Sethra nodded. "Sorcery," she said.

The pale woman spoke. Her hair was very black, and her voice soft. "His lead sorcerer is named Ori—"

"Ori!" I heard myself say.

"What is it, Vlad?" said Morrolan.

"Nothing," I said, embarrassed. "Never mind."

The woman looked at me, or, rather, through me, then continued. "He is adept at reconnaissance spells; especially eavesdropping on councils. I have protected this meeting. We must always be careful to do so, and to avoid discussing our plans without protection. In battle he is unlikely to come up with anything we can't counter, but he'll keep throwing spells our way to keep our own sorcerers too busy to concoct anything big."

Sethra nodded. "Anything else?"

"Yes," said Aliera. "Why is he here?" She was looking at me.

Sethra turned to Morrolan, who said, "Because I wish it."

Aliera started to speak, then changed her mind and was silent.

The meeting broke up; Aliera and the Dragonlord I didn't know left, Morrolan and Sethra spoke together quietly about details of supply, occasionally venturing off into matters of military theory that I cared about as little as I understood them, and I sat there staring at the map. It was a psiprint, like the one Melestav had shown me, but was more detailed and even cleaner.

Eventually Morrolan noticed that I was still there. "What is it, Vlad?" he said.

"Huh? Oh, nothing. I'm just looking at the map. I like maps."

"Very well. You have no questions?"

"Oh, I have a lot of questions, but I don't know if you feel like answering them."

"Like what?"

"Like why plan for a retreat?"

Morrolan looked expectantly at Sethra. She said, "I prefer a defensive fight when possible, especially when the numbers are close, and these will be. We might, in fact, be outnumbered overall."

"I see. Well, actually, I don't. What are we trying to do?"

This time Sethra looked expectantly at Morrolan. He said, "We need to curb his ambitions. This can best be done by handing his army a severe defeat. Sethra feels she can best do this by convincing him to attack us. We have an edge in our engineering corps—that is, we can construct quick and effective defenses better than he can. So we're going to invade, and invite him to attack, and then beat him."

"All right. I think I get it. And then, what, you expect him to return the sword he stole?"

"Maybe. We may have to negotiate after that."

"What's so special about that sword?"

"The fact that he wanted it."

"But, of all the weapons in that room, why did he take that one?"

Morrolan nodded. "That's what I want to know. I trust we'll find out eventually."

"I see." I considered. "Is there any more you can tell me about Baritt?"

"What do you want to know?"

"For starters, what were the circumstances of his death?"

"I'm afraid I can't tell you that."

"Great."

"If your task were to be easy," said Morrolan, "you wouldn't be earning such a large fee for it."

"Don't play games, Morrolan."

"It's not a game," he snapped, and looked at me through narrowed eyes; I suppose the look was intended to intimidate me. It worked. He started to say more, then, I guess, decided that he'd cowed me enough and didn't have to.

To change the subject, I said, "Who was the pale woman?"

"The Necromancer," he said. "She will be in overall charge of our sorcerers."

" 'The Necromancer,' " I said. "I've heard of her. Heck of a name. Will she raise the dead for us?"

"If necessary," said Morrolan. "But I could do that. If circumstances call for it, she can open a gateway for us that will bring us to a place where eternities pass in an instant, and where life and death have no meaning, and where space can only be measured by the twisting of one's soul. An effective escape, if things go wrong."

I was sorry I'd asked. "Could have used her in the Paths of the Dead," I suggested.

He didn't consider that worth a response.

I said, "I wish I knew what this was all about."

"War," he said.

"Yeah. Over what?"

"In part, whether he's going to keep pushing boundaries."

"Is he pushing yours?"

"Not yet. But he will, if he thinks he can get away with it."

"I see. What else?"

He hesitated. "All right, I'll tell you part of it. Baritt was feared as a sorcerer. He had a great deal of influence within the House and within the Empire. He was very good at getting what he wanted. Before the Interregnum, he was Imperial Sorcerer for a few hundred years. He defended himself against various attacks from various sources with amazing success. He . . . well, he was very good."

"All right, I'm with you so far."

"He was too good."

"Excuse me?"

"He did things he ought not to have been able to do. He stood off armies on his own. At one point he defied the Imperium and made it stick. Things like that."

"Sounds like you."

"Yes."

"Well?"

"I've been wondering for years how he did it. I've come to the conclusion that he had help."

"What sort of help?"

"That's the question, isn't it? Either the aid of a deity or something else."

"Such as?"

"Such as he possessed something. Something powerful. Perhaps an object of some kind—"

"Say, a sword?"

"Perhaps."

"Say, a Great Weapon?"

"That's my guess," said Morrolan. "Based on the fact that it was stolen."

I nodded. "And so, you go to war to get it, because you want it, and you don't want Fornia to have it." I thought, but didn't say, *all of which is why you let him steal it in the first place.*

"Yes," he said.

"And I go to war because he irritated me."

"Yes."

"I guess that makes sense. You think this, whatever it is, will give you any problems?"

"Fornia isn't stupid. I was protecting Baritt's household, and he violated it. He must have expected reprisals. He knows he is likely to be facing Sethra Lavode, Aliera e'Kieron, the Necromancer, and, if you'll excuse me, myself. He's a fool if he isn't worried about what we can do. That means he thinks he's up to facing us. He must have some reason for thinking so."

"Uh . . . I see your point. What do you think? Could he be right?"

"Maybe. Still interested?"

"Do you know the Jhereg saying about wizards and knives?"

"Yes. Do you know the Dragon saying about trying to drown water?"

"No, and I'd as soon not. It might be too subtle for me."

Morrolan looked inscrutable and said nothing.

I went back to my flat and, in spite of the stiffness in my side, threw knives at a piece of wood.

No one taught me how to throw knives. I remain convinced that there is a better way to learn. But what I did, a few years ago when I decided it was a good thing to know how to do, was this: I set up a piece of wood against a wall, and I bought a bunch of identical knives and positioned myself exactly nine paces away from the target—just about all I had room for at the time. And I just started throwing them as hard as I could. From the beginning my aim was pretty good; there wasn't much damage to the wall. But I must have thrown four hundred of the things, varying my grip slightly each time, until I got one to hit point first. Then I suppose I threw another couple of hundred until I got it to happen again. And so on.

I have no idea how many thousands of knives I threw at how many pieces of wood before I could regularly stick one in the thing—from exactly nine paces. Loiosh, of course, would periodically make helpful suggestions about how I could convince an enemy to position himself properly.

How long did it take me to learn to hit a target from any reasonable distance? That's easy: I still can't do it reliably. It's a lot harder than you'd think to get the damn thing to go in point first. And even if you manage, it's hard to nail him so well that he's going to be taken out of the action; all of which might make it seem wasted effort.

On the other hand, if you throw a knife at a guy, he's going to duck. Besides, you might get lucky. Anything that may give you an edge when your life is on the line is worth putting some work into, don't you think? And another reason, just as important, is the satisfaction one gets from learning a skill—from learning how to do something you couldn't do before. It is a good feeling any time you're dissatisfied with life. And aside from all that, there's something relaxing about the ritual: deep breath, drop your shoulders, focus on the target, let fly.

So I went home and threw a bunch of knives at a defenseless piece of wood.

The next day I put in a real day at the office for the first time that week. It felt a little odd. I handled a few loan requests, checked on my various interests, sent one of my boys to jog the memory of a forgetful debtor, and had a pleasant lunch at a nearby inn called the Crow's Feet. Then I had a heart-to-heart talk with one of my people who was starting to use a little heavily and might become unreliable, kidded around with Kragar and Melestav, and got caught up reading the local scandal sheets, none of which had any interesting news. And no one tried to kill me all day. Not even any mild threats. It was refreshing.

The next day was Endweek, and most of the soreness was gone from my side; Aliera apparently did good work. I said as much to Loiosh, who suggested I hire her.

Whether I go in to the office on Endweek depends on how much I have going on; that day there wasn't much, so I figured to take the day off, and, that evening, maybe treat myself to a dinner at Valabar's. I mentally went through a list of possible dinner companions and came up with several options. The idea of spending the day finding a nice Eastern girl to share wonderful food with was entertaining. With luck, I figured, maybe I could even forget about this silly situation I'd gotten myself into.

It was about then that Morrolan made contact with me.

"What the fuck do you want?" I said pleasantly, as soon as I realized who had invaded my mind.

"Have I had the misfortune to interrupt something?"

"You have interrupted nothing; that's why I'm so irritated. What do you want?"

"If you are available, I should appreciate your company on a short journey."

"Grand. I assume it's dangerous."

"No," he said.

"You're kidding."

"Are you disappointed?"

"No, just startled."

"If you will meet me here—"

"Can you give me a couple of hours? I want breakfast, and to give it time to settle in before I teleport."

"Very well," he said, and the contact was broken.

I made myself an omelet with sausage, onions, teriano mushrooms, and red peppers. I lingered over it. Loiosh cleaned my plate while I cleaned the frying pan. Then I buckled on my sword, secreted little surprises in their appropriate places in spite of Morrolan's assurance, and donned my cloak—a lightweight one, because the breeze coming in through the kitchen window promised a warm day. Morrolan, most likely, was going to take us someplace cold, but if I'd taken the heavy cloak he'd take us someplace hot and I didn't feel like attempting psychic contact with him in order to ask what I should wear.

I didn't want to call up one of my own sorcerers, so I returned to the House of the Dragon, which turned out to be a mistake; Baron Lokran wasn't there so I had to waste a lot of time finding someone else who would and could teleport me to Castle Black; the worst part being that I had to reach Morrolan to ask him. But eventually I made it there, and I didn't lose my breakfast.

Lady Teldra gave me her warm Lady Teldra smile and, after a pleasant greeting, did not say, "The Lord Morrolan will join you in the library." Instead she said, "If you will be kind enough to accompany me, I will take you to where the Lord Morrolan awaits." Variation. Something different.

"Goodness, Boss. What does it all mean?"

"Glad to," I told Lady Teldra.

We went up the main stairway, as usual, but continued past the library all the way down the long and very wide hallway. It ended in a door, which brought us to another flight of stairs; these were straight and wide, and reached a landing that swept back in an elegant curve before straightening again. At the top was another hallway; this one I'd never seen before. It was also wide, and it curved gently. Teldra opened a door and gestured for me to precede her. I stepped onto a very narrow circular stairway; the stairs were made of iron and they went up a long way. The door closed behind me. I looked back. Teldra had not followed.

"*Maybe it's a trap,*" said Loiosh.

"*That isn't as funny as you think it is.*"

The stairwell was so narrow I nearly had to ascend sideways, and my shoulder kept rubbing against stonework. The metal rail was cold against my hand. There were a lot of stairs. It flashed through my mind that we were getting pretty high up, and then I almost laughed when I realized that we'd started about a mile up in the air, so this climb didn't change much.

At last we reached the top, where there was a thick, black door. I stood outside it like an idiot for a minute, trying to decide what to do, then I clapped.

"Come in," said Morrolan.

I opened the door. It creaked melodramatically. I wouldn't put it past Morrolan to have purposely installed a door that would creak melodramatically.

I was in a round room—about as big around as my flat. The lighting was provided by a pair of half-shuttered lanterns, which gave less light than whatever had lit the staircase on the way up, which meant that I wouldn't be able to see much until my eyes adjusted. I suddenly remembered, from the courtyard, seeing a single tower atop Castle Black. That must be where we were.

"*Brilliant, Boss.*"

"*Shut up, Loiosh.*"

"*Notice the window, Boss?*"

"*It's the only thing I can see.*"

"*How come it's night out past the window, and day when we walked up here?*"

"*I've been wondering the same thing.*"

"*That's creepy.*"

"*Yes, it is.*"

My eyes began to adjust. There wasn't much to see, just a low table and a couple of wooden chests. There were curtains all around the tower, and a set of curtains pulled aside from the window; hence there were windows all around the tower, several of them. At least six. Fewer than seventeen, which was both a relief and oddly disconcerting.

"Boss, when we saw the tower from below, were there any windows?"

"No."

"I hadn't thought so."

I also noticed that Morrolan was wearing his sword. Since Morrolan wasn't accustomed to walking around his home armed, there had to be an explanation. I wasn't looking forward to it. Especially because "armed" in this case meant Blackwand, one of the seventeen Great Weapons. Its presence did nothing to make me feel better.

He said, "Welcome to the Tower, Vlad."

"Thank you."

"There are very few permitted up here."

"Okay. Would you mind explaining the window?"

"I don't believe you have had the training necessary to understand."

"You're probably right."

"What is important, however, is that I can sometimes make the windows look upon what I wish, and that I can then travel to those places. This can be useful in bringing me to places where I do not have a sufficient mental grasp to teleport, or to a place which lies beyond the confines of what we consider 'the world.' "

"Handy thing to have around. Do you know any place that sells them?"

"And, of course, I can bring anyone I wish with me."

"Uh . . . I'm not sure I like where this conversation is heading."

"I have been attempting to solve the problem of determining exactly what Fornia took from that room, and the related problem of why I failed to notice anything significant about it."

"That's good, Morrolan. A nice mental puzzle will distract you from—"

"Regard the window, Vlad."

"Do I have to?"

But I did, and it was no longer quite black, but had become somewhat grey. A closer look revealed a certain reddish hue amid the grey. And then, near the top, I noticed a bit of orange-red color that seemed a great deal like the sky. The grey had taken on a texture, and suddenly, instead of looking at something mysterious and terrifying, I realized that I was looking at a mountain, with a bit of sky beyond it. Of course, there was no mountain that close to Castle Black, which made it mysterious and terrifying, but you can't have everything.

"Where or what is it?" I said.

"We are looking at Hawk Mountain, in the Kanefthali chain." Something in his voice made me look at him; he was exerting a great deal of effort, more than I'd ever seen from him before.

His left hand was clenched into a fist, turned up, and held stiffly out in front of him at about chin height, the elbow bent. His right hand and arm were moving, going through various gyrations while the fingers extended, contracted, wiggled, twitched, and generally appeared to have a life of their own. Morrolan's eyes were narrowed to slits, and he was breathing loudly, through opened lips, creating a very slight whistling sound through his clenched teeth.

The thought *Earth, water, fire, and air* came into my mind as I compared left hand, right hand, eyes, and mouth; but I strongly suspect it wasn't anything that simple. I've seen sorcery, and I've seen witchcraft, and this didn't look like either one. I wasn't at all certain I wanted to know what it was.

I looked back through the window, and it seemed to be moving—or, more accurately, it seemed as if we were moving. My knees suddenly felt wobbly and I didn't like it. I looked at Morrolan again, and he was still staring intently through the window. He was making aimless gestures with his hands, and there were beads of sweat on his forehead.

The mountain appeared to rush at us, and I actually felt a falling sensation. I stepped backward and looked for something to brace against. Then it slowed and stopped, and just outside the window, so close I could touch it, was a dirt path leading to a cave that looked to be about forty feet away.

My heart was still racing. I glanced at Morrolan, who now seemed entirely relaxed; only his breathing showed that he had recently exerted himself.

"What's going on?" I managed.

"We're going to ask—"

"We?"

"—our questions of someone who might know the answers."

"Why 'we'? What am I doing here?"

"Just in case."

"I thought you said there'd be no danger."

"I don't expect there will be."

He stepped through the window, and just like leaving an ordinary window of an ordinary house, he stood on the ground outside, on a rocky path, about forty feet from the entrance to a cave. I sent a suspicious look at the cave. I've never been that fond of caves at the best of times.

"But," continued Morrolan, "it never hurts to have an extra blade along just in case. They can be unpredictable."

"Who is they?"

"The Serioli," he said. "Come on."

"Wonderful," I muttered, and stepped through the window.

INTERLUDE: MANEUVERS

Some things you do, you never seem to be done with; years later they come back and remind you, slap you, beat you up. Here I am telling a story of what happened years ago, trying to remember how I felt back then, and—well, forgive the digression, but it belongs here.

Just today, Sethra the Younger returned from exile (Sethra Lavode exiled her off the world a few weeks ago in punishment for, well, never mind what for) and sent word asking me to wait upon her. I don't like her, she doesn't like me, and I couldn't imagine how this could be anything good. And there would be no reason for me to go if I had steered clear of Dragonlords and their business, but since Baritt died I've surrounded myself with them, and now I'm in love with a woman who used to associate with Norathar, who is Dragon Heir to the throne. All of which made it difficult to decline the invitation.

Sorry for the confusion—but that's what happens when you start in the past and the present comes up and bites you. And it's what happens when you hang around with Dragonlords. I'd always thought of Dragons, above all, as simple and straightforward—if something gets in your way, you draw and charge and keep hacking until either it's gone or you are. This is another thing I was wrong about. Watching Sethra put together her campaign, arranging for supplies to be where they were needed, anticipating movements and preparing possible countermarches, guiding her intelligence services—well, okay, war is more complex than I'd thought, so I suppose recounting it has to be complex as well.

"What in blazes could Sethra the Younger want of me, other than my life, which I'm not prepared to part with?"

"Couldn't say, Boss. But you know you're going to go find out, so why not admit it?"

There wasn't much answer to that, so I went ahead and made the arrangements, responding through proper channels, and arrived at Castle Black, where she is staying. We met in one of Morrolan's sitting rooms. She is odd; her features remind me quite a bit of Sethra Lavode's but all done in pastels, and Sethra the Younger was without the terrifying sense of agelessness and power; nevertheless, she has her own aura—a ruthlessness and lust for power that one might expect in a Jhereg.

She tried not to be obvious about how much she disliked me, but casual conversation was beyond her.

"The sword," she began abruptly.

"What sword?" I asked.

"You know damned well—" She stopped, swallowed, and began again. "The sword that was recovered at the Wall of Baritt's Tomb."

I admired the way she put that. "Was recovered." Whatever it was she wanted, it wasn't enough to make her admit . . . oh, skip it.

"What about it?" I said.

"I have it," she said.

"I know," I told her. "I didn't realize it at the time because I didn't know you. But I figured out who you were later. It's funny you should bring this up just now—"

"If you please, Lord Taltos," she said, as if addressing me by title made her lips hurt.

"Yes?"

She looked at Loiosh, riding complacently on my shoulder, then looked away. I heard Loiosh chuckling within my mind.

I thought about baiting her some more, just because this conversation was so obviously distasteful to her, but I refrained, mostly because I was curious. "All right," I said. "What does this have to do with me?"

"I want you to act as intermediary for me with the Lady Aliera."

"You want me . . . wait a minute." I couldn't decide which question to ask first. I settled on, "Why me?"

"Aliera doesn't care for me much."

"Well, come to that, neither do I. So?"

"Negotiations should be handled by a third party."

"Then why not Morrolan? Or Sethra?"

"As for Sethra Lavode, I believe she is still sufficiently vexed with me that I cannot ask her for a favor. And Aliera's relationship with Morrolan is such that she will automatically react with hostility to anything he suggests."

That much was true. But—"What makes you think I have any interest in doing you a service?"

She looked startled. "Oh, I'm not asking you for a service."

"You're not?"

"No, no. I intend to pay you."

I carefully controlled my reaction. "I see. Well, what is this negotiation about?"

"The sword, of course."

"Excuse me?"

"I want to offer her the sword we recovered from Fornia in exchange for Kieron's greatsword."

That threw me. I sat there for a minute, trying to figure out what it all meant, and then, to kill time as much as because I was curious, I said, "So far as I know, the sword we recovered from Fornia has nothing special about it. At least, insofar as any Morganti weapon has nothing special about it. Why do you think she'd be interested?"

"You know as well as I that there is more to the sword than that. If I don't know precisely what, that is because, well, that is because I have not yet taken the time to find out."

Because you aren't up to the job? I thought to myself. But that wasn't fair, of course. Several people, including Fornia, hadn't been up to the job. But it pleased me that, after snatching it, she hadn't been able to solve the problem either. I speculated that she'd been too proud to ask Sethra Lavode for help, but I had no way of knowing; maybe the Enchantress of Dzur Mountain had drawn a blank, too.

What I said was, "What would you do with Kieron's greatsword?"

I could see her trying to decide if I deserved an answer. At last she said, "Conquer the East. It would be a tremendous symbol for the leader of—"

"Spare me," I said.

She cleared her throat. "Yes, certainly. But you must see, you are the perfect choice. She trusts you, and even has some bizarre affection for you. And you could put it in terms that would make her see the mutual advantages. I don't know what the going rates are for such a service, but I have sufficient means to—where are you going?"

"To drink seawater. It'll leave a better taste in my mouth than this conversation. Excuse me."

And that was what Sethra the Younger wanted to see me about. It is, you see, all part of the same picture. It is not a picture I'd care to have on my wall.

Which doesn't keep me from continuing to paint it.

7

WHAT WAS THE QUESTION?

Loiosh said, *"No one's noticed you, yet."*

"Good."

I trotted to the top of the hill and took a good look around. The field on which my messmates were fighting was behind me, and farther behind me was the Wall; a long way off to my right was a match of cavalry against cavalry, and to my left was a company of bad guys marching at quicktime. They might be reinforcements coming to attack my own unit; I couldn't tell yet, and didn't want to wait around to find out. Ahead of me, about two hundred yards away, was a slightly higher hill, and on it was a body of soldiers, I guessed around twenty or thirty, standing alert and, I was fairly certain, protecting the sorcerers, in the center of whom would likely be what I was after.

"Okay, Loiosh. *Forward at a march.*"

"You march, Boss. I'll just sort of hang around."

"Or you could fly overhead and let me know if you see Ori in that group."

"Whatever you say, Boss."

He left my shoulder. I headed toward the hill, wishing I had some sort of plan. But, after all, there were only twenty or thirty of them; what was there to worry about?

I'd covered about a hundred and fifty yards when Loiosh said, *"They've noticed you, Boss."*

"Great."

I kept moving, because stopping would have been worse, although I didn't enjoy it. I was, not to put too fine a point on it, terrified. My brain was working hard trying to come up with what to say, what to do that would not only leave me alive but let me finish what I set out to do, but each step took an effort, as if my feet had their own idea and wanted me to stop and reconsider the whole idea of forward motion.

I'd had the same reaction, now that I thought about it, to stepping through Morrolan's window; I hadn't wanted to go, but I did. And both times, in a way, I was driven by the same thing: the desire not to look craven in front of a Dragon. Why should I care? There's another mystery.

I knew, as I stepped through that window, that if I looked around there would be no window behind me, but I had to look anyway. No, there was no window; there was, instead, a breathtaking view of three mountain peaks, laid out as if they had been built just for how they looked from where I stood. Two of them were capped with snow, stretching out before me, too far away to pick out details. There was a purple sheen to them, and it took a moment to realize I was looking *down* on them. Then I noticed the sharpness of the air, and the fresh tang. I pulled my cloak closer around me.

"Let's go, Vlad."

"I'm admiring nature," I said, but I turned and followed him up the path.

I bent my head as we entered the cave—I suppose from some odd instinct, because it was large enough for Morrolan to enter unbowed, which he did.

The light failed quickly; after ten paces I could no longer see. Morrolan and I stopped and he made a light spell that caused a radiance to shine out from his hand, not too strong to look at but very bright wherever he pointed. We continued. The cave became narrower and the ceiling lower. "Watch your head," he suggested.

"Notice anything odd, Boss?"

"No, Loiosh, it seems just like every other time I used a necromantic window to step through onto the top of a mountain and walk into a dark cave to meet someone of a half-legendary magical race. What are you talking about?"

"What do you smell?"

"Ah. Okay, point. I owe you a fish head."

What I smelled was brimstone. What it meant I couldn't say, but

I doubted it was a natural smell in that cave, at least as strong as it was. I glanced at Morrolan, walking steadily and emitting light from his hand. I could read nothing from his expression.

About fifty paces in from the mouth, the cave abruptly ended in a natural-looking wall that could not have been natural. Morrolan stood there, frowning at it, and I said, "What now?"

"I am uncertain of the custom," he said. "Whether we should wait or—"

There was a rattling sound, as of pebbles rolling on metal, followed by a low rumble, and a portion of the wall before us gave back, showing a narrow stone stairway heading downward.

"I think waiting is appropriate," I said.

He began going down the stairs.

There were only twenty steps, and those shallow, until they reached another stone doorway, this one standing open, and we continued, walking on flagstones that echoed sharply. The hall was narrow and the ceiling low; I took a certain pleasure in seeing Morrolan walk with his head bowed. The smell of brimstone grew even stronger.

"*I wonder what's for dinner?*" said Loiosh.

The hall ended without ceremony, leaving us in a nearly circular cavern about forty feet in diameter. The walls were rough and cavelike, the floor polished smooth, and the ceiling just high enough for Morrolan to stand straight. There was no furniture of any kind. A short person stood at the far end, looking at us with what would have been an expression of curiosity in a human or a Dragaeran. We approached until we were about six feet away, and then stopped. The being was skinny and ugly, wore what appeared to be blue and red silks in the form of layers of scarves, and as far as I could see, had no hair whatsoever.

He—I thought he looked like a he—gave no courtesy, but spoke abruptly, in a pleasant, flutey voice. His accents fell in odd, almost random places, and there was a certain clipped quality to his consonants, but there was no difficulty understanding him. He addressed Morrolan with the words, "Greetings, brother. Who are your friends?"

"*Did you hear that, Boss? Friends?*"

"*Shut up, Loiosh.*"

"Good day to you," said Morrolan, adding a sound at the end that was either the last cough from a man with Juiner's Lung or the

name of the Serioli we faced. "His name—your pardon—the Easterner's name is Vlad Taltos, the Jhereg is called Loiosh."

"You don't mention the fourth, because we've met already; but
why do you leave out the fifth? Because she is not altogether here?"

Morrolan frowned and looked at me. I gave him a helpless shrug.
I said, "I take it you two have met before?"

"Once," said Morrolan. "Far from here, but he told me where to
find him."

There was a story there, but Morrolan wasn't much given to
storytelling, and now wasn't the time to ask. I studied the Serioli, the
only one I'd ever seen, and tried not to look as if I was staring. He
wasn't so polite; he was looking at me, and at Loiosh, as if an odd
specimen of vegetation had just occurred in his garden and he wasn't
certain if it were flower or weed.

His complexion was very pale, almost albino, and his face was
more wrinkled than my grandfather's. His hair was thin, wispy, and
white, his eyes a pale, watery blue.

Morrolan said, "Who is the fifth?"

"Who indeed," said the Serioli, nodding sagaciously, as if Morrolan had said something wise.

Morrolan glanced at me again as if wondering if I had any idea
what the Serioli was talking about. I shrugged with my eyebrows.

"You don't understand?" said our host. "How droll. But leave it
for now."

"We've brought wine," said Morrolan, which was news to me.
"Would you care for some? It is from the East."

"Grateful," said the Serioli. "Shall we sit?"

Morrolan sat himself down on the floor, leaning against the wall,
legs stretched out, looking absurd. I sat next to him, but I don't know
how I looked. Our companion walked around a wall that I hadn't
seen was there—it blended into the back of the cave—and emerged
with three handsome wooden goblets. Morrolan produced a bottle of
wine and glass-cloth from somewhere, broke off the neck with a practiced hand, spread the cloth, and poured. Then he hauled out some
sweet biscuits wrapped in cloth and spread those out on the floor. I
ate one. It was all right. I wondered if it was the custom among the
Serioli for guests to bring the refreshments; I made a mental note to
ask Morrolan later, but I forgot.

I watched the Serioli eat and drink. I couldn't tell for sure if he had any teeth, but I almost became convinced he had no bones in his arms. I thought he looked graceful, Loiosh thought he looked silly. What good these observations did is, of course, a perfectly valid, if inherently rhetorical, question.

"You've brought good wine," said our host after eating and drinking for a few minutes. "And questions, too?"

"Yes," said Morrolan. "We've brought questions, but first there's the one we didn't bring, but found waiting for us when we arrived."

"Yes. You did not know of whom I was asking." Then he looked at me with his head tilted and his funny little eyes narrowed. "And you, too. Or are there secrets I am giving away?"

"None that I know of," I said. "Besides, I trust the Lord Morrolan completely as long as he has nothing to do with my business."

The Serioli made a wheezing sound accompanied by his whole face pinching up; I assumed he was laughing. He spoke in his own language, a clicking, snapping sound that seemed like one long word full of consonants and digestive trouble; it flowed naturally from his face, as if he ought to speak like that. Morrolan chuckled.

I looked at Morrolan and said, "All of which meant?"

"Three can keep a secret if two are dead."

I raised my glass to the Serioli, who said to Morrolan, "Let me then answer your question. You may be unaware of it, but by your side, descendent of Dragons, is—?" Here he croaked, coughed, and clicked something in his own language.

"Which means?" I said.

Morrolan answered, "Magical wand for creating death in the form of a black sword."

"Oh," I said. "Is that what it is?"

"Close," said the Serioli. "I should not, however, translate it as 'creating death.'" He paused, as if wanting to formulate the sentence before embarking on it. "It would be more precise to say 'removing life-substance.'" He paused again, "Or perhaps 'sending the life-substance to—'"

"Fine," said Morrolan.

"Our symbol for life, you see, is expressed in the phrase—"

"If you please," said Morrolan.

The Serioli looked at him. "Yes?"

"What—or who—is the fifth?"

"The fifth isn't entirely here. But your friend of the Old People should know."

"You should know?"

"Old People?"

"How should I know?" I said. "Old people?"

He made a growling noise in which words were hidden. Morrolan searched them out and said, "I'm not sure what that means. 'People from the invisible lights'?"

"Small invisible lights."

"Ah," I said. "Well, if you can't see them, I don't suppose it matters much how big they are." Then, "But were you speaking of Spellbreaker?"

"Is that what you call it?" He made his laughing sound again.

"What would you call it?"

"Spellbreaker," he said, "is as good a name as any, for now."

"You're saying I'm holding a Great Weapon?"

"No, you are not. Not yet."

"Not yet," I repeated. I let Spellbreaker, which I kept coiled around my left wrist, fall into my hand. I studied it. It seemed shorter than it had the last time I looked at it, and the links appeared to be smaller. "Not yet?"

"Someday, there will be a weapon—" He stopped and his lips worked. Then he resumed, "Someday, there will be a weapon called 'Remover of aspects of deity.' "

I repeated this name and shrugged.

"Godslayer," said Morrolan.

"If you wish," said the Serioli.

"What has this to do with my chain?"

"Everything," said the Serioli. "Or nothing."

"Do you know, I get tired of people speaking in riddles."

Our host made his laughing sound again. I wrapped Spellbreaker around my wrist. "Fine," I said. "How do I find this weapon?"

"Uh . . . Boss? Why do you want to?"

"I'm not certain I do, but—"

"To find it, you must first find—" He clicked some more.

I looked at Morrolan. "Artifact in sword form that searches for the true path." He looked at the Serioli to see if the translation was approved.

"Not far off. But I am uncertain if 'true path' would be precisely the way to say it. I might suggest 'an object of desire when the path is true.' The form of 'path' is made abstract by the final 'tsu.' "

"I see," said Morrolan. "Thank you."

I wondered if Morrolan had any idea what he was talking about. Probably, since he spoke the language. I said, "Would you like to tell me more?"

"The two artifacts were, or are to be, created together—"

"Excuse me, but is there a simple explanation for this 'were or are to be' thing?"

"No."

"I didn't think so. All right." I dropped it. Whenever anyone starts talking about the odd things time can do, I think about the Paths of the Dead, and I didn't care to think about that just then.

"Some of our people," he continued, "desired divinity and crafted artifacts to find and then destroy those who sit on the Thrones of Judgment. One of these became something other than what it had been designed to be; it became a device for the finding of—well, for the finding of whatever the wielder wished to find, based on the principle that all of life, including the desire of will, is part of—"

"If you please," said Morrolan. "The other?"

"The other was taken by the Gods, and an attempt was made to destroy it."

"I can imagine," I said under my breath.

"Both are now lost; when one is found, the other is likely to turn up."

"And what I have—"

"What you have," he said, staring at me with an expression I couldn't read, "is a gold chain that is useful for interrupting the flow of energies from—" He concluded the sentence with another word or phrase in his own language. I looked at Morrolan for a translation, but the Dragonlord was chewing his lip, frowning, and seemed to be busy with thoughts of his own. That was all right; I could make a pretty good guess.

I said, "Well, that's certainly something to think about. But I believe Morrolan brought us here to ask you something."

Morrolan blinked and looked at me. "Pardon?"

"I was suggesting that you ask our friend whatever it is you wanted to ask him about."

"Oh. I already have."

"You—all right."

"Loiosh, did you catch any psychic communication?"

"No, Boss. But I might have missed it. This character is weird."

"You think?"

Whatever information Morrolan had been after, he'd clearly gotten it. He made a few courtesies, which I did my best to mimic, then, bowing, he led the way back out of the cave. As we walked, I said, "I forgot to ask why the place smelled of brimstone."

He didn't answer.

Once we were back outside, I said, "So, how do you make the window reappear?"

He didn't answer that, either, but made a few nonchalant gestures in the air, and it occurred to me that there was no reason to make the window appear; he could simply teleport us to Castle Black. I'd have suggested that I preferred the other method of travel, but he didn't seem to be in a mood to listen.

My bowels twisted and the mountains vanished, and we were back in the room which we'd first left, and without so much as a pause Morrolan said, "Thank you, Vlad, I am glad to have had you along."

"Mind if I sit for a moment?" I managed. It wasn't just the aftereffects of the teleport, it was the realization that I'd have to teleport again when I left.

"Not at all."

He drew a curtain over the window we'd lately walked through. I looked around the room again, just to kill time. For the center of power for a powerful sorcerer, there wasn't a whole lot there: the table, two chests. And the windows. I counted nine of them. Then I counted eight of them. Then I counted nine again, then I counted ten. By then my stomach had settled down so I quit counting and stood up.

"Feeling better?"

I looked for traces of a sneer and didn't notice any. "Yes, thanks. Lead on."

He brought us back down the narrow metal stairway and through the labyrinth of Castle Black—a labyrinth I was beginning to learn, thanks to Fentor and the work I was doing on Morrolan's security (which I know I haven't mentioned much, but it doesn't really come into this story; there was a fair bit of work involved, and some interesting things happened, but I don't want to take the time to go into it right now).

"So," I said. "Would you care to tell me what you learned?"

"Of course not," he said. "Would you care for a drink?"

"No, thanks. I'm teleporting."

"Ah, yes, certainly." He reached into his cloak and removed a small purse.

"No, no," I said. "This one's gratis."

"Indeed?"

"Yes. I learned enough to pay for the experience."

"Oh? And . . ." He decided not to ask what I'd learned because he knew very well how I'd answer.

Loiosh said, *"Did I miss something? What did you learn?"*

"Nothing. I just wanted to give Morrolan something to think about."

"I hope it was worth whatever he was going to pay you."

Morrolan said, "Are you still determined upon the course of action to which you previously referred?"

"I beg your pardon?"

"I said—"

"No, never mind. I think I got part of that. Yeah, I'm still willing to do what I can to mess up this guy's program, if you think it'll help."

"Good. We will begin the muster tomorrow. The following day you may, if you are still willing, of course, report to your unit, Cropper Company, at noon. It will be assembling on the lea below Castle Black, north of the stone wall. Look for a green banner with a black horn upon it."

I opened and shut my mouth a few times, then said, "So soon?"

"If you can give me a good reason to delay, I'll consider the matter."

"I'll think about it and get back to you. But can't I just teleport to someplace where I'll do some good, instead of joining a company?"

"What makes you think the enemy will allow teleports anywhere in the area? Or, for that matter, that I will?"

"Will you?"

"No."

"I see. Well, what about your window?"

"I won't be here, I'll be with the army."

"Oh."

"Any other questions?"

"Uh . . . Why that company?"

"Is there another you'd prefer?"

"I haven't a clue, Morrolan. I just wondered what it is about them—"

"They'll be in the van during the first stage, which makes it most convenient for your activities, and Cropper, the Captain, is easier to work with than some. Anything else?"

"Yeah. How do I get home? I don't feel like doing my own tele-port."

"Where are you going?"

"My office."

"I'll bring you."

"You mean you'll send me?"

"I was thinking of bringing you. I'd like to see where you work."

"Heh. That'll shake up the staff," I said. "Sure."

"Then open your mind and think of your office."

I had him bring us to the street outside, pointed out some sights to him while I recovered, and noticed that he was attracting a certain amount of attention: Dragonlords aren't often seen in the company of Easterners. On the other hand, no one wanted to stare too bla-tantly; people mind their own business in my neighborhood.

I led him through the various fronts and up into the suite of rooms I worked out of. Melestav looked up when I came in, then saw who was behind me and nearly sprang to his feet.

"Melestav," I said, "the Lord Morrolan."

Melestav didn't find anything to say, which amused me. Morrolan looked around. "If I didn't know better," he said, "I should say that this was the office of an advocate."

"What were you expecting? Bottles of poison and shelves of gar-rotes?"

"I'm not certain," said Morrolan. "Perhaps that is why I wanted to see it."

"Here's where I work," I said, leading the way. Kragar, whom I hadn't noticed, stepped out of our way.

"Excuse me," I said. "Kragar, the Lord Morrolan."

"We've met," said Kragar.

"Forgive me if I don't bow," said Morrolan.

I showed him in, and had him sit in the chair opposite me. "So," I said, "you need more time to pay me back. Well, maybe we can work something out."

"There is a disparity," he said, "between what you do and the surroundings in which you do it. It is interesting." Which was when I suddenly realized that he wanted to be here because he wanted to learn about me—that is, he was learning about a potential ally or possible enemy, in much the same way he would investigate military positions, or I would study someone with whom I had business. It was reasonable, but it made me very uncomfortable.

"I had the same reaction, a few days ago."

He stared at me hard for a moment, then continued looking around my office.

"*Ask him if he wants a job, Boss.*"

"*Maybe later, Loiosh.*"

"Well, thank you, Vlad. I'll be going now."

"I'll show you out," I said, and I did, then returned to my desk, sat down, and said, "So, Kragar, it's like this, you see. . . ."

He waited for me to continue, his eyes narrowed, his head tilted, and his expression one of intense suspicion. At length, when I refused to finish the thought, he said, "What was he doing here?"

"Checking me out. But that isn't what I wanted to talk about."

"Oh?" he said. "It must be my latent Dragon instincts that tell me you've either done something stupid or you're going to ask me to do something unpleasant, or both."

"Both, I think."

He nodded, his expression unchanging.

"I'd like you to run things here while I'm gone. It'll be at least—"

"That's both, all right."

"—a couple of days, maybe a month or more."

He frowned and thought about it. At last he said, "I don't much like the idea. I'm an executive officer type, not a commander. That's how I like it, you know."

"I know."

He considered some more. "Offer me a lot of money."

"I'll give you a lot of money."

"All right."

"Good."

"What will you be doing?"

"Following up on your idea."

"Which one?"

"Sabotage and sundry nuisance for an army."

"I see."

"Morrolan has assigned me to a company."

"I imagine he has."

"Anything I should know about military life before I show up?"

He laughed. "I don't know where to start. For one thing, expect to hate it."

"Oh, I do."

"For another, if you start letting yourself get pushed around—I mean by your messmates, not your superior officers—it'll never stop, or else you'll have to kill someone, which won't be good for anyone."

"Got it."

"And for another, if your messmates even suspect you aren't going to be holding up your end in battle, they'll make your life miserable."

"One question."

"Go ahead."

"What's a messmate?"

"I can see," said Kragar slowly, "that you're going to need a great deal of preparation for this."

If you follow Dockside Road as it meanders generally east and a little south (following the docks, amazingly enough) you'll eventually reach a place where it opens up into a market area, from which Bacon Street springs off down a hill. Assume that the wind is from the north or west because if it is from the south or east you won't make it that far, and you'll soon see a row of short, squat, ugly brick buildings wedged right up against a very low section of the cliffs of Adrilankha. These are the slaughterhouses, and they're positioned so when the meat has been sliced, seasoned, smoked, salted, and packed it can be dumped over the cliff on shipping nets, from which it can then be stowed in the holds of the merchant ships which will try to get it to its destination before too much of it has become too disgusting to be eaten.

Go on past it, and hope the wind fortuitously changes direction right about there (nothing, but *nothing*, smells as bad as a slaughter-house on a hot day) and you'll start climbing up again, and somewhere in there Bacon Street becomes Ramshead Lane, and you'll notice that the stench diminishes and changes (garbage doesn't smell quite as bad as a slaughterhouse) but doesn't go away and that the dwellings are mostly wood, and packed tightly together, and un-painted, and you're now in South Adrilankha, and you are welcome to tell me why you bothered to come in the first place. I was there because I had family in the district.

I knew the streets here almost as well as I knew my own area, so I paid little attention as we walked past bakeries and tanners and ironmongers and witches and prostitutes, following the turnings in the road and occasionally nodding at anyone who dared to make eye contact with me, because I don't go out of my way to be intimidating to other Easterners. It is a relief, in any case, to see people who are sometimes bald and sometimes fat and sometimes short and some-times have whiskers, because Dragaerans can't manage any of these things—what they see as better I see as more limited.

We passed a street minstrel who was singing in one of the more obscure Eastern languages, and I dropped a few orbs into his instru-ment case.

"Boss, was he singing what I thought he was singing?"

"A young man tells his beloved of his love for her."

" 'My little hairy testicle—' "

"It's a cultural thing, Loiosh. You wouldn't understand."

We came to a street called Strangers Road, and south of it was a neighborhood called Six Corners where everything changed at night; I know of nothing like it anywhere else in Adrilankha, or in any part of the Empire. But here is a fish shop during the day; at night the unsold fish are thrown away and it becomes a place to buy homemade untaxed liquor, especially brandy. Next to it is a boot-maker's, until night, when the boots are locked away beneath the floor and it becomes an untaxed gambling hall. That baker goes home for the day, and another man comes at night, opens the back, unfolds rows of mattresses, and turns the place into one of the most wretched brothels in the City.

I rather preferred the district in the day, though at night it felt more like home.

And then, just after passing out of Six Corners, we eventually reached a small witchcraft supply shop at the corner of two unnamed and unmarked streets, and I walked in under the awning, setting the chimes ringing. I was greeted at once by Ambrus, the cat, who emerged from under the hanging rugs and was followed by my grandfather, who parted them carefully before stepping through. "Hello, Vladimir," he said. "It is good to see you. Sit down and have tea."

Ambrus crouched before me, preparing to spring. I made a basket of my arms, caught him, and carried him past the rugs and into the shop or the house—it was the same place and hard even for me to tell which items were for sale or use by customers and which were strictly personal. For example, you'd think the self-portrait was personal, wouldn't you? Just goes to show you. Loiosh and Ambrus, having established their relationship early on, determinedly ignored one another's existence.

I sat in a grey stuffed chair, set the cat on my lap, and took the small, delicate porcelain teacup from my grandfather. It was painted blue, and the tea was red. I squeezed lemon into it, added a trace of honey, and said, "How are you, Noish-pa?"

"I am as always, Vladimir."

In other words, he knew I had something on my mind and that I wasn't just coming over to visit. The thing is, I often come over just to visit, so how did he know? But never mind that. I took a tiny sip of tea, because I knew it would be very hot. It was; it was also very good, and not in the least bitter. I could have gotten by without the honey. I should have sampled it first. I said, "I have joined the army, Noish-pa."

His eyes widened, and I was delighted to have actually managed to startle him. He said, "You have joined the army?"

"Well, after a fashion."

He leaned back a little in his chair, which was a great deal like the one I was sitting in. I suddenly realized that my own furniture tended to be like my grandfather's, as opposed to the hard wood and lightly padded stuff I had grown up with while my father was alive. "Tell me of it," he said.

"I was attacked not long ago. Beaten and threatened. It was by a man who had no reason to attack me, except to warn me to leave him alone. I'd have left him alone if he had left me alone. Now I'm going to hurt him."

"By enlisting in an army?"

"An army that is soon to attack him. I will be engaging in various special services—"

"Do you think this a good reason to enlist in an army?"

"Of course not, Noish-pa."

He cracked a quick, gap-toothed smile. "But you are doing it anyway."

"Yes."

"Very well."

He knew me, and knew when it was worthwhile to try to talk me into or out of something. He rarely tried to change my mind in any case, even when he might be able to. Loiosh flew over to him and accepted having his chin scratched. Noish-pa said, "What then do you ask me?"

"You were in the army once. What should I know?"

He frowned. "Vladimir, that was a different circumstance. I was a conscript soldier in an Eastern army; this is not the same as volunteering in an army of elfs."

"I know that."

"And we were soundly beaten in our first and only battle."

"I know that, too."

He stared off into the distance. "You will do a great deal of marching; protect your feet. Stay out of the way of officers—try not to be noticed. Do your share of latrine duty, but not more than your share, though you won't need to be told that. Sleep when you can, but you won't need to be told that, either. Trust your officers, even though they will not be trustworthy; you must trust them anyway because it is worse if you don't."

The implications of that last suggestion went home, and, in a certain sense, I became aware for the first time of just what I'd gotten myself into.

"It's not too late, Boss."

"*Yes, it is.*"

I remembered to drink more of my tea before it got cold.

"Are you hungry, Vladimir?"

"A little."

"Come, then."

We went back into his little kitchen, and I sat on a stool at the tiny counter while he made the one thing I've never been able to get to come out right: It is an Eastern bread, only slightly raised, and pan-fried in a very light olive oil. I think the trick is getting the oil at exactly the right temperature, and judging when to turn the bread, which is just before it shows any obvious signs of needing to turn; the dough was pretty straightforward, unless Noish-pa was hiding something, which would be unlike him. In any case, I've never been able to get it right, which I regretted anew as soon as the first one hit the oil and released its aroma.

I watched my grandfather as he cooked. His concentration was total, just as when he was crafting a spell. The comparison between cooking and witchcraft has been so overdone that I can't make myself discuss it, but I'll mention I was reminded of it again.

I let the first "loaf" (it looked more like a large, raised square of light brown dough) cool just a bit. I took a clove of garlic, cut it in two with my teeth, and coated the top of the bread with it. When I could hold the bread without burning my fingers too much, I bit into the garlic, let it explode in my mouth, then followed it with a bite of bread. I closed my eyes to enjoy the experience, and when I opened them Noish-pa had put a glass of red wine next to my elbow. We ate in silence for a while, and I enjoyed it until I realized that this would be one of the last decent meals I ate for a while. I wondered if it would be possible to teleport out of camp late at night, get something to eat, and teleport back. No, they'd doubtless have teleport blocks in place to make sure the enemy didn't show up for reasons other than cuisine.

"*You've really done it this time, haven't you, Boss?*"

I didn't even tell him to shut up. I embraced Noish-pa and walked back through South Adrilankha. Not much time had passed, and the street musician was still there, this time singing something about a cockroach wearing leather pants. In a better mood I'd have laughed, but I still put some more money into his instrument case, just on the chance that it might bring me good luck.

I wanted to spend the next day preparing myself for what was coming; the trouble was, I had no idea how to do so. I wasn't even certain what to pack, except to make sure I had my most comfortable boots and, of course, a good assortment of weapons. I laid them all out with a heavy cloak, a spare shirt, some extra hose, and shaving gear, and stared at them, thinking they were inadequate and ought to tell me why, then I stuffed them all into a satchel and headed over to the office because I couldn't think of a good excuse not to.

Neither Kragar nor Melestav had much to say to me, from which I deduced that Kragar had, at least, hinted to Melestav about what I was up to. And, after all, what was there for them to say? Melestav kept shaking his head; Kragar smirked periodically. I didn't think it was all that funny.

I canceled a couple of unimportant meetings because I just didn't feel I could do them justice. I couldn't decide if I hoped there'd be nothing to do so I could go home and fret or if I wanted to be kept busy with my mind elsewhere. After an hour or so of hanging around being irritated I decided I didn't care and that I'd just take the rest of the day off. I'm the boss; I can do that.

I paced around my flat. I tried to read but kept getting distracted, so I went to a club that had music but only found it irritating, so I went to another club that had Fenarian brandy, and that helped. I wondered how many times, down through the ages, has Fenarian brandy or its spiritual equivalent, so to speak, come to the help of a man the day before he became a soldier.

Hell, that was stupid. I was *not* becoming a soldier. I was enlisting, as a formality, so I could march with an army and do nasty things to the enemy; I was certainly not going to be around for any battles. I drank some more brandy to that thought, then went home and went to bed, and some time later I fell asleep, and then I got up late the next morning and enlisted.

8

IN THE ARMY NOW

Fifty yards away there were about twenty Dragonlords, and among them, to the best of my knowledge and belief, were sorcerers skilled enough to be willing to take on the duties for an army. Now, don't get me wrong; I'm good at what I do. But marching forward across an open field, in plain sight, and just starting to cut away was not, it seemed to me, the best way to accomplish my goal.

"*Now what, Boss?*"

"*Funny, I was just asking myself that very question.*"

I walked forward about half the distance; I was certainly the object of their attention now. If I had arranged an attack from some other direction, and my approach had been merely a distraction, it would have worked perfectly.

Shame about that.

I unbuckled my sword belt, let it fall to the ground, raised my hands, and kept walking.

"*Got an idea, Boss?*"

"*No,*" I explained.

"*Well, that makes me feel better.*"

Now it was just one foot in front of another, but with the destination in sight. There was horrid inevitability to it, as if I were just completing a journey that had started weeks before, with a teleport to where Morrolan's army was bivouacked; everything after that had been just continuing the journey. Maybe I never should have started it. I certainly felt that way when I appeared on the lea beneath Castle Black.

Skip the teleport; it's getting as boring to relate as it is to do, though perhaps not quite so sick-making. I arrived near a wooden bridge that was larger than it had seemed from a mile up (go figure). It was a strange bridge, too, with a high arch and sticks jutting out at odd angles and, as far as I could see, nothing at all keeping it together. On the other side were two sentries holding spears, and behind them rows and rows of tents, all of them beige, all facing the same way, all of them an equal distance apart. A few banners fluttered in the light breeze. It was a bit cool out.

I looked for the banner Morrolan had described. I wondered what I'd have done if there were no breeze; how much confusion would that have caused? No, of course a sorcerer would have gotten up a breeze. In fact, maybe that's what happened. I could probably find out by performing a—

"*Well, Boss?*"

"*I'm procrastinating.*"

"*I know.*"

I sighed and crossed the bridge. It seemed solid enough, and, yes, as soon as I crossed it I was stepping into an area protected from teleports. The sentries crossed their spears in front of me. One started to speak, but I said, "Vladimir Taltos, House of the Jhereg, to see Captain Cropper by orders of Lord Morrolan."

They stepped out of my way, and one of them gestured to my left. I nodded, turned that way, and began strolling, with the camps to my right. The stream on my left gurgled and laughed at me. It was all bloody damned pastoral in that direction. Looking the other way, there was actually not much activity; I saw a few people sitting on makeshift stools outside of tents, but not many, and those paid little attention to me. There were also a good number of wagons at the far end, and I could see a few people unloading boxes into large, pavilion-like tents. Occasionally I'd hear laughter drifting over. A few small fires were going, and I could smell wood smoke and fresh bread.

"*There it is, Boss. Green banner, black horn.*"

"*Where? Oh. I see it. I'd been thinking of a Lyorn's horn or some-thing, not the instrument.*"

I crossed the hundred yards or so to the flag and looked around. There were no uniforms as such, but everyone had a little cap on, and each cap was decorated with a green badge with a horn on it;

they also wore sashes, with the same badge near the left shoulder. I drew a few curious looks from those assembled, all of whom seemed to be Dragons. One of them had a silver braid about his left shoulder. He was sitting on an empty wooden crate next to the banner. He looked up at me and said, "You want something?"

"I'm looking for Cropper. Uh, Captain Cropper."

"Who's looking?"

"I am."

He gave me an "I am not amused" stare and I reminded myself that I might be about to put myself in a position where this person would have control over my comfort, and maybe even my life expectancy. I mentally shrugged and said, "Baronet Vladimir Taltos, House of the Jhereg, sent by Lord Morrolan e'Drien, House of the Dragon."

He studied me a little, I guess trying to decide just how much of an attitude he ought to display at this point. Then he stood and said, "I'll tell him."

He went over to a rather larger tent, clapped, was admitted, entered, and reappeared. "Go on in," he said. I wasn't sure if I ought to salute, so I didn't.

Captain Cropper was old, probably getting close to three thousand, but had bright eyes, as well as bushy eyebrows and a pointed chin. He had a jacket with three silver braids around the right shoulder. He was seated on a rickety chair at a rickety wooden table and he was writing up reports or something. As I walked up he said, "I was informed that you were to be attached to my company. Welcome, I suppose. We will dispense with the swearing in because I'm not certain it would have any meaning, and I am unclear on your status with the company. I will find out in due time. For now, Crown will give you cap, sash, and bedding and show you to your quarters. And get rid of that thing."

"That thing" was, of course, Loiosh. It seemed we were going to have trouble right from the start. "That thing" said into my mind, *"Tell him if he gives me some of those silver things, I'll forget the offense."*

"Shut up, thing."

"He is required—"

"Sir!" He glared at me. I managed not to roll my eyes.

"Excuse me, sir. He is required for the operations I am to perform."

He worked his mouth like a horse and said, "Is it necessary that it go around on your shoulder?"

"I could stand on your head, Boss, but you might get tired of that."

"Yes, sir, it is," I said.

Cropper glared at me again. "Very well," he said. "That's all." And he turned back to his work.

He didn't seem to expect me to salute either. No one was expecting me to salute. I'd been looking forward to it, too—it's such a silly thing to do, when you stop and think about it.

I stepped out of the tent and found myself looking up at the man with one silver braid. I said, "You must be Crown, right?"

"Sergeant Crown," he snapped.

"Excuse me," I said, keeping all irony out of my voice. He had rather a square jaw for a Dragonlord, and very thick, bushy eyebrows. He wore a sort of jerkin that covered his arms to the elbows, showing off forearms that were thick and knotted with muscle and quite intimidating. I decided that if I ever had to go up against this man, I'd do so from a distance. I wondered if he was any good at throwing knives.

"Come along," he said.

"All right."

"Answer: 'Yes, Sergeant.' "

"Yes, Sergeant."

He grunted and turned away. I followed him. It occurred to me that achieving popularity was not the number one point on his program. He led me past the Captain's tent and then down a long row of smaller, identical tents, pitched in triangles with flaps all facing the same way. I was the subject of stares, all curious and sometimes unfriendly, from those sitting around outside of them.

He stopped at one and said, "These are your quarters. You'll find a cot, a blanket, canteen, and kit inside."

I said, "Yes, Sergeant."

"I see you have a sword. If you deem it, uh, insufficient, you may draw one of ours."

"Yes, Sergeant."

He turned away. There were two Dragonlords relaxing on wood-and-canvas backless stools outside the tent. They looked up at me.

I said, "And a very pleasant morning to you both."

It wasn't, really; there was a nasty wind that made it a bit cold, and it smelled like it was going to rain. I mention this because one of them, the woman, said, "It is, actually; at least compared to the last couple of days. I'm Virt e'Terics."

"Vlad Taltos."

"Jhereg?"

The question seemed curious rather than hostile, so I said, "Yes I am, or yes he is, depending on which you're asking about." I turned to the man and raised my eyebrows. He turned away.

"His name," said Virt, "is Napper. He's of the e'Drien line. Don't take him personally. Every squad needs someone like him to make bivouacs so unpleasant we look forward to battle."

Napper gave her a nasty look but didn't actually say anything.

"You may as well stow your gear," said Virt.

"Sure. Uh, what exactly does that mean?"

"Shove it under your cot."

"Oh. I can manage that."

Napper gave a snort which I couldn't interpret. Virt said, "For whatever it's worth, we may be moving out any day."

Napper spoke for the first time, saying, "What makes you think so?"

Virt pointed with her chin toward the supply tents. "The last couple of wagons have brought traveling rations. Besides, Sethra Lavode hates keeping her armies in bivouac. If she can't move them out, she likes to arrange billets."

"Don't matter," said Napper. Virt smiled and shrugged with her eyebrows.

At this point another woman walked up. She glanced at Loiosh, then at me. "You must be Taltos," she said. "I'm Rascha, corporal of your squad."

I bowed my head. "Uh . . . how do I address you?"

"By name is fine. And you don't have to salute."

"No one has made me salute yet."

She cracked a small smile. "I suspect no one knows quite how to deal with you." Of all the soldiers I'd run into so far, she seemed the most "military"—she stood straight and stiff, making her seem taller than she was, and she wore her hair short and brushed straight back from her forehead; her eyes were dark and narrow. She also carried a sword, which I noticed because she was the only one so far who did.

Virt said, "What's the story, Rascha?"

"Maneuvers this afternoon, and we'll probably be moving out tomorrow."

Virt nodded and didn't give Napper any "I told you so" sort of glance. Napper, on the other hand, gave a snort which may have been a response to either piece of news, or both.

"Move where?" I said.

Rascha gave me a quick glance, and said, "You'll know when we get there, Taltos," in a sharp tone of voice.

"Sorry," I said.

"Get your gear stowed."

"Right away," I said, and entered the tent, ducking low enough not to knock Loiosh off my shoulder. It was a bit cooler than it had been outside. There were four cots, and three of them had identical backpacks under them; I put my satchel under the fourth.

"You should have gotten a backpack, Boss."

"Good time to tell me."

I stepped back out. Rascha had moved on. I said to Virt, "The corporal seems easy enough to work with."

"Yeah. She's tough when it counts, though. She spent some time as a marine."

"A marine?"

"A shipboard soldier. They're the ones who go over the side and try to take a ship from the enemy. She saw some action in a skirmish with Easterners during the Interregnum."

"I didn't know there was a navy during the Interregnum."

"There wasn't, officially, but there was some fighting now and then around Northport and Adrilankha."

"Okay," I said. "Any idea where I might acquire a backpack?"

She shook her head. "Not around here, and we're not permitted to leave camp without permission. But I expect that when Aelburr gets back he'll be able to rig some straps for you. He's good at that sort of thing."

"Aelburr?"

"He's the other one who bunks with us."

"Oh. Where is he now?"

"He drew kitchen duty. He'll be back after lunch."

"Such as it is," put in Napper.

Virt added, "You can ask him about making you a stool as well; you'll come to appreciate whatever comfort you can find."

"I don't doubt that a bit," I said.

I sat down on the ground next to them. Yeah, a stool would be nice.

A little later there was the sound of drums, and my heart leapt to my throat, and I almost stood up and drew a weapon; I just barely saved myself from embarrassment by noticing that no one else seemed excited.

"That little tune," said Virt, "is called 'Graze the Horses.' It means lunchtime."

"It's our big excitement for the day," said Napper.

"True enough," said Virt. "Because of the danger. Grab your mess kit and come along."

Lunch was served up at a long table, which you walked along with your tin tray out so the cooks could put on it a hunk of tasteless cheese, as many biscuits as you could eat . . . in my case, that was about a third of one, and a piece of salted kethna that I wouldn't have served hidden in a stew full of lasher peppers. Then you filled up your collapsible tin cup with a horrid white wine and walked back to your tent to eat, and then down to the stream to clean your mess kit, and, then, perhaps, downstream to the latrines to divest yourself of what you'd just had the misfortune to consume. I fed Loiosh a bit of the kethna, and he liked it fine, which I think proves my point.

An hour after lunch were "maneuvers." We were called out and made to stand in a neat line, four abreast. On my left was Napper, next to him was a Dragonlord who turned out to be Aelburr. He was very tall—close to eight feet—and thin even for a Dragonlord. His black hair was brushed back like Virt's, and his arms were nearly as knotted as Crown's. In that formation, they marched us out to a field, where we had to do things like turn around all together, go from four abreast to eight abreast and back, spread out in different directions and come back, go from four abreast facing forward to thirty abreast and four deep, with proper distance between the lines, advance, retreat, quickstep, double-time, and all sorts of other things that every-one knew how to do except me.

We did this for about five hours, with a five-minute break each hour. During one of the breaks, I threw myself down next to the man who'd been behind me for most of the march.

"Not used to the work, Easterner?" he said.

I looked at him, and he didn't seem to be actively unfriendly, so I said, "Can't claim to enjoy it."

"Me neither," he said. He was a rather small man, almost mousy, and didn't give the impression of great strength, though he'd gone through the drills without being as winded as I was.

"But you're in it for the fighting, right?"

"Me? No. I've been in a few battles. I can't say I enjoyed them."

"Then why—?"

"Experience. I want to make a career of the Phoenix Guards. Or the Dragon Guards if the Cycle will be kind enough to turn for me. And you get along better if you start out with a few big fights under your belt."

"I see."

"What about you?"

"It's personal."

He laughed. "I would imagine so. The scuttlebutt is you know Sethra Lavode."

"We've met," I admitted.

"Is she really a vampire?"

"Well, she hasn't drunk my blood. At least that I remember."

He laughed again. "I'm Tibbs," he said.

"Vlad."

"A pleasure."

"The same."

And the drum started up, and we were off on more senseless maneuvers. The next rest period found me next to Virt and Napper again. Napper had a look of disgust on his face that didn't encourage conversation. Virt seemed her easygoing self, so I said, "Mind if I ask you a question?"

"Sure," said Virt.

"Why is everyone so . . . hmmm. I'm not sure how to say this.

I've dealt with Dragons before, and I'm used to, ah, I'm not used to being treated so civilly by them. No offense."

Virt smiled. "It's taken some effort," she said.

"Why the effort, then?"

"I can only speak for myself."

"Well?"

"We're going to war," she said after a moment. "We're going to be fighting. You'll be fighting next to me. I'd just as soon you didn't have any reason to let me be killed."

"Ah. I hadn't thought of that."

She smiled pleasantly. "It's probably in your best interest not to give me a reason to let you be killed, either. You may want to keep that in mind, Jhereg."

Napper looked up at me, then glanced away.

And again the drum, and again the marching and running, and then, a little later, we broke for practice in throwing javelins. I couldn't get anything like the distance most of the Dragonlords got, but I was awfully damn accurate. That gave me a certain amount of pleasure.

Then there was another drumbeat that announced time to sup. Supper was much the same as lunch except that a thin broth was substituted for the kethna. I sat next to Virt outside of our tent, and said, "Does the food get any better?"

"No."

"I see." Then, "Are most of these people volunteers?"

"All of us, of course. The units with conscripts have Teckla in them."

"Oh. Why did you volunteer?"

"I'm attending the Terics Academy, and one needs experience in battle before mastering theory."

"I guess that makes sense."

"Why you?"

"Why am I here? It's personal."

"Ah."

I decided after a moment that she deserved a better answer than that, so I said, "The guy we're going up against pissed me off."

"You're kidding."

"Nope."

"You joined the army because you're mad at the guy whose army we're fighting?"

"Yep."

She stared at me. "You know you probably won't get a chance to, uh, what do you Jhereg call it?"

"We usually call it killing," I lied. "And, yes, I know that. But I can be useful here."

"You're nuts."

"Thanks."

"But I mean that in the nicest possible way."

At that point we were joined by Aelburr, to whom I was then introduced. He seemed friendly enough, and agreed to modify my satchel and make me a collapsible stool. I said, "Is there anything I can do for you?"

"Yeah. Tell me how to win at S'yang Stones."

"Run the game, don't play it."

"I'm serious."

"So am I. It's a rigged game. In the long run, you can't win unless the guy running the game is an idiot. If you're really, really good at it, and you concede if you don't score well on your first couple of throws, and double-up every time you have an edge with your flat stones, and you get very good at tossing, you'll only lose a little, very slowly."

"Why is that?"

"Because in, say, a ten-fifty game you're paying twelve orbs for the stones, and you're risking fifty orbs if you lose, and if you win you only get back ten plus fifty, not including doubling, which works out even in the long run. So every time you play against someone as good as you, you lose two orbs. If you play against someone better, it's worse, and if you play against someone not as good, the luck factor is almost always greater than the two orbs you're losing. Usually about four coppers' worth."

"You've got it figured that precisely?"

"Yes."

He shook his head. "What about personal games, with no one running it?"

"That's different. Then if you're better, you should win."

"So how do you play?"

"Go for the big scores with your flat stones, and use the round ones at the end to knock off his big scores, and, if he gets a big advantage on the first round, surrender your ten and start over."

"I like to use my flat stones to knock out the other guy's early scores. Then I can get lucky with the round stones."

"Yeah, a lot of guys play that way."

"And I double when, well, you know, sometimes you can just feel that you're going to hit big?"

Sure you do. I said, "I don't know, I don't actually play a whole lot."

"Well, it seems like it works."

I thought, *I know exactly how you play, sucker,* but didn't say it. I said, "How do you do, overall?"

"I'm about even, or maybe a little up."

I almost said it with him. The consistent losers always say, "About even, or maybe a little up." But I just nodded and didn't say anything.

"Maybe I'll try it your way," he said.

"Let me know how it works."

"I will."

"So, why are you here?"

"Here? You mean, in the service?"

"Yeah."

He was quiet for a while, then said, in a low voice, "I've always dreamed of fighting under Sethra Lavode."

"Okay," I said. "I can respect that."

"It's better than the alternative, in any case."

"Oh?"

"My last posting was with a mercenary army. They've been hired to fight against her. I wouldn't care to do that."

"No," I said. "I wouldn't either."

A little later fires were lit, and we sat around them; apparently every three tents had one fire. Virt explained that, usually, the fires were where meals were cooked, but as this whole operation had been thrown together so quickly, they had gone to communal kitchens to save the extra work of dividing up the rations. I suppose that made some sort of military sense. Someone from one of the other tents said it only made sense if we weren't staying long. Virt said we'd be moving out any day, and explained her reasoning, which provided the subject for much lively debate and led to reminiscences about past campaigns that had involved a lot of waiting in bivouac.

"Well, Loiosh, what do you think of military life so far?"

"The food's good."

"Heh."

"And there's a lot of it."

"I didn't see a lot."

"That's because everyone hasn't been feeding you scraps."

"Everyone's been feeding you?"

"They sure have, Boss. I think they think I'm good luck."

"You're lucky they don't know you."

"Heh."

The conversation continued around me, and I occasionally put in questions, such as how they could tell the different drum calls apart, which were answered with the sort of patience I might display to a potential customer who wanted to understand the interest on the loan he was inquiring about. The drum, by the way, was called a juice-drum, and the peculiar sound it made was caused by steel balls rattling around inside the steel frame as it was struck.

Later they went on to talking about what they were going to do after the campaign. If they did what they said they were going to, I'd see a big increase in business at all of my brothels. Then they went on to telling humorous anecdotes, most of which I'd heard and none of which are worth repeating, although there were some particularly military ones that were interesting—most of these had to do with peculiar injuries, ways of bugging out of battle, or embarrassing things happening to officers (but never sergeants, for some reason). Loiosh thought some of the stories were funny, but then, he'd liked the food, too.

The drum started up again, and Virt explained that it was time to sleep. I wasn't used to sleeping on a set schedule, but I realized that I was sufficiently tired that it wouldn't be a problem, even with the unfamiliar bed and the nasty, prickly woolen blanket. And it wasn't; I rolled up my cloak for a pillow, lay down, and was gone.

The drum woke me up the next morning, beginning my first full day as a soldier. We were given ten minutes at the spring to make ourselves ready, which only barely gave me time to shave. I noticed various of my comrades looking at me out of the corners of their eyes as I did so, and I rather enjoyed it.

There were fires going by the cook-tent, so I went over there and discovered that not only was there no klava, but there was no cream or honey for the coffee, so I skipped it. I forced down a biscuit because I thought I might need it, then went back and heard that morning maneuvers had been canceled.

"I wonder why?" said Aelburr.

"Be grateful," said Napper.

"I have a guess," said Virt, staring over in the direction of the Captain's tent. It was very cold; I pulled my heavy cloak around me, thinking I'd trade half my territory in the City for a good cup of klava, and didn't say anything.

Rascha came by and wished us a pleasant morning. "What's the word?" said Virt.

"You'll know as soon as I do," she said, and continued on.

I studied the sky, hoping it wouldn't rain, but I couldn't tell anything. I knew Castle Black was somewhere above us, but I couldn't see it through the overcast, even though I knew that Morrolan would be able to look down and see us. It seemed wrong, somehow.

"Loiosh, what am I doing here?"

"If I knew, Boss, I'd be sure to tell you."

About forty yards away, over the Captain's tent, the banner of Cropper Company snapped and floated in the cold morning breeze.

The drums started up again, but we'd already eaten breakfast and it was too early for lunch. Virt stood up, smiling. "Do you know how to strike a tent?" she said.

I assumed she didn't refer to hitting it, so I said, "No."

"Time to learn, then," she said. "We're moving out."

9

Skulking About

Loiosh kept asking what I was going to do when I got there, and I kept saying I didn't know. *"I'll think of something,"* I told him.

"Why am I not reassured?"

"Getting close enough is half—what's that?"

"More of the same battle, Boss. Just not our part in it."

"Look closer, Loiosh."

"Oh."

Off to my right, a bit over a hundred yards away, was a large body of Easterners—no doubt the mercenaries I'd been informed of. They were far enough away that I wouldn't have been able to tell they were human except that I could just barely make out a beard here and there, and that was sufficient.

They were going up against a cavalry troop, and I could just make out Morrolan's form, sitting on a dark horse and laying about him with—yes, it had to be Blackwand. With each cut of that blade, another died—and died forever, because there is no return, reincarnation, no afterlife of any sort to someone struck down with that weapon. The beliefs among humans regarding what happens after the death of the body are varied, peculiar, and often silly; but a hundred yards to my right Morrolan was making the question moot.

In spite of all I had seen, it was this that sickened me.

I discovered that I'd gotten all the way to the knot of sorcerers and their honor guard on top of the hill. Before any of them could speak to me, I said, "Can we stop all this nonsense, please?"

"Good work, Boss," said Loiosh. *"You've gotten their attention."*

"That was my secret plan," I said.

They looked at me and I looked at them, and I realized with an almost profound sense of importance that I'd *stopped*. I'd reached the place. Whatever was going to happen would happen here, and then it would end, and a sudden, terrible delight filled me that, for better or worse, I was done marching. This meant, above all, that I was done marching in the rain.

It had started raining a little before noon the very first day I'd marched with Cropper Company, and sometimes it seems that it had rained ever since. We'd been marching for about four hours, and after the first I had decided I didn't care for it. The rain did nothing to change my mind. Marching through mud just isn't as much fun as they say, especially with a folded-up cot, a jury-rigged backpack, and a few pieces of tent on your back. I wore my heavy cloak because it was cold when we started, but at the first break I switched to the light one because marching turned out to be much harder work than I'd expected, and I became hot and sweaty inside the first mile. Then, of course, the rain started, so I was too hot while we marched, and too cold every time we had to stop because a wagon had gotten stuck in the mud and it was either in front of us and blocked the road or behind us and we weren't permitted to get too far ahead.

Virt kept looking around, as if trying to guess where we were going and what we were doing; occasionally she would make helpful observations about how the engineers would have been able to keep the roads passable if only there were wood in the region. Napper never said a word, but kept up a constant stream of invective through inarticulate grunts and hisses. Aelburr seemed cheerful, which was really annoying. Loiosh sometimes rested on my shoulder and sometimes flew over the company, enjoying his unexpected popularity and, fortunately, not making any wisecracks to me. I did my best to keep my thoughts to myself, mostly as a matter of pride.

Somewhere in there we crossed into enemy-held territory. I didn't notice it at the time, but put it together some time later when I realized that our commissary was no longer paying for the supplies we took from the locals. Years later I found out that Sethra had cut the entire army off from its supply lines—a move she was fond of. I guess she was good at it, too, because the food never changed.

Pity.

The rainfall grew heavier. It's funny how little I notice weather in the City; but it just doesn't matter that much. A little bit of sorcery will keep the rain off, and then I'm at the office, or wherever I'm going. Here it was different; most of us had the sorcerous ability to keep the rain off our heads, but that did nothing for the road, and you can only keep up a spell like that for a certain amount of time before you start to get brain-fatigued, and then it can slip and you can lose control of the energy. It would be humiliating to fry your brain because a Verra-be-damned *umbrella* spell got out of control.

Worse for a Dragonlord, though, because he'd be likely to show up in the Paths of the Dead and have to explain just how he Got It.

The Paths of the Dead.

I remembered them, then, as I was walking; I remembered thinking I'd never find my way out, and then saving myself, and Aliera, and Morrolan, with a homemade bit of witchcraft I hadn't known I could perform. And where were Morrolan and Aliera now? Probably snug and dry in Castle Black, waiting to teleport to wherever we ended up, while my boots went *flllp flllp* in the mud.

But it was my choice, and I knew I'd feel better when we made contact with Fornia's army and I did something nasty and disruptive to it. Maybe only one or two things, then I could bug out.

Yeah. . . .

"Boss, you've got to let the spell go."

I wanted to argue with him, but there's no point in having a familiar if you don't let him do his job. *"Okay, thanks,"* I told him, and got wet. Looking at the line of march, I was pleased to see I'd held mine longer than many of them. I also knew that there would be some brain-fry casualties from this march; I wondered if that was one of the things calculated out by Sethra when she planned her campaigns: "Well, we're going to lose one percent every day to brain-fry if the weather's bad. . . ."

"You're right, Loiosh. My mind is getting numb."

"Soggy, too, Boss."

"You're not as funny as you think you are."

We stopped then—this one an official rest, as opposed to waiting for a mud-stuck wagon. I gratefully took off my gear, unfolded the stool Aelburr had made me, and sat down.

"We're bound for interesting country," said Virt.

I looked around; it was plain, and flat, with never a hill and hardly a tree to break up the terrain. "It is?"

"Well, this is good ground to fight on, but that isn't what I mean. I mean we're moving toward a hilly area, and it makes me wonder if Sethra plans to bring us directly into a fight or if we're reserves, because if we're reserves, I'd expect us to start heading north soon."

"Well, I know we're in the van."

"You do? How?"

"Morrolan told me. That's why I'm assigned to this company."

She looked at me as if waiting for me to go on.

"Boss!"

"Bloody death, Loiosh. I am brain-tired, aren't I?" "Never mind," I told Virt. "I've already said too much."

"All right."

"I'm not a spy, though."

"I didn't think you were," she said. "And I pretty much assumed that you weren't along just as a soldier."

"Yeah."

"But we're in the van, are we? Then, at a guess, we won't have more than a two-day march. Three, maybe, if the weather stays like this."

"And then battle?"

"I wouldn't be surprised. Will you be around for the fighting?"

I looked at her and knew what she was thinking—was I going to be sharing the danger, or was I just along for the ride and would bug out as soon as they went into battle. The answer, of course, was that I intended to bug out.

"I'll be there," I told her.

She nodded.

The bloody damn juice-drum again, and I stood up, refolded the stool, and eventually we moved out. The rain gave a last burst, then tapered off to a drizzle.

"Can't Morrolan's sorcerers do something about the rain?" I said.

"Chances are they just did."

I grunted. "Took them long enough."

"You're starting to sound like Napper."

Napper gave her a quick glare. I said, "I'm starting to understand him."

He gave no indication that he wanted to be understood.

I said, "I've been given to understand that bitching is the universal right of soldiers."

She laughed briefly, though I didn't think it was funny. "Not in an elite corps," she said.

"We're an elite corps?"

"Didn't you know?"

"How am I supposed to tell?"

"See any Teckla? See any conscripts?"

"Ah. Okay, I hadn't known to look for them."

"Well, there you have it. How do you feel, being part of an elite corps?"

"Bursting with pride," I said.

"That's the spirit."

Napper snorted. The breeze picked up and I shivered, but the rain stopped completely soon after that, and I was able to perform a quick drying spell, and then I felt better.

We put a few miles behind us, then stopped where we were on the road and ate salted kethna, cheese, and biscuits. I ate three biscuits. They tasted much better after not eating a decent meal for a day.

"*If this goes on long enough, Loiosh, I'll have no more taste than you.*"

"*I weep bitter tears.*"

"*Reptiles don't weep.*"

"*And we have other natural advantages, too.*"

I filled a pocket with some extra biscuits to eat on the way. They weren't all that bad, really, as long as you didn't compare them to anything good.

The grey clouds that had gathered beneath the orange-red overcast were gone, and in the distance there were now a few hills to be seen. That meant we were probably climbing, very gradually, which realization made my legs tired. Periodically, the Captain would ride by on a horse, presumably to make us feel even more tired. I hadn't seen much of horses before, and watching the Captain ride by while we kept trudging didn't give me any great affection for them.

As the light failed the drums rattled, and we stopped and I watched the other three put up the tent, making certain to show me how the pieces fit together. Then we lit fires, ate an evening meal that was suspiciously like the one yesterday, and sat around in front of the fire. Rascha approached and said, "Aelburr and Vlad, first shift on picket duty tonight."

"Okay," said Aelburr.

"Vlad?"

"Yes?"

"Did you hear?"

"Yes."

"Then acknowledge."

"Sorry."

Rascha moved on. I said, "How long does a shift last?"

"Two hours," said Virt, "unless they decide we're in imminent, in which case time doubles and personnel triples."

" 'In imminent'?"

"In imminent danger."

"Ah."

"Which I don't think we are."

I looked an inquiry at Virt, who shrugged and said, "I doubt it."

Aelburr stood up and buckled on his sword. I did the same. He led the way past the rows of tents to where we could just make out the banner in the fading light. Crown was there, and pairs would approach him to be sent off; to us he said, "North edge, forty yards out," and pointed. Aelburr saluted and turned away. I also saluted, which earned me a glance I couldn't read, then I went after Aelburr. But I was pleased; I'd finally gotten to salute.

"What do we do?" I said. "Stand in place like idiots or walk back and forth like morons?"

He gave a token chuckle. "Stand in place," he said. "More or less, anyway. As long as we keep watching, and we don't stray out of call, it shouldn't matter much."

We were out there for two hours, and nothing happened, but it was spooky. At first there was a hum of low conversation from the camp, but that died fairly soon, and then it was quiet, and I was one of those guards whom I'd spent so much time figuring out ways of circumventing, or sometimes knocking out, or occasionally killing. All of those occasions presented themselves to my memory with a snicker of revenge. I wasn't really worried, because Loiosh was there, but it was a position I didn't enjoy being in. I tried to start a conversation, but Aelburr let me know that we were supposed to use our ears, and that if we were caught conversing Bad Things would happen.

"What does the military consider a Bad Thing?"

"Latrine duty."

"Sold," I said, and shut up for the rest of our shift. We were relieved right on time by a couple of soldiers I didn't know and who didn't seem interested in either conversation or latrine duty. I followed Aelburr to the tent, which I couldn't have found on my own, and I climbed into my cot just an instant after I fell asleep.

Thirty hours later I got a practical demonstration of what "in imminent" meant. My feet were a day more sore, my legs a day more tired, and my spirits a day nastier. Virt seemed slightly amused at either my discomfort or my annoyance; Aelburr seemed lost in thought, and Napper, still scowling as before, appeared the only sane one of the lot of us. In any case, our entire tent was informed we'd be doing four hours of picket duty in the middle of the night, which made Virt nod sagaciously, Napper scowl menacingly, and Aelburr shrug philosophically. Then, an hour later, Rascha called me aside and informed me that I was excused and was not expected to do picket duty after all, and then she turned away before I could ask her why. I cursed under my breath.

"What is it, Boss? You enjoyed it so much last night that you want to do a double-shift tonight?"

"No, I just resent the implication that I'm not as reliable as anyone else."

"Getting a bit touchy, are we?"

"Bug off."

About then a mixed group of strangers—say a hundred of them— came rolling into camp on wagons pulled by horses. By mixed I mean I identified at least a couple of Vallista, and a few Teckla, and some Dragons. I looked an inquiry at Virt, who said, "Engineers."

"Ah. What will they be engineering?"

"Defenses. Earthworks. Bulwarks. We're apparently going to be required to hold this position."

"This position? Where in blazes are we?"

"You'll see the Eastern Mountains in the daylight."

"Oh. I guess we made good time today."

"We did at that." I recalled Sethra's plans, and then wished I hadn't known them, because I suddenly got the impression that our entire company was a marker on a gameboard that she was going to be maneuvering around with no concern for the individuals who comprised it. In an effort to distract myself, I strained my eyes eastward, but in the failing light couldn't see any mountain.

"We're pretty high up, Boss; I can tell you that much."

"How?"

"It's noticeably harder to fly."

"Why should it be harder to fly just because you're starting higher?"

"That's for you higher order animals to figure out; we avians just do our business on instinct."

"You're not an avian, you're a reptile."

"I still don't know why it works that way."

"If you had opposable thumbs you probably would."

"You want to drop that opposable thumbs bit, Boss?"

I suddenly had the impression that there was something I'd meant to do, something I should be thinking about, something . . . oh. Right.

"Who is it?"

"Morrolan."

"What do you want?"

"Aren't you even going to thank me, Vlad?"

"For what?"

"There's never been a soldier born who wasn't grateful to get out of midnight guard duty."

"I see. No, I don't think I'm going to thank you. I take it this is a good night to act?"

"The Captain is expecting you, and I'll be there."

"On my way," I said, relieved to know that I hadn't been let out of picket duty because they didn't trust me, and then annoyed with myself for caring.

I made my way through the camp toward where the Captain's tent should be.

"This way, Boss."

"Thanks."

It was very dark by this time, but I found it with Loiosh's directions and by hearing the flap of the banner. Then I wandered around it like an idiot until I found the entrance. The worst part of this nonsense was that I kept finding myself doing things I wasn't good at, and that meant looking stupid, in front of myself if no one else, and I've always hated that.

I clapped outside of the tent.

"Enter," said the Captain, and at the same time I heard Morrolan's voice: "Please come in."

"Well," I said, stepping in. "How pleasant that we should all run into each other here."

"Sit down, Vlad," said Morrolan.

I did so. I tried to read the expression on the Captain's face, but I couldn't quite make it out. But from the instant I'd stepped into the tent, things were different, and I think he sensed it: I was no longer one of his soldiers; now I was something else, though he wasn't certain what. I suspect I enjoyed the sensation more than he did.

"Their nearest outpost is three miles northeast of us," Morrolan began without preamble. "We can expect an attack tomorrow."

"Which means I have things to do tonight."

"Yes."

"What, exactly, do you want?"

Morrolan said, "Captain?"

The Captain's eyes widened, then he grunted, as if it all made sense to him now. "Let me think. We're still planning . . . uh . . . ."

"You may speak in front of Vlad."

He grunted again. "We're still planning a withdrawal to the southeast?"

"Yes."

He considered some more, then said, "How much of his army are we facing?"

"About a third. We know another third is marching to reinforce, and he probably has a division that's trying to move around our flank."

"What if he decides not to attack? Maybe he'll wait for the other divisions to arrive. Functionally, they're an outpost; they're losing a big part of their advantage right from the start if they launch an attack."

"They may not; if they don't, we'll attack."

The Captain shook his head. "We're an advance guard. I don't like the idea of attacking."

"We won't commit a great deal of force, just enough to encourage a counterattack."

"Right. I know. But if they don't counterattack?"

"We have sufficient force to overrun this outpost. If they won't counterattack, we'll take it and let them try to take it back from us. As far as Sethra is concerned, that's just as good."

"She's the general."

"Yes, she is. But, in any case, Fornia is very aggressive. Sethra thinks he'll test us tomorrow."

"All right. In that case, assuming he *is* planning a morning assault, anything that will delay it for even an hour or two would be useful. I'd like to give the engineers a little more time."

Morrolan nodded and said, "Vlad?"

I shrugged. "I don't know this work. How would I go about it?"

"There are a number of possibilities," said Morrolan.

The Captain said, "Do you care if they identify it as sabotage right away?"

"All things being equal, it would be better if they didn't, but that's not a high priority."

"Okay, then. What if you just went in and put holes in their water barrels? They're going to need coffee, or at least water, before they go into action. That should set them back a bit."

"Not very elegant," I said. "But I should be able to do it."

"I have a better idea," said Morrolan, with a sudden glint of humor in his eyes. "I believe you are going to like this, Vlad."

"I'll just bet," I told him.

Thirty-four hours earlier I had been on picket duty, assigned to make sure no one could get in the camp unseen; now I was on the other side, trying to do exactly that. This side felt more natural to me, and my new sympathy with the opposition didn't get in my way.

Loiosh flew overhead, keeping an eye out for exactly where they were stationed, as I moved slowly toward where I had been told the enemy was camped. My feet made no sounds, my grey cloak blended into the night, and in my left hand was a small rod that would alert me well before I crossed the line of any sort of detection spell.

"*Anything, Loiosh?*" I asked, just because the silence was hard on my nerves.

"*Not yet, Boss.*"

"*Maybe they've packed up and left.*"

"*I'll believe it if you will.*"

Then, "*Found 'em, Boss. Three of them, straight ahead of you.*"

"*I'll bear to the left, then.*"

"*It's clear that way.*"

I kept moving, not too fast, avoiding any abrupt motions. Now I could see the embers of campfires, which not only gave me a target but made it harder for me to be spotted from within the camp. I remembered from last night that I'd only rarely looked back toward the camp; my attention had been focused outward. Still, I made certain not to stand between any of the fires and the picket spot Loiosh had identified.

There should have been an interior line of pickets as well, and there probably was, but I didn't see them and they didn't see me. Once I was in the camp it was easier; the fires had mostly burned down, and nearly everyone was asleep. I walked with confidence, as if I belonged there, and the few guards who were wandering around pretty much stared through me.

"*Do you see their banner?*"

"*Forty yards, this way.*"

I went that way. Light glowed from the overlarge tent to which Loiosh directed me, the flickering light of lamps. As I got closer I heard low voices—officers, no doubt, discussing plans for the morrow, when our "advance guard" would be "tested" by their "outpost."

There was a guard posted right in front of the tent, a very inconvenient place. But that was all right.

"*Okay, Loiosh. Take it away.*"

"*I'm there, Boss.*"

He launched himself from my shoulder and swooped on the guard, missing his head by about three feet. The guard swore and took a step back. Loiosh swooped again. The guard drew his sword and took an aimless swipe into the air. I drew a knife from my belt and found the flagpole.

It took about a second to cut the rope, and the banner slid down silently. Another second, and I was holding the banner in my hands. I slipped into the darkness behind a nearby tent and said, "*Okay, Loiosh. I've got it. One down.*"

"*I'll be there in a while, Boss.*"

"*Loiosh . . .*"

"*Oh, come on, Boss. I'm having fun.*"

"*Loiosh.*"

"*All right, I'm coming.*"

Someone from inside the tent called, "What's that ruckus?" but I didn't hang around to hear the answer.

The others were easier; they were next to dark tents that had no sentries posted outside of them. It was just a matter of being careful and, as always, not getting caught. All in all it took about an hour, and then another twenty minutes to work my way back to our own lines.

Just for practice, I snuck past our own sentries and made my way to the Captain's tent. There was a sentry there, too, but to him I announced myself. He glanced at the bundle in my arms but didn't seem to recognize what it was. He announced me, then pulled aside the flap. The Captain and Morrolan were sitting around the Captain's table, drinking wine. I tossed my bundle onto the floor and said, "I'll have some of that, if you've any left."

"I think we can spare some," said Morrolan.

The Captain looked at the banners and laughed. "Well done," he said. "How many did you get?"

"Eleven."

"Well, well. We've captured eleven colors and haven't drawn sword. I wonder if history records its equal?"

"I very much doubt it," said Morrolan.

I drank some wine. Wine tastes especially good after you've pulled off something scary and you're easing up on muscles you hadn't known were tense.

"Any trouble?" said Morrolan.

"Nothing Loiosh couldn't handle."

"*Heard and witnessed, Boss.*"

"*Shut up, Loiosh.*"

The Captain said, "We ought, then, to have gotten a couple of hours' reprieve while they rig up some new colors, but we can't count on it. That means I still need to check on the earthworks."

"And you, Vlad," put in Morrolan, "should catch some rest. To-morrow you stand to battle."

"Heh," I said. "What makes you think I'll be there?"

He shrugged and didn't answer, which left nothing to say, so I finished my wine and went off to get some sleep.

I think Morrolan's little scheme worked. At any rate, it wasn't until the ninth hour of the morning that they commenced their as-sault on our position.

10

RUN AWAY! RUN AWAY!

I scanned the faces before me; mostly I was looking at warriors, all of them large and, well, scary-looking. Most of them were Dragonlords, but I saw at least two Dzurlords among them. They were all noticeably lacking in sympathy. Behind them were the sorcerers, and, though I couldn't see him, I knew Fornia was behind them somewhere, watching the progress of the battle—the slaughter—and making decisions that would let his forces do more of the slaughtering. That, after all, was what war was about.

Someone came forward, a Dragonlord I'd never seen before. He said, "I am Jurg'n e'Tennith. You are here to ask for terms?" He seemed doubtful. He probably didn't think Morrolan would send an Easterner.

I said, "Not exactly."

"To negotiate, then?"

I was considering how to answer this when someone else pushed his way through the warriors, and I recognized Ori. He said, "He's no negotiator; he's an assassin. Kill him."

Well, I reflected, that certainly put the negotiations on a different footing. Now would be a really good time to hear the juice-drum signaling "charge," and have the company come suddenly to my rescue. Unfortunately, I'd left them rather far behind, and any drum I was likely to hear would be support for those in front of me; not that they needed it.

All of which reminds me that I never much cared for the sound of the juice-drum, and provides another splendid opportunity to leave you hanging for a while. Don't worry, I'll come back to the fight in a little bit.

Where was I? Oh, yes: the juice-drum.

I'd pretty much hated it since the first time its call had woken me up earlier than I'd had to get up since I quit running a restaurant. It had woken me up even earlier than usual the morning of the attack. That day there wasn't a nearby creek, so those in charge had set up casks of water. I forced myself to shave. Shaving in cold water, by the way, isn't as much fun as they say. I decided it was a good omen, however, that I didn't cut myself. Virt, who was next to me at the water casks, explained that one difference between an elite corps and the usual sort of conscript army was that we were trusted to get our- selves up in the morning; in a conscript army the corporals came through the tents throwing everyone out and striking them with sticks if they weren't fast enough.

"And they aren't killed?"

"Corporals are hardly ever killed by conscripts. Officers, now, have to be a little careful."

I wanted her to explain that, but the juice-drum cut in again, and I realized with a kind of horror that I recognized the particular rattle and bang as the call to breakfast. Of course, there was a kind of horror associated with breakfast, too.

I tried forcing plain coffee down my throat, but only managed a swallow before I had to give up. Around me, everyone was swilling the stuff like it was peach brandy. I shrugged and ate a few biscuits, washing them down with water. Then I wandered back toward our tent, and only then noticed that, during the night, dirt had been piled up between us and the enemy camp, forming a kind of wall. Okay, now I knew what earthworks were.

Someone I didn't recognize came by and dumped a pile of javelins in front of the tent. Aelburr, who was standing there, picked up three of them, Virt did the same. That left six. I looked at them, then at Virt, then I picked up three of them.

Aelburr said, "You know how to use one of these?"

I thought he was asking about the javelin until I noticed he was handing me a whetstone. Wisecracks passed through my mind, but I only said, "Yes," and took it. He passed me a small flask of oil. There was already, all around, the scraping sound of weapons being sharp-

ened. I added my voice to the chorus, but I only sharpened the javelins and my sword; I was feeling a bit bashful about my collection of
nasties.

The bloody damn drum called out again. I hadn't heard that drum
call before, and I hated it that I could tell it was unfamiliar. I asked
Aelburr what it was. "It's called," he said, " 'Corporal's Tears.' It
means squad leaders report to the Captain. They're getting final instructions for the battle." My heart skipped a beat, but I kept my face
expressionless.

*"Loiosh, keep your eyes opened for a good time to make myself scarce.
Preferably before the fighting starts."*

"Noted, Boss."

I continued sharpening javelins. Virt said, "How far did you
throw that thing?"

"About sixty-five or seventy yards."

"All right, ignore the first command to launch; if you wait for
the second they should be in about the right place. The first throw
is just for annoyance anyway; the last two we send at them quickly,
and you can aim."

"From that far away we should have time for more than two
casts."

"You'd think so, wouldn't you? But over this kind of terrain, you'd
be amazed at how fast they can cover ground at a charge. Depending
on what sort of troops we're up against, of course."

"Do the javelins do any good?"

"A little. We dent some shields, anyway."

"Shields? They have shields? Why don't we get to have shields?"

"Do you know how to use a shield?"

"Uh . . . no. But still they'll have them."

"Probably. As I said, depends who we're up against. If it's cavalry,
they won't have shields, but then we'll have other problems."

"Cavalry?"

"Or it might be a spear phalanx, in which case the javelins will
be pretty much a waste of time, and we'll have to countercharge and
try to flank them. It's up to the enemy what they throw at us. That's
the advantage of attack."

"So, what do we have instead of shields?"

"We're light infantry. We have javelins and the capability to maneuver quickly."

"Oh, good."

"Boss, why do you care? You won't be there."

"I know. But I can't help thinking about what it would be like. This is no place for a self-respecting assassin."

"You knew that all along."

"Not viscerally."

The engineers came by, with more dirt to unload, build up, tramp down. I realized for the first time that as they went they were also digging a ditch in front of the thing. Virt and I watched them.

I said, "What do they do when it rains?"

"Hope there's a lot of wood around."

"For what?"

"For—"

And the juice-drum started up again.

"I've heard that one before," I said.

"Strike camp."

"Ah."

I was able to be a bit more help this time, and soon we had our backpacks in place, and, with our stools packed, we sat or knelt on the ground. There was no sign of the camp except for the pits where the fires had been. Then there came another call, this one I didn't recognize. "Let's go," said Virt. "Leave your pack by this mark and take the line."

"All right."

She walked toward the earthwork. Rascha motioned us toward a position, and I found myself between Virt and Napper. Napper wasn't scowling now; his eyes gleamed and as I watched he licked his lips, then bit them, first the top, then the bottom, then licked them again, and repeated.

"You okay?" I said.

"This," he said. "This is what it's all about."

"Oh," I said.

"Here they come," he said, his lips pulling back into a grin.

Oh, good. I was about to take a step back and get myself lost behind the lines when I noticed Virt looking at me. I stuck my javelins in the earthwork in front of me, drew my sword, and transferred it to my left hand. Maybe they'd throw something back at us and I could pretend to be hit, roll backward, and get out that way. No, that didn't sound practical. Maybe—

Virt clapped me on the shoulder. "You'll do fine, Easterner. Everyone—at least, everyone who isn't an idiot—is a little nervous before his first battle. You're worried you won't stand up to the test. It's normal. But once things get hot, you'll do fine. Trust me."

I'd never heard that line before, but it still sounded trite. For how many soldiers had words like that been the last thing they ever had spoken to them? Damned reassuring.

They appeared in a line in front of us, all at once. A whole lot of them. More than there were of us, I thought. They seemed to be walking at a steady pace, and I guessed the distance at about two hundred yards. A long way.

"Heavy infantry," said someone.

"Aim low," said someone else.

Virt tapped me on the shoulder. I jumped, but she was polite enough to ignore it. She said, "Their shields won't be long enough to protect their legs, and they'll naturally raise them once we release our javelins, so—"

"Got it," I said.

I guessed there were at least four or five thousand of them, which was more than ten times the number of our Company. Of course, it was more than just our Company on the line. I wondered how many of us there were all together. Not as many as there were of them. Soon they were close enough so that I could see they carried spears.

"Conscripts," someone said. "They'll break if we make it hot enough for them."

Napper was gnashing his teeth next to me, as if it were all he could do not to charge out at them. Aelburr, just beyond him, was tapping a javelin against the ground and whistling.

"Boss, what are you waiting for?"

"I can't run while she's watching me."

"Why not?"

"Because . . . I don't know. I just can't."

"Boss . . ."

"Loose javelins!" came the call from somewhere, and everyone except me did so. The enemy had gotten much closer, say a hundred yards away, and as our javelins flew they broke into a run. The flight of the javelins looked like we'd picked up a piece of black metal and thrown it as a body, dropping in on an enemy—

"Loose javelins!"

—who might not even have noticed for all the good they did, as I threw mine and instantly lost sight of it, and then I remembered that I was supposed to aim low, but the idea of aiming was beyond me as I picked up my second, readied it, and—

"Loose javelins!"

—threw it, and who knows where it went, because they were *awful* close now, as I picked up my third—

"Prepare to engage!"

—and transferred it to my left hand while switching my sword to my right as they made it to the ditch, and over it, clawing at the earthworks, and everyone was yelling, including me, and there was this annoying wooden shield in my face, so I stuck my javelin into it and used it as a lever to force the thing away and then cut someone's face open, and I kept trying to move ahead, but there was this damned mound of dirt in front of me and I cut once more, hit someone's shield, then dropped to my knees and cut at the side of someone's legs, and then Virt was pulling me backward and saying, "Vlad! Vlad! It's over! Didn't you hear the drum?"

I stood there, panting for a moment, then, moved by exhaustion or disgust, I wasn't sure which, I pitched forward onto my face, rolled over onto my back, and lay there staring up at the sky and breathing. Oddly, it was only then that I became aware of screaming and invocations to various Gods from all around me. There was also some quieter moaning from nearby, but I didn't turn my head to look at it. I had an idea of what I'd see if I looked: bodies strewn here and there, many of them alive, some of them missing portions of themselves. The sound told enough of a story.

"You injured?"

"No," I heard myself say, and I wanted to laugh because the question was funny. Of all the things I could have said I was—hurt, damaged, destroyed, demolished, ruined—she'd asked the one question to which I had to answer "No."

Napper's face suddenly appeared above me. I couldn't read his expression because his face was upside down. There was blood spattered all over him, clothing and face. It seemed natural. He said, "You'll do, Easterner."

If I'd been able to move, I think I would have killed him.

I spent about five or ten minutes lying there before someone I didn't recognize knelt down next to me.

"We'll have to get that jerkin off," he said.

"I beg your pardon?"

"The jerkin has to come off."

"Shouldn't we be introduced first?"

His smile came and went, like he'd heard that sort of thing before, and someone behind me grabbed my shoulders and pushed me up, and he started to pull my jerkin off.

"Wait a minute," I said.

"You'd rather bleed to death?"

"I—" I looked down and saw a gash in the jerkin, and there was a great deal of blood coming from it. Be damned. I *was* injured. Well, that gave me some justification for lying flat on my back staring up at the sky.

The funny thing was I still didn't feel anything. But, yeah, I'd managed to get myself cut. I didn't look closely, but it was within a couple of inches of the same place I'd been cut a few days before. My grandfather would have told me my fourth position guard was drifting up. My grandfather, no doubt, would have been right. I'd have to—

"The jerkin?" said the physicker.

"Go ahead," I told him.

He pulled the jerkin off, dropping four knives, a couple of shuriken, and three darts onto the ground. He gave me a look. "What?" I said.

He shook his head. "Lie down."

"I can do that."

He poured something onto my side; it felt cold, but there was still no pain. However, I did feel a few drops of rain on my face, then a few more. The first couple felt nice. After that I hated it, and I only wanted to get out of the mud.

Mud.

Gods, but I hate mud. I'd never noticed it before, but now I think I'll hate it until they bury me in it. I had always thought my boots fit well, until the mud kept trying to pull them off my feet with each step. Sometimes it would succeed well enough that I had to step out of line, adjust, then run to catch up, and even without that I felt like I was constantly out of breath just from the extra effort. The water that leaked into my boots wasn't that much fun either. And now I was lying in it.

I began to shiver, which, more than the knowledge of the wound, made me feel weak and vulnerable. The physicker did a few things I'm not sure of, probably sorcerous but maybe not, then he slapped a bandage onto my side and put some sort of cloth against my skin that held the bandage in place. They were both instantly soaked with water; maybe they'd have carried me to someplace dry if I were more seriously injured or if there were any such place.

The rain increased to a driving torrent, and I hated it.

"Why didn't you tell me I was wounded?"

"I was afraid if I did it would start to hurt."

"Oh. You're pretty smart for a guy with no opposable thumbs."

"Thank you so much."

"That should do," I was told. "Take it easy with that side for a few days."

Physickers always say things like that. What exactly did he mean? Was I supposed to avoid having any more holes put in it? Good plan. I'd go with it.

"Okay," I told him. "Thank you."

He grunted and moved on. There were no more screams, but there were still a few moans that I could hear over the sound of rain striking wooden shields, metal swords, and whatever else was there to make sound against. Whoever had helped with my jerkin now helped me stand up, which made my side hurt, but not badly, which was just as well since I don't much care for pain. It turned out to be Aelburr. I said, "Anyone else hurt?" which of course was a stupid question, but he knew what I meant.

"Napper lost some skin on his left hand, but nothing else."

"Can't one of our sorcerers stop this Verra-be-damned rain?"

"I suspect our sorcerers are more exhausted than anyone else on the field."

"Oh. I suppose. Any idea what happens now?"

"We've picked up our wounded and our javelins, that's always the first thing. Now, I imagine, we'll re-form and—" The juice-drum cut in again. I was getting very tired of the thing. Aelburr paused, then said, "Or maybe we retreat to a prepared position."

"What does that mean?"

"With luck, it means the higher-ups had this in mind all along. Without luck, it means we're running and they don't want us to fall apart."

"Oh. Yeah. I didn't have to ask: They had it planned."

"How do you know that?"

"Uh . . . I'm an Easterner. We know things."

He didn't look convinced, but he did help me find my pack, get my heavy cloak out and on, and then put the converted satchel onto my back. That hurt, too, but I could carry it.

"Carry it on the wounded side," said Aelburr.

"Excuse me?"

"If you carry it on the healthy side the wound will open up."

That made too much sense for me to ignore it, so I did as I was told, then made my way up to the mudworks, which were vanishing into the field, and stared out; I could just make the enemy out through the drizzle, formed in a solid, even line, not moving, about a hundred and fifty yards away.

The command came a little later, and this time it was in plain words: "Fall back!" Seemed like a fine idea. Rascha came along and formed us into something like a line, and then Crown yelled something and everyone else turned around so I did, too; we began to move, in one long line, the Captain to the extreme right, our backs to the enemy. We started out at a quick trot, which I can safely say that everyone in the company was better at than I was, but I kept up. Eventually, on command, we dropped it back to a fast march, which we kept up much too long, and then we halted and turned and waited.

The rain stopped at last, and it was followed by a bitter wind that was only partially blocked by my rain-drenched cloak. Happiness, I decided, would be a nice campfire, proving once again that happiness is minor misery where before was extreme misery, if that ever needed proving. But there was no fire, and we waited.

At the time I had no idea what was going on, or how our part fit into Sethra's grand design, nor, to be honest, did I give it even a passing thought; but it is rare that a foot soldier has the chance to ask questions of his commanding general over a glass of red wine, and I had that advantage, so I ought to give you the benefit of what I was able to learn, later, when I had the leisure for curiosity.

Most of the division led by Morrolan had been about half a day's march away from us the entire time, and while we pulled back after their first attack, they were advancing. The engineers had been killing themselves preparing a defensive position for just this circumstance, and it was Sethra's hope (though not, she says, her expectation) that their entire corps could be lured into battle against our company and the other companies in the van, which would hold them just long enough for Morrolan's division to arrive and scatter, trap, or crush them. Of course, it didn't work that way, and what happened instead is that we fell back to the "fortified" position and stayed there for an entire day convinced we were to be attacked any minute, and then we abruptly broke camp and marched away in another direction entirely, which turned out to be due east, rather than the southeast that Sethra had originally planned on. I don't know what led to the change; none of my business, I suppose.

I found it annoying, but everyone else seemed to take it as just part of the routine. The rains plagued us for the next day, and most of the conversation was about incompetent sorcerers who couldn't manage the simplest weather control, and speculations about whether the whole thing was the work of Fornia's sorcerers. We could all see that the weather system above us was too large and complex to be considered "simple" but that didn't stop the remarks. I'd have hated to be a sorcerer; I'd have had to kill someone.

At the end of that day's march, with the rain still coming down, all of us soaked to the skin, and the ambulances having already carried our wounded back toward the rear, we held services for the nine soldiers in our company who'd been killed. The Captain gathered us together in formation facing the presumed enemy (I don't know if they were five hundred yards from us or twenty miles at that point) and stood there flanked by tall torches, so we could see him. The bodies lay naked in front of us, wounds hidden, torsos glistening with rain and the embalming oils that would preserve them between here and Deathgate. I knew they were dead because they were the only ones present who weren't shivering.

The Captain spoke of the pride of the House of the Dragon and promised the souls of each of the fallen that they would be sent to the Paths of the Dead, where he was confident they would be received with honor. He named them, and their rank (none higher than corporal), and asked the Lords of Judgment to look kindly upon them, and then said a few words in the ancient tongue of the House of the Dragon.

I felt as out of place as I'd ever felt anywhere, and I kept waiting for my natural cynicism to rescue me, but it was off catching up on the sleep that the rest of me wanted. Loiosh, too, was silent, and there was little talk as we broke up into squads and returned to our tents. I did ask Virt, in a quiet voice, how these things were handled, and was told that the bodies were to be placed on wagons and an honor guard sent to convey them to Deathgate Falls.

"Beyond that," she said, "who knows?"

Well, I did. At least, I had a pretty good idea, but it didn't seem right to say so. I was the only one in the company who had personal experience of what lay beyond Deathgate; I was also the only one in the company who had no right to the knowledge and the only one who, if killed in action, would not be sent there.

My natural cynicism finally appeared, but by then it was time to sack out for the night, so I could arise, rested and alert, and spend another day marching through rain and mud and eating bad food.

After a couple of days, the rains realized that we weren't going to quit so they stopped, and even the overcast became higher and thinner. There were mountains before us now: the Eastern Mountains in general, and Mount Drift in particular; I remembered it from the map. There was no more rain at all, as we had reached the dry lands west of the mountains; by whim of the Gods or freak of nature, the eastern slopes of the mountains were lush and forested while the western would have been desert were it not for the mountain streams, washes, and rivers that made their way across.

Now that the rain was gone, however, it was too hot, much too hot for marching, anyway. Both of my cloaks were stowed, my pack weighed a million pounds, give or take a couple, and even the little uniform cap was an irritation; the first thing everyone did when we stopped was take it off. On the other hand, I learned then what it was for: It kept the dust out of our eyes as we marched. Apparently cooling spells, or even wind spells, were too much work for the sorcerers of the company, and so those of us who knew a little sorcery, which was fortunately most of us, took turns attempting to summon up a breeze. This broke down by the second day of marching, after which we just put up with it.

I was now consuming six or seven biscuits at a meal, to show to what depths the human animal can be reduced. And we still had no idea to where we were marching, nor for what purpose. Well, I had a vague idea, thanks to having been at the one planning session, but it is one thing to hear elaborate strategic plans; it is quite another to spend a week marching with no knowledge of what was ahead except, in the most general terms, that we'd probably fight at some point. Stopping was a relief, but now, ironically, there was little reason to stop. We were on a good road cut by someone sometime for some reason through the harsh, rocky ground, but even the ground would have been passable, so we just trudged on and tried to make it to the next water break without screaming or choking on the dust kicked up by those in the front. My side did feel better.

Eventually, late one evening, we reached the Eastern River. I had assumed we would stop there, but whoever was in charge—that is to say, Sethra Lavode—wouldn't hear of it. We were to cross at once, we heard. I studied the river in the fading light and would have scowled but I didn't want to look like Napper.

There were grey, water-smoothed stones on the far side of the river, and smooth sandy banks near us; I'm willing to listen to explanations for that if you have any. Beyond it Mount Drift was getting close, and its companions were appearing tall and impassable. Impassable didn't bother me, because I didn't think we were going to pass them; as opposed to the river, where the engineers were already at work with wooden planks, floats made of sheep bladders, and prefabricated fittings. The river was wide here, and fast, but, we were informed, not more than four feet deep. "Not more than four feet deep" had a sound I didn't like. The evening, ironically, had turned quite cool, so walking through water, for which I'd have traded my best dagger the day before, had, now, nothing to recommend it.

"Are they going to ask us to ford it?" I asked Virt, gesturing significantly at the engineers busily putting together their makeshift bridge.

"That's what I'd do," she said irritatingly. "We should have a force on the other side before we start to bring the wagons across, and the sooner the better."

"Why?" I said, just because I was annoyed.

"Well, we have to figure the enemy is nearby; we've been skirting his territory for days, and he can't let us just wander anywhere."

I mentally pulled out the map of the area. Oh, *that's* where we were. Okay, that made sense; once we crossed the river, we could follow it downstream right into the heart of Fornia's territory; if Sethra wanted to force him to attack us, that would be the way to do it.

The drum ripped out, and by now I had no trouble recognizing the call to form up and prepare to move. We did, grumbling. Virt and Aelburr seemed like the only two in the company who didn't mind; just my luck to be in the only squad in the company with two irritatingly cheerful footsloggers. I made a remark to that effect to Napper, who nodded glumly.

Rascha approached before we started across and said, "Taltos, you're a bit shorter than the rest; if you want to wait for a wagon you can."

"I'm fine," I said.

"Boss, I'm never going to figure you out."

"Shut up."

The Captain led the way, dismounting and leading his horse across, then we moved out, and got wet and cold and fought the current, and climbed up over the rocks on the other side and moved back about a hundred yards from the bank. Eventually fires were lit, and we put up our tent by their light, and they served the food, and we sat around the fires getting warm and dry, which translated to happy, which in turn translated to not too discontented.

At the next fire over, they were playing S'yang Stones, and I knew that Aelburr would be there, maybe following my advice and winning, but more likely playing his own game and losing. I thought about playing myself, but sitting by the fire was too pleasant. Napper was off somewhere; the rumor was he'd formed a liaison with a woman in another company. I ended up sitting next to Tibbs, who kept trying to find humorous anecdotes that I thought were funny, and failing. When he got to the one about the headless private carrying the legless corporal back to the physicker, Loiosh said, "*Aw, c'mon, Boss. That was funny.*"

"If you say so," I said.

"*If you stay in the army long, Boss, your sense of humor is going to vanish entirely.*"

We were joined by a young-looking Dragonlord; in the flickering of the campfire he seemed little more than a boy. Tibbs said, "Hey, Dunn. Where have you been?"

"Fishing."

"Catch anything?"

"No."

"Told you."

"I had to try."

"Yeah, you did, didn't you? This is Vlad. Vlad, Dunn."

"I've seen you."

"*A nice guy, Boss; he's fed me.*"

"*All right, Loiosh. I won't kill him, then.*"

Dunn and I exchanged greetings. Tibbs said, "What are you looking so glum about?"

Dunn said, "Crown says I still can't carry the colors next time we go into action."

"Congratulations," said Tibbs. "Why are you so all-fired anxious to be killed?"

Dunn didn't answer. Tibbs shook his head and remarked, "You should have been a Dzur."

"I'd challenge you to a duel for that," said Dunn, "but there aren't enough of you."

Tibbs gave a short, barking laugh.

Rascha came by about then, wished us all a good evening, and said, "You may want to sharpen your weapons tonight."

Tibbs said, "You think we'll see action tomorrow?"

"Nothing's for certain, but it looks likely."

We nodded and thanked her for the information. I went back to the tent and borrowed Aelburr's whetstone, then returned to the fire and put it to use.

Loiosh said, "*What about the whole plan to bug out when the fighting starts, Boss?*"

"Shut up, Loiosh."

INTERLUDE: DEFEND

I spent last night with Cawti, an Eastern girl who has agreed to marry me. She has a wonderful smile and a good hand with a dagger, and she knows how to listen. We lay in my bed, pleasantly exhausted, her hair all over my chest and my arm around her shoulder, and I spoke with her about the proposal from Sethra the Younger. She listened without a word until I ran down, then she said, "And?"

"And what?" I said.

"And why did you expect anything different?"

"Well, I don't suppose I did."

"Are you still angry?"

"Not so much. Like you said, I should have expected it."

"And what about her proposal?"

"What about it? Can you imagine me accepting it?"

"Certainly."

"You can?"

"I have a great imagination."

"Among other things, yes. But—"

"But, if she hadn't been so annoying, what would you have thought about it?"

"Why should I care?"

"Aliera."

"What about her?"

"She's why you should care."

I sat up just a little, found a glass of a very dry white wine that we'd kept cold by setting it in a bucket of ice. I drank some, then held the glass for Cawti. She squeezed my shoulder by way of thanks, and I said, "You think I owe her something?"

"Don't you?"

"Hmmmm. Yeah. What with one thing and another, I suppose so."

"Then you should probably tell her about the offer, so she can decide for herself."

"I hate the idea of doing a service for Sethra the Younger."

"Yes, I know. I hardly blame you, but . . ."

"Yes, but."

The wine went down nicely. A welcome breeze came through the window.

"I think it's going to rain," said Cawti.

"I'll speak to Aliera tomorrow," I said.

"Would you like me to come along?"

"Very much," I said.

"All right. I think I'm sleepy now."

"Sleeping comes highly recommended as a cure for that."

"You think? Next you'll tell me that eating is a good cure for hunger."

"Temporary, but it'll take care of the symptoms. Are you hungry?"

"Yes, but I'm more sleepy."

"Then we'll have breakfast tomorrow. One problem at a time."

"Good idea," she said sleepily, and nestled into my shoulder.

"I wonder what Aliera will say. She doesn't think much more of Sethra the Younger than I do."

Cawti didn't answer. If she wasn't already asleep she was close to it. I set the wineglass down next to the table, then pulled the covers up. Outside, it began to rain. I thought about shuttering the windows, but it was too much work, and the rain smelled nice.

That was yesterday. This morning Cawti and I found Aliera in the library of Castle Black. Going there today, after spending so much time thinking about, remembering, those first few times I'd been within the walls of that peculiar place, caught me up. I looked at it as if seeing it anew—as I'd first seen it years ago before war and love and war. To me Castle Black has always seemed palatial, with the grand, sweeping stairway and the three great chandeliers lighting the enormous hallway, all of them decorated by artwork one might expect to find in the Imperial Palace itself, artwork that is violent and beautiful at once, as, I suppose, are the Dragons at their best.

At their worst they are brutal and ugly.

Aliera said, "Greetings, Vlad, Cawti."

We both bowed. Cawti said, "How is Norathar?"

"Adjusting. Becoming reconciled. She'll make a good Empress."

I glanced at my betrothed, but if the subject was still painful for her, which I was certain it was, she gave no sign of it. Every once in a while I wondered how the House of the Dragon felt about its next Empress having once been a Jhereg assassin, but chances were good I'd be long dead by the time the Cycle turned, so I didn't give it that much thought, and it was one of the things Cawti and I still had trouble talking about so I don't know how she felt about it.

I said, "I have a proposal for you."

Aliera put down her book—I didn't catch the title—and tilted her head. "Yes?" she said, in a tone that indicated, "This is bound to be good."

"It comes from Sethra the Younger."

Her green eyes narrowed and appeared slightly grey. "Sethra the Younger," she repeated.

"Yes."

"What does she want?"

"Kieron's greatsword."

"Indeed? The sword of Kieron the Conqueror. She wants me to give it to her. Well, isn't that sweet."

"I'm just passing on a message."

"Uh-huh. And what is she offering for it?"

"I think you can guess, Aliera."

Aliera studied me, then slowly nodded. "Yes, I suppose I can, at that. Why don't you both sit down."

She looked at us, her grey eyes squinting. She held her wineglass, a fine piece of cut crystal, so that the chandelier made a rainbow through it that decorated the dark wood table next to her.

"What do you two think?" she said at last.

"We're delighted, of course," I said. "We'd like nothing better than to have Sethra the Younger butcher a few thousand Easterners."

She nodded. "There's more to this than that, however."

"Yes," I said. "There is."

"I'm surprised you're even bringing me the proposition."

"I wasn't going to," I said. "But Cawti talked me into it."

Aliera turned an inquiring gaze at Cawti, who said, "It's something you should know about."

She nodded. "Morrolan claims to have an idea what it is, but Sethra the Younger claimed it, and he didn't have the—well, he chose not to dispute it."

"If you get it," I said, "he still won't. Unless you give it to him."

"It may be," she said, "that, whatever it really is, a Great Weapon, as we suspect, or something else entirely, it has been trying to come to me all along."

I thought back on the Serioli, and on the Wall, and on everything that had happened, and I said, "That is a disgusting thought."

She turned her glance to me, frowning as if I'd spoken in a foreign language, but continued her thought without answering me. "If so, to fail to take it would be to ask for more trouble, and greater."

"On the other hand," I said, "I seem to remember Kieron the Conqueror promising to come after you if you gave his sword away."

"Yes," said Aliera. "And that is, of course, another advantage."

11

BREAKFAST WITH CHEF VLADIMIR

There was a certain amount of doubt in the eyes of the soldiers in front of me, either because they weren't all that happy about cutting down a single unarmed Easterner or, more likely, because Ori was not authorized to give them orders. But for whatever reason, they hesitated; Ori, on the other hand, did not. He took a step forward, and as his arm came up, I let Spellbreaker fall into my hand, and then there was something black and ugly crackling and coming toward me.

And here my memory plays tricks on me again, because I know how fast such things move, and so I know I didn't really have time to make the cold, disinterested observation that I remember making, and I certainly wouldn't have had time to deliberately fall over backward while swinging Spellbreaker before me, and to listen to the crackling in the air, and notice that particular odor that accompanies thunderstorms, and be simultaneously planning what I was going to say if I were still able to say it, but that's how I remember it happening, and if my memory is to defy reason, well, I still have to go with my memory, and so there is the smell, the crackle, the roll, and even now the muscle memory of Spellbreaker's weight in my hand, and the feel of the ground beneath me, and even a small rock that bruised my shoulder as I hit, rolled, and came up, aware that my left arm was numb, and my brain was going *tick tick tick* as I made deductions and decisions and was able to keep my voice cool and rational as I said, "That was uncalled for, Ori. Do it again and I'll destroy you. I'm here to talk, not to kill, but if I change my mind I'll burn you where you stand even if your bodyguards slice me to ribbons in the next instant. Now stop it, and we'll talk."

I caught his eye and held it, and for a moment I didn't even notice the twenty-odd Dragonlords who might or might not be about to cut me down. I waited. Before me stretched gentle, green hills; behind rose the cliff called the Wall, with the plain flat monument to Baritt, his "tomb" standing up before it; and around me were the Eastern Mountains; they all seemed to hold their breath with me. I wondered if I were to die here. It would have been appropriate if I'd had some sort of premonition, but I don't get premonitions, at least, not reliable ones. In any case, I'd had no premonition when I had first reached the Eastern Mountains.

At their feet, I had learned when we first reached them, long miles from where I now stood, the day arrives suddenly. For once I was almost glad to be made to wake up early, because otherwise I should never have seen the red and gold tickling the peak of Mount Drift in the false dawn, with the overcast, very high and thin, looking like a product of the mountain, and the splintered light turning the camp into a giant field of mushrooms and the river into a ribbon of purple.

Forgive me; you know we hardened soldiers are all philosophers, and philosophers are all poets. Well, actually, we hardened soldiers are usually drunks and whoremongers, but philosophy's a good way to pass the time in between.

I was poetically given latrine duty that day. Rascha explained, apologetically, that there hadn't been enough "defaulters" to do the job, so lots had been drawn, and my name had come up. But I could breakfast first. I took it philosophically.

I won't spend a lot of time describing latrine duty, but I can say it wasn't as bad as I thought it would be—a lot of digging, mostly, and, in any case, everyone else was involved in digging more earthworks under the guidance of the engineers, so it wasn't much more work than what everyone else was doing, just slightly more unpleasant. I did get a laugh out of a few of my comrades by taking a piece of salted kethna, throwing it into the pit I'd just dug, and covering it over. "Just thought I'd cut out the middle part," I explained.

But I learned one thing of real value that impressed itself upon my consciousness even more than it had during the march, which is when I first began to suspect it: A Dragonlord squatting over a field toilet looks no more dignified than anyone else in that position. That is knowledge I am happy to carry with me.

We held the position on the riverbank for three days, three relatively pleasant days, in fact. It was hot, but we didn't have anything to do except relax or bathe in the river, and, best of all, no one tried to kill us. I had thought we were waiting there with the expectation of being attacked, but I learned later that, in fact, what we were doing was letting the other divisions move into position for a three-pronged attack on the heart of Fornia's realm. Fornia, of course, was busy with marches and countermarches to defend against exactly this. We heard rumors of skirmishes on our flanks, and they turned out to be true, but they were only minor, unimportant little probes of our defenses— unimportant, that is, except to whoever was killed or maimed in the actions. Since the fatalities were all in other companies, we didn't have funeral services for them.

Most of our time was spent sitting around gabbing—or, in the case of Napper and me, complaining. Most of the conversation was pretty low on the scale: sex and liquor, with drugs and food coming second. The rest of the conversation was at a considerably higher level—there was very little middle ground. Philosophizing, as I mentioned before, is a highly respected activity. At one point I said to Virt, "The trouble with you Dragonlords is that to you killing is so impersonal."

She raised an eyebrow. "That's not what I'd expect to hear from a Jhereg."

"How so?"

"I'd thought some of your associates were in the habit of having people killed for business reasons."

"Sure," I said. "But one at a time."

"I imagine that's an important distinction to whoever gets it."

"Well, no; but it matters a great deal to everyone else in the neighborhood."

"Maybe to the House of the Dragon," she said, "the means must be broader because the ends are more sweeping."

"Excuse me?"

"We're not fighting for control of this-or-that brothel, but for this-or-that barony. While that may not be better, it is certainly bigger, so there would naturally be bigger forces involved."

"You think that accounts for it?"

"It is, at least, the most widely accepted theory, and I believe it."

"Uh . . . 'the most widely accepted . . .' There are theories about this?"

"Oh, certainly. There are theories about every aspect of war."

"I see. And are they useful?"

"Some more so than others. But the ones that aren't useful are usually entertaining."

"I see. I hadn't thought of 'entertaining' as having much to do with war."

"No, you wouldn't have. And the idea that it might be probably disgusts you." I didn't say anything. After a moment she said, "Haven't you ever been in mortal danger and discovered after it was over that you'd been having the time of your life? Haven't you ever taken pleasure in making detailed plans, pleasure that had nothing to do with how good, or bad, or important, the end result was? Can't you imagine the pleasure in setting up a complex problem and watching the pieces line themselves up, and all the forces come together, and having things work out the way you wanted them to?"

This, of course, set me thinking of Assassinations I Have Known. I said, "Yes."

"Well?"

"Yes, but."

She nodded. "Go on." It occurred to me suddenly that she was enjoying the conversation. Then I realized that I was, too. Was this significant of something?

I let my mind run and my eyes wander; she waited patiently. I said, "Well, maybe it's just numbers. But it seems that the more lives are being lost, the more important the cause ought to be. Don't you think?"

" 'Ought' is a tricky word. So is 'important.' "

"I can't deny what you say about danger. Yes, certainly, even though I try to avoid putting myself in danger, I know what you mean about the feeling of, well . . ."

"Of being fully alive?" she said.

"Yes, that's it. But that's me, and maybe even the guy I'm facing, if he's another volunteer. But what about those conscripts you've mentioned?"

"They're Teckla," she said.

"True," I admitted. "Okay, back to 'ought' and 'important,' then—"

She laughed suddenly. "You'd make a good tactician. I don't know about strategist, but certainly a tactician."

"I don't think I want to know why," I said.

"All right, then. Back to 'ought' and 'important.' They're moral judgments, aren't they?"

"Is that illegal in this dominion?"

"Not at all. But, traditionally, they're considered too important to be trusted to foot soldiers."

"Ah, tradition," I said. "Well, do you believe that?"

"Of course not," she said. "At least, no one can help thinking about the why's of what we're fighting for. And it does no harm, as long as you don't think about it just when someone is trying to skewer you."

"Well then," I said. "Let's get down to specifics. Fornia is as power-hungry as—well, he's power-hungry." I'd been about to say "as Dragons always are," but caught myself. "So is Morrolan. Their lands are next to each other, and Morrolan wants to make sure Fornia isn't able to threaten him, and, of course, Fornia doesn't want his lands invaded, so they make up a pretext of insult, and a few tens of thousand of us start hacking at each other. How do we fit that into 'ought' and 'important'?"

"You're here for much the same reason, aren't you? Fornia offended you, so you're going to kill a few perfect strangers?"

"I'm one man. I'm not commanding an army to do my killing for me."

"You think Morrolan should challenge him to a duel?"

"No, I think Morrolan should kill him."

"How? Assassination?"

"Why not? Anyone can be assassinated."

"So I've heard," she said dryly. I expected her to start in on the cant about how horrid it was to assassinate an enemy compared to honorable battle, and I was all set with a tirade about the death of one versus the death of hundreds or thousands, but she didn't go there. She said, "And, if he succeeded, what would then happen? Do you imagine Fornia has no friends, no family, none who would take offense?"

"If no one knew—"

"Is that how it usually works, my dear Jhereg? When someone is killed in your House, is it not usually known who benefits from his death?"

I didn't have a good answer; she was right. In the Jhereg, you usually wanted it known who had the guy shined; that way it served as a warning to the next guy who might think about committing whatever offense had put a polish on the victim.

"All right," I said. "I concede the point. Assassination would be impractical in cases like this."

"Well, then?"

I grinned. "There's always negotiation."

"Certainly," she said. "As long as you can threaten war, you'll always be able to negotiate."

"I was kidding."

"I know. I was being serious."

"You'd make a good enforcer. I might not want to give you your own territory, but I'd certainly hire you to collect debts."

For an instant she looked annoyed, then she gave me a smile and said, "All right. Well taken."

"Who is that?" I said, gesturing with my eyes.

"Who? Oh. His name is Dortmond. I'm not sure what line he is of. He's been in the company for most of two hundred years. He certainly knows how to campaign, doesn't he?"

"Except that he has to carry it all."

"He's big enough. It all collapses, and I believe he's been known to bribe the wagoners to bring some of his excess along."

The man in question was a couple of tents down from us. He was, indeed, a very large man, of middle years, with long hair and good features for a Dragon. He had his cap pulled down over his eyes and was sitting in front of his tent on what seemed to be a canvas-and-wood chair, complete with back. His feet were on a small footstool of similar construction, and by his elbow was a table, on which sat a wine bottle; a goblet was in his hand, and he was smoking a large black pipe. I watched him for a moment. The complete soldier, all his spare energy devoted to wresting luxury from the tedium of camp life.

"You should see the inside of his tent," said Virt.

"Oh?"

"Double-sized cot with extra padding, pillows, and bug netting. He's painted the bug netting, too; it shows a mountain scene with a wolf howling."

"That *is* a lot to carry."

"The cot is awfully comfortable, though."

"How—never mind."

Virt didn't answer the question I'd almost asked, but silently watched him along with me. He probably expected to serve as a foot soldier all his life, perhaps someday reaching the rank of corporal. He gave the impression of perfect contentment with his lot. Virt seemed to share my thoughts; eventually she said, "There are worse lives than that of the soldier, you know."

"Evidently," I said. "But you'll never be content with it."

"Me? Oh, no. If I'm killed in battle, it'll be on the way up the ranks."

"And what about Napper?"

"Him? You know, I think he's every bit as contented with his life as Dortmond."

"What about her?" I asked, gesturing toward a slim lady who had just walked up to Dortmond. "She looks, oh, I don't know. Peaceful. Nice. Friendly. Something like that."

"Neera e'Lanya. She is. As sweet a girl as you'd ever meet. She's the peacemaker whenever two people in the squad start getting on each other's nerves."

"And now you're going to say that, in battle, she turns into a berserker, right? Dragon rage, spitting, killing with her bare hands?"

"You got it."

"She's really like that?"

"She really is."

"Dragons are weird," I said.

After the evening meal, such as it was, I was called to the Captain's tent once more, and once more the Captain seemed a bit nervous, and once more Morrolan was there.

"Well, Vlad," he said. "Are you prepared to strike another blow for freedom?"

"Is that what we're doing?"

"No, but it sounds better than helping a wealthy and powerful aristocrat maintain his wealth and power."

"Have you been listening in on my conversations?"

"No, why?"

"Never mind. What do you want me to do?"

"Fornia," said Morrolan, "likes to send troops into battle with a full belly. It—"

"The dastard," I said.

"—would be to our advantage, then, if that proved to be impossible."

"I imagine. You're expecting them to attack?"

"It seems likely. They've brought up a number of units, and ours are still arriving. The longer they wait, the stronger we are. Mill's brigade should be arriving sometime tomorrow morning between the eighth hour and the ninth; if they're here before the action begins, we should be able to mount a nice counterattack."

I nodded and didn't express my thought about how "nice" a counterattack was likely to be. I said, "All right. Yeah, I'll interfere with their breakfast. You have something specific in mind?"

He did. I laughed, though it wouldn't be all that funny to the soldiers on the other side. I said, "Won't that just put them in a bad mood?"

"Yes. No doubt their officers will blame it on us and give them good rousing speeches. But it'll also disorganize them and delay their attack. And, of course, it won't help their morale to realize that we can get in and out of their camp any time we like."

"Well, that's what I signed on for," I said. "Where are they?"

"Downriver about half a mile."

"Right along the river?"

"Yes. For the same reason we are."

"We could make use of that, you know. We could mess with their drinking water or—"

"There are traditions involved, Vlad; we don't do that. Officially."

"Officially?"

"I mean nothing organized. But I've never heard of a unit that was upriver of the enemy who could resist a few pranks, at least."

"You must tell me about them."

"Another time."

"All right. In any case, it should be easy enough, with them right next to the river. How many of them are there?"

"More than there are of us," he said. "But then, we're dug in pretty good. Why do you need to know?"

"I have to know how much I'm after, don't I?"

"Oh. Yes." He did some calculation. "More than one wagon, probably more than two, fewer than six."

"Ah. An exact science, I see."

"Plus, of course, whatever they've already taken off the wagons."

"Right. Plus that."

"They won't have unloaded much; they won't know exactly when they'll be moving out. Of course, your target will be toward the rear."

"Okay," I said. I did some calculating, trying to figure out the best way to go about it; difficult, without complete information. "It'll be easier if I have some help. A lot easier."

The Captain spoke for the first time: "How much help?"

"Two should do it. Just extra hands to speed matters up."

"I don't want to lose valuable troops."

"Glad to hear it. I doubt they want to be lost. I know I don't."

He started to respond, glanced at Morrolan, cleared his throat, and said, "Perhaps some of your tent-mates, to keep the gossip down."

"They'd do."

"Who's your corporal?"

"Rascha."

"Very well, I'll speak with her."

"Good enough," I said. "I'll set off around midnight."

He nodded. Loiosh said, *"This should be fun, Boss."*

"Sure, Loiosh. Maybe you'll get a promotion out of it."

I went back to my tent and pulled my cloak out of my satchel. Virt and Napper were sitting in front of the fire, sharpening their weapons. Aelburr was inside, catching a nap. He opened one eye and said, "Not going to sleep like a sane person?"

"A sane person wouldn't be here."

A corner of his mouth twitched and he went back to sleep. I stepped out of the tent and sat down next to the others.

"Nice night," said Virt.

It was, actually. I hadn't noticed. I realized that I didn't notice the weather unless it was bad. Napper, however, said, "She means she doesn't have picket duty tonight."

"How 'bout you?" I said.

"No. Probably tomorrow, though."

"Tomorrow," said Virt, "we'll be somewhere else. Either upriver or downriver."

"There will still be picket duty, though. And, most likely, worse weather."

"True enough," I said, because I agreed with him. I checked the various goodies in my cloak, then checked the time and found that I had a few hours to wait, so I set about sharpening my blade.

A little later Rascha came by. She gave me a funny look, worked her mouth a couple of times like she was having trouble talking, then she said, "Aelburr! Virt!"

Virt said, "I'm right here, you know."

Aelburr poked his head out and said, "Yeah?"

"You're both assigned to Taltos here for tonight."

I felt them looking at me while I studied the top of the tent in front of me, just to see if it was straight.

"What is it?" said Virt.

"He'll explain," said Rascha with distaste, and moved along quickly.

They both gave me inquiring looks. So did Napper. The top of the tent was reasonably straight. I said, "It's nothing much. I've been asked to cook tomorrow."

Napper made a grimace. Virt said, "There's something you're not telling us."

"Yeah, well. I'll explain later."

"How much later?" said Aelburr. "Is this going to interfere with my sleep schedule?"

"Think of it as picket duty. Sort of."

The three of them exchanged glances. "All right," said Virt. "When *are* you going to explain?"

"Around midnight, we're going to take a walk. We'll go past our own pickets. Then I'll explain."

"Ah," said Aelburr. "An adventure." He didn't look pleased.

Virt said, "I don't know how good I'd be at sneaking around."

"You don't have to be either silent or invisible; you just have to not be heard sneaking or seen skulking."

"Excuse me?"

"Once we get to, uh, where we're going—"

"I like the sound of that."

"—you hide behind any handy objects, but in getting to them you just walk. Don't crawl, and don't try to walk silently. If there's any of that to be done, I'll do it. And you'll be going without your swords."

"How did we get so lucky?" said Virt.

I shrugged. "You have the good fortune to bunk with me. Not only do you get to listen to me snore, you also get to go and get killed with me."

Napper cleared his throat and looked at me with narrowed eyes.

"Sure," I said. "You can come, too."

He nodded.

Soon after midnight we set out, creeping along the river. At roughly the halfway point between the pickets, I stopped and sketched out the plan in a whisper; then I motioned them to follow me before they could ask questions I didn't want to answer or, more important, think about what we were doing. Having them thinking would do no one any good.

Loiosh spotted the enemy pickets and guided us past them. I don't think any of my little band figured out what Loiosh was up to; they just followed me. That was best. Once past the pickets, we had to remain hidden until Loiosh and I could identify the cook-tent. We entered the enemy camp and I had them wait while Loiosh and I searched. The supply wagons were near the mess-tent, which was both good and bad for my purposes. The cook-tent was less than thirty yards from the river, which was good.

"Well? Are they guarded?"

"Four guards, Boss. Moving rightwise around the wagons and the tent. You want to try the same trick we used last time? That was fun."

"No. Too much danger they figured it out. And I won't discuss your idea of 'fun.' "

"What then?"

"We wait."

"Clever, Boss. Do you think if I had opposable thumbs I could come up with plans like that?"

"Shut up, Loiosh."

I returned to where my compatriots were hidden, and, in the flickering half-light of the enemy campfires I indicated that we would just be sitting there for a while. I couldn't see their expressions. I was just as glad.

It was neither warm nor pleasant, but they were used to waiting for action, and, for that matter, so was I. We waited a little more than two hours for the guard to change, assuring us of several hours before they were relieved again. I had their movements figured out. And there had been no one checking on them. Loiosh said, "If this had been your operation, Boss, you'd have gotten all the details before you went to work."

"If this had been my operation, Loiosh, I would have hired someone else to do it."

I signaled to my temporary squadron that they should stay there, and I moved a little closer to the guards. I drew a dart from my cloak, waited for the guard to pass by me, then threw the dart into his back. He cursed.

"What is it?" said someone.

"Something bit me."

"Bees sleep at night."

"Well, that makes me feel better."

"I'm just saying—"

"I better see the surgeon; I'm starting to feel queasy."

"You have any allergies?"

"Not that I know of. What is there that bites around here?"

He didn't get an answer, because the woman he'd been talking to was out cold by this time. At least out cold, maybe dead, because a blow to the top of the head with the hard pommel of a dagger can kill, even if you don't intend it to. Fortunes of war and all that. And then, as the man succumbed and collapsed, I stuck a dart into the woman to be certain—the poison on the dart probably wouldn't kill her, but it wouldn't make her feel any better, and, in any case, neither of them would wake up any time soon. I hoped I hadn't killed either of them; I hate killing people I haven't been paid for. Were this a Jhereg operation, it wouldn't have come up. Jhereg operations are cleaner.

So, okay, you don't need the details; I took care of the other two guards as well, and I didn't kill either of them for sure, though I may have hit one a bit too hard. . . .

Oh, skip it. I went back to the others and motioned for them to follow me.

The rest of the job involved one decision: Was it safer and easier going to the water or from the water? One was quicker, the other safer; I opted for quicker. I was fairly certain I could vanish into the night if by chance I was seen, but I doubted my companions could. I called them close and whispered, "If there's an alarm, we go straight into the river, drop everything, and swim downstream as far and as fast as we can, okay? Remember to get rid of your boots."

They nodded. I didn't think they were very pleased with the prospect. We entered the mess-tent and took care of business there, which took only a few minutes. While we did so, I had Loiosh smell the wagons so he could tell me which ones we were interested in.

"Three of them, Boss."

"Good show."

I left the tent first and looked around in spite of Loiosh's assurance that all was clear, then I led my little band over to the wagons and pointed out the ones we wanted. There was a little more light here, and I could see them wondering how I knew. I resolved not to tell them.

We dumped kerosene over them. Now was when we had to be fast, because no one is going to pay much attention to someone half glimpsed who is moving about the camp as if he belongs there, but the smell of kerosene is strong and sets off alarms in anyone.

It only took a minute or so to drench the wagons, then I signaled that we should retreat back toward our own camp. Virt looked a question at me, presumably, How are we going to set them on fire? I smiled back at her and led the way.

We made it past the pickets without incident, at which point Virt said, "How are you going to start the fire from here?"

"Oh, I don't know." I picked a stick, drew on my link to the Orb, and started it burning. "I'll think of something," I said, and handed it to Loiosh, who flew off into the night.

They stared in wonderment for a moment; none of them, I think, had any previous clue of Loiosh's intelligence. Just for fun, I led them past our own pickets.

Once back in camp, all three of them reacted as I should have expected: laughter bordering on the hysterical, which was a little terrifying in Napper's case; and, along with the near hysteria, an unreasonable desire to continue being silent, as if the habit had been ingrained for life in the few intense hours.

Eventually they quieted down, and then Aelburr whispered, "Hope they like toast," and they all burst into giggles again, with hands clapped over mouths to keep it quiet, which, of course, made it even funnier. I found myself laughing with them, until we were informed that if we didn't quiet down at once we'd be put on report. Napper, tears streaming from his eyes, tried to whisper something that struck him as funny about that, but couldn't get it out, and the effort made him laugh even harder.

Virt, however, hysterics or not, was not anxious to be put on report, so she gestured that we should follow her. She started jogging toward the river, then veered away to stay within the boundaries of the camp. I wondered what she was up to when my question answered itself; it is hard to stay hysterical when you're out of breath from running, and hard to run when you're out of breath from laughing. In a few minutes, we weren't laughing anymore, and Virt led us back to our tent.

It actually worked; I, at least, fell asleep quickly, and I think the others did as well, and there was really nothing more to the incident until breakfast the next morning, when we each took our biscuit and looked at it.

"Yes," said Napper. "They taste rather better today than they did yesterday, don't you think?"

Whatever happened in the next few hours, I decided, getting a pleasantry out of Napper counted as a moral victory.

12

A FEW BUMPS AND BRUISES

Sounds broke in to interrupt my stare-down with Ori: the sounds of Easterners being slaughtered. Mostly screams—and screams that were different from the cries of the wounded, because these had the edge of terror. I realized then that even from here I could feel the presence of Blackwand. On the field below me, to my right, Easterners were dying and my side was winning; the souls of my kind were gone, swallowed up, vanished forever, destroyed; and my side was winning the engagement. You could say I had mixed feelings about this.

On the other hand, if I wanted to present myself as a negotiator, it did put me in a stronger position. As I considered this, another interruption came, this one in the form of someone pushing through past the honor guard and coming up next to Ori.

It was about here that everything speeded up and slowed down; that is, things began to happen faster, but it seemed as if I had more time to observe and think it all over, to weigh the options, note the dangers, and be afraid.

"Well," I said. "My Lord Fornia. I hadn't expected to find you here."

He didn't appear any better disposed toward me than he had been when last we met, which, now that I thought about it, was only about a quarter of a mile from this very spot. Coincidence, if you like. I don't, terribly. I did think, for a moment, about taking a shot at him; the reasons against were legion, including not having much chance of killing him, having less chance of escaping alive, and being certain that Morrolan wouldn't thank me even if I managed. But I did think about it.

Ori said again, "He's an assassin. Kill him."

I said, "Oh, let's not."

Fornia said, "No, he's not here to assassinate me. Whatever his threats, Morrolan would never countenance such an act."

"In war, my lord? In battle?"

"On the other hand," said Fornia, "I do not believe you are here as a negotiator. Morrolan would no more send an Easterner to negotiate with me than he would send a Jhereg to assassinate me. So what *are* you doing here, exactly?"

The warriors stared at me; behind them, no doubt, were more of Fornia's sorcerers. I turned my head and gestured to the battle to my right. It was worse than it had been; I could make out Morrolan, and around him, even from this distance, I saw corpses lying in heaps. Or, at any rate, bodies; I didn't have to be there to know they were dead.

I turned back to Fornia. "They're getting closer," I said. "Morrolan and his brigade. With Blackwand," I added.

He didn't seem unduly worried. I went on, "Morrolan didn't send me to kill you or to negotiate with you. He didn't send me at all. I'm here on my own."

"Indeed," said Fornia. "Do you, then, imagine you can kill me, here, now?"

Why wasn't he worried? If Blackwand was coming for me, I'd be worried. I'd be more than worried, I'd be bloody terrified. "No," I said. "Or, perhaps yes, I could, but it is not my intention to try."

His eyes strayed to the carnage below, now noticeably closer than when I'd reached them. He seemed unconcerned. "What then?" he said.

"I want to stop the slaughter."

He gave a short laugh. "You *have* become a soldier. Soldiers have wanted to stop the slaughter as long as the profession has existed."

That I believed. That, at any rate, had been my desire since the first time I was in battle. No, I suppose, since the second time; the first time was too confused, the second time, the morning after we had burned up the enemy's biscuits, is the battle I have the clearest memory of, and the greatest feeling of disgust, at least up until this point. It all seemed to happen slowly, with a neat succession of images burning themselves into my memory.

That time, the engineers, instead of digging the ditches and building up the earthworks, passed out shovels and guided us in doing so. The ground, I remember, was soft and easy to work with, a fact the engineers never let us forget. The air was dry—almost throat-parching dry—but cold. The sort of cold where any little bump or bruise has an additional sting to it. I hoped we wouldn't be doing any fighting, but I expected we would, and I was right.

So we dug a deep ditch and piled up dirt until it reached the height of our chests, and whether our clandestine activities in the night had anything to do with the fact that we were able to finish before they attacked, I don't know, but I'd like to think so. It makes me feel useful.

The juice-drum gave the call, "Rubbing Elbows," which meant to form the line, and we did, under Rascha's guidance. We were each given three javelins, which we stuck into the ground near us. Rascha had a spyglass, and her first word as she studied the enemy that was just too far away to see with the unaided eye was "Cavalry." Then she said, "Pass the word for pikes." Then, almost at once, "No, never mind. They're re-forming."

This time Loiosh did not suggest I bug out; he probably didn't know why I'd stayed in the line last time, any more than I did, but figured there was no help for it and I was just bound and determined to remain for the fight.

Rascha continued studying their lines, occasionally making aim-less gestures with her left hand; I assumed some sort of spell to help her see or to counter any clouding spells the enemy might be using.

"No cavalry," said Virt. "You won't have to fight your own kind yet."

"Good," I said, meaning it.

She said, "Smart, too. I wouldn't send horses against ditches and earthworks."

"What would you send against us?"

"Well, certainly not a spear phalanx—they don't like ditches and they hate earthworks. I'd say either mounted infantry or heavy infan-try, like last time."

"Mounted infantry?"

"Ride like bastards up to the ditch, dismount, and come right over. They could get here awful fast, and the horses will shield them

from javelins once they've dismounted. Why do you ask? We'll know
for certain in a few minutes."

"Just killing time."

"Best to be killing something," put in Napper. His eyes were
shining and he kept baring his teeth.

I shook my head. "You really like this, don't you?"

"Yes," he said. "And so do you, you just don't want to admit it."

"Mounted infantry," said Rascha.

"Good call," I said. "So, what do we do? Think the Captain will
pull something clever?"

"Nothing clever to be done, really. We just have to hold this
spot. Maybe Sethra will send someone in on their flanks, maybe not.
Depends on how much of their forces they've committed and, well,
on a lot of things we don't have any way of knowing."

I grunted.

Crown, from far down the line, called, "Make ready."

I drew my sword, transferred it to my left hand, and picked up a
javelin.

"You really ought to borrow a heavier blade," Aelburr told me. I
grunted again.

Virt said, "We'll be lucky to have time for two throws before
they're on us."

"Yes," said Aelburr.

That meant one for me.

Rascha said, "Aim for the horses." That was funny; how was I
supposed to aim for anything else? We could now see the line
clearly—it stretched out to more than cover us; we were flanked on
both sides, then. But that, of course, was not my concern. Whoever
was guiding the battle was supposed to make sure our line didn't get
rolled up, and if whoever that was blew his job, it wasn't my concern.

It was, of course, my life. I remembered what my grandfather had
said about trusting your officers even though you know they aren't
worthy of trust. My hand was cramping from gripping the javelin
tightly and I made an effort to relax it.

I wasn't used to this. Analogous situations in the Jhereg just
weren't analogous.

"You know, Loiosh, I don't think I'd care to make this a career."

Whatever answer he was going to give was masked by an intrusion into my head. It took a minute for me to figure out what it was, then I realized that it was Kragar, choosing just then to get in touch with me.

"What is it, Kragar?"

"Nothing important, Vlad, but—"

"Then forget it, for the love of Verra. I'm just a little busy right now."

"Okay. Later."

I looked up again, and there were many horses riding down on us, and Rascha said, "Javelins ready!" We all prepared to throw; I prepared to ignore the order to throw until I had at least some chance of hitting something. I wondered abstractedly if this time I'd be able to follow the flight of the javelin as it left my hand. I wondered if—

"Loose javelins!" called Rascha, and the sky darkened again. I waited a moment, then threw, instantly forgot that I wanted to see where my javelin ended up, and transferred my sword once more to my right hand.

Someone screamed, and someone yelled, " 'Ware sorcery!" so I let Spellbreaker fall into my hand, and I noticed that there were an awful lot of horses writhing about on the ground. At first I thought someone had strung a trip-wire, then I realized that they were the result of the javelins, and then I wondered why I hadn't thought of stringing trip-wire myself, or, at any rate, why someone hadn't thought of it, and then some guy came bounding up out of the ditch in front of me so I stuck my sword through his neck and he went down.

There was shouting, screaming, and the clashing of blades, but it all became a sort of noiseless noise, and I remember having the illusion that I was in my own universe, with no directions except forward; anything to the sides was someone else's problem. It was odd, and it was also odd how much time I had to think, to observe, to plan, and to act. Someone else bounded up, off balance and sword flailing as if he'd been propelled by something behind him, and I remember being able to pick my target, wait for it to line up, and to hit it. Then a hand appeared, and I cut it, and then I intercepted some sort of spell with Spellbreaker without being aware of how I spotted it. Then two came over at once, and I gave one a good cut across the legs while the other struck at me. I slipped to the side while holding my rapier up at a sharp angle—I even remember calculating the angle to keep the blade from breaking—and when I'd deflected it I stuck him one in the stomach. He fell forward, so I let a dagger fall into my hand from my left sleeve, stuck it into his throat as he lay on his back, and recovered Spellbreaker from his chest, where I'd dropped it.

I wiped my brow, dragging Spellbreaker in front of my eyes; its gold links were small now; no doubt that meant something. I waited for the next man to try to get past me, but there wasn't one; the assault was over.

I stood there and looked myself over, until Loiosh said, *"Relax, Boss; not a scratch."*

"Okay."

Then I looked for my tent-mates. Virt was on her knees breathing heavily, but didn't seem to be bleeding. Napper had one hand on the earthworks, the other holding his sword, as he watched our retreating enemies, and I had the impression he was willing them to return. Aelburr was sitting on the ground, grinning, shaking his head, and cradling his left arm with his right. He caught me looking at him. "Son of a bitch," he said, but not angrily, more as if he were commenting on the weather. "Dislocated my fucking shoulder."

"Next time," said Virt, looking up suddenly. "Try cutting them instead of throwing them around. For one thing, that way they aren't in such a hurry to crawl back over."

"I'll keep that in mind," he said.

I looked an inquiry at Virt, but she didn't provide any details. She opened up her water flask and helped Aelburr drink some, and presently the surgeon arrived. I walked away a little, because I don't like watching surgeons, physickers, healers, or anyone else whose job it is to undo the sort of thing I'm so good at doing.

Rascha came by about then and directed those of us who didn't need treatment to pick up javelins and make sure they were unbroken, which was sufficiently mind-numbing to be relaxing after the battle.

We had not, it seemed, been in the worst part of the engagement; there were places where the carnage was much worse, and Jhereg— normal-sized ones—were circling overhead. Sometimes one would come a little too close and someone would hurl a stone or a javelin at it.

"Why is it, Loiosh, that they hate Jhereg so much but like you?"

"My winning personality, Boss?"

"Yeah, that must be it."

By the time I got back, the bodies were neatly stacked, and the seriously wounded were gone, and the walking wounded had, for the most part, been tended to. Napper had gotten over his battle-fury and was himself once more. "We should attack," he said disgustedly.

"Good thinking," said Virt. "They only outnumber us about three to two."

"Don't matter," said Napper.

"And we'd be leaving our protection, which is the only way we survived the attack."

"Don't matter."

"And they could probably bring a spear phalanx against us."

"Hmmm. Matters," said Napper.

"What," I asked, "is a spear phalanx?"

"A unit specially designed to wipe out units like us."

"Oh."

"Think of a solid wall of very big shields with ranks of spears sticking out of them, and those in back, who aren't even in danger, pushing the ones in front at you."

"I see. Well, no I don't, but I'm convinced I don't want to."

"I've been through one of those," said Virt. "I didn't much care for it. I probably wouldn't be here if we hadn't had help."

"What sort of help?"

"They don't like getting hit from the flank while they're engaged in front. They especially don't like it when it's heavy cavalry."

"Do we have heavy cavalry?"

"Probably. I'd still rather skip that fight."

"Okay," I agreed. "I won't order it."

"Thanks," she said. "Which reminds me. That business last night."

"What about it?"

"Are you—"

I was saved from having to evade another question by the juice-drum, which told us to form our line again.

"Here they come again," said Rascha.

"Bugger," I said.

Napper stood and bounded back to the earthworks, his eyes shin-ing.

"More mounted infantry," said Rascha. "Ready javelins."

You don't need to hear about the second assault, or the third. We survived, and more died. Virt picked up a gouge on her left leg that didn't amount to much, and I got a bruise on my forehead that knocked me down and would probably have been fatal if I hadn't been rushing my opponent; she caught me perfectly, but it was the flat of the blade. Things got hazy for a bit, and I don't know what became of her, but then it was over, and, while we were awaiting the fourth assault we got word to retreat. Napper didn't like it, but I was delighted.

Rascha came by and gave me a new cap, since I'd lost mine in the last assault, and Virt, limping along next to me, said that the bandage around my forehead made me look like a real warrior. I made scatological culinary recommendations.

"Loiosh, I just want you to know, for the sake of my familiar having complete information, that my feet hurt."

"I think you're cheating, Boss. Everyone else has to either carry on without complaint or be known as a complainer. You get to complain without anyone knowing it."

"Because I had the foresight to show up with a ready-made listener to complaints."

"That's a new job for me. Do I get a raise?"

"Sure, Loiosh. Your salary just doubled."

"Heh."

We didn't start the march until fairly late in the day, so we stopped blessedly early, posted the extra pickets, and settled in to a hasty but well-organized camp. I suppose the art of setting up camp has a whole lot of theory behind it, too. Maybe that was what Crown was so good at; I don't know.

I had the second picket duty, which gave me the dubious pleasure of sleeping a little less than four hours, standing guard for four, and then sleeping another hour and a half before having to get up. We weren't attacked during the night, which I wondered at. In fact, I wondered why we never launched attacks during the night. I wondered if it was some sort of agreement among Dragons, the way the Jhereg won't have you assassinated in your own home or in front of your family.

Turned out I was wrong, it was all a matter of generalship and the art of war, about which I know nothing now and at the time knew even less. You see, I somewhere got the idea that good generalship would have a lot in common with running the organization and that there would be a great deal of similarity between battle tactics and, say, planning an assassination. I found out later that I was wrong. Oh, in very general terms, sure there are some similarities, but not in any useful way. I was speaking with Sethra Lavode about the Wall of Baritt's Tomb and the campaign leading up to it. I said, "You have this reputation, you know. I mean, as being a great general. You were Warlord I don't know how many times, and—"

"What about it?"

I had to cast about for words. It's hard to tell the most powerful sorcerer and perhaps greatest general in history that you weren't impressed with how she did her job. She might take it wrong. After mumbling a bit, I finally said, "I don't know. It's just that the whole time I was marching and waiting and sneaking around and fighting and marching again I kept waiting for you to make some brilliant maneuver, or some great stroke, or pull some trick, or something."

"How many tricks do you use in your work?"

"Huh? I'll use a trick any time I think I can get away with it."

"So will I," said Sethra Lavode.

"But you usually don't?"

"Tricks, feints, sneak attacks, night attacks, they all work better if they're on a smaller scale. A unit, maybe a company, that's about it. Once you have anything larger, the chances for miscommunication and mistake become too great. And there's always more of a chance for error on attack than defending even in the most simple operations, so if you add something tricky it gets much worse. That's one reason I prefer to defend whenever possible."

"So that's why we kept holding positions and then retreating after we'd won?"

"Those skirmishes you're talking about—"

"Skirmishes?"

"All right, Vlad. Those battles, then, that you won, you couldn't have actually won if you had remained. Fornia wouldn't have attacked if he hadn't been pretty sure he could overrun those positions eventually. We had to keep drawing him after us."

"Well, I suppose that counts as a trick, then."

"Maybe. Except, of course, that he knew very well what I was doing."

"Then why did he do what we wanted?"

"Because it was what he wanted, too. He wanted to try to get past our advance positions so he could divide our forces, which would have put me in a very uncomfortable position. It was a race, if you like. I needed to hold him off long enough for all of our forces to be in position; he needed to break through and separate us so we couldn't combine. And then, of course, the big, decisive engagement. However much planning you do, you don't really know until the armies meet and have it out. Even if your position looks perfect on paper, or even if it looks utterly untenable, you don't know until someone calls for an attack and the fight happens."

"Okay," I said. I tried to phrase my next question, then gave up just as she figured it out.

"The reason," she said, "that I have been successful is that I pay attention to details. The fewer details you miss, the greater your chances of winning."

"Well," I said. "That much *is* rather like assassination. Or so I've heard."

"I don't doubt it. It means keeping open lines of retreat and communications, and always knowing how you're going to feed and water the troops, and where they'll be camping, and what sort of ground they'll be crossing at every point, and the nature of your officers and where their strengths and weaknesses are, and how much dependence to place on which intelligence reports, and how far to push a particular victory, and how to salvage as much as possible from a given defeat, and so on and on and on. The details—the little things that lead to your peace, instead of the enemy's."

"Lead to peace?"

"Peace is the goal of war. Didn't you know that?"

"Uh . . ."

"Come, Vlad. Until there is peace, you haven't won. That is, you haven't accomplished your goals. On the other hand, it is worth re-membering that, until there is peace, you also haven't lost."

"I guess I hadn't looked at it that way."

"You have never had to."

"Yeah, I suppose."

"The other reason I've been successful, I think, is that I'm very aggressive. And of course, my reputation helps. They think of me as being a great general, which makes the enemy afraid to be aggressive, which makes me a great general." She laughed a little. "But my usual approach is to give the enemy every chance to make a mistake, and then I punish him when he does, and the biggest mistake may be not to be aggressive enough, which is one mistake I never make."

"Aggressive on defense?"

"Certainly, Vlad. After all, it's always the defender who starts the war."

"Excuse me? Then it was Fornia who started the war with Mor-rolan?"

"Yes, indeed. That made him the defender, and that was why so much of my effort was involved in bringing him over to the attack."

I shook my head. "I don't see how it is that the defender starts the war."

"It isn't that complicated. The attacker doesn't want war. The attacker wants to conquer. If the defender would simply allow him to do so there would be no war."

"Uh . . . Sethra, I think there's something wrong with your logic."

"No," she said. "There isn't. It's counterintuitive, but it isn't wrong."

I thought all that over, remembering the battles and the retreats and the marches, and I said, "Assassination is easier. Or so I've heard."

She smiled and made no answer.

But that, as I said, was months later. At the time I just sat in camp along with everyone else, stood picket duty, marched, and griped. I think of that period as "the long march," although it was made clear to me that it wasn't long by anyone's standards except mine. I don't know exactly where we marched—I keep meaning to find a map and trace the route—but we usually had the Eastern River on our left, and we always had the Eastern Mountains on our right, and we kept going north; and then one day we turned around for no

6

STEVEN BRUST

apparent reason and headed back south, almost exactly retracing our steps. No one except me, it seemed, found that infuriating, but I was annoyed enough to make up for the rest of them. My comments on the subject met with shrugs and puzzled looks until I stopped talking about it.

The weather for the most part stayed dry and cold. The cold wasn't too bad, because marching kept me warm, but I learned that dry wasn't all that much better than raining, because we were now passing through an area that hadn't seen any rain in some time, and so whenever we were on a road, which was most of the time, the troops in front kicked up dust that we had to eat all day—even worse than before. Dust so thick you walked with your cap down and tried to keep your mouth closed, but you couldn't because your nose was plugged up. A few of my comrades had handkerchiefs over their mouths and noses; I tried that, but breathing became difficult so I stopped. Periodically someone would conjure up a cross breeze just to give us some relief, and even I took my turn at it, but we couldn't keep it going all day without a major weather-working, which was expressly forbidden by the Captain—something about interfering with "stated objectives of the Brigade."

Excitement, what there was of it, came in the form of raids from the enemy, usually directed at the supply trains that came along several miles behind us. We would hear about them because we'd suddenly be ordered to halt, we'd have to take battle positions, and then we'd wait, and then we'd be ordered back in line and we'd set off marching again.

Then, one day, we made a sharp turn, put our backs to the river, and headed toward the mountains. There began to be a feeling of urgency, or maybe *purpose* is a better word, but I'm not sure where it came from. It grew colder as we climbed still higher, and the Eastern Mountains loomed ever larger. One peak in particular seemed to be our destination; a very tall, reddish-looking mountain with, it appeared, nothing whatsoever growing on its side. One evening, before the light failed, we stopped a few miles away from it, and I saw just how steep it was; it seemed to rise straight up from the ground, its top lost in the overcast.

The funny thing was, I didn't recognize it until the next day, when, after only a two-hour march we reached its foot, and Loiosh dived into my cloak with a psychic squeal, and then I looked around and said, "I'll be damned."

"Then don't get killed," said Virt. "But what is it this time?"

"I know where we are."

"That's good. Where are we?"

"That piece of rock," I said, "is Baritt's Tomb."

She nodded and looked around the area: a few hills here and there, and off to the southwest a flat plain covered with rocks and low grass, then a tall hill beyond. I could suddenly imagine warriors on each of those hills, and others charging across the plain.

"Good ground for fighting," she said.

13

Soldier's Stew

Just a few short minutes before, the approaching battle had been terrifying. Now it was also loud. I felt this awful sense of urgency, that I should be doing something *now*, but I just stood there, and so did Fornia. It did accomplish one thing—which was to give myself time to think. What was Fornia accomplishing by doing nothing? Why was he letting me, an enemy, just stand there like that?

Was he delaying, too? If so, why? The only thing he could want was for the battle to close in on him, and what would that get him? I would have given whole worlds to know what he had in mind. I wished—

I did a quick check. Yes, indeed, there was a teleport block in place. But. Maybe.

Time. I needed time. I needed time to find out why Fornia needed time. Well, okay, so maybe he'd be willing to give it to me.

"What are you going to do when they get here?" I ventured.

"You'll see," he told me.

"Do you expect me to just wait here?"

"Do as you wish."

"*Kragar!*"

"*Vlad?*"

"*Kragar, I need Daymar. Now.*"

"*Daymar?*"

"*Now.*"

"*Uh . . . how do I—?*"

"*I'll give you my location, you pass it on to Daymar, and warn him there's a teleport block up.*"

"How can he get past a teleport block?"
"Damned if I know. But he said—"
"Yeah, he might at that. I take it this is urgent."
"You might put it that way, yes."
"I'll see what I can do."
"Hurry."

Yeah, Daymar. He might be able to help me. I didn't terribly enjoy calling on him; I hadn't much enjoyed what he'd done last time we'd met. That had been . . . what? Two weeks ago? Less? Impossible. In that time I'd fought in three engagements, marched halfway around the world through rain, mud, and dust, and come to here, to this place: the Wall of Baritt's Tomb.

There had been nothing, at first, to indicate that stopping there was any different from any of our other temporary halts, except for the obvious one that we had halted early in the day. But there was no rush to put up defenses, and no indications we'd been given a position we would be holding against an attack. I found out later that this was because the original plan had been for us to be part of a major attack against one side of Fornia's army, but that this had changed when Sethra, at the last minute, had learned how Fornia had deployed his forces.

"Deployed." That's a military word. I learned it from Sethra. I'll have to make sure to use it on Kragar sometime, just to see his reaction.

Virt and Aelburr scraped out a fire-pit while Napper and I pitched the tent. "No wood around here," said Aelburr.

"So we freeze?" I said.

They ignored me. Virt said, "The wagons should be across in a couple of hours."

I looked at Napper. "Coal," he explained.

I felt stupid and didn't say anything.

We went through the rituals of setting up camp, but I kept looking up at that mountain, the flat slab extending up until it became lost in the overcast. Occasionally the giant Jhereg would swoop down and Loiosh would dive into my cloak. The Wall had been dedicated to Baritt's memory, and as long as it stood it would bring him to mind whenever it was seen or even mentioned. I thought back to meeting him. Would someone by now have mentioned the Wall? Would he care? It seemed a shame, not to mention ironic, for him not to know that there was a monument to his memory.

On the other hand, I hadn't much liked him.

Three hours later we had a fire going and water heating. Aelburr made something called Soldier's Stew, which involved crumbling a lot of biscuits into boiling water along with the rest of our rations, and molasses, and it should have been disgusting, but he added some basil, mushrooms, toeroot, and nutmeg that he'd picked up somewhere, and the thing was all right; we sang his praises the rest of the day.

We did picket duty early in the evening, and so were able to get a good night's sleep, and the picket assignments indicated no enemy nearby. The next day some of the company drew out a squareball field, wrapped a bunch of rope around a rock to use as the ball, and played a good rousing game while the rest of us stood around and yelled encouragement and obscenities. The injuries weren't nearly as bad as a full-scale battle would have been but were bad enough to get us yelled at by Crown and cursed by the company physicker. I did, however, resolve never to get into a fair fight with Dortmond. That was okay, I had no intention of ever having a fair fight with anyone. There was more S'yang Stones that night, and someone pulled out a reed-pipe and a bunch of them sang bad songs off key, and Aelburr made more Soldier's Stew.

At one point, I found Rascha, Virt, Dunn, and Aelburr standing looking out over the flat field nestled between the hills. "That's where they'll be," Rascha was saying. "They'll spread out between those hills, Dorian's and Smoker's, command both of them, and try to hold us off from there."

"If we fight here," said Aelburr.

"Well, yes," said Rascha. "But the sergeant hasn't given any indication that we're going anywhere."

"I think it'll be here," said Virt. "What I don't understand is why we haven't taken positions on those hills ourselves."

"You're the expert," said Rascha. "What do you think?"

"I think the only thing that could keep the Captain's grubby paws off those hills is orders from above."

"Good thinking," said Rascha.

"You've heard that?" put in Dunn. "We've had specific orders about them?"

"Only a rumor, but that's what I've heard."

"But why?"

Rascha looked at Virt and gave a bow. Virt said, "To entice an attack. Same reason we haven't built up any defenses. Sethra wants them to attack us, and she's making it as attractive as possible."

I said, "Will they fall for it?"

"It isn't a matter of falling for it," said Virt. "They'll know how we're laid out. If we're offering battle on favorable terms, they'll take it."

"But then they wouldn't be favorable terms for us."

"It isn't that simple," said Virt.

"Then don't try to explain it to me," I said. I wandered away. It was too pleasant a day to think about fighting. There was a breeze whipping south along the mountain that brought cool air, but it wasn't yet cold, and it was dry, and not even terribly dusty. I came upon Dortmond, who was sitting back in his chair, feet stretched out, smoking a pipe. He opened one eye and said, "Well, it's the Easterner who fights like a Dragon. Wine?"

"Sure."

He pulled a beautifully carved wooden goblet from a canvas bag at his feet, filled it from a bottle next to his hand, and passed it to me. I tasted it. It wasn't wine, it was brandy; even better as far as I was concerned.

"To the soldier's life," he said.

I didn't care to drink to that, but I did care to drink, so I raised my glass and swallowed.

"How did you get this stuff?"

"The victualer is a friend of mine, and a few of the provisioners owe me some favors, and there's always a little spare room in some of the supply wagons."

I drank the brandy. Loiosh, who had been flying about collecting scraps of food, found me and landed on my shoulder. Dortmond eyed him. I said, "Do you believe he's good luck, too?"

"Sure. Why not? We've had good luck during the whole campaign, haven't we?"

"Have we?"

"Well, are you alive?"

"Haven't checked lately."

He refrained from the obvious wisecracks and poured me more brandy, still calling it "wine." He said, "I think the campaign has been pretty lucky, all in all." He reached into the canvas bag once more, removed a loaf of bread and a large chunk of cheese. He broke off some of each and passed them over to me. It was a smokey meiren cheese, very sharp and good. The bread was stale but not moldy, and much, much better than biscuit. He broke off some more cheese, held it up, and Loiosh flew over and took it from him in one claw, holding it almost delicately while feeding himself. I watched him eat: nibble, chew, swallow, wipe mouth on wing. He was rather more civilized than I.

"Luck," said Dortmond.

"*I feel sick, Loiosh.*"

"*Good cheese, Boss.*"

I said, "So tell me, what are you going to do after the campaign is over?"

"Me?" said Dortmond. "I'm going to go fight another one."

"Why, for heaven's sake?"

"Because," he said, "I like it."

"You're not looking for promotion?"

"No. I like it where I am."

"And if you get knocked on the head in one of these battles?"

He closed one eye, tilted his head, and said, "You're a cheerful son of a bitch, aren't you?"

"Just curious."

He shrugged. "All right. Well, you have to die sometime."

"Yeah, I've heard that before. It doesn't strike me as a good reason to rush into it."

"Have some more cheese."

I did. A little later a woman I didn't know came over and joined us. He gave her some cheese and brandy; I took the hint and made myself scarce. Back by our own tent I met Napper, who scowled, I suppose just on principle, and said, "Are we going on any more of your expeditions?"

"Did you enjoy it?"

"Yes."

"I don't know. Maybe. Hey, Napper."

"Yeah?"

"Do you ever wonder what it's all about?"

"What, the war? Why, do you know?"

"Yeah, sort of."

"What, then?"

"Fornia stole something Morrolan wanted."

"Oh. Seems reasonable. We should go steal it back."

"I doubt it will be that simple."

"You're probably right." I thought, but didn't say, *Besides, that would end the war, and you'd hate that.* Then I thought, *Yeah, it would end the war. Maybe I should do that.*

"*Sure, Boss. It'll be easy.*"

"Well, but it might be possible."

"*How?*"

"If we get to a decisive battle, Fornia will be there, and if Fornia is there, the sword will be there."

"*Sure, just walk up and take it.*"

"I don't know, Loiosh. Maybe—"

"*Maybe you'll get yourself killed, Boss.*"

"Everyone's got to die sometime."

"*Heh.*"

"And it'll probably be safer than standing to battle."

I had him on that one; he shut up.

We were joined by Dunn, Tibbs, Virt, Aelburr, and Rascha, and the bunch of us sat around and I listened as they told stories, most of them funny and not terribly complimentary toward officers, about various campaigns they'd been on. Rascha announced light picket duty again, which I went off and did, then I went to bed once more.

It was one of the most pleasant days I've ever had.

The next morning we watched as a cavalry troop rode in and set up camp near ours, and, shortly thereafter, we saw the movement of more of our infantry. I recognized Aliera riding a light-colored, spotted horse alongside the infantry column; I wondered if she knew how much those who marched beside her hated the dust she was kicking up. They made camp to the west of us.

Things changed with the new arrivals. Nothing drastic, yet it was unmistakable. There was a bit more snap to everyone's motion, and a little more saluting here and there, as if to look good in front of the conscripts. There was no fraternizing between corps, either.

Late in the afternoon, word spread through the camp that Sethra Lavode had arrived; Aelburr claimed to have seen her. Shortly after the evening "meal" a young-looking Dragonlord I didn't recognize arrived at our tent and said I was to follow him. Virt shot me a look. I shrugged, collected Loiosh from one of his scavenging expeditions, and followed.

We went through the camp and into the camp of the conscripts. I tried to spot the differences between their camp and ours, but there just wasn't all that much; except, of course, that these were mostly Teckla rather than Dragons and there were certainly a great many more of them. But they had the same sort of campstools we were using, and the bits of conversation I caught seemed about the same, the expressions on their faces were no different from those in our camp. Make of that what you will.

At the far edge was a large pavilion tent, and it was to there my nameless escort directed me. I clapped and heard Sethra's voice telling me to enter. I did and was directed to a chair between Morrolan and Aliera—not a terribly comfortable position, by the way—with Sethra and the Necromancer sitting across from me. I had obviously interrupted some sort of discussion: Aliera had a look as if she were about to froth and spit; Sethra's brow was furrowed; and Morrolan kept making glances at his cousin as if she were an unidentified creature that had appeared in his soup. The Necromancer seemed only barely present; I wondered where her thoughts were while suspecting I was glad not to know.

"Well, Vlad," said Morrolan after I was sitting and drinking bad wine. "How are you enjoying the life of a soldier?"

I shrugged. "Loiosh likes it more than I do."

"I've heard," said Morrolan, "that he has been adopted by your company as mascot."

"Yeah. He's insufferably smug about it."

"*Hey now, Boss. That's not fair.*"

"*Truth isn't, Loiosh.*"

Sethra said, "You've done some good work, I am told."

"Sure," I said. "For what it's worth."

"I think it was worth something," said Morrolan.

"Maybe," I said. "I don't know. I don't have enough of an idea of how our little company fits in with everything else that's been happening."

"You saved some lives in your company," said Morrolan.

"Okay," I said. "But none of those battles were decisive."

"The next one will be," said Sethra.

I digested that. "You're ready, then?"

"I hope so," said Sethra. "But, more important, Fornia is. He has to make a stand somewhere, and this location has symbolic importance. He won't be able to pass it up."

"Symbolic importance," I repeated.

Sethra gave me a half smile. "Don't start," she said. "It also has a great deal of strategic importance; as far as he can tell, we're backed up against the mountain, and—"

"As far as he can tell?"

"We have lines of retreat, Vlad. Northward. Let me worry about that part of it."

"Sorry."

"In any case, this will be a good place for him to win a battle. He'll fight here. He has to. From here, I can push straight into the heart of his realm. Besides, if he can hold us for a few days, he has another division coming up."

"He does?"

"He sent his third division all the way around the other side of Chengri to cut me off from my base of supplies."

"That doesn't sound good."

"Well, if we're stuck here for three or four days it won't be good. You'll start getting hungry. But I don't plan on being stuck that long; I plan on pushing through him while I have the advantage of numbers. He knows that. He'll fight here."

"I believe you," I said. "What exactly do you want of me?"

"What we want," said Morrolan, "or, rather, what I want, is exactly what you said you wouldn't do, way back when this all started. I want you to get that sword from Fornia."

"Funny about that," I said. "I'd just been thinking the same thing."

"I still don't like it," said Aliera, evidently continuing a discussion I'd missed the beginning of. "If we're going to do that, why not go all the way? Hire a thief and just be done with it."

"For one thing," said Sethra, "we don't know any thieves."

"Vlad can put us in touch with one."

"And for another," said Morrolan, "that wouldn't accomplish what I want. I don't just want the sword. I have a perfectly good sword." Here he touched the hilt of Blackwand. "I want it taken from him."

"You want him humiliated," said Aliera.

"Call it defeated," said Morrolan. "And defeated at every level. Both militarily and by losing the very item that caused the war."

"If you defeat him," I said, just to be argumentative, "won't he have to give it up?"

"Military defeat," said Sethra, "is not an all-or-nothing proposition. I believe we can hand his army a major defeat. That doesn't mean he'll be powerless, and it doesn't mean he can be compelled to surrender all of his forces. To do that would require a far greater campaign than this one, more costly in every way, riskier, and with the danger of Imperial intervention."

"We've been talking it over for some time," said Morrolan. "And we cannot leave him in possession of the artifact, so we must take it. Once we've taken it, we cannot leave him unbloodied, or he'll try to take it back. So we have to get it from him and, at the same time, bloody his nose."

"And you want me to do the getting."

"If you'd like."

"I'd like. How do you suggest I go about it? I suspect sneaking into his tent at night is going to be trickier than the other stuff I've been doing, and, really, I'm not a thief by profession or training."

"No," said Morrolan. "And that wouldn't do what we want anyway. We need it removed from him during the battle."

"Excuse me? Why?"

"Because I don't know any way to get it after the battle. He isn't going to leave himself vulnerable; he'll retreat, probably return home, and at that point we *would* have to hire a thief to get it."

"That may not be a bad idea," I said.

"I don't employ thieves," said Morrolan.

"Didn't you just ask me to steal something?"

"To remove it from him in the middle of a battle, yes. We do not countenance assassination either, but making targets of senior officers while in combat is not only proper but recommended."

"Too nice a distinction for me, Morrolan. I'm just a hardworking Jhereg. But what about before the battle?"

"If you do that, there won't *be* a battle, Vlad. He'll pull back, reform, and launch his own campaign to get it back from me, maybe years from now."

I shook my head. "How am I supposed to go after the thing while we're fighting? How will I even find him, much less the whole question of getting to him."

Sethra spoke up. "For one thing, we're going to position your company in such a way that you'll be as close as possible to his command center."

I wondered how Virt would feel if she knew how her general was deciding on the order of battle. I resolved not to tell her.

I said, "I still don't see how I'm supposed to get out of a pitched battle, all the way to their command post, find Fornia, and extract the weapon from him."

Aliera said, "I don't either. I think the whole idea is idiotic."

"As for getting the weapon from him," said Morrolan. "As I said a moment ago, making targets of senior officers is an accepted tactic."

"Oh. So now you want me to kill him?"

"If necessary."

I shook my head. "If I'd wanted to kill him, Morrolan, I would simply have done so. Days ago. It isn't clear to me—"

"You won't be alone," he put in.

"I won't?"

"If you require assistance, we can supply you with as many subordinates as you wish."

"That," I said, "may make a difference."

"*Boss, are you nuts?*"

"*Some people think so, Loiosh.*"

"*Add me to the list. You can't—*"

"*Maybe I can, Loiosh.*" Aloud I said, "How much time do I have to think it over?"

"I don't know," said Sethra. "Fornia is bringing up troops all the time. Of course, so are we, and faster. Right now, delay works in our favor, so I would expect them to begin the attack soon."

"What does 'soon' mean?"

"Probably tomorrow morning."

"Yeah, that's soon."

"Tell me your decision through Captain Cropper," said Morrolan. "Just give him the message to give to me, don't reach me psychically; I want this going through proper channels."

"Why, for the love of the Gods?"

"Because that's how it's done."

"All right," I said. I stood up. "Have a good council."

"Do you need a guide back?" said Morrolan.

"No, thanks."

I left the tent. It had become dark and cold; I should have brought a cloak. Loiosh guided me back, and I was glad to find the fire; it felt like home.

"Well," said Virt. "Did you see her?"

"Sethra? Yes."

"And?"

"There will most likely be a battle tomorrow. A big one."

"Did you get another mission?" said Napper.

"An interesting question," I said. "I'm not certain."

"Well, if you need anyone—"

"Noted. Thanks."

Virt said, "Battle tomorrow, hm?"

"So it seems."

"We don't have any bulwarks built up."

"Yes."

"So either we're spearheading an attack or we're bait."

"Or both," I said. "I suspect both."

Virt shook her head. Aelburr sat there stirring the fire and not talking.

Virt said, "So, what's she like?"

"I don't know," I said. "I've never met any other vampires to compare her to. Excuse me, I'm going to take a walk."

"Don't go too far," said Virt. "We're in imminent, and up for picket duty in half an hour."

"Half an hour," I repeated. "I'll be there."

I stayed within the pickets and walked around the perimeter of the camp. I tried to focus on the decision I had to make, but the fact is I've never been good at just thinking about things, so I didn't get anywhere except around in a circle; my thoughts kept drifting over my recent experiences: fights, and marches, and sitting around fires. I didn't come to any conclusions about those, either, and then half an hour was up and I returned to our tent, where I collected Aelburr, Napper, and my heavy cloak, and we went off to picket duty, where we were not allowed to speak, which pleased me.

Picket duty passed without incident, and I passed the time without reaching any conclusions. Then I went to bed and got a few hours of sleep. The next day we were woken up appallingly early, even for the army, and ordered to move our camp a hundred yards closer to the Wall and a little north to the top of a small hill. Virt said, "The other option, of course, was that there was no point in having us erect defenses for a position we weren't expected to hold."

She seemed much cheered by the idea until Aelburr said, "Then why aren't we putting up defenses here?"

"Maybe we'll move again," she said, straining her eyes to the north, where we could make out plenty of activity but couldn't identify it yet.

Virt pointed to the hollow to our left and said, "Two spear phalanxes."

"Which means?"

"It means we aren't defending a flank. That's good, if you value a long life."

"Then I'm glad."

"On the other hand, if we're attacking, we may be sent against their flank."

So we finally got breakfast. I chewed a couple of biscuits, washed them down with water, and followed the company colors until I found the Captain, staring at the enemy through a telescope and talking to Crown. He looked at me when I approached and said, "Yes?"

"Morrolan asked me a question last night. He said I was to give you the answer to relay back to him."

He stared down at me and scowled, evidently not entirely pleased with being a messenger for a Jhereg. "Very well," he said. "What is it?"

"Tell him I said yes."

The Captain opened his mouth, closed it, nodded abruptly, turned to Crown, and said, "See to it the Lord Morrolan gets the message."

"Yes, sir," said Crown. He saluted and set off to find a messenger. The Captain returned his attention to the enemy. Just because I felt like it, I saluted before returning to my squadron.

14

UPS AND DOWNS

I kept thinking that I could put it all together if I were smarter. Whatever Fornia was up to should have been subject to deduction, but I couldn't figure it out. Of course, I was aware that figuring it out might not turn out to be useful; just because you know what someone is doing doesn't necessarily mean you can stop him. That was Sethra's attitude; her approach to this battle was straightforward, and fundamentally without deception, and it seemed to be working—at least to judge by the fact that a press of Morrolan's troops, including himself and Aliera, were pushing their way toward Fornia's command position.

On the other hand, the Eastern mercenaries, though retreating, had not yet broken. Nothing was yet decided, except that a large number of people had died here, and more were going to.

As I studied Fornia's face, I saw him concentrate briefly, and an instant later a mass of cavalry appeared in a long row over the lip of the hill behind us, about a hundred yards distant.

I watched, suddenly and temporarily oblivious to my own situation. The column rode down the hill, in no apparent hurry. I tried to estimate their numbers, but I'm not very good at that. At least several hundred, though, maybe a thousand, and as they drew closer I saw they carried spears.

As they came closer they spread out into a single line, and I couldn't help but admire the way they went about it; neat and precise, they formed up to charge into Morrolan's forces. I risked a glance at Morrolan, and saw him, now a bit back from the fighting, talking to someone and pointing at them.

"Watch closely," said Fornia. "Now it gets interesting."

I kept watching, and saw, behind the cavalry, a mass of infantry reach the top of the hill and begin marching down.

In military terms, Fornia had "committed his reserves." In my terms, things were going to get even uglier. I'd have done something if there had been anything to do. I admit I even gave another thought to trying to take Fornia down, but his personal guard had failed to be distracted by the battle; they were still watching me.

The decisive moment was approaching; not the best time for me to be indecisive.

Fornia said, "Are you prepared to hear my terms, then?"

"No," I said. "I don't have the authority to accept them."

He chuckled. "That doesn't make you the ideal negotiator, then."

"The negotiator will be arriving shortly, if you'd lower your tele-port blocks—"

He laughed. "Don't count on that, Jhereg."

"It isn't a trick," I said.

"Oh, I believe that. It's much too crude to be a trick. But I have no intention of opening myself up to accidents. If your negotiator wants to show up, he can do it the hard way."

I was trying to formulate a response when Daymar appeared, either blasting through the teleport block or coming in around it; I don't know enough about either sorcery or psychics to tell you how he did it. But there he was, floating, cross-legged, about six inches off the ground.

"All right," I told Fornia. "The hard way, then."

There was an instant where I wasn't certain if they were going to strike us both down, but they were well trained, and they waited for the order. The order didn't come.

I suddenly felt Daymar's presence in my mind. It was shocking, and not entirely pleasant. For one thing, I'm not used to people I hardly know being able to communicate with me psychically; for another, well, imagine being gently picked up by a relative stranger who you can tell could crush your body with one hand if he wanted to. Sure, I said *gently*, but he's still a stranger, and he could still crush you. As I said, I did not terribly care for the sensation.

"What do you want?" he asked in a sort of psychic whisper—as if he were being very careful not to burn my brain out.

I said, "That fellow, him. That's Fornia."

"Well?"

"I want to know what he's up to."

"Certainly," he said, as if I'd asked him to pass me the tray of sweetmeats. Just how good was he, I wondered. I mean, his mind was strong, and he'd clearly trained it, but was he good enough to pull the information I wanted out of Fornia's mind? Well, he'd pulled information out of Kragar's mind.

Thinking of Kragar makes me, in retrospect, realize just how far away from my own world I was. He had picked exactly the wrong moment to get in touch with me, and then I never heard back from him until I thought of it, days later, when we were positioned to make a charge or await one in front of the Wall. I had suddenly thought of it, then, and gotten in touch with him.

"Kragar? It's me."

"Howdy, Vlad. How's the army life?"

"You should know."

"I tried to warn you."

"For the most part I hate it," I told him, "but then people try to kill me and I really hate it."

"It wasn't the trying to kill me part I didn't like, it was all the rest of it."

"I can sympathize with that. What was it you wanted?"

"A guy wants to open up a new game in our territory."

"A guy? What guy?"

"Don't know him. Jhereg, seems small time. He's willing to give us our usual cut, and he's willing to provide his own protection, but I didn't know if that would be too many games for the area."

"That was a while ago; what did you do?"

"I told him to go ahead."

"And?"

"Seems all right so far."

"Okay. Good. Anything else?"

"No, everything's quiet."

"Wish I could say the same."

"Oh?"

"Building up to a big battle here."

"I assume you're staying out of the battles."

"Not exactly."

"What? You're fighting? In the line?"

"I haven't always been able to avoid it."

"Do something conspicuous and you might make corporal."

"Let Loiosh make the wisecracks, Kragar. He's better at them."

"Sure, Vlad. Anything else?"

"No, I'll talk to you later."

I stared out at the place where the enemy gathered. It suddenly occurred to me that if Kragar had done something conspicuous no one would have noticed. That might explain some things that I'd never ask him about. As good an explanation as any.

I found Napper was watching me. I guess I don't always hide it well when I'm communicating with someone psychically.

"If your lips didn't move, Boss, it would—"

"Shut up, Loiosh."

"Well?" said Napper. "We got something to do?"

I shook my head and went back to watching the enemy gather across the field. There were now banners on most of the other hills, including the ones Virt had said we should have taken when we got here.

Someone came walking down the line passing out biscuits and cheese. I had several of the biscuits, ate the cheese, and drank some water. I turned back to Napper to ask him why he was so damned eager to get killed when there came the rattle of the juice-drum again, another call I didn't recognize. I knew, however, that I wasn't going to like it, because Napper broke into a grin.

"What's that one?" I said.

" 'Time to Be Alive,' " he said. "It means to form up for a charge."

" 'Time to Be Alive,' " I repeated. "Is that someone's idea of irony?"

He didn't answer.

Rascha came along and placed us where she wanted us—elbow to elbow, hardly room to move. I realized that this was the first time I would be taking part in a charge; everything I'd done up to that point involved standing there and keeping the enemy from over-running us; from our success, I was not encouraged about being on the other side. Napper was on my left, Aelburr on my right.

The Captain came out in front of our line, riding a dark-colored horse that seemed much too small for him; his feet didn't reach the ground, but it seemed like they could if he just stretched a little. The effect was vaguely comical. He spoke in a loud voice that carried easily, though he didn't seem to be shouting.

"We will," he announced, "be attacking light infantry, very much like ourselves. They have no bulwarks nor ditches, and they number significantly fewer than ourselves; however, we will, as you see, be attacking uphill. We will go at a brisk march, charging the last hundred yards. We will take the hill and hold it until relieved." No one commented on the fact that yesterday we could have taken the hill by walking up it and planting our colors.

He continued, "I will expect you to maintain formation until we meet their line. We will have additional support from the sorcerers corps, especially defensive. If we keep our lines dressed and strike quickly, I do not anticipate any difficulty. That is all. Attend to your squad leaders."

He rode off to the far end of the line, drawing his sword as he did so. It seemed like a functional sword; maybe he'd use it. I hadn't recalled seeing him in any of the action hitherto. But I might not have noticed.

Crown took a position in the middle, just ahead of us. He, too, was holding his sword. I realized my pulse had quickened. I said to Virt, "Do they have javelins?"

"Probably," she said. "Almost certainly." Then, "Do javelins worry you?"

"Not at all," I said. "I'm looking forward to trying to catch one in my teeth."

"That's what we need: fighting spirit."

I assumed she was being ironic, but I couldn't tell for certain. Crown gave a signal, and the colors moved out. The rest of us followed.

"War," Sethra Lavode once explained to me, "consists of missed opportunities alternating with narrow escapes, and it usually ends when someone, somewhere, fails to commit a timely error." If I'd had that discussion with her before the Wall of Baritt's Tomb, it might have done me some good. Or, I don't know, maybe some harm; in any case, I wouldn't have been as surprised by what happened.

We went forward, straight into an unmoving mass of warriors.

They stood shoulder to shoulder about halfway up the hill. The hill, by the way, had a long and gentle slope, deceptively gentle. It looked like it might be possible to run up it without being winded well before you reached the enemy position. This turned out not to be the case. I was already breathing heavily before we broke into a run, and so were Virt and Aelburr. We kept getting closer, and I kept wondering how I was supposed to fight in this condition. And at the same time I was both dreading and longing for the signal to charge.

And then they launched their javelins at us.

When we had thrown, it had seemed as if we had launched a single, vast, sheet of metal at the enemy. Now I was on the other side, and it seemed just like that. Then, I had wondered how the enemy kept coming at us; I still wondered. Now, after it is all over, I still wonder.

But I kept moving.

Then Crown waved his sword, and the colors surged forward, and I heard Rascha's voice, somewhere to my left: "Charge!" I couldn't go any faster up the hill, but everyone around me was able to, so I did too, and the effort distracted me from noticing what effect, if any, the javelins had had on our forces. Then they launched a second barrage, and this time I noticed: Virt stumbled and went down, and I remember thinking that I wished it were possible to stop and help her, and I still don't know why it wasn't, but I kept running. There was a horrid yelling, and I realized that I was making some of the noise myself.

There was a third barrage of javelins, which did some damage, to judge by the screams around me, and then a fourth, during which one went screaming past my ear and made Loiosh yelp psychically, and then we met the enemy.

The noise is what I remember most about that first instant, a screeching, groaning thunder that filled my skull and became something greater than noise, that went beyond the pain from my ears. It encompassed the battle like a shroud, and everything that happened was twisted and dulled by the din—out of which it was impossible to isolate what was causing any of it; it was just one unending roar. And through it, I kept trying to go forward, and I couldn't.

Now look, I think I'm more than a match for just about any of the swordsmen you care to name. For one thing, I'm good with a blade, but more important than that, I fight in a way they aren't used to: We Easterners have our own ways of fighting that I can use to take advantage of the fact that I'm smaller and quicker than they are. This mostly involves staying out of the way of those big monster blades they use, not giving them a good target, and never putting myself into a position of setting my strength directly against theirs.

Okay, now that I've said that, you probably already see the problem. I was not out there fighting against another swordsman with the object of killing him or taking him out of combat; I was out there trying to get myself past a certain point along with several hundred others, and at no point did I really have the chance to settle in and actually fight someone. I ducked a lot, and scampered back and forth, and I'd occasionally make a halfhearted jab in the direction of one of the defenders, but there was just no way for my fighting advantages to be of help, whereas all of my disadvantages were multiplied.

It's nothing short of a miracle that I wasn't killed inside the first twenty seconds after we met their line. The very first instant someone brought a big old sword cutting down at my head, and I still don't know how I got out of the way. He certainly would have killed me if he had followed up on that first strike, but I guess he got distracted after that. For whatever reason, I picked myself up (no, I don't remember falling or dropping to the ground or whatever I did) and charged again, and someone came within a whisper of disemboweling me. I don't remember gasping for breath while this was going on, but I must have been. I just remember thinking in a strangely detached way, *That's two; the third will probably kill me.*

Then Loiosh said into my mind, *"To the left, Boss!"* which accomplished two things. The first, and most immediate, was that it caused me to look to my left, where someone was drawing a bead on me with a sword swirling over his head. The second thing was that, somehow, it transformed me from a soldier into what I was. Or, to put it another way, it reminded me that I had more weapons than my sword—although that isn't accurate either, because I didn't exactly *remember*, because I never made a decision, but the next thing I knew I had put three shuriken into his chest, which slowed him down a bit, and while he was trying to decide how badly he was hurt, someone—I think it was Aelburr, though I'm not sure, cut his legs out from under him.

I went back to looking ahead of me, and when I attracted someone's attention I threw a knife at her, missing, but I guess making her decide to look elsewhere for entertainment.

How long did our assault last? Well, I saw in the log book where it was recorded at four minutes. To me it seemed longer and shorter. Longer because at the time it seemed to go on and on; I kept thinking that something had to break, but nothing did. Shorter because I can't account for most of it. I usually have good memories of fights because my mind is always working, keeping track of the movements that training has made instinctive and making notes for future reference, but in these battles it had been different, and in this one in particular I can only account for about a minute of the fight, and then we were retreating back to our own lines with Rascha shouting to maintain our line. I remember seeing our colors and telling myself, *Okay, we didn't take them, but we weren't broken.* I didn't know that the color bearer had gone down, and his replacement, too, but I suppose that didn't much matter; what did matter was that we retreated in order and looked threatening enough doing so that whoever was in charge of the company that had just repelled us decided not to counterattack.

Which is part of what I meant earlier when I spoke of mistakes. I am fairly sure they could have broken us if they had charged immediately. They had elevation working for them, and we were at least a little demoralized, but, probably because we looked like we were retreating in order, or maybe because we'd killed some officer, or maybe just because the enemy commander lacked backbone, they didn't attack.

It was only when we had retreated all the way back to the bottom of the hill and an additional hundred yards besides that I became aware that there was fighting going on around us. We had, it seems, been only one part of a major battle, which I should have known but had never thought of until, motionless and recovering my breath, I noticed dust clouds from several of the hills around us, and the movement of troops, and opposing banners awful close together.

I didn't watch, however, because I couldn't see much and didn't want to anyway. I overheard various remarks about who was winning where, but they didn't agree with each other so I concluded that no one knew.

Presently Virt came up next to me, and it was only then that I remembered she'd gone down. Aelburr said, "Good work, slackard."

"Good move on their part," she said. "If they hadn't knocked me down we'd have won."

"Yeah," he said. "You'd have taken the position by yourself."

"Damn right."

"What happened?" I said.

"The bastards missed my knee, that's what. Thigh wound, about as clean as you could ask. I'd have kept going up the hill but I felt like taking a nap."

"You and Napper," he said, which was when I realized that I hadn't seen Napper since the fight, but then I noticed him almost at once, lying on his back just past Aelburr; as near as I could tell he was sound asleep.

I tried to decide how I felt about that, but gave up and threw myself onto the ground next to him.

"Behold the grim aftermath of battle," remarked Virt.

Loiosh tells me I caught a nap myself after that, and I can't prove him wrong. In any case, the juice-drum brought me to my feet with "Rubbing Elbows," the call to form a defensive line. I looked around the battlefield, aware that I'd been resting my eyes for a little while, and saw that the scene had changed; our colors now occupied a hill we hadn't been on before, and I could just barely make out fighting a long way to the right. They were, I supposed, attacking our flank. (Well, no, they weren't, as it happened; it was some sort of complicated diversionary move to cover an envelopment on the other side that never happened, but I didn't find that out until much later.)

I asked Loiosh, who had been strangely silent since we charged, if he was all right.

"Boss, we don't belong here."

"I know. What's your point?"

"We should cut out."

"Can't do it."

"Why not?"

"For one thing, I've agreed to a job."

"Do you see any way to do it?"

"*Not at the moment, but—*" I said aloud, "Where do you suppose their command center is, Virt?"

She pointed to a hill about four hundred yards south of us. "I'd be there," she said. "It commands a good view, and it's hard to tell for sure, but I think it's pretty steep. It would be easy to defend, easy to retreat from, easy to advance from. I'd certainly have my sorcerers there, and probably my command post. Why?"

"Just curious," I said.

Napper gave me a look. "You got something?"

I shook my head and didn't answer.

Aelburr sat down with his head in his hands, his long knees drawn up. Farther down the line, Tibbs was in the same position. Virt, though still standing, had a look that matched their poses. Napper wasn't glowering; he was just staring at the ground in front of him.

I said, "We got beat, didn't we?"

Virt nodded. "We got beat," she said.

Napper glanced at me. "Maybe they'll come at us now," he said hopefully.

I agreed with him, but didn't feel hopeful, so I didn't say anything.

Presently Rascha came along the line. Virt said, "We're expecting guests?" She nodded. Virt said, "How bad did we hurt ourselves going up the hill?"

"Could have been worse," said Rascha.

"Which means?"

"Fourteen killed or missing, twenty-six wounded. It could have been worse," she repeated, and moved along the line.

"Sure," murmured Virt. "It could have been—"

"Why don't we have javelins?" said Aelburr, looking up suddenly.

Virt used the sort of language soldiers have traditionally used in such circumstances. I was impressed.

For someone who had never touched a javelin two weeks before, I certainly had become attached to them. I suppose charging through a storm of them and actually feeling what it was like on the other side had a lot to do with that. What was worse, however, was the feeling that, if things had broken down badly enough for our javelins to go missing, what else was liable to go wrong?

DRAGON

199

The answer was, something big went wrong, but fortunately it was in the enemy's camp: They failed to attack us. Another example of what Sethra was talking about, I suppose. I did ask about that, too, but Sethra didn't know why they failed to attack that day. As far as I was concerned, I watched them, tense and more than a little scared, for several hours. Around us the battle continued, but it was a day of missed chances and maneuvering, or so I've heard, and what I saw was a great deal of marching and almost continuous skirmishes, but no real battles except for our charge up that hill.

Lucky us.

A couple of hours later we were issued javelins, and a little after that we were issued more biscuits and cheese, and this time we each got a strip of salted kethna to chew on. By then we were entertaining hopes that they wouldn't attack and fears that we'd be ordered to go after them again. But we weren't. Late in the afternoon, Rascha came by again. "They're shifting," she said.

"Leaving the hill?" said Virt.

"Now we can take it," said Aelburr.

"I assume they're being replaced. We'll find out tomorrow who we'll be facing."

"Tomorrow," said Aelburr.

"Tomorrow," I said. "I like that word. That's a good word. Tomorrow."

"But we have to stay alert for night attacks," she said. "Extra picket duty all around, and like that."

Napper moaned suddenly. "What is it?" said Virt.

He stared disgustedly at his javelins. "We have to set camp again."

"Life is rough," said Aelburr.

"Might as well get to it," said Virt.

We struggled to our feet.

"Tomorrow is going to be ugly," said Aelburr.

"I hope so," said Napper. "We going to take whatever that hill is called tomorrow?"

"Dorian's Hill," said Rascha. "And yes, I think we are." She moved off down the line. Loiosh and I kept our cynicism to ourselves.

INTERLUDE: COUNTERATTACK

The day after our visit with Aliera I sent a message to Sethra the Younger in care of Lord Morrolan.

"She'll be pleased," I told Cawti.

"There have been no promises," she said.

"Yes. But you know Aliera will agree. Eventually."

Cawti nodded.

That was the day before yesterday. Yesterday I finished telling my story, as far as I felt like going, and came home in time to prepare dinner for Cawti. I was planning to treat her to a three-fish three-pepper stew with leeks and white wine, because no woman who has tasted it can resist me. Oh, okay, maybe I'm stretching a point. But it is good. So I did my shopping (I enjoy shopping for food, and if I ever achieve real wealth, I think I'll continue to do so), returned home, started preparing the oysters (yes, yes, I know oysters aren't fish), and was interrupted by Loiosh telling me that someone was clapping at the door. I started to yell "Come in," when Loiosh said, *"It isn't Cawti."*

I opened the door and found myself staring up at Sethra the Younger. My mouth fell open. She looked down at me. I swallowed and said, "Would you care to come in and sit down? I'm afraid it falls short of your standards for a domicile."

"Save it," she said, stepping in. "I'm not here to criticize your decorations." She paused, looked around, then said, "Although I must admit I find your home surprisingly tasteful."

Tasteful? I have furniture that one could sit on, and floors that are clean, and walls that hold the place up. I have one shelf of knick knacks with sentimental value. Home is where I go when I sleep; the only room I've put much thought into is the kitchen. But okay. Maybe she meant she expected to find it a kethna's nest with peeling walls, bloodstains, and rusted weapons lying about, I don't know.

But I said, "Okay, why are you here?"

"Can't you guess?"

"No. If it was about the trade you want to arrange with Aliera, I'd have expected you to send for me."

"And would you have come if I had?"

"No," I said.

"I hadn't thought so." She unbuckled her sword belt, and I noticed its size at once. She carefully set it on a table, and then sat down. I gritted my teeth and brought out some wine. She said, "Perhaps we should send for Aliera and get this done."

"Actually," I said, "I had plans for the evening."

I could see her forming the words "Break them" and then changing her mind. After a moment she said, "Are they breakable?"

"Perhaps. If you can convince me—" There was another clap at the door.

"Loiosh?"

"Yes."

"My plans for the evening," I said. I went over to the door and admitted Cawti.

She took in the scene at once; I saw her notice the sheathed sword on the table. I said, "It wasn't my plan. She wants to finish things tonight."

"Why not?" said Cawti.

"Why not indeed?" said Sethra the Younger.

I could have made some answers, but I decided the question was rhetorical. "All right," I said. "Then someone should reach Aliera. Who wants to do the honors?"

"Why don't you?" said Sethra the Younger.

"All right," I said, and composed my mind for the contact.

I reached Aliera more quickly than I'd have expected to. I guess I was getting to know her. I had mixed feelings about this.

"What is it?" she said without greeting, preamble, pleasantry, or anything else I hadn't expected.

"*Sethra the Younger is here.*"

"*There? Where is there?*"

"*My flat.*"

"*What does she want?*"

"*To conclude the transaction.*"

"*I haven't agreed to the transaction yet.*"

I said aloud, "She hasn't agreed to the transaction yet."

"Then let's talk about it," said Sethra.

"*Then she suggests you talk about it.*"

"*I—very well. Can you give me a picture?*"

I did so to the best of my ability. It got me enough into her head that I could tell what she thought about the best of my ability.

"*Very well,*" she said eventually. "*I'll be there directly.*"

"Well?" snapped Sethra the Younger.

"She'll be here."

She nodded.

We sat in uncomfortable silence for a few minutes; Cawti sat next to me and held my arm. Aliera clapped outside the door; I let her in.

Sethra the Younger stood up. They gave each other slight bows over mutual glares.

Sethra said, "You know the bargain I propose."

Aliera said, "You should never have received the weapon in the first place."

"Received it?" she said, and I remembered, then, that final encounter at Baritt's Tomb. It hadn't stayed with me because I hadn't known her then. She said, "I didn't receive it, Lady Aliera. I took it. I used it. I—"

"I remember. I was there."

"Yes, you were, weren't you?" She turned to me. "And so, I believe, were you."

"You could say that," I told her.

She nodded. "But, Lady Aliera, I believe the weapon should be yours. What is your opinion?"

"My opinion is that you want the sword of Kieron the Conqueror. My opinion is also that I'm no haggler."

"Well, then?"

"Then if you want it, come take it."

"I could do that," said Sethra the Younger, touching the hilt of the blade next to her.

"Not in my house, you don't," I said, but they weren't listening to me.

I concentrated hard and, very quickly, reached Morrolan.

"What is it, Vlad?"

"A favor."

"Oh?"

"Grab Blackwand and get your ass over here. Now."

He didn't ask why, or what was going on, or anything else. Whatever else you say about Dragons, they understand when it is time for action.

The same, of course, can be said for Aliera and Sethra the Younger. They had drawn their swords and were circling each other in the parlor.

I hoped they wouldn't destroy too much furniture.

15

SCRATCH ONE JERKIN

The instant after Daymar appeared was another moment when I felt like I was about to be snuffed out, but I wasn't. A little piece of my mind that likes to comment on what the rest of me is doing suggested that I was getting tired of almost getting cut to ribbons every few seconds, and then answered itself by pointing out that it was, at least, better than actually getting cut to ribbons.

"You think he can do it, Loiosh?"

"Probably. But you need to give him enough time, Boss."

"Any idea how much time is enough?"

"Not even a wild guess, Boss."

To Fornia I said, "This is Daymar, my associate. And, just to be clear about things: You're right. I'm not a negotiator. On the other hand, I was not sent here to kill you, and I have no intention of trying to. I only hope you'll be as reserved with regard to me."

He laughed a little. "Why should I be?"

"Curiosity. To find out what I'm doing here."

"I've never been all that curious. Any other reasons why I shouldn't do as Ori says?"

"Because you don't kill prisoners, and I surrender."

"Boss!"

"Any other ideas?"

He nodded. "That will do." He addressed his personal guard, then: "Search him carefully, and I especially want that gold chain in his hand. Bind him well and send him to the rear for quest—"

Someone whispered in his ear. He listened carefully, then put his telescope to his eye and studied the field somewhere over my left shoulder.

"Not quite yet," he said as three of his bodyguards moved toward me to carry out his orders, leaving me saying to myself, "Now what, smart guy?"

I guessed, from where Fornia was looking, that the subject of the message he'd just received was Dorian's Hill, where I had recently left the rest of my company in the middle of a battle, which I was certain was no more fun than it had been yesterday, when, after an entire day of fighting, I'd gotten myself good and properly nailed.

We had woken up yesterday morning to discover Dorian's Hill was deserted. Empty. Unoccupied. This provided the subject for that morning's breakfast conversation. There was constant chatter all around me, and I kept hearing the word "trap" find its way from the buzz and hum.

"What do you think, Boss?"

"The hill we spent yesterday trying to take is suddenly empty, and yet they think it might be a trap? What suspicious minds."

"I meant, do you think you'll be ordered to occupy it anyway?"

"Oh." I studied the hill in the morning light: green, harmless, a few shrubs on the top, only long grasses and a few sharp grey stones on the way up. The only sign of yesterday's action had been that the grasses were a bit tromped down. The hill was just sitting there. If it were human it would have been twiddling its thumbs, staring at the sky, and whistling. *"Probably,"* I told Loiosh.

At least they didn't keep us waiting. We were given breakfast, and within a few minutes after eating we were formed up, and the Captain rode out in front of us. He turned and faced the line, and said, "We will occupy the hill and immediately begin preparing to defend it. To that end, the engineers will accompany us. We can expect to be required to defend it at once."

"No shit," said Napper under his breath.

The Captain was done talking; Crown stepped out and led us up the hill. It was much easier this time. The walk wasn't even tiring.

"It's going to be a fight once we get there."

"I imagine so," said Napper.

"No, I mean they'll have something special waiting. Sorcery, or some traps they put up there. Something."

"Don't matter," said Napper. It was hard to argue with him, so we just walked for a while.

"It's just us," said Virt as we neared the top.

"Excuse me?"

"We're by ourselves up here. Just the company."

"And the engineers," said Aelburr.

"And the engineers."

"Oh," I said. "Not enough, huh?"

"Not enough," said Virt.

Aelburr said, "Trap within a trap?"

"Maybe," said Virt. "Which makes us bait."

"Grand," I said.

"Don't matter," said Napper.

In a way, it was irritating to just stroll up the hill that had caused us such agony the day before, but I didn't say anything about it because I knew what Napper would say, and if he said it again I was going to have to kill him.

We reached the top, and before we had even caught our breath Crown called out, "Form a perimeter, begin constructing earthworks. Engineers to the fore."

They passed out shovels and instructions, and we dug ditches and piled dirt for about half an hour, during which time javelins were distributed. We stopped working when the fog rolled in. Thick fog, blanketing the entire hill; it came up with only seconds of warning.

"I wonder if it's magical," said Virt as we scrambled for our weapons. That was irony, by the way.

Crown's voice cut through everything: "It's safe to breathe," he said, scaring me all over again, because it hadn't occurred to me it might not be.

"Form your line and stand ready!"

A whole lot of swords were drawn from a whole lot of scabbards.

"Where's our line?" I said.

"Right here, I suppose," said Virt.

I recognized a voice that cursed from my left. "What is it, Napper?"

"Tripped in the bloody ditch."

"Hurt?"

"No."

"Can't bring up a wind," said someone. "They've got it blocked."

I let Spellbreaker fall into my hand and searched for something to use it on, failed to find anything, and wrapped it around my wrist again.

That was the moment when I realized that I was surrounded by an elite corps and was grateful for it. They had to have been as terrified as I was; a single, isolated company, having walked into what we all knew was a trap, and now we were blind; yet there was no sign of fear from anyone around me. They just waited, coolly, swords in hand.

Well, I certainly wasn't going to be the first to panic.

The silence itself was terrifying, until I realized that, without anyone's having said a word, everyone was listening intently. An obvious thing to do, which I would have thought of myself if I hadn't been scared half out of my wits. I mentally cursed. Being frightened wasn't new to me, but letting it interfere with my efficiency *was* new, and very bad. What would Loiosh say?

Loiosh . . .

"*Loiosh, can you—*"

"*On my way, Boss.*"

He left my shoulder soundlessly. I can usually hear the flap of his wings, but he is capable of flying silently when he needs to. I'm like that, too, now that I think of it. The air was still and there was no sound but that of a few random birds squawking overhead; why is it mountain birds always have horrid voices? Presently Loiosh reported. I said, "Corporal!"

"Quiet," said someone.

"Bug off," I suggested. "Corporal!"

"What is it?" she whispered in my ear.

"Relax," I said in a normal voice. "They aren't within earshot on this side."

"How—?"

"There are about fifty of them on the west side of the hill, coming up quietly. Right now they're between sixty and seventy yards below the ditch. More of them are at the bottom of the hill on the southeast side, waiting."

"How—?"

"Loiosh," I said.

"I see."

She clapped me on the back and moved off. If Loiosh had been popular before, I reflected, now he'd be a hero. And impossible to live with.

Presently the hero returned to my shoulder.

"*Good work,*" I told him.

"*Thanks, Boss. Just proves you don't need opposable thumbs to be a hero.*"

I had nothing to add to this observation, so I added my voice to the silence, wondering if Rascha was going to make any use of the information. I'd about decided she wasn't when I heard the command, "Loose javelins!" from somewhere behind me.

The javelins flew without noise. It was eerie. Then, very faintly, we heard a brief scream from far away, quickly cut off; at least one of the javelins had struck home.

"Loose javelins!" came again. This time I recognized Crown's voice.

Someone else screamed—maybe there were two. It was strange and terrible, unable to see five feet in front of me, Virt and Aelburr indistinct shapes at my side, trying to guess what was happening from the sounds.

I never did find out exactly, but you can probably guess as well as I can. Nothing more happened for about ten very, very long minutes, where most of my activity involved reminding myself not to grip my sword so tightly my hand cramped. For excitement, I'd switch the sword to my left hand, wipe my right hand on my jerkin, and switch it back.

And then, finally, a breeze came up, and, in an instant, the fog blew away like so much smoke and it was daylight again, and there was no enemy in sight closer than the foot of the hill, and I felt like a fool for having been so frightened. I imagine they called off the attack when our javelins fell into them, assuming our sorcerers had penetrated the fog. But whatever, Rascha came by and ordered us back to digging ditches and piling dirt, which work lasted maybe two minutes before the enemy began moving up the hill in force.

"Here we go," said Virt needlessly.

Aelburr began whistling, then broke off abruptly. The look on Napper's face was familiar by now.

For the record, I didn't have any sympathetic thoughts about an enemy's going through what we'd gone through the day before; I was just pleased to be on the other end. We released javelins five times as they made their way up, and I could see we did some damage. By the time they reached us, I think they were having doubts about the whole idea, so when Sethra sent a company that, I learned later, was called Tuvin's Volunteers up the hill to attack them from behind, they broke before they even got there. I never bloodied my sword during that battle; the whole affair was slick, sweet, and easy, and it would have been perfect if it had decided anything, but the enemy broke back down the hill, skirted around Tuvin's people, and made it back to their own lines, where we watched another company come up to reinforce them.

Tuvin's company was pulled back to threaten the same maneuver rather than joining us to reinforce our position, so we watched and waited. Those who had been injured by our javelins crawled off the field as best they could or were captured by Tuvin's company. A few of them, of course, wouldn't be moving again ever, and they remained where they were.

They gave us about twenty minutes before they began moving up the hill again, a whole lot of them even with the units they dispatched to hold off Tuvin.

We threw more javelins, and they came, and we held them off. This time my sword got bloody, but I had learned: A few of my surprises got bloody, too, and when it was over, and they went scampering down the hill, we were still intact, breathing hard, but with the feeling that it could have been worse. Napper suggested it would be next time, and Virt didn't disagree, only it wasn't, as far as I was concerned, because the third attack that day came from the southeast, and I was facing the southwest, so all I did was stand there, listening to the yelling, the screaming, and the crashing sounds from seventy yards to my left, and waited to be sent in if needed, but presently it was over. We took a few casualties, but they took more, and then we got a breather.

The top of the hill had plenty of room to set up camp, which we did, while keeping an eye on the enemy below. When it was done I took a stroll around the hill. I looked to the north, where I could see the camp of our reserves, stretching all the way from the stream to the Wall. Between us and the Wall, to the northeast, was a smaller hill—"Beggar's Hill," I learned—which was occupied by two companies whose names I never learned. We held the north, and from there we were brought barrels of water and biscuits and salted kethna, and more javelins. The best part of receiving the supplies was that it drove home the fact that we weren't cut off, and where supplies could come, troops could, too, if they were needed. Where it was easy to feel isolated, this was no small reassurance. Good for morale, as Virt would put it.

To the west was the stream, a little spinoff from the Eastern River. It ran straight south until it emptied into Khaavren's Sea, some three hundred miles away. To the southwest were a couple of smaller hills, occupied by the enemy, and from there they were mustering to attack us again.

Earlier there had been fighting to the west, all over the fields between our hill and the ones they occupied, but now everything was quiet. Three hundred miles is too far away to smell the sea, so I'm certain the very faint tang was more in my mind than in my nose, but the wind was coming from the south. I don't know.

"Watching them muster?" said Virt.

"Yes. More of them, this time."

"We getting reinforced?"

"Don't know."

We watched some more.

"A lot more of them this time," I remarked.

"Well," she said, "if I were the enemy commander, and our assault had failed three times, and I wanted to make a fourth, I don't think I'd attack with fewer men. But that's just me."

"Shut up, Loiosh."

"I beg your pardon?"

"Never mind. Private joke."

Aelburr came up next to us. "Our side again," he said. "Napper felt left out last time."

"Wouldn't want that," said Virt.

The enemy began moving up. The juice-drum explained that it would be best if we formed a defensive line. I chose not to argue with the juice-drum.

They came slowly up the gentle part of the slope. Very slowly. I strained my eyes until my vision began to blur, then said, "*Loiosh, are they carrying something odd?*"

"*I've been watching, Boss. They're all carrying a stick or something, but I don't know exactly what it is. I'll go check.*"

But he didn't have to, because Virt's eyes were better than mine. "What by Deathgate are those things?"

"That's what I've been wondering," I said.

"You know, it makes me a bit nervous to see an enemy approaching carrying things I don't recognize. It makes me—wait. I recognize them now. Rascha!"

The corporal came over. "What is it?"

She gestured down the hill. "Javelin shooters."

"Bloody damn," said the corporal. Then called, "Sergeant!"

A moment later I heard Crown's voice say, "Drummer! Beat 'Kiss the Ground.' "

"*That sounds entertaining, Boss,*" said Loiosh as the drum started up with a call I hadn't heard before.

I turned to ask Virt what it meant, but Virt, and everyone else, was busy lying down on the ground. I made a quick deduction and joined them. When the drum stopped, I said, "Javelin shooters? I don't like the sound of that."

"No. You won't like the effect, either."

"What—?"

"Here they come!" yelled Rascha, and a mass of javelins flew over our heads, save for a few that landed, point first, in the ground near us. Down the line someone began cursing, very creatively, in a low, even, conversational tone of voice. One of the javelins had fallen about two feet from my right hand, and was sticking out of the ground; it was much smaller than the ones we were throwing, and had feathers near the back, and, at the very end, the wood had a small notch.

"Take a length of green, bendable wood," said Virt. "Put a string to it, and you can use it to shoot those things a long distance. Longer, even uphill, than we can throw our javelins downhill."

"A shield would be nice to have along about now," remarked Aelburr.

"We just going to stand here and take it?" I asked.

"I doubt it. Most likely—"

She was interrupted by the juice-drum. "I recognize that one," I said.

" 'Time to Be Alive,' " said Virt. "We're going to charge them."

"Oh, good," I said.

"Any other ideas?" she said, standing up but remaining hunched over.

I waited for the order to charge. If I got myself killed doing this, not only would it be annoying to me, but Morrolan would be irritated that I risked myself this way instead of doing my job. There just wasn't any good reason to be here. I glanced over at Aelburr and found that he was looking at me. I managed part of a smile and turned my eyes back to the enemy.

Crown walked in front of us, about ten feet down the hill, appearing utterly unconcerned by the javelins falling around him. He waved his sword.

"Give them a good yell as you go," he said. And added, "Charge!"

Well, it was better than just lying there waiting to get a hole punched in me.

So I charged down the hill, sword in hand, and then I was back in my tent with a familiar face looking down at me.

"We were sent help," said Virt. "Otherwise I don't think we'd have made it."

"What sort of help?"

"A platoon of cavalry from one side, three companies of heavy infantry from the other."

"We grind them up?" I asked.

"No, but we escaped."

"Everyone all right?"

"Aelburr took a scrape in the shoulder, but no one got it as bad as you. And Napper had himself a fine old time."

"Oh?"

"He laid about in grand style. I think he took out six of them all by himself."

"Maybe he'll get a decoration."

"Yeah, and we both know what he'd say about that, don't we?"

I grunted.

She said, "How are you doing?"

"I feel fine."

"Yeah, well, they've got you pretty doped up."

"Do they? Really? I feel normal."

"You wouldn't say that if you could see your eyes rolling around."

Now that she mentioned it, I was having a bit of trouble focusing. I said, "My back feels wet. I'm not still bleeding, am I?"

"No blood. They got this gunk all over your back, for the burns."

"Burns? From what?"

Loiosh butted in at that point, saying, *"Boss? You okay? You've been out cold forever."*

"I think I'm all right. What happened?"

"I don't remember. You got hit by something. A spell. I must not have seen it coming."

"That's two of us, I imagine."

I said, "Where am I?"

"In camp. Top of Dorian's Hill."

"Did we delay their attack?"

"What?"

"The expedition. Burning up their biscuits. Did it—"

"That was days ago, Vlad."

"Oh. My head is scrambled."

Virt said, "You got caught by some spell, straight in the back. You don't remember?"

"I don't remember anything. Well—"

"Well what?"

"I don't remember anything that actually happened. I think."

"You think?"

"Was there a little girl on the battlefield? You know, a child?"

"No, I think I can safely say there wasn't."

"Then I can safely say I don't remember anything about the battle."

"That's probably just as well, then."

I tried to fill in the intervening time. Presently I said, "So their trap didn't work."

"So far, at least. And if Sethra or Brigade or whoever was planning a countertrap, that didn't work either. We're expecting a night attack, though."

"Don't wake me up for it."

"I won't."

"I was kidding."

"I wasn't. You're out of it tonight. Physicker's orders. He also says, by the way, that you're to stay on your stomach all night. I hope you can sleep that way."

"I always enjoy the chance to learn a new skill," I told her.

"As for fighting," she said, "we'll see how you're doing tomorrow."

"If there is a tomorrow."

"Oh, there will be. Somewhere. Now excuse me. The others want to know how you're doing."

"I'm touched."

"If you need help, you can . . ."

Her voice trailed off. What had she been about to say? See the physicker? Then why didn't she complete the sentence? Because the physicker wouldn't be able to do anything more than he'd done? Just how bad was I hurt, anyway?

"Just how bad am I hurt, anyway?"

"You'll live," she said.

"That's good to know. What else can you tell me?"

"Nothing."

"Okay. Well, thanks for coming by."

"You're welcome."

She left me alone.

"*What happened, Loiosh?*"

"*I don't know any more than you, Boss. Whatever got you, I caught a bit of it myself. I don't remember.*"

"*Are you all right?*"

"*I think so.*"

"*I don't like it that I got hit in the back, though. I mean, was I running?*"

"*Maybe, but I don't think you're smart enough for that. More likely you got turned around during the fight. Or—*" He broke off.

"*Or what?*" I said.

"*Well, it's possible it was our own people. I mean, if they were coun-terattacking, reinforcing us, and using spells . . .*"

"*Right.*"

Over the next several months, by the way, I started to remember more and more of it. I eventually got a pretty clear memory of getting hit: the feeling of having my muscles contract almost to the point of breaking my own arms and legs; the feeling that my eyes were trying to pop out of my head; the peculiar sensation of every hair on my body suddenly standing up; and watching the battle progress around me as I slowly fell over. But I still have no memory at all of what led up to it—the time between the beginning of the charge and the point where I was hit is completely gone.

All of which is to say that if you want war stories to tell your grandchildren, don't get hit by sorcery.

There, you ask for a story and you get useful advice out of the deal.

At the time, however, I remembered none of it, and that was scary, too. *"Wish I knew how bad I was hurt, Loiosh."*

"What good would it do to know?"

"I'm scared anyway. It would be nice to know if I had cause to be."

"Well, Boss, if we can judge by what remains of your jerkin, your back got hurt pretty bad."

I thought that over and decided I didn't care for it, and I suppose I fell asleep for a while, but I didn't sleep well; I had all sorts of odd dreams.

16

A WALK IN THE PARK

"Got it," said Daymar into my mind and into the silence of Fornia, his honor guard, and his sorcerers all staring at me and waiting for me to do something. Relative silence, I should say; there was still a battle moving toward me. Had Daymar actually succeeded? Pulled the information out of Fornia's mind, just like that? Well, I had to believe it.

"Let's have it, then," I said.

"Wait!" said Fornia to those of his honor guard who were moving forward to search me. They stopped and looked at him, while he stared at Daymar, then at me, then back at Daymar. He had evidently felt Daymar invade his mind and he had evidently taken it personally. I wondered if that had pushed him over the edge—if he would now order us killed out of hand. Hell, I would have.

The trouble was, that wouldn't help him any, and would undo the good fortune—from his perspective—of my having arrived here, because, of course, my being here would likely draw Morrolan; so the Easterner's showing up, while puzzling, and thus worrisome, had fit in so well with his plan to have a face-to-face meeting with Morrolan in the middle of the battle and engage him so he could— Oh, *that's* what was going on.

"Good work, Daymar," I said aloud. And to Fornia I said, "You don't know exactly what it is, either. And you're only guessing about how to bring it out. That was a possibility that hadn't occurred to me."

Ori stared back and forth between me and Fornia, and the other sorcerers and the bodyguards also seemed uncertain about what had just happened and what to do about it. Fornia said, "I suspect killing you here will draw him to me anyway; I think I no longer need you alive."

Now, that was unfortunate for me.

I said, "Remember, I surrendered."

"Spies can be executed."

"I'm in uniform," I said, remembering from somewhere that that might matter.

"Then you'll look properly military when—" He broke off, staring over my shoulder.

"Boss, don't look now, but we've got company."

"Who?"

"Napper."

"What?"

In spite of his warning, I looked. And there, about fifty yards away, was Napper, sauntering up the hill, come, no doubt, to get in on the action. Did this change anything? Well, yeah, it did change one thing—it put my back to Ori, and that caused a panic that, I suppose, was inevitable after what I'd been through the day before, so I spun back and almost set off a melee right there. I can't believe, with Napper showing up right then, that Fornia would have done anything except have us killed at once if there hadn't been sudden cries from the honor guard—Morrolan's band was on the verge of breaking through—thus giving him other things to think about than this pesky Easterner and his odd friends.

He addressed those of his guard who had been about to bind and search me, and said, "Guard them, all of them. Kill them the instant they do anything suspicious," then he turned back to his war.

That was good. Twice in two days would have been uncalled-for, even if I lived through it.

I almost hadn't lived through it the first time. I even dreamed that I didn't. I half remember several of the dreams, but in one that I remember most of I was sent over Deathgate Falls, and in the Halls of Judgment (which looked a lot different in my dream than they did when I'd actually been there) the Gods all thought it was the greatest joke in the world that I was asking to be admitted, and in the confusion of the dream I tried to explain that I deserved to be admitted

as a Dragon, and they just couldn't stop laughing. It sounds funny to
tell, but I woke up in the middle of the night in a sweat, breathing
hard, and shaking.

I got out of bed because I suddenly couldn't stand to be lying
still. I walked out into the quiet of the camp; the mountain air was
cold on my chest, but felt good on my back, which was hot, like I
had a localized fever.

"Where are you going, Boss?"

"I'm not sure. I need to walk."

"The physicker's tent is this way."

"I've gotten plenty of physic."

I slipped past the pickets, almost out of habit. "Am I going the
right way, Loiosh?"

"What do you mean, Boss? You're not heading toward the enemy,
but you're going downhill."

"That's what I meant. I wouldn't want to present myself to the enemy
just yet."

"Then where are we going? Are we finally getting out of here like
sensible people?"

"I'm not sure."

"Because if we are, you've forgotten a few things."

I made my way down into the darkness, my eyes straining to pick
out a path from the bits of light from distant campfires. Loiosh landed
on my shoulder.

"Ouch."

"Sorry, Boss. You should have a jerkin on."

He was probably right. I had no jerkin, no cloak, no boots, no
sword, Spellbreaker was back next to my bed, and the only weapons
I carried were two paper-thin throwing knives concealed in the seams
of my trousers. I hadn't been out of doors this naked since I joined
the Jhereg, and there was something exhilaratingly spooky about it.
It was a cleaner fear than what I'd felt in battle, and the pain of
stepping on rocks with my bare feet was clean, too, and so was the
cold. I hadn't realized how much I needed to feel clean.

I slipped past another line of pickets, effortlessly, and for a while
I entertained the illusion that I was the wind itself, that I didn't feel
the cold, rather I *was* the cold, and none could see where I went, but
they would feel me pass by a prickling of the hairs on their necks. I

was naked but invisible, helpless but omnipotent, and I was lost in the world I all but owned. Certainly, it was false; in the streets of Adrilankha I owned the world, but this was a desert filled with soldiers; the feeling was different, and illusory, but it was there. I made no sound, and, had anyone been looking, I don't think he'd have seen more than my breath in the night air. My awareness of those around me came, above all, from the faint sounds of breathing, and I knew that Loiosh, as silent as I, was above me in the night, in the wind.

A single bush, like a sentry, waves to say with a laugh that it, at least, sees me, and I wave back though my arm doesn't move; a pebble between my toes is a burden which I reject, so it rolls away in search of its own reason for being; my time is filled with empty space, and my space with empty time, and my legs can't move so I must float float float through the armies of the world, clashing forever on the battlefield of my mind where all is in motion and nothing moves and the Cycle looms overhead, and at its top is the Dragon, glaring, plotting, scheming, protecting its young by devouring the souls who are cast loose to roam the night and come to me for protection that I cannot give, for I am in no place but everywhere, and there is no end to the night that is me.

How long I walked, or where, I don't know; nor do I know how far my mind wandered on a journey of its own, but somewhere in the night real thoughts returned, and practical matters impinged on my consciousness and brought me a few steps closer to home.

I found that I was thinking, for example, about just how big Morrolan's army was. My own unit—I couldn't help thinking of it that way—was one company out of scores in one brigade out of dozens. I passed tent after tent, all the same, all full of Dragons and Dzur and Teckla who would be going out the next day to cut and hack at Dragons and Dzur and Teckla on the other side. I walked through the camps as one might travel in a dream, apart from it all, and it came to me that the power I held as a Jhereg was nothing to the power of a Dragonlord, who could, on a whim, command so many to do so much. If I had such power, how would I use it? And what would it do to me? Did that explain why Morrolan was the way he was? There are stories that, in his youth during the Interregnum, he had entire villages put to the sword in sacrifice to the Demon Goddess

that she might grant him knowledge of the Elder Sorcery. If the
stories were true, did I now understand why? Was it that, having such
power, he used it merely because he could? And would I be the same
way, given the chance?

I came to the river and turned north, walking by still more camps,
and supplies, and pickets to whom I was invisible. That was my own
power, and I was using it, I suppose, because I could, and maybe there
was my answer. To my right were several large pavilions, some with
lights showing within. Perhaps Morrolan and Sethra were meeting
even now to plan the destiny of the thousands assembled here—
because they could.

And what of Virt, and Napper, and Aelburr? They were all volunteers, professional soldiers, who fought—why? Because if they died
bravely they would receive high status in the Paths of the Dead? Or
have a chance to be reincarnated as a commander who could lead
others into the sorts of battles that led to their own deaths? That
didn't account for it, but I couldn't get any closer.

None of my answers satisfied me.

I stepped out into the river, just a few feet, and felt the bitter
current against my legs and the sand between my toes. I stood there,
alone amongst thousands, and only then became aware that my knees
were trembling, and that I felt light-headed, and that my arms were
without strength. Whatever the sorcery had done to my mind, which
was, apparently, a great deal, it had also taken a lot out of me physically. I wondered if I'd be able to fight the next day. I began to shiver
uncontrollably, but I stayed where I was. It would be wonderfully
ironic if I passed out from weakness and drowned in two feet of water.

"You have any answers, Loiosh?"

"To what, Boss?"

"To why Dragons are the way they are."

"That's easy, Boss: They can't help it."

Well, there was maybe something to that, but it was hardly sat-
isfying. When I thought about it, the differences in character among
Morrolan and Aliera and Virt and Napper, to pick four, were greater
than the similarities. What was the common thread? Put that way,
the answer was obvious: Once having decided on a course, motivated
by greed, or by anger, or by the highest moral outrage, they attacked
with a ruthlessness that would excite envy—or disgust—in a hard-

ened Jhereg operative. I tried to decide if this were inherently a bad thing, and I could come to no conclusion. Fortunately, no conclusion was demanded of me.

I did, however, come to two other conclusions. The first being that, if one were forced into the service of a Dragonlord, one was better off serving a Dragonlord who was better at being ruthless than the other Dragonlord. The second being that the river was bloody damned cold, and that it was surpassing stupid for me to be standing in it when I hardly had the strength to remain upright.

"I bid you a pleasant evening, Lord Taltos."

The voice came out of nowhere, but I must have subconsciously known there was someone around, because it didn't startle me.

"Who is it?"

I turned around. At first I couldn't see her, but then she came up to the edge of the water and nodded to me, and then I recognized her. It took me a moment to reconstruct where I had met her before, but it came back to me at last.

"You're the Necromancer," I said.

"What are you doing?" she asked me.

I considered the question carefully, then said, "Dreamwalking, I think."

Her head tilted. She was very, very thin, wispy, and her skin was so pale it almost glowed against the darkness and against the black of her garments. "I didn't know Easterners did that," she said.

"Neither did I."

"I sense that you've been injured."

I turned enough to show her my back, then faced her again.

"I understand," she said.

"Excuse me?"

"I understand why you're dreamwalking."

"Ah. But I'm really here, aren't I?"

"How do you mean that?"

Crap. Even while dreamwalking there was only so much mysticism I could take. I said, "I mean that if I drop dead I'll be really dead, and my body will be found here in the morning."

"No."

"No?"

"No. Your body will actually float downriver from here, at least as far as the next bend. If you climb up on the shore—"

I laughed, probably more than it was worth.

"You did that on purpose, didn't you?"

"Did what?" she said.

"Made me laugh. Brought me back."

"Oh. Well, yes. You may have to fight tomorrow."

"Not the way I'm feeling now."

"Oh? Oh, of course. You were hit hard, weren't you? Come here for a moment."

I did, walking up to the bank until only my ankles were in the river, and she reached out and cradled my face in her hands. Her hands were very, very cold, and I tried not to think about what was touching me. I looked into her eyes, and it seemed she was a long way away, speaking to me from another world. I got the sense that speech for her required effort; she didn't think in words the way I did, she probably thought in—no, I didn't want to consider what forms her thoughts might take; I probably couldn't understand them anyway.

She closed her eyes for a moment, opened them, and said, "Go back to your camp and sleep, dream-walker. You'll feel better in the morning."

"Right," I said. "And I'll think this was all a dream."

"Maybe. Maybe it is."

"We've been through that."

"Go back to your tent, Easterner. Go to sleep. Dream of bearded women."

"Excuse me? No, never mind. Don't explain. I don't want to know."

Now that I was myself again, the wind was really cold, especially on my wet legs. And the rocks hurt my bare feet. And I had to work to slip past several sets of pickets, more of them than I remembered from getting there.

"*Well, she was pretty weird.*"

"*Who was, Boss?*"

"*I hope,*" I said after a moment, "*that you're joking, Loiosh.*"

"*Ummmm.*"

"I've just had a conversation with the Necromancer, Loiosh. A real conversation. Out loud and everything. You really didn't see her?"

"Boss, I didn't see her, I didn't hear her, and I didn't hear you talking. You just walked out into the river, stood there for a while, and walked back."

"Grand," I said. "Just grand. I get myself into the army, stand up in battles I have no business in, get nailed in the back by sorcery, accept an impossible assignment to be carried out in the middle of it all, and then, just to top things off, I have to go have a mystical fucking experience. This is just great."

"Whatever it was, Boss, I think it helped. You're sounding like yourself."

"Oh, thank you so much, Loiosh."

I made it back to the camp, and to my tent, and to my cot, and I remembered to lie down on my stomach, and it was only then that I realized that whatever weakness I'd felt before was, if not gone, at least diminished. I tried to make sense of it, but I must have fallen asleep, because then it was morning, and I got up to the sound of the drum before I remembered that I probably wouldn't have had to. Rascha was outside the tent when I emerged, bare-chested and blinking.

"You all right?" she said.

In spite of everything, I managed to give her a straight answer. "A bit wobbly on my feet, and my back itches, and I could use about another forty or fifty hours of sleep, but yeah, I'm okay."

"Think you can take a spot on the line?"

"Sure."

"Good. We had some casualties."

"Did they attack last night?"

She looked at me. "Just before dawn. Glad we didn't wake you up."

"I think you could have burned the tent down without waking me up."

"Today, I think."

"Hmmm?"

"I think today will settle things."

"Oh. That's good."

"Yes. And our end of it shouldn't be too bad. All we have to do is hold this hill. Unless, of course, the powers-that-be change their minds and have us do something else."

"Holding the hill might be rough enough," I said.

"Maybe. Go get some food in you."

"Good idea," I said.

I went back inside and grabbed my jerkin and inspected it. I found that it no longer had a back—just a big hole, about a foot in diameter, with ugly burn marks around the edges. I started to feel queasy again.

"Boss—"

"Yeah. Impressive, isn't it?"

"What are you going to do for a jerkin?"

"I brought a spare."

"Oh. Good thinking."

I put it on and my back started itching. I filled the ribs and sleeves and the collar from my old shirt, then put a light cloak over it, and made sure that I was properly packed. I ate three biscuits and drank a lot of water, then got myself shaved and cleaned up as best I could.

My knees felt very shaky by then, and I wasn't looking forward to taking a spot on the line. If I'd remembered what I had promised Morrolan I'd do I might have panicked, but my brain was still a bit scrambled and that didn't occur to me until later. The experiences of the night before came back in pieces, and I kept wanting to think of the whole thing as a dream, but I couldn't convince myself, and then I made the mistake of asking Loiosh, who confirmed that at least some of it had actually happened.

When I returned to the tent, I found Rascha sitting with Virt and Aelburr. I sat with them, and soon after that Crown came along. "Morning, soldiers," he said cheerfully. "Today we take them."

Rascha nodded. "What do you think of the earthworks on the southwest side? They got pretty messed up last night."

He nodded. "It wouldn't hurt to build them up again."

Dunn came over then. He said, "Sergeant, I'd like—"

"No," said Crown. "Mora's taking the colors. If she goes down, then you're up. So stick by her. And keep her alive, if you can. You can answer to Dortmond if she shines."

"Yes, Sergeant. Thank you, Sergeant."

Dunn walked away. I shook my head. "I just don't get it."

Crown looked me up and down. "No, you wouldn't, would you?"
He walked off.

"I think," I said, "that I've just been insulted."

"Don't let it keep you up nights," said Virt.

From farther down the line someone called out, "Here they
come," and we walked up to the remains of the earthworks and waited
for the assault to begin.

They came, and we held them off, and they came, and we held
them off. The whole time Loiosh remained on my shoulder, maybe
for whatever effect it might have on anyone who faced me. I kept
asking him why he didn't get to somewhere safe, but I didn't get a
satisfactory answer, just questions to which I couldn't give a satisfactory answer. My legs kept wanting to buckle—residual effects from
getting hit the day before, but I never quite collapsed at the wrong
time. If the Necromancer had actually done something, well, it must
have worked.

After the second attack, Virt said, "Have you noticed that every
time they attack they've been knocking away at the earthworks?"

"Uh . . . you're right."

"And that they attack with more troops each time?"

"Right again," I said. "You're on a roll. Don't stop now."

"They're forming up for another charge," she said.

Rascha came by and said, "Up to the line again. Where's Aelburr?"

"I'll sit this one out, I think," he said.

That was when we noticed that he was flat on his back, bleeding
from two distinct chest wounds and another on his right leg. "Physic!"
came the call, from Rascha and Virt at the same time.

As the physicker approached, Virt said, "We're awfully cut up.
Do we have anyone left to plug the holes?"

"No," said Rascha. "We've got holes everywhere. About twelve
percent casualties. And, from the looks of things, I don't think we
can expect any support from Brigade."

"Oh," said Virt.

"Time for someone to think of something clever," I suggested, at
which moment the juice-drum gave the call to prepare for a charge.
I said, "That wasn't the sort of clever I was thinking of."

Virt said, "This should be interesting."

"Interesting?" I said. "We're too weak to defend, so we attack? That isn't sound military practice, is it?"

"No," said Virt.

"Well good," I said. "See? I've learned something."

"I'm sure it will do you a lot of good next time you enlist." She paused. "It's been done before, though. And it isn't that bad an idea. One time, at Kipper Bay, we—" She broke off abruptly and pointed. "I'll tell you the story later," she said optimistically.

They were coming up the hill, and there was something horribly determined about how they came. I didn't like it at all. We prepared to go down the hill. I liked that even less. At least we had elevation on our side.

One way or the other, we were going to settle it right now.

"Well," said Loiosh. "Here you are."

"No shit," I said.

17

THE LIMITATIONS OF WIT

I turned back toward Fornia and stood there next to Daymar as Napper approached from behind me to my left, and the whole bloody war approached from behind me to my right.

Napper got there first. He came up next to me, holding a short, heavy sword that was streaked with red. I glanced over at him, and his eyes were shining, and he wore a delighted smile all over his face. I said, "Napper, meet Daymar. Daymar, Napper. And that is the Count of Fornia. Anyone bring wine? Cheese? I could manage some biscuits."

The three who had been assigned to watch us didn't think I was very funny, but neither did they construe my remarks as suspicious enough to cut us down. "Your weapons," said one of them.

"*Daymar, can you break through the block and get us out of here?*"

"*No,*" he explained gently. "*They strengthened the block after I broke through it.*"

"*Pity,*" I said.

"*If I can get about half an hour—*"

He might as well have asked for half a year. "*Yeah, well, I'll let you know.*"

"Weapons," repeated the soldier. "Now."

"What's the plan, Vlad?" said Napper, loud enough for everyone to hear.

"The good news is that we're negotiating," I told him. "The bad news is that I surrendered."

"You what?"

"On the other hand, if he plans to kill me, I'll have to say the surrender is off. In the meantime, you'd best give the nice man your sword. I would, too, but I don't have one."

"Carefully," added the guard. "Unbuckle the belt and let it fall."

He looked fairly tough. So did the others. I didn't like Napper's chances against all three of them. One was between us and Fornia, the others flanked us. Napper began to comply, with exaggerated slowness.

"I don't suppose, Daymar, you know what they're doing?"

"No," said Daymar. "He has me blocked." Daymar sounded hurt.

Orders came barking out from somewhere in the group, and swords were drawn. I drew in my breath, terrified all over again, but the honor guard and the sorcerers turned to face the approaching battle. For an instant, with all the movement, I had a clear shot at Fornia, but then it was gone before I could have taken it even if I'd been so inclined.

There was an odd, unreal quality to the whole thing that lingers in my memory even now. I stood with Daymar on one side of me and Napper on the other, with the whole war, or at least a crucial part of it, rushing down on me, with Fornia amidst his honor guard and sorcerers turning away from us as if we were suddenly no part of their world and certainly no threat to them.

Well, okay, we *were* no threat to them.

I knew what Fornia was doing, I knew why he was doing it, I knew where it would lead; and there wasn't anything I could do about it.

There's a certain frustration that players of S'yang Stones get when their best shots fail and their opponents keep getting lucky breaks. I've seen it, and I've had it happen to me. You start just throwing your stones, even the flat ones, almost at random, as if you want to punish yourself for your bad luck by playing badly. I was feeling the same thing right now.

Was I making a bad play out of frustration, or was I really getting the odds I needed, now that the battle was loud and everyone had their backs to us?

I threw a shuriken into the throat of the man in front of us, the one who was threatening Napper, and then planted a knife in the throat of the one to my left; I heard Napper draw his sword, and by

the time I turned around the third of the guards was dead and Napper
was finishing off the one I'd started on. I caught a glimpse of Daymar
staring, wide-eyed.

Better yet, Fornia hadn't noticed, nor had any of his group.

Napper said, "What's the plan?"

That almost made me laugh. A little demon in my head wanted
me to say "Kill them all," but I resisted temptation.

"Boss, does this situation seem a little absurd to you?"

"Absurd? Well, among other things, yes."

Then Morrolan's band reached Fornia's honor guard, and the
game was being played in earnest.

I saw Aliera, now dismounted, standing next to Morrolan; around
them were several others I didn't recognize, and behind them—where
she came from I couldn't say—behind them, mounted, was Sethra
Lavode, holding the weapon I knew to be Iceflame. They were all of
them heading straight for Fornia, who was waiting with the patience
of a gambler who has staked everything he has on one throw and
knows, now that the coins are spinning, that all he can do is wait
and see which way they land.

My task was simple, put that way: just reach my hand out and
scoop up the coins before they stopped spinning. And somehow con-
trive not to have my hand cut off.

Now *that* was a thought.

Good. I had a thought. All I had to do was combine thought
with opportunity and I'd have something else: a chance.

I tried to make contact with Morrolan, but either I didn't know
him well enough or he was concentrating on his mayhem too hard,
or both. Probably both. I knew Aliera even less, but it was a worth
a try—

And at that moment Fornia's honor guard fell back toward us as
a body, struck by Morrolan's attack—or, more exactly, the remnants
of the Eastern cavalry that was being pushed into Fornia's honor
guard—and the three of us had to scramble or be trampled down.

"The plan," I told Napper, "is not to get killed."

"We could attack from behind."

"And get maybe two each at the most before they wiped us out.
I don't think so."

Now, you must understand that, as we were speaking, we were

also running to get away from the retreating honor guard. This left me facing the northeast, the highest part of the hill. I touched Napper's arm and said, "Look. What's that?"

He stopped in his tracks, watching another mass of humanity head toward us. "That's the hammer," he said. He gestured back over his shoulder and said, "And that's the anvil."

"Well, we had to expect him to have reinforcements handy once Morrolan started breaking through."

"That makes me feel better," said Napper.

Daymar, who had been silent this entire time, said, "I think I am perhaps no longer useful here."

"Does that mean you can teleport now?"

"Not exactly. I was thinking of a different method."

I thought of Morrolan's window and an idea began to form. I said, "Tell me about it."

He stared at me with a puzzled expression and said, "I was thinking about running."

"Oh," I said. "I hadn't thought of that."

The battle continued pressing toward us, and the approaching company looked to be light infantry.

"Do you think Morrolan will reach Fornia before the reinforcements arrive?" said Napper.

"If Fornia has his way, he will."

"Beg pardon?"

"I have to do something," I said.

"Like what?"

"Something clever."

We backed up a little farther. "Clever," said Napper, "will only get you so far."

I didn't answer, because things had gotten even louder, and that just wasn't the right moment to be philosophical. The light infantry was closing on us quickly, and on the other side Easterners were dying, and to the smells of battle that I've already refused to describe once we can add the distinctive and equally unpleasant smell of dead and dying horses.

What Napper said was reasonable, though: Fornia's plan wasn't "clever" in the usual sense; rather it was a bold, calculated gamble, like redoubling the bet when the pattern is in your opponent's favor but one perfect throw could give you the game and you're down to your last flat stone.

"Napper," I said aloud. "I think it's time to die valiantly. What do you think?"

"Yes!" he said.

"How 'bout you, Daymar? Want to join us?"

"In what?"

"We're going to attack, of course."

"Oh. Very well," he said.

"He's not armed," pointed out Napper.

"I most certainly am," said Daymar, sounding slightly offended.

Well, he wasn't carrying a blade, but I believed him.

"All right," I said. "That one, with his hair in a queue, is Ori. He is preparing a split-second teleport as part of Fornia's plan to, well, never mind. The important thing is to kill him. Killing Fornia will be harder, because he is surrounded by his honor guard, but it isn't as important either. It is Ori who has to die."

"All right," said Napper.

"Very well," said Daymar.

"Any questions?"

There were none.

"Charge," I said conversationally.

We walked forward at an even pace. I had evidently drawn a dagger at some point, and I held it in my right hand. Spellbreaker was in my left, swinging in circles. It had grown longer somehow, to almost three feet, I think, and the links were bigger; its swing covered my whole body, and Daymar on my right and Napper on my left.

Napper said, "Should we give them a yell as we go in?"

"No," I said. "We should say nothing. No more talking."

"You're going to strike them in the back, without warning?"

"Yes."

"I don't—"

"You volunteered for this. We're doing it my way. If you don't like it, take off. In either case, keep quiet."

"Yes, sir," said Napper. It didn't occur to me until later to wonder if he was being ironic. Thinking about it, I don't believe he was.

Yes. Battles are decided, Sethra told me, when timing and momentum and courage all come together and, at just the right moment, someone fails to make a critical mistake and doesn't manage to miss a vital opportunity. An opportunity that, perhaps, no one quite realized was there, because it is just all too confusing to have a complete grasp of everything that is happening. I was right in the middle of it, and I still don't know enough about who was doing what to give a complete picture. But I have my incomplete picture; I have to be satisfied with that, and you will, too.

As we approached, I reached out for Daymar, who was astonishingly easy to make contact with, and I said, *"What is Ori doing?"*

"Which one is Ori again?"

"That one."

"Oh. I don't know what he's doing exactly. They're still blocking me. But he's concentrating on a spell of some kind."

"Doing one, or preparing to do it?"

"Oh, he's preparing to do it. He's—what's the word? Poised. Yes, that's the word. He's poised to do a spell."

We hadn't stopped walking forward, and by this time we were ten feet behind the sorcerers, who were just behind Fornia and his honor guard. Ori was facing away from me.

I walked up and stuck my knife squarely into his back.

He screamed, and everyone turned around and looked at me as Ori spasmed and dropped to his knees. I couldn't see the expression on Ori's face, but I wasn't terribly interested in it, either. Fornia, however, stared at me wide-eyed.

"I hope," I said, "I haven't interfered with your plans."

"Kill him," said Fornia. "Kill all three of them."

And likely they would have, too; except that, at that moment, Morrolan broke through the final line of Eastern cavalry, and, amid the cries of people and horses, they charged Fornia's honor guard.

Fornia was thrust back toward me, which might have made it an excellent chance to kill him but I couldn't because I had to get out of the way of the large, very plain, unadorned Morganti greatsword he was swinging at my head. I did so, falling to the ground and rolling. I continued to roll away, not knowing exactly where Fornia and the Morganti blade were, and making the calm, rational decision that I needed to get away from them both, and besides, it was all I could do in the midst of my panic.

"Boss! Boss! You can stand up now!"

It's always embarrassing to panic in front of Loiosh. I stood up, and for just an instant, no one was around me and nothing horrible was happening in my immediate vicinity.

Then I spotted Fornia, about twenty feet away. He held both hands on the hilt of the sword, holding it at about waist height. Napper, his back to me, stood facing Fornia. Neither of them moved. It took me a second to realize that I could see a few inches of the point of the Morganti greatsword sticking out of Napper's back.

Napper dropped his sword, which fell, point first, very slowly, then stuck in the ground and swayed back and forth, also slowly. Nothing else moved in the entire world; Fornia and Napper were like twin sculptures, and would hold that pose until the world dissolved into the dreamstuff of the Gods, as my people say it will someday. But even then, the essence of Napper would never come back, and the shadowy remembrances of him in the minds of people like me, his comrades, would be all that would ever again exist of him.

And still they both stood, mutually transfixed.

Then Fornia looked at me, Napper unceremoniously fell to the ground, and the world started up again.

My moment of panic was over, replaced by a kind of hollowness that isn't all that bad a way to feel in such circumstances; at least it didn't keep me from observing, anticipating, and acting. I threw a couple of knives at Fornia just to let him know to keep his distance and began working my way toward Morrolan. At this point, the light infantry finally reached us. They flowed past me—I guess they figured that, being an Easterner, I had to be one of their cavalrymen—and Fornia was momentarily lost from sight.

I tried to spot Morrolan, but, ironically, now that he was within a knife-throw I couldn't see him. I kept looking.

Thinking back on it, this was what I had always imagined a battle to be like: constantly dodging, moving, trying to look in every direction at once, and never really sure of what I ought to be doing. The actual battles I had been in had certainly had elements of confusion, but at least I always knew what I had to do, and I could always concentrate on one direction. I guess the difference was that there were no actual lines here: Everyone was mixed up with everyone else, the entire thing being broken up into an endless, chaotic series of one-on-one or two-on-one fights. I could just imagine how often those who were actually participating had to stop and check caps or sashes to make sure they weren't about to strike down someone on their own side. Probably a few people got hit because they took too long to be sure, and almost certainly a few people got hit because the guy in front of them didn't take long enough.

At length I spotted Morrolan, just a glimpse of him through a temporary part in the sea of struggling humanity, and I moved toward him. If, by the way, you're wondering what became of Daymar, I still don't know. Maybe he was around the entire time, mixing it up with the enemy in his own way and doing what damage he could, but I suspect he took to his heels right around the time Fornia was destroying Napper. Can't say as I blame him much.

I skipped around a few fights, shuffled, dodged, and tried to spot Morrolan again. On the way, I passed by Napper's lifeless and souless body, and had another, very brief, moment of panic until Loiosh said, *"He's not here, Boss. Not in sight, at least."* I kept going.

I wrapped Spellbreaker around my left wrist again and grabbed Napper's sword from where it stuck out of the ground, even though it was too heavy for me, and moved toward where I'd seen Morrolan, hoping that I could trust Loiosh's perceptions and that Fornia wasn't about to appear swinging at the back of my head.

But no, Fornia wasn't coming after me just now, he was coming after Morrolan. And Morrolan seemed pretty pleased about it. They faced each other in a spot that sensible people had stayed away from, circling each other, and both apparently delighted by the encounter. Just beyond Morrolan I saw Aliera and a couple of other officers I didn't recognize, and they also seemed quite happy with this state of affairs.

In fact, everyone was happy about it except me, and I wouldn't have minded either except that I knew what Fornia was up to. The fact that I'd killed Ori had certainly messed with part of his plan, but he was going merrily on with the rest of it, I suppose trusting himself to find a way out when it was over. Or maybe not caring if he found a way out; he was, after all, a Dragon.

"No way around it, Loiosh."

"Boss—"

"I know. But I hate letting people get away with things. It offends me when they think they've put one over on me. It's a pride thing."

"You've been hanging around Dragons too long."

"Lieutenant Loiosh—First Jhereg Assassins—Charge."

"Whatever."

It was less of a charge than a stroll, but I carried it out, hardly planned and barely thought about, as neatly as any assassination I'd ever done, and under the circumstances that is no small thing. I did my calculations during the half dozen paces that separated us: I still didn't want to kill him, and didn't want to get close enough to that weapon to be so much as scratched by bad luck should he spasm; but I couldn't let him fight Morrolan with that weapon. I held Napper's big, heavy sword with both hands and toyed with it a bit. I wished I'd had more time to get a feel for the thing.

I came up directly behind Fornia. Morrolan spotted me, although I was awfully close before he did; he probably doesn't know how I did that, or maybe he just thinks he was concentrating too hard on Fornia. But the look on Morrolan's face warned Fornia, who took a step backward and started to turn, and when he was part of the way around I stepped in and swung Napper's sword down in a long over-head arc such as no Eastern fencer would ever execute and I put everything I had into it, knowing that if I missed I was dead and worse, but that it would likely take all my strength.

I struck him just above the wrists, and his scream was instanta-neous and a joy to my ears. The force of the blow left my own weapon embedded in the ground, but I was done with it anyway. Before I could think about what I was doing—because, I assure you, thinking would have done me no good at all—I picked up the Morganti great-sword by the pommel, and ignoring the hands still wrapped tightly around it, I tossed it in Morrolan's general direction, being careful not to throw it actually *at* him, because I knew he might take that wrong.

Fornia sobbed.

His honor guard closed on me, and I did something I had been wanting to do for several weeks: I turned and *ran*.

My plan at that point was to run as fast as I could and as far as I could and not stop until I reached Adrilankha, and if I happened to be going in the wrong direction, well, okay, so maybe I'd make a bit of a detour; they say the world is round, after all.

As I dashed by, I saw someone stoop to pick up the Morganti

sword that Fornia had recently held—I didn't even notice at the time which side had recovered the thing—and that gave me even more reason to run. Adrilankha, here I come.

I didn't actually make it that far—it was more like fifty feet before I was stopped. The command, "Hold it!" was so sharp and so, well, commanding, that I found I had obeyed before I actually thought about it. I turned around and found I was looking up at Sethra Lavode, atop a horse that, with my equine expertise, I can assure you was dark colored and very big. It looked at Loiosh and tossed its head, snorting like Morrolan had on one or two occasions. Loiosh didn't dignify it with an answer.

Sethra said, "Where are you going, soldier?"

"Uh . . . I think you have me confused with someone else," I said.

"I doubt it," said Sethra. "In any case, there's no reason to run now; the battle is nearly over."

I looked at where I'd just come from, turned back to Sethra, and said, "You're kidding, right?"

"I'm not kidding. Your unit routed the enemy from Dorian's Hill and drove them almost right up to the Wall. That would have been Fornia's moment to bring up his reserves, except that he was busy just then and didn't get around to it. Besides, Morrolan informs me that Fornia is dead now, anyway, and we have the weapon that caused all the trouble, so there isn't all that much to fight about. I expect a general surrender within the next few minutes, as soon as they can find someone with sufficient authority to surrender to us."

I looked again. "If you say so," I said.

Sethra seemed amused. "It's over, Vlad. Trust me. I've done this sort of thing before. You should have run earlier, when it would have done some good."

"I know, I know."

"Now you might as well wait here, with me."

"You're not going to send me back into battle as punishment for desertion?"

"The punishment for desertion is beheading. Being sent into battle is a reward."

"You mean that, don't you?"

She looked serious for a moment, and said, "Yes."

She was right, though. I don't mean about being sent into battle,

I mean about the whole thing being pretty much over. Within half an hour the fighting had stopped, there were banners piled up all over the field, and Sethra, Aliera, and Morrolan were all involved in negotiations with their previous enemies. The war was over. If I chose to, I could convince myself that I had had a major part in winning it. I would have preferred to forget the whole thing, but that was harder.

We eventually formed a camp on the hill where we'd lately fought with Fornia, his sorcerers, and his honor guard. Most of the honor guard had fallen to Blackwand and to Kieron's greatsword (Aliera's actions in the battle were much discussed, although I hadn't actually seen much of her). I sat far away from the action, but eventually Virt found me. She had a brand-new scar on her face and a noticeable limp.

"Hey there," she said. "So you bugged out, huh?" She sounded more bantering than hostile.

"Yeah," I said. "I bugged out."

"I've heard about it. Probably not accurately, but I've heard. Good show."

"Thanks."

"And I've heard about Napper. We're going to have services for him this evening. Aelburr and I would like you to help us anoint him."

"What's the point? There's nothing left for Deathgate."

"I think you know what the point is."

I took a deep breath, then I nodded. "All right. I'll be there."

She moved on. A little later, Rascha came by. She said, "Good work, soldier."

"Thanks," I said.

"I also convey congratulations from Crown, and from the Captain."

"Thank them for me."

She started to say more, then snapped a salute and walked off. A little later Sethra walked by again. She said, "You should know that Cropper has recommended you for a Dragonshead Medal. I declined on your behalf, with thanks, but I thought you should know."

"Thanks," I said. "And thanks."

How did she know me so well? I suppose that's part of being a general, or maybe part of being Sethra Lavode. I knew that in a few days or weeks the idea of being recommended for a medal by a Dragon warrior would be pretty funny, but right now a ceremony would be nothing more than an irritation. They'd be giving out a lot of medals this evening, and I didn't have much interest in hanging around to watch, much less participating. I just wanted to go home.

I said, "Will Napper receive one?"

"Yes."

"Good."

She wandered away, and a little later Aliera came up and stood over me. I looked up at her, and then away. When she didn't speak, and the silence was becoming uncomfortable, I said, "I understand you did a lot of killing today. Congratulations. Did Morrolan get the weapon?"

"No."

I looked up. "No? What happened to it?"

"It was picked up by the officer at whose feet it landed when you threw it. She claimed it as battlefield spoil. Hard to argue with."

"Oh."

"Morrolan was wondering why you jumped in when you did."

"Fornia had a plan; I wished to stop it. Besides, I told him I'd get the damned thing."

"Wasn't Morrolan well on his way to stopping Fornia's plan anyway?"

"No, he was well on his way to helping Fornia carry it out."

"I don't understand."

"As Napper used to say, it don't matter."

"No? Well, maybe not. But tell me: Do you understand us a little better now than you did when you signed up?"

"No."

"I think you do," she said.

I didn't answer, and presently she walked away. At least she didn't salute.

Later that night I met up with Cropper Company and helped anoint the bodies for Deathgate. There were thirty-four dead, and many more in various stages of recovery. Dunn was among the dead, having fallen carrying the unit colors, just as he wanted. I had the awful feeling that some of the company were jealous of him. No one, of course, was jealous of Napper. And, pointlessly, Virt and Aelburr and I rubbed the oil onto him so his body would remain whole until he went over the Falls, where his body would eventually rot anyway. Then came the ceremonies for the dead, and the awarding of decorations, and then we were done, and back to our tents.

Virt and Aelburr and I sat around and watched the fire burn down. I said to Virt, "You got what you wanted, didn't you?"

"Yes," she said. "And so did you."

"Yes," I said. "I did."

"Was it worth it?"

"Yes. Just barely, but yes."

"That's how I feel."

"Sometimes winning is painful, but it's always better than losing."

"Hear, hear," said Aelburr.

The teleport blocks were down, and I could have returned to Adrilankha that night, but I told myself that I was in no mood to have my insides scrambled, so I spent one more night in the tent, and it was only the next morning, when confronted with salted kethna, bad coffee, and biscuits that I said good-bye to Virt and Aelburr, suggested they come visit me sometime, and teleported back to my own street, where I found a place that served decent food and I ordered klava, hot muffins, boiled goose eggs, and a thick slab of bacon, with onions.

I lingered over breakfast, then headed back home for a nap. I figured I'd earned a day off. Tomorrow I'd go back to making crime; it was so much kinder than war.

Epilogue: Trophies

When it was over, my dining room table was suitable for firewood, and the upholstery on two of my chairs was suitable for rags, but my favorite chair had escaped with only a slight nick in one leg, and my carpet had no blood on it. Sethra the Younger lay next to the window box, half conscious, her eyes rolling about in her head.

Morrolan, who had broken up the fight, much to Aliera's disgust, stood between them and addressed me: "You knew all along, didn't you?"

"Excuse me?"

"I mean, back during the battle. You knew."

"I only knew what Fornia had in mind, and I didn't find that out until the end."

"Why didn't you tell me?"

"My job was to get the weapon. I got it. I didn't much care who ended up with it."

"But you knew—"

"Yes, dammit, I knew. And now you know. There was a Great Weapon concealed inside that blade Fornia had taken from Baritt, just as you suspected. I assume it was Baritt who concealed it, and that he did it for reasons of his own. Fornia was able to find it, but didn't know how to release it from its concealment. His idea was that if it clashed with another Great Weapon, it would emerge. I tried it tonight. It worked."

"And Fornia," said Aliera before Morrolan could compose a response, "set up his battle so that he would cross blades with a Great

Weapon, either Blackwand or Iceflame. He could," she added reflectively, "have just challenged Morrolan to a duel and gotten the same result."

"He probably would have," said Morrolan reflectively. "But I launched a war, and he was never one to turn down a challenge like that."

The weapon in question lay on the floor midway between Aliera and where Sethra the Younger sprawled. All around it were pieces of the greatsword in which it had been hidden. With its concealment gone, it appeared as a dull, black short sword. No one touched it.

"You could say thank you," said Morrolan suddenly.

Aliera said, "For what?"

"For saving your life, cousin. Do you think you could have gone up against a Great Weapon?"

"Yes. Besides, Cawti was going to stick a knife in her back."

Morrolan looked at Cawti, who was leaning against the wall with her arms folded. She dimpled and dropped Morrolan a curtsy. I was surprised that Aliera had noticed. Aliera added, "And Loiosh was going to attack her, too, I think. She never really had a chance. If you hadn't butted in—"

"If Morrolan hadn't butted in," I said, "we wouldn't have discovered the Great Weapon, which I take to be—what did they call it, Morrolan?"

"It is called Pathfinder."

"Well named," said Aliera. "It found its way to me, eventually."

"To you?" said Morrolan.

Aliera stepped forward, bent over, and picked it up, transferring Kieron's greatsword to her left hand. "Yes," she said.

"And what do you suppose Sethra the Younger will say about that?"

Aliera unbuckled the sheath she wore on her back and tossed it onto the floor near Sethra. Then she put Kieron's sword next to it. "She'll say we have a bargain," said Aliera.

"You know, Vlad," said Morrolan, "I've suspected for years now that there were things you never told me about the Wall of Baritt's Tomb."

"There were things I didn't want to think about," I said. "Some of it I still don't want to think about, and some of it I still don't remember clearly. But you told me to get that sword—you didn't, by the way, tell me anything about how to go about it or what to do when I'd gotten it—so I went and got the sword. And—as I say, that's all I remember."

"That's all you remember, is it?"

"My memory sometimes plays tricks on me, Morrolan. Just a couple of days ago, I suddenly remembered a few things about our trip to Deathgate that I'd forgotten up until then. Maybe, someday, I'll remember more about this."

"You expect me to believe that?"

"You have to believe it; you're in my house. Next time I'm at Castle Black you can call me a liar if you want." His lips twitched. I added, "And with everything you knew but didn't tell me, you have no cause to come down on me about not telling you everything."

"Hmmm. I may concede on that point," he said. "I'll have to think about it."

"Do that," I said. "In the meantime, why don't you get your things, including that"—I pointed to Sethra the Younger—"and leave me alone. I'm sure she wants to go plan the invasion of the East, and Aliera wants to play with her new toy, and you, well, maybe you'll want to go start another war or something."

"Vlad—"

"Never mind, Morrolan. I just want to relax now."

"I'll send someone over to clean up the mess."

"No, I can get it. I'll see you . . . sometime."

He nodded.

They gathered up Sethra and headed for the door. Aliera carried Pathfinder. Morrolan started to say something at the door, then shrugged and walked out. What they did after that I neither know nor care about; the Wall of Baritt's Tomb was finally over for me, except for the final telling. And at the cost of a table and a couple of chairs I considered it a pretty good deal.

I sat down in my favorite chair, and, because the others were destroyed, Cawti sat in my lap. I leaned my head back and closed my eyes.

"That," I said, "is what the Dragons call negotiating."

"Mmmm," she said. "What now?"

"As I said, I'll clean the place up tomorrow. Eventually I have to go put this whole thing behind me by having a last session with an odd metal box, and then—what day is it?"

"Farmday."

"Right. Valabar's won't be too busy. Thinking about all those months of bad food has made me want something good, and I'm in just the mood to have someone else cook it and bring it to me and then wash the dishes."

"My treat," she said.

"Mine. I'm finishing a job and getting paid."

"All right. When are you going to go talk to the box?" She leaned her head on my shoulder. Her hair smelled of sandalwood and was very soft.

"Soon," I said. "But not instantly."

Loiosh flew over and landed on my shoulder. I didn't much want to move, but it would be good to have the whole thing finished. I opened my eyes and looked at the wreckage of my flat, thought back on my days in the army, and stroked Cawti's hair.

If just surviving can be counted as a win, I was way ahead of the game.

ISSOLA

This one is for Cynthia.

Acknowledgments

Thanks to Dave Shores, University of Minnesota Department of Chemical Engineering; and to all past and present members of W.I.N., whose help cannot be overstated; and, always, to Adrian Morgan, who started it all. For criticism, I am indebted to Teresa Nielsen Hayden, Pamela Dean, Will Shetterly, and Emma Bull. Special thanks on this one to John Robey. Thanks to Terry McGarry for great copyediting. Finally, thanks to Don Hill for showing me how to generate a bit of additional income while waiting for the book to finish itself, and to all those schlimazels who tried to run down my aces.

I've heard it said that manners are more complex in primitive societies—that it is easier to give accidental offense in, for example, the Island kingdoms of Elde or Greenaere, or among the Serioli, or the Jenoine, or the various kingdoms of my own Eastern people, than among the more civilized Dragaerans.

You must allow me to observe that it is invariably Dragaerans who point this out. One can imagine finding a Dragaeran who will not insist that the Empire has achieved the highest imaginable pinnacle of civilization; but then, one can imagine the Emperor presenting one with the Imperial Treasury, too, if one's imagination is active enough.

Yet even among the Seventeen Great Houses of the Empire, there are differences in what is considered proper behavior in various circumstances, and it is worth noting that, if you look hard enough, you will find that there are always very practical reasons for some phrase or action being considered polite or rude under certain circumstances. To pick an obvious example, among my own people, when arriving at the home of an acquaintance, one is expected to pound upon the door with one's fist, whereas among the Dragaerans, this is considered rude. I will not insult you by explaining why, in a culture rich in sorcery and steeped in paranoia, it is a bad idea to touch the door of someone's home. The practical has become a matter of courtesy.

In the Jhereg, the House to which I belong (and the criminal Organization for which I used to work), it is considered rude, when asking to meet with a superior or an equal, to arrive at the meeting first, whereas among the Dragons it is rude not to be first if you've done the inviting. The Dzur remain seated when greeting new arrivals to their tables at public or private houses; the Lyorn invariably rise. Except that the Dzur meeting the Lyorn might rise, knowing the Lyorn custom, whereas the Lyorn . . . well, you get the idea.

It is all very confusing.

As an Easterner, and, in several different ways, an outcast, I have had the opportunity to observe many of these customs and considerations of proper behavior, and so, on the assumption that you might one day have the chance to visit some of these fascinating and delightful people (okay, then, these irritating and obnoxious jerks), I herewith submit a small treatise on manners in the Dragaeran Empire. I hope you find it useful. But, in case I made an error somewhere, and you inadvertently commit a minor breach of etiquette, please, don't tell me about it; I have my own problems.

1

ADAPTING BEHAVIOR TO ENVIRONMENT

Just because they really are out to get you doesn't mean you aren't paranoid. If they've been after you long enough, paranoia can become a reflex.

Interesting things, reflexes: if you pay attention to them, you'll stand to learn some interesting things about yourself. This is one reason I avoid paying attention to my reflexes.

But sometimes I can't help it.

Let me pick an example at random:

I awoke almost instantly from a sound sleep to active stillness, and before reaching for a weapon, or dodging from a possible attack, or even opening my eyes, I reached out, mentally, psychically, for contact with my familiar. My mind to his, I said, *"What's going on, Loiosh?"* At that instant, all I knew was that something had happened to wake me up. I didn't even remember where I was, though one patch of ground in the wilderness is much like another, and that's where I'd been sleeping lately.

My first real clue that there might be a problem came when he didn't make any wisecracks. Instead there was a moment of mental silence, if you'll excuse the expression, and then Loiosh said, *"We may have been hunted down, Boss."*

"Well," I said. *"That wouldn't be good."*

Pretending to be calm to my familiar helps me to actually be calm. Loiosh accepts this as part of his job, and doesn't give me grief about it, much. In the meantime, without any conscious decision on my part, I was holding a neat, slim stiletto in my hand. Reflexes again.

I remained still, counting on Loiosh to tell me if and when I ought to move. While I waited, I contemplated my circumstances—in particular, the sharp, nasty stone that had insinuated itself onto the ground between my shoulder blades. I had a thick layer of darr skin between me and the ground, and a thin layer of chreotha fur between me and the sky.

"*Brigands, do you think, Loiosh?*"

"*Brigands come in bands, Boss. Whoever this is, there's only one of him.*"

"*So the Jhereg is more likely.*"

"*Or something else entirely.*"

I heard Rocza shift, caught the faint psychic whispers of Loiosh telling her to stay still. Just to fill you in on the basics, in case we haven't met before, Rocza is Loiosh's mate, which I'm sure must answer every question you have.

"*Coming closer, Boss.*"

"*Do I have a target, yet?*"

"*No.*"

"*Do you have any suggestions?*"

"*No. But I'm not worried, Boss. I'm sure you'll come up with a plan.*"

Reptiles are cold-blooded; a reptilian sense of humor will naturally display the same characteristics. This, in spite of being hunted and hounded by a massive and murderous criminal society that wants nothing less than the destruction of my soul, is probably the greatest burden I carry.

"All right," I said, ignoring his remark. "*Fly as silently as you can away from whoever it is, and circle around. As soon as you see—*"

I was interrupted by the ostentatious clearing of a throat, followed by someone saying, "I beg your pardon for disturbing you at such an hour, Lord Taltos, but I'm certain you must be awake by now, and I'm afraid if I come any closer you might do something I'd regret."

I sat up, the knife poised for throwing. "You can't be who you sound like," I said.

"I am, though."

"It's not polite to lie."

She laughed. "Nor to accuse a friend of lying."

"You can't be—"

"It is, Boss."

"Well," I said after a long moment. "I'll be skinned for a norska."

"Probably," said Loiosh. "But not by her."

I heard her come a little closer; Loiosh could now see her, but I can't see as well at night as he can.

"Don't feel bad, Boss. We can't all have adequate vision."

"At least both of my eyes face forward, scavenger."

"Mind if I make a light?" I said.

"Please do."

I stood up slowly, put my knife away, and found my firekit close at hand. I lit a candle and held it up and away so we would both be illuminated. There was, fortunately, little wind. I saw her standing before me, looking very beautiful and incredibly out of place. She gave me a courtesy, and I bowed in response.

"Lord Taltos," she said.

"Lady Teldra," I replied. "Welcome to the wilderness."

She looked around. "Yes. Well, shall I start, or should it wait until morning?"

"If it is urgent enough to track me down in the middle of nowhere in the middle of the night, can it wait until morning?"

"It can, Lord Taltos. My urgency was to find you before you moved on, thus making the search more difficult. Again, I apologize for disturbing you."

"Not to worry. Did you bring any blankets?"

"I . . ."

"I know how difficult this must be for you, Lady Teldra, and I can't wait to hear about what brought it all about, but, believe me, we'll both be better off if you let me handle things for tonight. I'd prefer it that way. Please."

"Very well."

"Did you bring any blankets?"

"No."

"Is anyone following you?"

"No."

"Are you—forgive me—are you certain?"

"Yes."

I studied her face. Lady Teldra was worried about something. She was worried enough about something that she had allowed it to appear on her features, and something was wrong enough for her to have deliberately woken me up. This was almost more startling than her sudden appearance in the forest between Appertown and Ridge.

Startling. Yes.

When one knows an Issola, such as Lady Teldra, one gets so used to the grace, elegance, and manners of the House that one forgets its other side. The issola is a beautiful white bird. I'd seen several during my recent travels. One usually saw them standing, graceful and lovely in the early morning or late evening, in swamps or the shallow banks of rivers. They stand as if their only reason for being were to look lovely and graceful. And then the issola would be holding a fish in its beak, and you'd never see it strike. And then the fish would be gone in a single swallow, and the issola would be standing on one leg, looking lovely and graceful.

Lady Teldra looked lovely and graceful. I felt plain and clumsy. On the other hand, now that the adrenaline was no longer coursing through my system I realized that I was still pretty tired.

"Let's sleep," I said. "You can share my furs, as long as you don't get forward with me."

"My lord—"

"I'm kidding. Climb in."

I blew out the candle. It had been a long time since I'd slept curled up with a warm body—it brought back memories that I'd been trying to suppress, and the fact that she wasn't human did little to help me forget. There had been a time when, every night, I had gone to sleep next to a woman I loved, and, even better, woken up with her. Those days were over and beyond recall, and allowing myself to dwell on them could take from me the edge I needed to stay alert and alive.

It took a while, but eventually I fell asleep, and when I woke up it was dawn, and she had climbed out of the furs and had a fire going.

"Have you klava?" she said, when she saw I was awake.

"Not even coffee," I said. "But we're within a few miles of a town."

"Really? I'd have thought you'd stay at an inn, then."

"Loiosh works better out here, and these days I'm thinking more about survival than comfort."

"I'm sorry," she said, and seemed to mean it. But, of course, she was an Issola: she would always seem to mean it. In the light of dawn, I saw that she was dressed in white and green, in a gown suited less to the wilderness than to her duties at Castle Black, home of the Lord Morrolan, where she'd welcome you into his home, serve you wine, and convincingly seem delighted to see you. For almost the first time in the years that I'd known her, I wondered: Just exactly what *were* her duties for Morrolan?

She looked an inquiry at me, then held out her hand. I nodded and Loiosh flew over to her, landing delicately. Her hand was stiff and slightly tilted, her elbow sharply bent: she knew the technique, though as far as I knew she'd never held a jhereg before. This failed to startle me.

"A pleasure to see you," she told my familiar.

He gracefully lowered his head until it was below the level of her hand, then raised it again.

"I believe," said Lady Teldra in an amused tone, "that I am being mocked." I heard Loiosh giggle inside my head. He turned around on her hand, launched himself, and returned to my right shoulder. Rocza, by now on my left shoulder, shifted and wriggled, which she often did in the morning. It probably meant something. There are many interesting facets to the character of the wild jhereg—poisonous reptilian scavengers of the jungle—but for some reason I got stubborn and decided not to learn about them. I imagine Teldra knew a lot about the wild issola.

"I'll bet you know a lot about the wild issola," I said.

"I know a bit about them," she said. "But, your pardon Lord Taltos, I should imagine that isn't the question foremost on your mind."

"No, foremost on my mind is breakfast. There's bread, cheese, and the remains of a dried and salted wild boar in my pack, as well some dried gammon and jerky in my pouch. Help yourself while I vanish for a moment and get myself a little cleaned up. There's a stream about a hundred feet this way, just over that rise."

"Thank you, my lord. I found it earlier."

I went off and did what was necessary and filled my water flask. When I returned Teldra had broken off several chunks of bread and, while they toasted on the rocks next to the fire, she was cutting up strips of cheese to lay across them.

"No questions before you eat?" she said.

"Exactly."

"I can respect that."

The bread started smelling good. When she put the cheese over it, and the boar, my mouth started watering. The cheese was a smokey honin; I usually prefer something sharper, but it went well with boar. We ate, and I passed the water flask over. I almost apologized for the lack of wine, but Teldra would have been mortified to hear me apologize, so I didn't. The food was good. As I ate, I fed bits to Loiosh, some of which he passed on to Rocza.

When I was done eating, I wrapped my furs and few possessions in their leather cords so I could leave in a hurry if I had to. As I did so, I said, "Let's have it, then."

"Where should I start, Lord Ta—"

"Vlad," I said. "I'm sorry, Teldra, but titles just don't work with the surroundings."

"Very well, Vlad. What would you like to know first? How I found you, or why I wanted to?"

"Start with how you found me; it might be more urgent. If you can find me, perhaps the Jhereg can find me."

"Not the way I did."

"Oh?"

She said, "Do you remember Morrolan's private tower, and the windows in it?"

I stared at her for some few moments, then said, "Oh. No, I don't suppose the Jhereg is very likely to find me that way. I don't think. Although the Left Hand—"

"Oh, that isn't the whole of it. By themselves, the windows could bring me here, but couldn't find you. I—"

"That's a relief."

"—had help."

"Of?"

"Well, Kiera the Thief, for one."

"Kiera. Yes." I did not believe Kiera would betray me, or do anything she knew would put me in danger without a very good reason.

"She knew more or less where you'd be—what part of the Empire, that is. She said you'd been nursing a sick boy back to health, and that he lived in this district, and that she expected you to be escorting him to his home by now."

"True enough."

"And then, once I knew the general area, I got more help. Sethra Lavode."

"Oh, her," I said. The most powerful sorceress and wizard in the world, yeah, well, I wasn't surprised she could find me. Especially because a year or so ago, when we had run into each other near Northport, she had said something about—"Loiosh?"

"Yes. She gave me a means of tracing him."

"*Well, is my face red.*"

"*Shut up.*"

"So," I said. "You had help from both Kiera and Sethra."

"Yes."

I watched her face, but if she knew anything, she betrayed nothing. Well, neither would I.

She said, "What happened to your hand?"

I looked at my maimed left hand, turned it over, and shrugged. "A sorcerer tried to eviscerate me from across a room, and either his aim was off, or I was too fast with Spellbreaker. Or not fast enough, depending on how you want to look at it."

"How did this come about, Vlad?"

I shook my head. "Later, Teldra. We're still hearing your story. For myself, I wouldn't care, but you know how curious Loiosh gets."

She flicked me her smile again; my familiar did not deign to make a rejoinder. Rocza, at that moment, flew off into the trees, probably thinking the breakfast scraps inadequate. Of the three of us, she seemed most happy to have spent the last few years away from cities.

"Shall I start now, or ought we to find Klava first?"

I'm not an Issola, but I can sometimes take a hint. "Sure," I said, standing up. "This way."

We hiked in silence at first; Teldra picking her way carefully, me just walking. I had, over the last few years, become something of a woodsman, albeit unwillingly. It seems that Teldra never had, and I allowed myself to enjoy a certain feeling of superiority.

"Kiera never explained what happened to the boy," said Teldra after a while.

"Not that much to tell," I said. "If I were just a bit more cynical,

I'd say it was a debt of honor. He was hurt in my service, so I tried to help him."

"And you succeeded?"

"The Justicers are debating that one. I think so, at least in part."

"Where is he now?"

"Back with his family, not far from here." I recalled his family's reaction to his return, and then their reaction to me, and refrained from giving Teldra any additional information.

We reached Appertown, with its post office, dry goods store, and inn. The latter, which boasted a faded sign that had once been red and seemed to have a chicken's head painted on it, was almost deserted, but the three Teckla occupying a table in the back quickly looked away from Teldra while trying to glance at me covertly. If I had been wearing my Jhereg colors, instead of the nondescript leather I now affected, they wouldn't have dared to look at me, either.

The hostess, a Teckla who was too thin to give me much confidence in the food, seemed a bit wary as she asked what we wanted.

"Klava, if you have any," I said.

"Klava?" she repeated as if she'd never heard the word before.

"If not," said Teldra, "we should be glad of coffee."

"We have a klava press somewhere," she said. "But—"

"You must have eggshells," I said. "Have you any vanilla bean?"

"Oh, I'm certain we have that. But I don't know how to make the filter."

"I do," I said. "If you'll allow me into your kitchen—"

"Vlad," said Teldra softly. "I think coffee would do, wouldn't it? As long as there is honey and cream."

"Very well," I said. The hostess sent Teldra a look full of gratitude and scuttled off for coffee. She brought back two mugs, along with a pitcher of thick cream and a jar of honey. Teldra gave her a smile that our hostess probably valued more than the money we'd leave with her later. Along with the coffee, she brought us each a sample of the house bread—a small, round loaf with a hole in the middle, cut horizontally and lightly toasted. I tried it.

"Not bad," I said. "This would be good with smoked pinkfish and buttercheese."

"And a bit of onion," agreed Teldra.

As I mixed the proper proportions of my coffee, Teldra said, "How *do* you brew klava?"

"You don't know?"

She smiled. "I can serve it with the best, but I've never needed to learn how to brew it."

"You press coffee through a filter made of eggshells and wood chips with vanilla bean, then reheat it so it almost boils, then you pass it through a cloth to remove any oils brought out by the reheating."

"Wood chips?"

"Hickory works well, also fegra, cherrywood, and crocra. It's the wood, or combination of woods, that makes each version unique. Well, and how much vanilla you use. Also, some people add cinnamon, but I don't; cinnamon is just as good if you add it later. Everyone has his own recipe. Valabar's does it best, but they do everything best. I miss Valabar's."

"Is that all you miss, Lord Taltos?"

The expression on her face made it seem like light banter rather than an intrusive question, so I said, "Maybe one or two other things. And, even though we are enclosed by four walls, I still consider this the wilderness."

She smiled. "Very well, Vlad."

I took another sip of coffee and missed Valabar's. This inn was a single-story building, stretching back quite a ways from the road, and built of molded brick with what had once been very nice woodwork around the windows; but now the wood was old, scratched up, and showing signs of dry rot. There was no actual bar, such as Adrilankha's inns always had, but just various tables with glasses and bottles sitting on them. We sat near the front door; two doors led back, no doubt to various sleeping rooms, and another went back to the kitchen. I always notice the entrances and exits when I'm in a new place, although there haven't been many times in my life when noticing actually did me any good. It's just one of those things you do, like warming up your muscles before and after fencing practice. I once asked my grandfather, who taught me fencing, how, were I ever jumped by brigands, I could convince them to wait while I warmed up. He just rolled his eyes and gave me a flank strike, which I parried, causing the tip of his weapon to whip past my guard and leave a nasty welt on my forearm. After that I made my questions more serious.

"Would you like to share your thoughts, Vlad?"

"Have you ever had a practice saber whip around the bell of your weapon and leave a welt on your arm?"

"Why, no, I can't say I have."

"Then you wouldn't understand."

She laughed. You never know if an Issola is laughing to be polite. I resolved not to try to be funny around her.

"How long do you think that will last, Boss?"

We finished our coffee at about the same time and called for more, which was brought with a cheer and alacrity that showed the hostess had fallen under Teldra's spell. No surprise there.

I said, "So Kiera told you how to find me, Sethra did the locating, and Morrolan let you go into his tower and use one of his Magical Mystical Powerful Transcendental Wizard Windows to get here. What I'd like to know—"

"Not exactly," said Teldra.

"Oh?"

"Morrolan didn't exactly let me use the window."

"Go on."

"Morrolan . . . that is, I didn't ask him."

"You didn't ask him."

"I couldn't. I didn't—that is, I don't know where he is."

"I see. I begin to see. I think I begin to see."

"Perhaps I should begin at the beginning."

"Arbitrary. But still, not a bad choice."

"Almost a minute, Boss. Good work."

"Shut up, Loiosh."

"Well, to begin with, then, the world was made when the gods created a ball of amorphia to hang—"

"Maybe we should let Loiosh make the jokes."

"But you're the only one who can hear him."

"Believe me, Teldra, that's a blessing for you."

She smiled. She had dimples. I tried to remember how many Dragaerans I'd met who had dimples. Plenty of humans did, but I didn't recall seeing many on Dragaerans.

"Early in the morning, four days ago," she said, "I received a message from Her Majesty, the Empress, asking Morrolan to extend his hospitality to a certain Lady Marquana, House of the Athyra, who would be in the area on Imperial business."

"What sort of Imperial business?"

"Does it matter?"

"Probably not, but asking questions makes me feel smarter."

She dimpled again. "In point of fact, Vlad, I don't know."

I shrugged. She continued, "I went to find Morrolan, and he wasn't in the library. I attempted psychic contact, and failed to reach him."

"Is that unusual?"

"Unprecedented."

"Really? He's never been busy?"

"If so, he has told me in advance. The only time I have been unable to reach him is when he has been, well, off the world."

"Off the world?"

She studied me. "You know something of those windows."

"Ah. Yes. And this didn't happen often?"

"Twice before, and both times he told me ahead of time he would be out of touch, and left instructions about what to do in case of trouble."

"What were those instructions, Teldra?"

"To reach Sethra Lavode."

"Not Aliera?"

"This was before Aliera had, uh, re-emerged. I agree that, now, Aliera would be the obvious person to speak with first."

"And so did you speak with Aliera?"

Teldra tilted her head and smiled suddenly. "Why do you remind me so much of an Imperial Inquisitor?"

"Damn," I said. "I was aiming for Third Floor Relic."

"Who?"

"Ah ha."

"Ah ha?"

"I've just proven that you're not Sethra Lavode. Did you speak with Aliera?"

"She's gone too," said Teldra.

"My goodness," I suggested. "Four days, you say?"

"Yes."

"No message, no word, no communication?"

"No message, no word, no communication."

"I see." I tried to wrap my head around the idea that something might have happened to Morrolan and Aliera. It was hard. They'd always struck me as, for all practical purposes, indestructible. But Teldra had sought me out in the wilderness, and that meant, however unimaginable it might be, something serious had happened.

I forced my mind back to business. "So when did you make contact with Sethra?"

"As best I remember, Your Equitableness, it was—"

" 'Your Equitableness'? Are the Justicers really addressed that way, Teldra?"

"I thought you'd know."

"I never had an advocate, so I've never heard the forms used."

"Oh. I believe that's the term."

"It sounds silly, doesn't it? Want more coffee?"

"Yes, please, Your Equitableness. If you don't mind my asking, why didn't you hire an advocate?"

"Having an advocate makes one look guilty."

"But the Orb—"

"The Orb is an awfully literal-minded thing, Teldra. They asked their questions, and I answered, and they looked at the Orb, and then they let me go. And, speaking of questions, I think I'd just asked one."

"Very well, Your Equitableness."

I sighed. "Okay, I get the point. I'll just let you tell it."

"After we get more coffee. If I were a Justicer, I'd require you to find a place that served klava."

I signaled the hostess for coffee, which was supplied with oppressive good cheer.

Presently, Teldra said, "Morrolan and Aliera were gone, and with no message. I tried for psychic contact with each of them, and failed. After a day, I spoke with various people in the Castle—Fentor, whom you know—"

"Yes."

"And Surill, whom I believe you have not met."

"Correct. Who is he?"

"She. She currently leads Morrolan's circle of witches." I had heard that Morrolan had such a circle, though he rarely spoke of them and I never asked. "They were unable to help, though Surill said she had tried to reach Morrolan through her own means as well. So I sent a messenger to Dzur Mountain, to Sethra Lavode."

"A messenger? Why?"

"To get her a message."

"But—"

"I don't know her well enough for direct contact, Vlad. Not everyone does, you know."

"Oh," I said, feeling sheepish.

"She sent a message back asking me to visit her at Dzur Mountain, so I did."

"Oh, yeah? How's the old place holding up?"

Teldra gave me a look. "We had a long talk. Sethra explained to me about Phoenix Stone, gold and black, and the blocking of psychic contact. She also, in my opinion, seemed worried."

"To paraphrase Seapur," I put in, "if Sethra's scared, then I'm scared."

"Yes," said Teldra. "Your name came up."

"How did that happen?"

"In connection with gold and black Phoenix Stone."

I fingered the cords I wore around my neck, which had a sample of each. "Yes," I said. Then, "What if they're already dead?"

"They aren't."

"Who told you that?"

"The Necromancer."

"Ah. Yes. Well. She'd know, wouldn't she?"

"Sethra believes you can help find them."

"Did she say how?"

"Not exactly. She mentioned something about Aliera's Great Weapon, Pathfinder, and some sort of link between it and some artifact you carry."

"Spellbreaker," I said.

"She didn't give it a name."

"That's the name," I said. "What does she want me to do?"

"Return with me to Dzur Mountain."

I drank some coffee.

"Boss, it isn't the same as returning to Adrilankha."

"*I know that, Loiosh.*"

"*If you'll be safe anywhere—*"

"*I know, Loiosh.*"

"*And if there's anyone you owe—*"

"*I know, Loiosh.*"

"Sethra thinks I can help?"

"She does."

"And she thinks Morrolan and Aliera might be in trouble?"

"She thinks it probable."

I considered a little longer. Teldra was courteously silent. Exactly why I had to consider, I don't know; certainly the idea of returning to any of my old haunts, when the Jhereg had a large price on my head, was scary; but there was never any doubt about how I would decide. I guess I just needed a few minutes to work it through my viscera.

I had just about decided when Teldra said, "Vlad, it would be wrong of me to put unfair pressure on you, but—"

"Oh, go ahead, Teldra. What is it?"

"Do you remember Sethra's servant?"

"Tukko. Yes."

"He knows how to brew klava."

"He does? Verra! What are we hanging around here for?"

"I'll pay the shot," she offered politely.

2

Being a Good Listener

This is, I suppose, as good a time as any to tell you a little bit about myself. I was born human in a world of Dragaerans, an outcast in their Empire, so I learned how to get paid for killing them. Small, weak, and short-lived by their standards, I learned how to seem larger, stronger, and to stay alive. I became a part of a vast criminal domain within the Empire; got married, had my marriage fall apart, and so angered the Organization that, as I said earlier, they were now avidly hunting for me.

That's enough for now; it's too depressing to dwell on. Besides, I didn't have much time to think about it, because soon we had walked beyond the edge of Appertown, and Teldra said, "If you would remove the Phoenix Stone, can you be teleported? That is, if it is still on your person?"

"Yes," I said. "I keep a small box with me that I can put them in. It's made of—never mind. As long as the stones are in the box, they have no effect."

"Then, if you please, do so."

I swallowed. I had no reason not to trust Teldra—I *did* trust Teldra. But it still wasn't easy to bring myself to remove the artifacts that had protected and hidden me for the last few years. While I was hesitating, she was standing, motionless, with the air of one who expected to be waiting for a long time and had no trouble doing so.

I removed the cord from around my neck and secreted it away. The instant I closed the box, I felt horribly vulnerable. The hairs stood up on the back of my neck, and I kept slipping into Loiosh's mind to see, through him, if I smelled anything suspicious in the area.

"*Relax, Boss. Even if they detect you instantly, they can't*—"

"*I know.*"

"I apologize," said Teldra, "for the discomfort of the teleport."

I didn't say anything. In fact, thanks to an amulet I had of my grandfather, there would be no discomfort; were I an Issola, I'd have told her. But then, were I an Issola, I wouldn't be in this situation.

Teldra closed her eyes. Her lips began to move soundlessly, which is something some people do when in psychic contact; presumably she was in touch with Sethra, but I couldn't ask without interrupting her, and that, of course, would be rude. Presently her eyes opened. She nodded to me, accompanying the nod with a gracious smile, and beckoned. I took a step closer to her; there was a moment of disorientation, and I stood in a place I had thought never to see again: the Grand Hall of Sethra's Keep high in Dzur Mountain.

I've heard it said, "By his home shall you know him," and we all know that we must pay attention to anyone who reverses the subject and the auxiliary verb in his sentence, so let me tell you a bit about the home of Sethra Lavode. A bit is all I can tell you, because I don't know Dzur Mountain all that well. For example, I can't tell you how far down into the mountain her dwelling extends. I've been told that the mountain is riddled with natural caves, caverns, and tunnels, and that some of these connect to the areas she has carved out for herself.

One of these was where I had first appeared, long ago, in the company of Morrolan. It had seemed then that I was deep in the heart of the mountain and had to climb a long stone stairway to its peak; I have since learned that I was close to the top, and that when I emerged in Sethra's living area we were hardly closer: Dzur Mountain is very, very big.

She had a library, but somehow I had never gotten around to inspecting it, so I can't tell you what she reads. On one side of the library are a few well if plainly furnished guest rooms, some of which I have used from time to time; on the other is a wide spiral stairway that leads up to the kitchen, or down to a hallway from which one can reach one of three dining rooms of various sizes, two of which I'd eaten in, and the third of which, the Grand Hall, I stood in now; a sitting room where I'd once insulted Sethra (an insult stopping just smoke's weight short of mortal); and two doors that go I know not where. At the end of the corridor is another spiral stairway: I don't know where this one leads to going down, or how it goes up, because it seems to me that it should lead directly up into the middle of the library, but there isn't a stairway there.

There is little decoration. It is as if, over the millennia, she had lost patience for anything that attempted to brighten what was naturally dark, ornament what was naturally plain, enliven what was naturally severe. There were no bright colors in Dzur Mountain, yet nothing was rough; rather everything was subdued but smooth, as if her home were a monument to the effects of time. Her furnishings were all simple and comfortable, with cushions on hard stone chairs and light provided mostly by simple oil lamps or candles. There was little to show her history; or, indeed, that she had a history—that is, her home was noticeably lacking in those oddities one picks up over the years as gifts from friends, or objects acquired from traveling, or trophies won from enemies. The one thing of that kind was in the library, where there was a device covered in glass, with spinning metal inside. I had asked her about it, but Sethra denied knowing what it actually was and refused to say how she had acquired it or why she valued it. Other than that, as I say, there was nothing to which one could point and say, "Sethra Lavode has this object because it means something to her."

I admit that I have, from time to time, speculated on why she had arranged her home like that, but I kept coming up against the same question: Were I somehow to achieve her age, how would I want to surround myself? And to this question I could not know the answer, which would always end the speculation, leaving me only observations.

And that about concludes what I know about the home of Sethra Lavode—not much, considering how often I've been there. I've heard a great deal more, of course, running from the probable to the preposterous: labyrinths deep within the mountain where she conducts monstrous experiments; high towers in the very peak where she communes with the dead; hidden passageways to the Halls of Judgment; concealed rooms full of treasure; and so on. But I don't know anything about these (except I can pretty well deny the passageway to the Halls of Judgment: if that really exists, she owes me an apology for sending me the hard way). Little is known, more is suspected, and much is guessed at.

And there you have Sethra Lavode as well, which ought to prove the point about reversing the subject and the auxiliary verb.

I didn't see Sethra at once, so I turned around, and there she was: tall, pale, undead; she had forgotten more of sorcery, even the forbidden sorcery of the ancient world, than anyone else would ever learn. She was a vampire, but it didn't seem to bother her much; and to those who told stories of her it was almost superfluous, like hearing that the guy who is going to cut your heart out plans to kick you in the shin when he's done. Her origin was in prehistory, and some had come to believe that she was the living personification of the world itself, that it would end when she ended. I doubted this myself: I mislike the idea of a living personification being undead.

Her features were those of a Dragonlord, except that, if one looked for it (as I did), one could see hints of the Dzurlord in the shape of her ears and her eyes. She dressed in black, black, black—the only hints of color upon her today were a red stone about her neck, a yellow stone on a ring on her right hand, and the blue hilt of Iceflame at her hip. She wore enigma as if it had been created for her alone.

Teldra bowed to her very deeply—more deeply than I had ever seen her bow before. Sethra acknowledged it as if it were her due. I nodded, Sethra nodded back.

"Sethra Lavode," I said. "It has been some time." Now, there was an ambiguous remark for her to play with if she cared to. She didn't. She held out her arm, and Loiosh flew to her, allowed his chin to be scratched, and then, just to show his high regard for her, he bent his head to allow her to scratch the scales that concealed his ears: a special mark of honor, because jhereg are very protective of their ears. I don't know if Sethra appreciated the honor. While she paid attention to Loiosh, I pulled the box from my pouch, opened it, and put the cord back around my neck. I felt better right away.

"Welcome to my home," said the Dark Lady of Dzur Mountain. "Please come with me."

"Always a pleasure," I said, and we followed her up to the sitting room, where she asked if we cared for wine.

"Klava," I said. "I was promised klava."

Sethra smiled. "And you?" she asked Teldra. "The same?"

"If you please."

Tukko emerged, shuffling, blinking, and twitching. "Klava," said Sethra Lavode.

Tukko did an imitation of a snake testing the air, gave a twitch that might have been a nod, and shuffled out again.

I watched him leave by a far door. "Just how old is he?" I asked.

"Younger than I am," said Sethra.

I nodded. "I just asked to give you another chance to be enigmatic."

"I know." She studied me. "You are looking well, Vlad."

"The outdoor life agrees with me," I said.

She went through the motions of smiling, and said, "And you, Lady Teldra. It is good of you to come, and I thank you for bringing our wandering Easterner with you."

"It was only my duty, Lady," said Teldra. "I must, in turn, thank you for your help, and your hospitality."

The mention of hospitality was Tukko's cue to emerge with a tray bearing two mugs of klava, a jar of honey, and a pot of thick cream. Teldra received hers with a smile of thanks; she took her klava as it came. I fiddled with mine until it looked right. It tasted right, too. I had missed it even more than I thought I had.

"The simple pleasures of civilization," I said. "I haven't tasted klava since Northport."

Sethra didn't bat an eye at the mention of Northport, even though—never mind. She said, "Perhaps we should turn our attention to business. Or would you rather wait until you've finished your drinks?"

"No, no," I said. "Drinking klava while talking business brings back all sorts of pleasant memories of happier days when I could sit around with like-minded fellows, contemplate my various affairs, and decide whose leg should be broken that morning."

Neither of them gave me the satisfaction of reacting, but Loiosh said, *"You're so sentimental, Boss, that I almost can't stand it,"* and flew back to my shoulder, evening up the weight. Rocza, by the way, had not moved the entire time. Presently, Tukko returned, this time with a tray full of some kind of raw dead thing, and set it down on the stone table in front of me. Loiosh and Rocza flew down and began nibbling. Neither Sethra nor Teldra jumped when they flew down.

This is significant because pretty much anyone will be startled by a winged thing suddenly flying right in front of him.

I noticed for the first time that Tukko's hands always seemed to shake, but when he was carrying a tray, the tray never shook. I wondered if his various ills were an act, and, if so, why?

"I thank you on behalf of my familiar," I said.

"You and they are most welcome," said Sethra.

I sipped more klava. Damn, but I had missed that stuff.

"Morrolan and Aliera are both alive," said Sethra abruptly. "Or, at least, they were alive yesterday. They have, therefore, achieved a state where we cannot communicate with them. That means they are either surrounded by gold Phoenix Stone, or they have left the confines of our world. And, until we know otherwise, we must assume they are being held against their will, and that must involve someone with a great deal of power—perhaps even a god, though I consider that unlikely. No, I fear what we are facing is rather more powerful than a god."

"Good," I said. "I wouldn't want it to be too easy."

"No, Vlad. Wrong response. You should say, 'How can I help?'"

I snorted. "If I say that, you're liable to tell me."

"There's that danger," she admitted.

"What do you think happened?"

"I have no idea."

"Don't lie to me, Sethra."

"Vlad!" said Sethra and Teldra together, in entirely different tones.

"Oh, stop it. Sethra, my whole lifetime has been less than the flap of a wing to you, but to me, I've known you for a long time. You wouldn't have sent for me without knowing something, or at least having a strong suspicion."

"Vlad—"

"No, Sethra. Don't even. Morrolan used to pull that stuff on me. Go, do this, but I'm not going to tell you any of the reasons behind it. My bosses in the Jhereg were experts at it: Kill this guy, you don't need to know what he did. I'm done with that sort of rubbish. Where are Morrolan and Aliera, why are they missing, and what is all the other stuff you aren't telling me?"

Lady Teldra opened her mouth, but I cut her off. "No," I said. "I won't go into it like this. I want to know."

"Do you, then?" said Sethra, almost whispering. There was something in her voice I had never heard before: something chilling, and powerful, and very dark. I was in the presence of the Enchantress of Dzur Mountain, and I was daring to question her. For one of the few times since I'd known her, I felt the power of legend bearing down on me; I sat there, silent, and took it; I could say nothing, but I didn't crumble, either. She said, "Do you really want to know, Vladimir Taltos, Easterner, Jhereg, and renegade?"

"Yes," I said, though it took considerable effort; and even more effort to keep my voice level.

"And if I don't tell you, what then? You'll leave Morrolan e'Drien and Aliera e'Kieron to their fate? Is that what you're telling me?"

I looked into her eyes, which I discovered I had been avoiding. They were black and went on far past forever; the focus on me was terrible. I controlled my breathing as if I were fencing, or reaching the climax of a spell. "Are you going to make this a test of wills, Sethra? Is that it? You will threaten to leave them to their fate if I won't help, or I must threaten if you won't answer my questions? Is that how you want to play this game?"

"I don't want to make it a game, Vladimir Taltos."

Looking into her eyes, I saw again Aliera's face as I returned to life after the Sword and the Dagger of the Jhereg had taken me down; and I saw Morrolan in his Great Hall defending me from the Sorceress in Green, and, I recalled faces, incidents, and conversations that I didn't want to remember. Then I cursed. "All right," I said. "If you push it, you'll win. You're right. I owe them both too much. If one of us needs to back down, I will—I'll go run your Verra-be-damned errand for you, like a two-orb street Orca hired to bust heads. But—"

"Then I'll answer your questions," said Sethra, and I shut my mouth before I made things worse. "I'll answer you," said Sethra, "because you're right, you deserve to know. But I will speak of matters I have no wish to reveal so, damn you, be grateful."

"I'll be grateful," I said.

Teldra stood abruptly. "I shall be in the library," she said, "in case you—"

"Please," said Sethra. "I wish you to stay."

"I . . . very well," said Lady Teldra, and sat down again.

Tukko emerged, and I realized that my klava had gotten cold. He replaced it, freshened Teldra's, and left.

"Where should I begin?" she mused. I held my tongue in check and waited.

"Perhaps," she said, "I should ask: Who are the gods? No, I've already taken a false step. That is not the question: Ask, rather, *What* are the gods? What freaks of chance, what hidden talents, what cataclysmic events combined to produce those whom your people worship, and mine strive to emulate? What are they, why are they, what do they do? Is their power acquired only because there are those who worship them? Is their power, in fact, imaginary? There are no simple answers to the question you have asked, because everything is tied to everything else."

I drank klava, and listened.

"Part of the answer to the question I have posed is this: The gods are beings who are able to manifest in at least two places at once, and yet who are not subject to the forcible control of any other being; this latter marking the difference between a god and a demon." That much, actually, I knew already, but I let her continue. "An interesting ability, and one that implies many others. The Jenoine, for all their talents and skills, cannot be in two places at once. Many of the gods, of course, can be in many, many places at once. I don't understand entirely how it works; I am neither god nor demon."

"I don't think I've ever met a demon," I said. "Unless a certain Jhereg who goes by that name means it more literally than I think he does."

"You have," said Sethra. "The Necromancer."

I stared. "She's a demon?"

"Yes. But I suggest you don't try to control her; she is liable to take it wrong."

"I'll take that advice to heart."

She nodded and continued. "As I say, this one skill implies many others. How did they acquire this skill? Some of the younger ones have been taught by some of the older ones; I was once offered godhood. But this still begs the question: Whence came the oldest of the gods, and how did they acquire their abilities?

"We must go back a long way, Vlad. A long way even to me.

Before the Empire, and even before the thirty-one tribes that became
the Empire."

"Wait. Thirty-one?"

"Yes."

"Uh . . . why thirty-one? I mean, is the number significant of anything?"

"Not as far as I know. It's just the number of tribes there happened to be then. And please don't interrupt; this is difficult enough."

"I'll try."

She nodded. "Your people came first, my good Easterner. I imagine that doesn't startle you, perhaps you guessed it, or were told something of the kind by Aliera, who indulges in much enlightened
speculation. Well, I tell you now what is no guess: Your people pre-
date mine. How they came here, I do not know, but I know they
arrived, they were not produced by Nature, as were the dragon, the
dzur, the jhereg, and the Serioli. Yet even these were changed by—
but no, all things in their proper time.

"Your people were here, though in what state I cannot say, and
the animals, and were found here by others, by those we call the
Jenoine. I don't know what they call themselves, and I don't know
where they're from, except that it isn't here. They came here, as your
people came here, only later."

Yes, I had known some of this before, too.

"There is so much we don't know, Vlad; that we can't know. I
have said nothing of what I saw, what I later learned, what I have
since deduced, because of all that I don't know. Were those who
came here representative of all Jenoine? Were their actions typical?
What were their motives when they arrived, and how did these motives change? Is the word 'motive,' as we understand it, even meaningful when discussing them?"

That was a rhetorical question if I'd ever heard one, so I didn't
answer it.

"You have met Verra, her you call the Demon Goddess. That
name—but never mind that now. She is of yet another species, and
was brought to this world as a servant of the Jenoine. She was there
when they began their experiments with the plants and the trees, and
then with the animals, and then with the people who came to be
called Easterners: changing some of them a little, some of them a

great deal, some of them not at all. Improving, in certain cases, upon them: extending their lifespans and the abilities of their minds, and making into them the people who came to be called Human. Yes, Vlad, our beings and even our languages come from your people, and you can take whatever pride in that you care to. Aliera, of course, refuses to believe it, but it is true."

I had a pleasant moment imagining taunting Aliera about that, but Sethra was still speaking.

"From what Verra has said, I would guess that they were, in their own minds, benevolent; but one must sift her words to discover this, for she hates them. She was their servant, and they were not kind to her. For that matter, she was not kind to them, either. Of this, I know only what hints she has dropped, and a few words from Barlen, her consort, but it is clear that it was Verra, and a few others, who sabotaged their work, who created the Great Sea of Amorphia, who unleashed upon the world that which we call sorcery, who themselves became the first of those we know as gods, and who destroyed all of the Jenoine who then lived on this world.

"I have lived through Adron's Disaster, in which those same powers were unleashed a second time upon the world, and the Lesser Sea was created. The Great Sea, in area, is seven times that of the Lesser Sea; I cannot, in my own mind, imagine the cataclysm of the moment when it came into being, that instant when for the first time the Unknowable took form."

This was something I didn't care to imagine.

"But," continued Sethra before I had to mentally go there, "the Unknowable is, by definition, formlessness: the totality of content, with nonexistence of form. What happens when the Unknowable takes form? One answer is, it ceases to be unknowable. As soon as there was a Sea of Amorphia, there had, sooner or later, to be a Goddess named Verra to codify and define the Elder Sorcery that could manipulate it; and a Serioli named Cly!ng Fr'ngtha that made the Elder Sorcery tangible by embodying it in objects blurring the distinction between animate and inanimate; and a Human"—she meant a Dragaeran—"named Zerika to craft an Orb that would make this power subject to any mind that could discipline itself to learn the patterns and codes by which the Orb translated the raw power of amorphia into the fingers that shape reality. Now the Unknowable is knowable again, and it is a power such as exists, so far as I know and so far as the Necromancer has been able to discover, nowhere else in the universe—in any universe, for there is more than one, as the Necromancer has demonstrated."

I had some trouble with this, but just sort of mentally stored it away for future consideration, and kept listening.

"So in our world, thanks to the gods, there exists this power, and, somewhere, are the Jenoine, filled with lust for the power, and hatred for those who destroyed their brethren—or so I believe we might think of their feelings and not be too far from the truth.

"Who is it, Vlad, who might protect us from this jealous and angry species, who see us all as the rebellious objects of science—as test subjects placed in a maze who not only escaped it, but killed the observers and now in their arrogance operate the maze as they please and will not let those who built it so much as observe? Who might protect us from the Jenoine?"

I guessed what the answer was going to be, and I was right, but I didn't interrupt.

"The gods," said Sethra. "Above all else, that is their task.

"The place we call the Paths of the Dead sits, as I think you know better than most, both in and out of our world, and at its heart is the place we call the Halls of Judgment, because our legends tell us that this is where we go upon death to have our lives judged. And, as far as it goes, this is the truth. I know how your mind works by now, Vlad, and I see the glimmer of understanding in your eyes; I suspect that you begin to glimpse the true purpose of the Halls of Judgment."

I swallowed. She was right, I was getting a glimmering.

"Yes," she said. "It is there that the gods sift souls as a Serioli sifts for gold in a mountain stream. The gods search for those who can be useful to them in their long war. It is in the Halls of Judgment that they sometimes glimpse pieces of what to us is the future, and try to interpret these glimpses, and prepare to meet each threat as it develops. And as they sit those who are considered worthy are brought to them, upon death, for this reason. It is a way of building the forces to protect their world."

"Their world?" I said, catching significance in that.

She nodded. "Yes. Their world, not ours."

"I see."

"Yes. As they review the dead, some they have no use for; these are allowed to reincarnate, or are taken to be servants in the Paths of the Dead—those who wear the Purple Robes. Others have skills that might someday be useful, and those are held in the Paths of the Dead against that use, or reincarnated into circumstances where their skills can develop. A few study for the Godhood themselves, and a tiny number are sent out once more, as Undead, because their usefulness in the world has not expired with their lives. I became one of these latter some years ago."

I nodded. "Okay, I think I'm starting to get it."

"Yes? But here is where it starts becoming complicated."

I rolled my eyes.

"Stop it," she said. "That expression is not your most endearing. Listen and try to understand."

I sighed. "All right."

She nodded. "I have told you about the gods and the Jenoine, but there are other factors, and chief of these are the Serioli. You have never met one, but— You have? I didn't know or have forgotten. But I am sure you know little about them. I know little about them, though I have had more to do with them than any other human being in the world.

"The Serioli are native to the world, which neither your people nor mine are. In some measure, perhaps they resent us both, though most of them recognize that we are not responsible for what has been done to us. But above all, they resent the gods, because the gods, in a very real way, rule the world. The Serioli did not evolve as a people to be ruled—who would so evolve?

"It was the gods who sent the dreams that inspired Kieron the Conqueror to gather the tribes and move east, and the visions that led Zerika to create the Orb; thus it was the gods who created the Empire that drove the Serioli from their homes, that destroyed much of their culture, killed many of them in battles. They—and while it is hard to speak of a whole people as if they had a single voice, here I think I am not too wrong—they hate the gods. This does not always make them friends of the Jenoine, but it does make them the enemies of the gods. Do you see?"

"I think so," I said slowly.

"And some of the Serioli believe that an enemy of their enemy must be their friend."

I nodded.

"The gods," she continued, "are forever seeking ways to seal our world, so the Jenoine cannot reach us. And factions among the Serioli keep searching for ways to allow the Jenoine access. And into this conflict come those Serioli who, years ago, crafted those half-living, half-inanimate artifacts called the Great Weapons, each of which is, in one way or another, obviously or not, directed against the gods."

I blinked. "The Great Weapons are—but that doesn't make any sense. Why—? Okay, never mind. Keep going."

"I never said it would be simple."

"Yeah."

"Where was I? Ah, yes: the Great Weapons. Jenoine are very hard to kill, Vlad. We know of no poison that works on them, their internal organs are duplicated; they have no spine to sever, and they have an almost perfect natural immunity to the disruptive effects of amorphia. They regenerate when injured, and I have seen them, on more than one occasion, resist even powerful Morganti weapons, as if their very souls are hidden away from their bodies. But this cannot be, because the Great Weapons can kill Jenoine. The Great Weapons are the only reliable way to kill Jenoine—if you can survive long enough to find a way to strike, and if you don't miss and if they fail to defend against it.

"Do you see the contradiction, Vlad? Do you see the irony?"

"Yeah, I'm always good with irony."

"I know. You always have been, even in the days before the Empire I remember that about you."

"I . . . okay."

"Do you see it?"

I nodded. "The Great Weapons were created to destroy the gods, but now they're being used to defend the gods. Cute."

"Yes. We who carry the Great Weapons are the appointed of the gods—even those of us who, like Zungaron—"

"Who?"

"Never mind. Even those of us who have one only by accident and have not the least clue what it is for, or what to do with it. If we defy the gods, by intention or accident, we are likely to find life difficult. And yet, we are the only humans whom the gods have reason to fear, and to hate."

I blinked. "I've never envied you, Sethra. Now I envy you even less."

She smiled. "The result," she said, "is that we must look out for each other—the reasons for that should be obvious."

I nodded.

"The gods hate our weapons and need us who wield them; the Jenoine fear our weapons and hate the gods. Do you understand?"

I nodded again.

"Think back to your own past, Vlad: I know what Aliera told you about your past lives, so consider her words now. Millennia ago, back in the days when we were creating an Empire, though only Zerika knew that we were doing so, the seeds of all of this were planted. Consider those you know of who were once your family, and those who mattered to you in a time too faded in the mist for you to imagine, much less remember. Kieron is gone now, and remains in the Paths of the Dead awaiting his moment. I, who had some importance in the tribe, am here, watching the Great Weapons, observing the Jenoine, listening to the gods, and trying to see that nothing upsets the balance.

"I think we were all, even then, marked out by the gods. I can't say I like it much, or that you should, but there it is. Now Aliera has been taken, and Morrolan as well. Who could and would take them both?

"A human agency? I wonder if there is anyone who could take two such as Aliera and Morrolan, and hide them from me. But, even if such a person exists, he could not hide them from the Necromancer. If there was a human involvement, then, it was in the service of someone more powerful.

"The gods? An unlikely possibility, but one that cannot be overlooked. I did not overlook it; I have ways of finding out such things, I used them, and I believe the gods have nothing to do with this; indeed, some of them are rather concerned by it. Perhaps a rogue god, and this could still be true, but such a one would have trouble hiding from Trout, who knows the motives of the gods. No, I do not believe it was any of the gods.

"A demon? No, the demons have their own lives, and no concern for our world, except when they are summoned; and that only begs the question of who did the summoning and why?

"The Serioli? I doubt it, because I have never heard of their doing anything of the kind, but I hope it is the Serioli, because if it is not them, then it is the Jenoine. The Jenoine, who wish the weapons to be used against the gods—which, after all, is what they were designed for.

"I know you, Vlad: you are uncomfortable with things like causes and reasons, however much you ask for them. And however much you protest, you are and always have been happiest when you had a single task you could accomplish, without worrying about the whys and the consequences. Well, but you asked, and so I answer. Our friends are in danger. And it may be that much else is in danger as well; until we know more, it is impossible to say for certain if this is part of a move against the Empire, but we certainly must be aware of the possibility. You may be able to help ward off a threat to the Empire, you may have the means of helping those who are your friends and mine; it seems to me that you certainly have a duty to try, and I would have told you nothing except that, but you wanted the whole story. The whole story would have taken longer to tell than you expect to live, Easterner, but at least I gave you a piece of it. I hope you're happy."

3

DROPPING IN UNEXPECTEDLY

Once again I had allowed my klava to get cold; once again Tukko appeared and brought me more.

All right, so the Jenoine had taken short, cocky Aliera, and tall, arrogant Morrolan, her cousin. I confess that a little part of me was pleased that someone had shown them they weren't as ultimately tough as they acted. But other parts of me couldn't forget that, well, that we'd all saved each other's lives more than once, and that they had both been kind to me when they had no good reason to, and that, however irritating I might find them, we had a lot of history among the three of us, and, though it hurt to admit it, even some affection.

I spent a moment reliving memories that I won't share with you. Preparing and drinking the klava brought me back, at least to the point where I was able to speak. "Of course I'll do what I can, but saving the world just isn't my style, Sethra. I specialize in smaller things: breaking legs, collecting debts, knocking off the occasional squealer. You know, small stuff."

Neither she nor Teldra replied. At length I said, "Okay. What do you need me to do?"

"There is a procedure," she said, "that I believe might work. You must be the one to do it, however."

"Uh . . . if I ask why me, will I get an answer lasting less than an hour?"

"Because you have the chain you call Spellbreaker."

"I see. Well, actually, I don't."

"Use Spellbreaker to make contact with Blackwand, then follow the link through one of Morrolan's windows."

"That's it?" I said.

"That's it. Your artifact should be able to connect to the Great Weapon, even across necromantic boundaries, because Blackwand should always be able to sense, at some level, what is happening in those windows. Or so I think. It will either work, or it won't."

"Yeah, I imagine those are the options. The question is, what then? I mean, if it works, what do I do?"

"Improvise."

"Improvise?"

"How can I say what to do, when I don't know where you are going, or what you will find there?"

"You know I don't care much for improvising."

"I know. But you are good at it."

"Thank you so much."

"And you don't rely on sorcery; you have other abilities."

"Great. Once I open up the way, if it works, and I get there, if I do, will I have any help?"

"What about me, Boss?"

"Shut up, Loiosh."

"No," said Sethra. "There will be none to give you."

"I see. I just go in, and improvise. While I'm improvising, what will you be doing?"

"Waiting."

"Can you, I don't know, keep an eye on me? Maybe yank me back if I get in over my head?"

"I don't know how. If I can't reach them where they are, I don't know how I'd be able to watch you there."

"Uh . . . magic?"

"If sorcery worked there, I don't think we'd be having this problem, and I can't think what other magic we might use. Unlike you, I'm not a witch."

"If you'd asked, I could have taught you. But you're saying that witchcraft will still function?"

"It should; that's one reason I wanted you for this."

"Witchcraft is not usually useful—"

"Have you forgotten the Paths of the Dead, Vlad?"

"I've tried to." I had visited the place where the dead hang around like old Dragonlords with no battles to fight except the ones they've already lost, and, even though I was living at the time, I just didn't enjoy the experience enough to dwell on the memory.

She didn't answer. I said, "How about the Necromancer?"

She cocked her head to the side. "That *is* a thought, Vlad. And not a bad one at that."

"See what a good vacation will do for the creative powers?"

"I'll speak to her."

I ran it through my mind. "Sethra, do you understand what you're asking me to do?"

"Yes."

Yes, of course she did. She was, to begin with, a Dragon; moreover she had led armies. She had no problem ordering people off to get killed—it was a way of life for her.

"Before I go jumping into this, tell me one thing: Do you have any reason to believe I might get out of this alive?"

"Oh, yes, certainly," she said. "I have a high regard for your skills."

"Ah. My skills. Well, that's reassuring."

"Don't underestimate yourself, Vlad."

Anything else I said would sound self-pitying, so I shut up; but Teldra said, "I will go along."

Sethra and I looked at her. She had said it as if she were announcing the wine she intended to serve with dinner.

"Teldra," said Sethra at last. "I am not certain you are qualified for this mission."

"Perhaps I am not," she said. "But I am not quite as helpless as you, perhaps, believe I am."

"Nevertheless," said Sethra. "This is the kind of activity that Vlad is trained for"—this, by the way, was news to me—"and you are not."

"Are you certain of that, Lady?" said Teldra. "I speak not of Vlad's training, but perhaps with what lies before us, my talents would not be useless."

"I see," said Sethra slowly, considering her words. Sethra had obviously picked up some meaning that had escaped me entirely. "Yes, you may be right after all."

I said, "Sethra, would you mind explaining this to me? I think I'm missing something."

"Yes, I believe you are," said Sethra.

"It is difficult to explain," said Teldra. "But, if you wish—"

"I'm changing my mind about explanations," I said. "Just tell me if I need to know."

"You don't need to know," said Sethra.

Teldra said, "And then?"

"Yes, you ought to go along."

"Then let us begin at once," she said.

"No," I said.

"Is there a reason to wait, Vlad, or is it that you need time to gather your nerve."

"No, my nerve is far too scattered for mere time to gather it. But if I'm going to go off and get killed I'm going to finish my Verra-be-damned klava first. Now please give me some peace to enjoy it."

Sethra smiled. "Do you know, Vlad, whatever happens to you, you do certainly remain yourself."

"That's good. I haven't had as much practice being me as you have being you. But does that mean I get to finish my klava?"

"By all means," said Sethra. "While you do so, I'll attempt to reach the Necromancer."

Sethra's face went blank and I stopped watching her, because it is rude to watch the face of someone having a psychic conversation with another, and it was hard for me to be rude while Lady Teldra was sitting there. I drank klava. It really was very good.

"The Necromancer," said Sethra presently, "will be there, and will attempt to monitor the proceedings, but she cannot guarantee her success."

I grunted and drank the rest of my klava. I enjoyed it. I remain grateful that they permitted it. Sethra still seemed to be amused. I could not, of course, guess what Teldra was thinking.

"Okay," I said at last. "I'm done. Let's go get killed. Is everybody ready?"

Sethra shrugged. "For now, I have nothing to do."

"The teleport," I said. "I'm a little out of practice."

"Very well, I think I can manage that."

I hid the two specimens of Phoenix Stone, one gold and one

black, in their box, and once more I felt naked, but I was too frightened by the idea of the Jenoine to let a little thing like the Jhereg worry me unduly. Isn't it funny how the tiniest change in circumstances can alter all of your priorities?

"*Ready, Loiosh?*"

"*Oh, sure, Boss. Couldn't be better.*"

"Ready," I told Sethra. Teldra stood next to me, and Sethra, without, so far as I could tell, so much as furrowing her brow, caused the sitting room to vanish, and the courtyard of Castle Black to appear around me.

I felt like saying hello to it; I had a lot of memories tied up in that place, and not all of them were even bad. It was big, and it was a castle, and it was made all of black marble shot through with veins of silver, and it floated a mile or so in the air, and no one except me thought there was anything strange about that.

I guess you could say similar things about Morrolan, if you wanted to return to an earlier theme. I replaced the cord about my neck.

"I propose," I said, "that we head straight up the Tower and do this, or at least attempt it, because I don't want to give myself time to think about it."

"Very well," said Teldra.

The familiar doors opened to us as we approached them. I said, "Are you not frightened at all?"

"Would you rather I were, Vlad?"

"Good question. I'm not sure."

In and up and around and about; and add a few more prepositions to the mix, and eventually we were climbing the narrow metal staircase up to Morrolan's Tower. I'd been there before. It was not one of the places I missed.

"There ought to be a guardian here," I said.

"Pardon?"

"We shouldn't be able to just walk up and do this. We ought to have to fight our way past some sort of legendary half-man half-monster that has guarded this place since the beginning of time, and cannot be harmed by any weapon, nor moved by any words, nor evaded by any motion."

"I see," said Teldra. "Why?"

"I don't know. A warm-up for the rough stuff."

"Do irony and grey laughter help ease your fears?"

"Yes."

She nodded. "Was that a rude question on my part?"

"I'm not sure. I'll get back to you on that."

I pushed open the door over my head. It fell over with a boom and I caught the faint odor of formaldehyde, which I hadn't remembered from before. I climbed up and looked around. From my previous experience, I knew better than to count the number of windows; besides, all of them except one were covered up. The view out the open one was of a deep purple with pinpoints of light dotting it here and there; it reminded me a bit of the sky in the East. It actually took me a moment to realize that the Necromancer was already there, standing very still against the curtain between two of the windows. Teldra came up behind me and carefully shut the trapdoor.

"Vlad," said the Necromancer. "It is a pleasure to see you again."

I didn't know how to respond to her; I have never known how to respond to her. In some ways, she was more enigmatic even than Sethra Lavode. She looked creepy; I imagine on purpose. She was thin, even for a Dragaeran, and dressed entirely in dull black, without even silver buttons, and she was very, very pale, and she was an expert in what I think of as death, but, from what I've picked up of her conversation, she sees as something entirely different; to her "place" doesn't mean the same thing as it means to me, nor does "life" or "the soul." What to the Athyra are issues of epistemology and ontology are to her matters of engineering. I made a fervent wish that I would never arrive in a circumstance where "place" and "life" and "the soul" became matters of engineering.

It is wishes like that that get you in trouble.

How in blazes had I gotten myself mixed up with weirdos like this in the first place?

"Your natural charm, Boss."

"Shut up, Loiosh."

Once again, I removed the cord from around my neck, and put away the Phoenix Stones. This time, I remember feeling nothing in particular as I did so. I allowed Spellbreaker, a gold chain of small links, just less than two feet in length, to fall into my left hand from where it was coiled around my wrist. I looked at it. It was made of the same substance as the gold Phoenix Stone I had just put away, but it was different. Things had been done to it. Someone, some Serioli smith, I believe, had worked it, shaped it, and made it into something very special—exactly what, I had only gotten hints of over the years, like the Serioli who, when I asked if it was a Great Weapon, said, "Not yet." Heh.

This time, the links of the chain were very small; perhaps a quarter of an inch long, which meant that there were more of them than on other occasions, when the chain had been, say, fourteen inches long and each link had measured an inch and a half. For some reason, I found the idea that the number of links changed to be more disconcerting than that the overall length of the chain would vary.

I turned my eyes to the window, then back to the chain. In my mind, I drew a picture of Blackwand, Morrolan's weapon. Or, rather, I tried to draw a picture of Blackwand; but it kept sliding away from me.

"Help, Loiosh."

"I'm there, Boss."

I pictured it in its sheath, though I had seen the damned thing naked. About five feet in length, it was: a longsword, as some called it, the hilt smooth and black, the guard a simple crosspiece, gleaming like silver; on top of the hilt a piece of smooth, glistening black stone, that stone called Verra's Tears, which was obsidian that had been smoothed away by Black Water. The scabbard I had seen Morrolan use most recently—he had several—was very plain, and seemed to be leather, although there had to be more to it than that. It was an old sheath, and there were a few threads coming loose at the seams, and a slight tear in the leather near the very top.

With Loiosh's help, the picture became clear, then very clear, then clear enough that I became frightened, then Lady Teldra was next to me in response to something I said, then there was a motion from around my shoulder, then I sent Spellbreaker out into the window in front of me.

And it all worked, just like Sethra Lavode had said it would.

Shame about that.

The window blurred and shifted, filled with lights, and darkness, and indistinct shapes. Herds of animals I didn't recognize grazed upon green fields beneath a sky that was a peculiar grey; strange appendages like fingers worked upon a small metallic object, striking it with a tool; a mountain peak appeared below me, stark against a sky that was black, black, black; there was an ocean of green, waves that seemed huge and that crashed against the window but didn't pass through; a young girl who may have been human or Dragaeran and who I might or might not have recognized made impossible eye contact with me; an athyra-like bird screeched horribly and fell along a wooded path, then vanished into nothing as it landed; violet sparks came from a wheel that spun at incredible speeds, though to no purpose I could imagine; a man with a pen made odd scratches on a long roll of parchment; deep under water, a strange creature with scales all of green and yellow worked upon a piece of red fabric, embroidering it with a thin silver needle and blue thread. And all of this with no trace of sound—that, perhaps, the most peculiar thing of all.

Now the window shows darkness pierced by flickerings of light as of a storm, the source of the light beyond the scope of my vision, but in those flickerings I see Blackwand, itself, only barely more real than in my vision, until suddenly I realize that, though it is concealed in its sheath, and that sheath attached to a familiar figure, I *feel* Blackwand; and that tiny portion of my brain which remains free to have opinions and feelings regrets that we have been successful.

Teldra and I, in perfect unison, following Spellbreaker, took one step forward through the window. There was no sense of disorientation, the way there is when teleporting, nor was there the delay. In a way, I think this made it worse—the changes were sharper than any I had known before, and it was lucky that I didn't have to defend myself at once. The first thing I noticed was that I felt heavier—perhaps the result of a general protection spell against anyone who doesn't belong, or it might also be some natural property of the place. The air smelled funny, sort of sweet, with a queer kind of tang in it. There were no sounds; what had seemed to be a flickering light was some sort of dim lamp, forty or fifty feet away, that was hanging from the ceiling and swaying back and forth, and it was in this light that I saw Morrolan and Aliera, which was the second thing that struck me; but the first demanded my immediate attention.

"*Loiosh, where is Rocza?*" I was, to be honest, surprised at the sinking fear I felt in the pit of my stomach.

"*I had her stay behind. I didn't want to worry about her.*"

I was equally surprised by the relief that flooded through me. *"You could have told me."*

"It was a last-minute decision."

I turned my attention to the Dragonlords we had come to rescue. They were both sitting on the floor against a stone wall, with what seemed to be iron manacles on their wrists, and they were both awake. Both had their weapons with them.

Morrolan cleared his throat and said, "Welcome. I find myself filled with the desire to say something like, 'What took you so long, Vlad,' but I fear that you, Lady Teldra, might take it wrong, so I will refrain."

"Damned decent of you," I said.

"Hello, Vlad," said Aliera. "I wondered who she would send into this trap."

"It's a trap?" I said. "Why, now, that's hard to believe."

Morrolan snorted.

I said, "How did they come to leave you your weapons?"

"Do you imagine," said Aliera, "that they would be willing to touch them, or even come near them?"

"I see. So you have your weapons, but are unable to move."

"Well, you probably noticed that you have no link to the Orb."

"Uh," I said, because, in fact, in all the disorientation, that little fact had escaped me. "Let's see if we can get you out of those things."

"Good luck," said Aliera.

"Oh?"

I inspected them. There was a fair bit of slack—enough to reach the plain, white ceramic chamber pots a few paces from the wall (the contents of which I didn't bother to inspect), but not much more. The chain was thick, and seemingly of some material a lot like iron, but smoother, and—

"There's no lock. They don't open."

"Noticed that right away, did you?" said Aliera.

"Bugger," I suggested. "How did they get them on you in the first place?"

"I don't know," said Morrolan.

I looked at them. "Well, so here you are, unable to move, to escape, or to act in any way. Good. There are a number of things I've wanted to say to you both over the years."

"Funny, Vlad," said Morrolan.

"*I thought it was funny, Boss.*"

Teldra said, "Do you think our arrival here has been detected?"

"I have no way of knowing," said Morrolan.

"I'd have to assume so," said Aliera.

"Well," I said. "That ought to make things more interesting. Does anyone have a suggestion for getting you two out of those manacles?"

"You should have brought Kiera," said Aliera.

"Yeah," I said. "Right. What could I have been thinking of to have forgotten to have a Kiera in my pocket?"

I knelt down next to Morrolan and studied the manacles. They were completely smooth, as if they had been created, fully formed, around his wrists out of some material I had never encountered before; something very hard, dull grey, and at least as strong as iron.

"How did you get here?" said Aliera.

"The windows in my tower," said Morrolan. "He used Spell-breaker to find Pathfinder."

"Blackwand, actually, but yes."

"So is the window still open?"

I said, "No," at the same time Morrolan said, "Yes."

I said, "Uh, I defer to your expertise."

"Yes it is," said Morrolan, "but I know of no way to reach it without using powers to which I have no access from here, so it may as well not be."

Aliera said, "Have the Jenoine access to such powers?"

"Excuse me?" said Morrolan.

"Can they use your window to reach our world?"

Very softly, under his breath, Morrolan cursed. "I hadn't thought of that," he said.

"I should imagine," I said, "that Sethra didn't, either."

Morrolan and Aliera were cousins, both of the House of the Dragon. Morrolan was the sort of fellow who would restyle his hair every week or so, and take great care of his nails; and in his youth, had put entire villages to the sword when the mood took him. Aliera was short for a Dragaeran (still taller than me, of course), compact, brilliant, and more fond of a good duel than of any other entertainment you cared to name. They were both better sorcerers than I'll ever live to be, though a bit overshadowed by their association with Sethra Lavode; but that only meant they were often underestimated.

They both carried Great Weapons; these were rarely underestimated.

Morrolan didn't hate Easterners as much as you'd expect; Aliera didn't hate me as much as you'd expect. Exactly how I got mixed up with these two is a long story, and probably not worth repeating, but, over the years, it is possible my association with them had done me more good than harm—at least up until now.

I studied where the chains from Morrolan's manacles joined the wall, and there was nothing there to work on—it was as if the chains were built in when the wall was first constructed. The wall itself seemed to be made of stone, except there were no stones in it, just one solid piece, as if someone had carved it out of a mountain. Well, why not? Sethra did something like that. Of course, her walls weren't so smooth as this.

"They don't seem to be in a hurry," I said.

"We can assume," said Aliera, "until proven otherwise, that they are watching and listening, and, since they know they have us all trapped, they have no need to be in a hurry, and by listening might get useful information from us."

"Such as the fact that they can use the window to reach our world," said Morrolan, "which we were just kind enough to tell them."

"And you are even now repeating, in case they missed it before."

"As if—"

"Oh, cut it out," I said.

I flipped two fingers to the world in general, just in case they were watching and the gesture was universal, then noticed for the first time that there didn't seem to be any doors in the room.

I took some time to look around the room a little more, feeling all eyes on me, but seeing no need to explain myself. The room was about two hundred feet by a hundred and fifty feet, and empty save for several tall metal objects that looked a bit like bookshelves, but were devoid of books. Most likely, this was some sort of storage room. And, as far as I could see, there was no way into or out of it. A good way to keep your property from being stolen. I'd have to remember that, in case I ever again had property to protect and the opportunity to protect it.

"There aren't any doors," I remarked.

Aliera and Morrolan gave me a look as if I'd just announced that knives were sometimes sharp. Teldra nodded solemnly, but I think she'd already noticed.

I thought about communicating with them psychically, but without the Orb it's damned difficult, not to mention exhausting.

Morrolan closed his eyes for a moment, then touched the hilt of Blackwand. "No one is listening to us," he said aloud.

Aliera's head whipped around, and she stared at him. "How can you know that?"

"Blackwand is not without power, cousin. Nor, for that matter, am I."

Aliera looked dubious, but didn't say anything more.

"Hey, Boss, do you think the Necromancer has been able to maintain contact?"

"I'd give whole worlds to know, Loiosh."

Aloud I said, "Why don't you guys tell me what happened?"

They both started speaking at once, which I ought to have predicted; then they glared at each other. Finally, Aliera nodded toward Morrolan, who shrugged and said, "I don't know. I was in the library, and then I was here, being used to ornament this wall."

"I," said Aliera, "was in my bedchamber." She said this as if being snatched from the library ought to give Morrolan no cause for complaint.

"You have no idea how it happened?"

"None," said Aliera. "I was there, then I was here, manacled. I had no sensation of time passing, or that I had lost consciousness, although that proves nothing. On the other hand, Pathfinder has no sensation of time passing, and that, I believe, does prove something."

"Blackwand and I had the same experience," he said. "Which I hope means that they have the ability to transport us, instantly, off our world and into manacles chained to a wall; because if not, it means they have the ability to interfere with a Great Weapon, and then I should be worried."

I chewed that over, then asked Morrolan, "You had no indication that, I don't know, your security system had been breached?"

"No," he said.

"Is this something they've been able to do any time, and just decided to now? Or do they have something new?"

"I've been wondering the same thing," said Morrolan.

"This doesn't give us much to work with," I suggested. "And I don't suppose either of you have any suggestions about getting out of here?"

They didn't.

I studied the chains that held them, and was wondering what it would take to break them, and what to do once they were broken, when Aliera said, "If we could reach Sethra—" which is as far as she got before our hosts finally decided to grace us with their presence.

4

Making Acquaintances

I was looking at Morrolan and Aliera, and saw their eyes suddenly focus on something over my shoulder, so I turned just as Loiosh gave a sort of agitated, undefined psychic squeal. I don't actually *know* that they appeared through the floor, but it seemed like it at the time; as if they sort of formed from the floor up. There were two of them.

I said, "Are those—?"

"Yes," said Morrolan. "That's what they look like."

"Heh. They're ugly enough, anyway."

It is hard to say what my first impression of them was. I saw them emerge, and my memory supplies their image; I don't know exactly what I noticed first. They were big—bigger than Dragaerans, I'd say more than nine feet tall, which I ought to have guessed from the size of the ceilings, but that's the sort of thing I always figure out after the fact. But whereas Dragaerans are thin, at least compared to humans, the Jenoine were broad, heavy, strong-looking, with thick arms, ending in hands with some reasonable number of fingers and one thumb per hand, but from where I stood they didn't seem to have any wrists. Nor hair of any kind. It was hard to see their faces, either, but there seemed to be two large, round eyes, both facing forward, and a mouth of some sort. They were naked, and, as far I could tell, sexless.

And I'll mention again, because it impressed me so much, that they were very big.

I hated the idea of trying to fight them. I felt Loiosh draw himself up and do the jhereg dance—which is what I call it when he tries to make himself look bigger. It is one of the things I don't make fun of him for, because I've caught myself doing the same thing in my own way, although just at the moment I'd have liked to make myself look smaller. Vanishing would have been even better.

"Don't draw a weapon," whispered someone, and it took me a moment to realize it was Teldra. I wasn't certain what good a weapon would do me, so I saw no reason to argue with her. Besides, if she had some inkling of an idea about what to do, she was a long way ahead of me. The thought did flash through my mind, in light of what Sethra had told me, to grab, say, Pathfinder from Aliera's side; but laying hands on another's Great Weapon is as close to certain death as you can come without having Mario after you.

But the thought did make me realize that neither of the Jenoine appeared to be armed. It didn't take a genius to realize that if they didn't carry weapons, it was because they didn't think they'd need any. This was not a comforting thought either.

At some point in there, it hit me that I was now in the presence of the Jenoine, of those half-mythological creatures that were spoken of in whispers, and the subject of as much ignorant speculation as Sethra herself. I had never truly believed in them, and now, here they were, and here was I, and typically, I had to worry about what to do about it, and I didn't have a clue.

Evidently, Lady Teldra did.

She took a step toward them, holding both hands in front of her, palms out, and emitted a series of sounds midway between a cat screeching and a hyena with hiccups.

"Be damned," murmured Morrolan.

I could see that, whatever else was happening, she had their attention. One of them moved a step closer to her, and, in a deep, rasping voice, spoke in the same language. If I could read the expression on that one's face, I'd guess it was mildly startled—its eyes, at any rate, had widened a little. Do facial expressions translate among species? There was another question for later contemplation. I was getting quite a collection of them. Evidently, I had thought it a good idea at some point to put Spellbreaker away; it was once more wrapped snugly around my left wrist. Amazing how light it felt that way, and how much heavier it got once I let it drop into my hand.

"*Loiosh, why does my mind wander whenever I'm terrified?*"

"It doesn't, Boss; your mind wanders whenever you're frustrated because you can't do anything."

"Oh."

"Or maybe it just always wanders and I don't notice it the rest of the time."

Teldra spoke again, the Jenoine responded. I waited patiently, like a prisoner whose fate was being settled by a magistrate while he stood helpless. It was enough to bring on the headache. I feel very fortunate not to be subject to the headache. There were many questions I should have liked to ask Morrolan and Aliera, but I was afraid it wouldn't be polite to carry on a conversation while Teldra was involved in screeching and coughing with the Jenoine, so I remained patient and tried to look tough and imperturbable—not for the Jenoine, who probably couldn't tell the difference, but for Morrolan and Aliera, who probably wouldn't care.

The conversation continued. I couldn't tell if Teldra was negotiating for our lives, laying down conditions to the Jenoine under which she wouldn't lay waste to their world, or asking if they knew any good recipes for klava.

I was just wondering if I'd be willing to try their version of klava, when the two Jenoine and Lady Teldra abruptly vanished. No fading, as of a teleport, and none of the shimmering and twisting of form that accompanied necromantic transportation, so this was something else entirely, and what should be surprising about that? Whatever it was, it was fast and neat—there wasn't even the rush of displaced air that I'm used to, which indicates to me that natural laws were being suspended, and that didn't surprise me, either.

"They're gone," said Morrolan, which was too obvious even for me to make a crack about how obvious it was.

"Now," said Aliera, "might be a good time to get us out of these."

"Good idea," I said. "How do we do that?"

Morrolan ignored me. "If Teldra is involved in negotiations," he said to Aliera, "we may jeopardize them by—"

"If Teldra is involved in negotiations," said Aliera, "it is in order to give us time to get out of here."

"What makes you think so?"

"Don't be a fool."

"Here we go," said Loiosh.

"Lady Teldra," I cut in, "did not leave our presence willingly."

That stopped them, at least for a moment. "How do you know that?" snapped Aliera.

"She vanished suddenly, without saying a word about it. It was rude."

"Good point," said Morrolan.

Okay, Vlad, I told myself. Teldra has just been taken away by all-powerful, legendary demigods; Sethra and the Necromancer are so far away that the term "distance" is meaningless; and Morrolan and Aliera are chained to a wall by some no doubt magical substance impervious to everything. That leaves you. Do something.

Morrolan and Aliera were looking at me, as if they expected the same thing. Well, fine. I tried to figure out what I needed to know, before I could even start formulating a plan. There were so many things. I didn't know what powers and abilities the Jenoine had, or, except in the most general terms, what their goals might be. Of course, I knew a bit about what Morrolan and Aliera could do, and Teldra—now, Teldra was a nice little mystery herself. I should have insisted on an answer from Sethra about why she was along. What is it she knew, or what skill did she have that . . .

Hmmmmmm.

"Morrolan, would you mind telling me, just because I'm curious, exactly what Lady Teldra does for you?"

"I don't understand, Vlad. You've seen her. She greets guests, she sees that they get where they are going within the Castle, and that I am informed about arrivals and departures. I thought you knew that."

"I did. I do. What else does she do?"

"Isn't that enough?"

"No."

He shrugged. "Well, that's what she does, enough or not."

I shook my head. "I'm missing something."

"He's an Easterner, Morrolan," said Aliera.

I bit back a smart remark, because Aliera's observation seemed to elicit an "Oh" expression from Morrolan. He said, "That's true."

"Okay," I said. "What is obvious to you that isn't to me?"

"The gods," said Aliera.

"What about them?"

"We consider them guests as well," said Morrolan. "Permanent guests of our homes, at all times; I had forgotten that you don't think of them that way."

"I don't see the point."

"Teldra," said Aliera, "is, in your terms, Morrolan's High Priestess."

"Ah ha."

"Ah ha?" said Morrolan.

"That's what I was looking for."

"Why?" said Morrolan and Aliera together, and I felt Loiosh asking the same thing.

"I don't know exactly. But I knew there had to be some connection there, and some reason Sethra agreed to send her, and because I need to understand all of these connections if I'm going to do anything useful."

Morrolan shrugged again. "Okay," he said. "Now you understand the profound truth that someone who knows how to be polite to a Dragonlord, a Teckla, or an Emperor might know how to be polite to a god as well."

"Not to mention a Jenoine," I remarked.

"Yes, a Jenoine, too."

"And she speaks their language."

"Obviously."

"What has that to do with her duties as High Priestess, or whatever?"

"Nothing," he said. "But she knows many languages. Many Issola do. It's a custom, such as Dragons knowing how to fight, and Jhereg knowing how to offer a bribe." I let that go. He said, "Is any of this important?"

"I don't know."

"Then, perhaps, you might turn your attention to doing something useful."

"Two problems, Morrolan. First, I'm stumped. Second, as Aliera said, if Teldra is talking to them, we may not want to irritate them during her negotiations."

"But as *you* said, Vlad, she didn't leave willingly."

"I know. But are you certain she can't talk them around? She's evidently used to dealing with beings who are far more powerful than she is; can you think of a better negotiator?"

He thought about that.

Loiosh said, *"I don't know if we ever want to cross them, Boss. I'm scared of those things."*

"They're worth being scared of," I said. "They'd kill without a second thought."

"I hate to say this, Boss, but so would you."

"Yeah, but I'm a nice guy."

"Try Spellbreaker," said Morrolan. I looked at him. "On the chains," he said. "Try Spellbreaker."

I looked at Aliera, who shrugged.

"Can't hurt," I said.

"What are you worried about, Boss?"

"Looking ridiculous."

"It was his idea."

I let Spellbreaker fall into my hand. It was only about a foot and a half long and the links were nearly an inch long. I took a step forward, and struck the length of chain connecting Morrolan's right wrist to the wall. The ringing sound was loud, though hearing the sound made me realize the room didn't echo as much as I would have thought it should. Nothing else happened. I felt ridiculous. I wrapped Spellbreaker up again. Morrolan shrugged; evidently he didn't feel ridiculous.

"If Spellbreaker is still changing, Loiosh, there's something that is still happening, I mean, something magical, even though we're no longer at home."

"Seems reasonable, Boss."

"And why am I so heavy? It's like I have to work to lift my arms."

"Yeah. Don't expect me to fly anywhere."

"So, okay, Sethra was wrong. There's sorcery here. Or, if not sorcery, something else; something that can make us feel heavy, and that makes it so hard to breathe. I'd really like to avoid having to fight here."

"Okay, Boss. But just for the record, where is it you haven't wanted to avoid fighting?"

That didn't deserve an answer, so I didn't give one. About then, I noticed something else, and cursed.

"What is it, Vlad?"

"I'm starting to get light-headed."

"Oh, that."

"What does 'oh, that' mean?"

Aliera said, "Try to take shallow breaths."

"Uh . . ."

"Try it. If you don't, you'll get dizzy."

"If you say so."

I tried to make my breaths shallow. At least it didn't make things any worse. I said, "Are they poisoning the air?"

"Not on purpose," said Morrolan.

"What does 'not on purpose' mean?"

"It seems to be the nature of the world. Just make your breaths shallow and you'll be fine. Soon you'll stop needing to think about it."

"Oh, good."

I took Aliera's hand and weighed the manacle in it. It was heavy, and seemed not too dissimilar to cast iron, maybe three-quarters of an inch thick. The chain seemed to have been made as one piece of it, and I saw no way to break it, or separate the chain. I studied where the chain joined the wall again, and still saw nothing. I probably would have started to get frustrated at that point, but before I had the chance Loiosh said, *"Boss, they're back,"* which gave me other things to think about.

"They're back" wasn't entirely accurate; only one of the Jenoine was back, but Teldra was with him, looking none the worse for wear, and holding something small and black in the palm of her hand. I permitted myself to hope it was a key to the manacles.

I held my tongue as she walked up to us; there's something about courtesy that's contagious. She said, "I have negotiated with the Jenoine."

I studied her face at that moment, I suppose feeling something momentous about to occur, and I couldn't get anything from her expression.

"They will release you, Morrolan and Aliera, if Vlad agrees to perform a task for them."

"I can hardly wait," I muttered, but either no one heard me, or they all ignored me.

"They want Vlad to perform a killing, a murder."

"Did you explain that I'm no longer in that line of work?"

"I made no agreement of any kind," she said. "I merely spoke to them, and they stated the conditions."

"And otherwise we'll be killed, I assume," said Aliera, as if she were being threatened with not being allowed to dinner.

"That wasn't specified."

"That's why we were taken," said Aliera, giving me a look. "In order to coerce Vlad into doing what they want."

"You'd think," said Morrolan, "that if that was true, they'd have taken Cawti, or better yet—" He broke off abruptly and scowled.

"They're separated," said Aliera.

"So?" said Morrolan. "Who knows how the Jenoine think, and what they know? They may not know much more of our customs, not to mention emotions, than we know of theirs."

"They know enough to have us here, bait for Vlad. You'll notice he's here."

"Makes me wonder what they would have done if you hadn't been along, Lady Teldra."

"Some of them speak our language," she said.

I cleared my throat. "I notice none of you are asking the obvious question."

"You mean," said Morrolan, "who is it she wants killed? It is obviously either Sethra, or a god, and you certainly aren't going to do it, so what difference does it make?"

"I should think a god," said Aliera judiciously. "Probably Verra."

Teldra bowed to her.

"Verra?" I said. "They want me to kill Verra?"

"Yes," said Teldra.

"Well, I have been annoyed with her now and then. I mean, I can't say I haven't thought about it."

"It isn't a joking matter, Vlad," said Morrolan.

"I think it is, Boss."

"That's two of us, if it comes to a vote."

"Did they have any suggestions as to how I was to accomplish this task?"

She held out the object in her palm. It was a small, black cube, perhaps an inch on a side. It didn't seem to reflect any light. "I am told," she said, "that this will bring you to the presence of the Goddess." With her other hand, she took from her belt a sheathed knife

I hadn't noticed before. "This is a very powerful Morganti dagger; it will be sufficient to, as they put it, prevent the Goddess from manifesting on our world."

"That means kill her," said Morrolan.

"Not exactly," said Aliera.

"Close enough."

I made some sort of grunting sound; I'm not sure what it meant, because I'm not sure what I was thinking. Teldra set the two objects down at my feet, then stepped back. There was something of ritual about how she did it; as if she were saying, "Here, now my work is done, and I say nothing about your work, what it is, or if you ought to do it."

I stared at the black cube and at the Morganti dagger. I could feel its emanations even from its sheath.

I said, "Teldra, do you trust them?"

"Vlad!" said Aliera. "You aren't considering doing it!"

"Yes," said Teldra. "I think they were telling the truth."

I grunted again.

"Look on the bright side, Boss: you've done a king, now you'll be able to say you've—"

"That's not the bright side. The bright side is the pleasure of rescuing Morrolan and Aliera. They'll never live it down."

Morrolan was staring at me. "Vlad, you can't be thinking about it. Think! Verra, the Demon Goddess. Your ancestors have worshiped her—"

"Leave it alone, Morrolan."

"Leave it alone? She is my goddess, too. How can I let you destroy her to save me?"

I laughed. "How can you stop me?"

"Vlad—"

"Oh, be still, dammit. I don't want to hear anything from anyone for a while, okay? Except you, Teldra, I want you to answer a question or two: Did they say anything about how long I had to make up my mind?"

"It wasn't mentioned," she said.

"Did they say anything about feeding us?"

"No."

Aliera opened her mouth to make another passionate and irritating plea, so I turned and walked away to the far side of the room. What I needed was time to think; usually needing time to think only happens when you haven't got any, but this time I at least had the chance to work a few things through in my head: Aliera and Morrolan wouldn't subject themselves to the indignity of yelling across the room, Teldra was too polite to say anything, and, for a miracle, even Loiosh gave me some peace.

So I ran a lot of stuff around my brain, for whatever that would do. The fact is, I don't think all that well when I'm just standing and thinking; I need to be talking, or doing something active, then the thoughts flow. But I did my best, and eventually sorted the matter out into several categories of things that I didn't understand. This was progress.

Categories, if you'll excuse a brief digression, are a useful way to get a handle on things you don't understand, as long as you don't get too attached to them and forget that things like to pop out of one category and into another, and that sometimes the whole category turns itself inside out and becomes something different. It's useful, for example, to categorize your target as a sorcerer, if he is one; but if you get too attached to your category it'll leave you embarrassed when he suddenly pulls a knife on you.

Just thought I'd share my reflections on categories.

In this case, I broke the unknowns down into: the abilities of the Jenoine, the plans of the Jenoine, and the nature of this world we were in.

I decided to start with the latter. I walked back.

"You have no link to the Orb, correct?"

Morrolan and Aliera nodded.

"Your Great Weapons seem to be behaving normally?"

They nodded again.

"What about time?"

"Excuse me?" said Aliera.

"I know time works differently in different places. I've been to the Paths of the Dead. Exactly how differently does it work here?"

"As far as I know," said Morrolan, "an hour here is an hour at home."

I shook my head. "No, I know that isn't true. How long have you been here?"

"I don't know," said Aliera. "Several hours."

"Several days," I told her. "Five, to be exact."

They looked properly startled. Before they could respond, I said, "What about Verra's Halls? How does time work there?"

"What difference does that make?" asked Aliera.

"I'm just curious."

Morrolan looked suspicious, and like he didn't want to answer. I glanced at Teldra, who said, "I don't know. I assume time flows the same there as it does at home, but I don't actually know."

"Okay," I said.

The reason that assassins make so much money is that, first of all, there aren't many who have what it takes to dispassionately murder someone; and, of those, there aren't many who can get away with it. I used to be one of them. Whatever there is in me that made me able to shove the knife, I still had. What made me able to get away with it so many times—sixty-three, to be exact—was that I understood the key ingredient: knowledge. You have to know things. You have to know everything there is to know about your target, about the environment, about your weapons, about your own abilities. Then you can make a plan. A plan built on ignorance can be worse than charging in with no plan at all; if you have no plan, you might get lucky.

I gestured toward the cube on the floor. "How do you use that thing?"

"All you need to do is hold it," said Teldra.

"Vlad—" said Aliera.

"Oh, stuff it," I said. "Morrolan, if I get you two out of those things, will you be able to get us out of here? Back home?"

He hesitated, then looked disgusted and shook his head. "Maybe," he said, "but probably not."

Aliera said, "Can you get us out, Vlad?"

"I'm still thinking about that," I said. "But even if I can I don't know how much good it will do."

"I would rather," she said, "be free to act, no matter what happens after."

"I understand that," I told her.

Either way was a gamble—picking up the cube, or attempting to free Morrolan and Aliera. I don't like gambling, especially when I don't know the odds; or at least the stakes. When possible, I'd rather be running the game than playing it. But now the Jenoine were running it, and I didn't even know the rules. I didn't know how to free them, and I didn't know if I could kill Verra. Freeing them might accomplish nothing; killing my Demon Goddess was not high on my list of ways to spend an afternoon.

I reached down and picked up the Morganti dagger; stuffed it into my belt. It wasn't easy to do—I'd never liked those things, and I could tell instantly that this was a particularly nasty one. Well, I suppose it would have to be, if they expected me to kill the Goddess with it.

Morrolan snapped, "What are you doing, Vlad?"

"Can always use a good Morganti dagger, right?"

"Boss, you're not going to—"

"I've got to do something. I'm bored."

"Oh. You're bored. Well, that's a good reason—"

"Drop it."

So I didn't have a plan. I did, as I stood there, start to get the seeds of what might, sometime, become a vague step generally in the direction of an intention. I may be stating that too strongly.

I took a good look around the room, noting the tall, thin metal shelves; the flat grey look of the walls; the height of the ceiling. I tried to fix it in my mind. I could not imagine what circumstances might lead me to try teleporting here, but that is the sort of thinking that goes with paying attention to details, in case you're curious about how my mind works.

My chest hurt. I tried to keep my breathing shallow, and to forget about how heavy I felt. It would be impossible to exert myself without taking deep breaths. I felt Aliera and Morrolan watching me. One step, and I was committed, and I still just didn't have enough information. But the only other option was standing around doing nothing, and that would only be effective for so long.

No, if I was going to do something, I had to have information, and there was no one here who could give it to me, which left only one option.

I reached into my pouch and pulled out two pieces of gammon. I handed one to Aliera and one to Morrolan. "If you're going to be helpless and miserable," I said, "at least you can eat a little."

They both accepted it, and they both looked like they were trying to decide if they should thank me, but neither said anything. I flexed my fingers.

All right.

"Lady Teldra," I said, "would you come here, please? Take my hand, if you would."

She did so, asking no questions but looking curious. Her hand was dry and cool. I reached down with my other hand, not letting her go, and picked up the small black cube.

Aliera said, "Vlad, what are you doing?"

The cube was very heavy for its size, but didn't seem to do anything except make the walls of the room turn a dull, ugly white. Or, at any rate, that was my first reaction; it took a moment to realize that Teldra, Loiosh, and I now stood in the Halls of Verra, the Demon Goddess.

5

PLEASANTRIES WITH DEITIES

Everything was too big and too white. The ceiling too high, the walls too far apart, the pillars spaced along the walls too big around, and everything the same uniform, ugly, chalky, pasty color. It was huge. It was only a hallway.

The next thing I noticed was that it was easier to breathe, and I didn't feel as heavy and sluggish as I had a second ago. It was only then that I realized that the little black cube had, after doing its job, neatly vanished.

"I got to get me one of those," I remarked. My voice sounded funny; it took me a second to realize it was because there was no echo—it was as if the corridor was absorbing the sound.

"I'll pass one along next time we get a shipment," said Teldra. Her voice sounded odd, too.

I had to look at her before I knew she was kidding. It was a very un-Teldra-like remark; I guess she was rattled too.

She said, "Where are we?"

"Where we're supposed to be. Or where we're not supposed to be, depending on how you look at it. But this is the home of Verra. I've been here before. Straight up ahead there, through those doors, is where I've seen her."

"You've been in her presence, then?"

"Yes, a couple of times. Once here, once elsewhere. Or maybe more often than that, if you use 'presence' loosely enough."

"We are surrounded by the color of illness; not very encouraging."

"I think it means something else to her."

"I suspected as much. But what?"

"I don't know, exactly. Is it important?"

"It is something I ought to have known."

"As Morrolan's High Priestess, you mean?"

She nodded. "Something like that can be important. And just in general, the more I know of the gods, the better."

"You must already know a great deal; maybe there are things you ought to tell me about Verra, before we go through those doors."

"Perhaps there are," she said. "But one thing I know, my dear Easterner, is that to you she is the Demon Goddess, and to me she is Verra, and we know her differently. Whatever I know might not be useful; indeed, it might mislead you."

I grunted. "Are the walls white?"

"Yes."

"I see them that way, too."

"Point taken."

"Then let's hear it."

"On the other hand," she said, smiling a little, "it may be that I can't tell you anything useful, and you're just procrastinating, because you aren't in a hurry to go through those doors."

"Point taken," I said, and started walking toward the doors.

"Wait," she said.

I waited.

"A god," said Lady Teldra, "is the living, sentient embodiment of a symbol."

"Oh," I said. "Well, that clears up everything."

"Your people, Easterners, might speak of a god of life, a god of death, a god of mountains, and so on. Isn't that true?"

"Sometimes," I said. "I think so. My education was a bit spotty."

"Those are all symbols."

"Death is a symbol?"

"Certainly. Very much so. Death, in fact, is a very powerful symbol because it defines life."

There were many things I could say to that, but I settled for, "All right, go on."

She looked around, gesturing to the walls. "We stand in the halls of a very powerful being; one with skills and abilities that surpass those of any mortal. By tradition, she represents the random arbitrariness of life."

"That's the rumor."

"Well, look around. Does her home appear random and arbitrary?"

I grunted, because I don't like giving obvious answers to pointed questions. "What are you getting at?"

"That she isn't just a symbol, she's also a person."

"Uh . . ."

"The tradition isn't wrong," said Teldra, "it is merely imprecise. She—" Teldra stopped and frowned, as if looking for the right words. "Your goddess," she said at last, "is capricious. At any rate, that is her reputation. It may be only that we expect a being with her power to behave with a certain consistency and decorum, whereas she follows her whims as much as any of us do. But don't depend on her."

"I shan't," I said. "I never have." That wasn't strictly true. At one time I did, but I had learned.

"Then that is all I can tell you," said Teldra.

"All right," I said. "Thanks. Let's go."

And we went, for several paces, until we reached doors that made Morrolan's look diminutive, and there we stopped, because, unlike Morrolan's, these didn't open as we stood before them.

"Maybe we're supposed to say something," I suggested.

"Maybe we aren't supposed to go in," said Teldra.

I studied the massive doors, and the corridor behind me. "Last time I was here," I told her, "there was a sort of fog in the hallway. Now there isn't. Do you suppose it means something?"

She shook her head; the sort of head shake that comes in answer to a question one doesn't know the answer to. I cursed under my breath, and, just because I couldn't think of anything else to do, clapped at the door.

Nothing happened.

"*Too bad, Boss. She's not home. Guess we'd better—*"

"*Shut up, Loiosh.*"

I then pushed at the door, because I'd have felt stupid if they opened inward and weren't secured. It didn't work, leaving me feeling stupid. The doors were filled with designs, all white-on-white, abstract designs reminiscent of embroidery from my ancestral homeland. All very nice. There were no handles on the doors. The space between the doors was wide enough to admit a pry-bar, or a knife blade, but I didn't have a pry-bar, or a blade with me that wouldn't snap from the weight of those doors. On the other hand, I had some spare knives. I pulled a stiletto from my boot, and was about to insert it between the doors when Teldra said, "Vlad."

I turned my head without moving the knife. "Yes?"

"Are you quite certain that breaking in is a good idea?"

"You're afraid I'll offend her?"

"Well, yes."

"You don't think killing her will offend her?"

She showed me a smile. "Vlad, we both know you have no intention of killing her."

"Do we know that, Boss?"

"Well, Teldra does, at any rate."

I turned back to the door, slipped the knife in, put some pressure on it, and promptly snapped the blade. The sound was dull and, like our voices, didn't echo. I stared at the hilt and the inch and a half of blade left in my hand, shrugged, and discarded it. It made more of a thump than a clatter as it fell to the floor.

"Okay," I said. "Next idea."

"You could pray to her," she said.

"Yeah," I said. "But what if she answered?"

"Do the gods answer, when you pray?"

"Sometimes. I've had her answer once, at any rate, and maybe twice. Or there may be other occasions I'm forgetting about. That's the sort of thing I'd like to forget. How do we get in here?"

"I don't know," she said. "You'd know better than me; you've had personal contact with her."

"Yeah. From which I know nothing except—" I put my face up against the door and yelled, "Verra! It's me, Vlad! You've had your joke, now open the bloody damn door."

The door began to swing inward. The last time I'd been here, the doors had opened outward. At least, I think they did. But this time they opened inward, and mists and fogs rolled out; the mist that had been in the corridor last time was now in the room.

"You can get the same effect with dry ice," I told Teldra.

"What's dry ice, Vlad?"

"It is an Eastern secret for keeping things cold. I learned of it from Valabar's."

"Witchcraft?"

"I guess so."

She nodded. "Shall we go in? I believe we've been invited."

"Yeah, sure, all right," I said, and stepped into the fog.

I walked forward with more confidence than I felt. I walked a long time, reminding myself that distances seem greater when you can't see, and the room was plenty big without help.

"Wall, Boss."

I stopped and cursed under my breath. Then I said, "Verra—"

There was a chuckle that seemed to come from all around me, and the fog cleared away and vanished—not going anywhere, just thinning out until it was gone, a process that took about five seconds. I was standing at the far end of the room; Verra sat on her chair, or throne, or dais, about twenty yards to my left and behind me. I made my way to the front of it and, while Teldra made some sort obeisance, I said, "What was that all about?"

She gave me an ironic indulgent look, if you can imagine such a thing. On the throne on the dais (all of white), she looked even taller than she was. She wore a hoodless robe that was mostly pale red with black embroidery. Her fingers were long and had an extra joint to them. Her hair, this time, was shoulder-length and wavy: a subdued brown with red highlights, and very thick, so it seemed to have an iridescent quality. Her eyes didn't glow, but it seemed like they ought to have.

She was my God—insofar, at least, as I had one. When I was a child, my grandfather had spoken of her, but given few details of the sort that might be useful, and my father never mentioned her at all, but it had been impressed upon my young mind that one made the proper observances at the proper times of the year. More than that, her power and presence were so deeply ingrained in me that all through life my thoughts would flash to her briefly at times of danger, or in moments of despair; and even in moments of great joy or triumph I would think of her, sending her my gratitude and the hopes that I would not be punished for enjoying my happiness.

When I had first met her in person, so many years ago, the shock had been so great that I couldn't assimilate it. At other times, I had felt her presence, but didn't know how often this feeling was only supplied by my imagination, and how often she had truly been with me. There were occasions, such as my one experience as a soldier of the line, when I could not imagine how I had survived without her having some hand in the matter, but she had never told me she actually did. Of course, I hadn't asked, either.

To know her as real—that is, a flesh-and-blood individual with whom I had spoken—was something I could never reconcile with the idea of a presence watching over me; perhaps watching me at times I didn't want to be watched. I had buried my own reactions, only to have them emerge as hatred some time later when she had visited misfortune upon my head, or maybe allowed misfortune to visit me, whichever. Since then I had tried not to even think of her, but in this I had failed, and now here she was, and to rescue my friends, I had to destroy her.

"Well?" I said. "Why the games?"

"An odd question," she said. I had forgotten the peculiar sound her voice had: not exactly an echo, but more as if there were two of her speaking, mostly in unison, but sometimes they'd fall a bit out of synchronization. She continued, "How can you complain of my treatment of you, when you are only here to assassinate me?"

"There is that," I agreed. "Goddess, may I be permitted to put a question?"

"Very well, assassin," said the Demon Goddess.

"Was this all your doing?" And, for a second, I actually had made Verra look astonished. Then the expression was gone. I continued, "The last time, if you recall—"

"Yes, Taltos Vladimir, I remember. But no, this was none of my doing. I did not arrange this, nor expect it. I did not expect you to arrive here; I did not think you would be able to do so without my assistance. Tell me, how *did* you manage that? I can't believe the Issola standing next to you accomplished it for you."

I wanted to say something like, "It's a trade secret," but even I have limits beyond which I won't go.

Teldra said, "Goddess, it was the Jenoine."

Verra nodded, slowly. "Yes," she said. "It had to be. Do you know who? Or which faction?"

"I was unable to learn, Goddess. I can tell you that one addressed the other by the honorific 'ker.' "

"Well done, Issola. It is a term used by what among the Jenoine is the equivalent of the military. It is useful information."

"I am only too happy to be of service," she said.

The Demon Goddess narrowed her eyes a little at this pronouncement, and said to me, "And you, little Easterner. Are you, also, only too happy to be of service?"

"I haven't decided yet," I said. "How many places can you be at once?"

"Well," she said. "You've been studying. Sethra Lavode, I take it?"

I grunted. "Yes, but I knew that much, at least, from a long time ago."

"Many," said the Goddess, in answer to my question. "But there is one place I cannot be, and your countrymen are responsible for that."

"An ancestor?"

"No. It was a blood prince, and you are of peasant stock."

That stung. "All right," I said. "Thanks for the compliment. I still want to know."

"I cannot appear among the Jenoine, Vlad, which is what you're really asking, isn't it?"

"Supernatural powers, immortality, and clever, too."

"Don't try my patience, Fenarian. I mean that."

I swallowed and nodded.

"Goddess," said Teldra, presumably breaking in to take me off the hook, "our friends are being held captive. Can you and will you help us?"

"Sit down here at my feet," she said, "and we'll talk."

Teldra sat on the dais as if there was nothing distasteful about doing so; I did my best to emulate her but I don't think I managed to keep the scowl entirely off my face.

"Speak," said Verra, and Teldra did so. I occasionally filled in a detail or speculation. Verra remained silent the entire time. She must have known some of what was going on, to judge from her comment about my being there to assassinate her, but she just listened and gave no hint about what she had known.

"There is more to this," said the Goddess when we were finished, "than you are aware of."

"No shit?" I said.

She gave me an indulgent smile, which did nothing to improve my mood. I felt Teldra's hand on my arm; if it had been anyone else, I'd probably have bit it.

Verra said, "I do not, however, intend to explain everything to you."

"Well, there's a new experience for me."

"Little Easterner," said Verra, "you seem determined to express your displeasure to me in more and more obvious ways until I take notice. Very well, I take notice. You are wroth with me because I have used you; because I have offended against your innate right to be a useless cyst on the hindquarters of life. Yes, well, you may continue to be wroth with me, because I intend to continue making you useful. You may attempt to kill me, in which case I will destroy you; or may continue to annoy me; in which case I will cause you sufficient pain to make you stop; or you may shut up and accept the inevitable."

I opened my mouth, Teldra squeezed my arm, I shut my mouth.

"Say, 'Thank you, Teldra,' " said Verra.

"Thank you Teldra," I said.

"Boss, where did this self-destructive streak come from?"

"Shut up, Loiosh."

Verra said, "I have been waiting for some time, and so has Sethra, for the Jenoine to put their plans in motion, without knowing exactly what form they would take, or, indeed, what those plans were. But we knew they were preparing something. Now they have begun, and we are only able to respond and react until we know more about their intentions."

I said, "Sethra once tried to explain to me about offensive-defensive strat—"

"Keep still," she said, and I suddenly felt like someone was driving a spike into my head. I gasped, and the pain went away.

"Very convincing," I said, when I could speak again.

"They have made the first move," said Verra, as if nothing had happened. "We don't yet know what it means. The Jenoine are, in some ways, not unlike the Yendi; they will have anticipated our response, and worked it into their plans. They will have secondary and

tertiary responses to our moves. Their objective will be concealed
under layers of illusion and misdirection."

I bit back a suggestion that she let me know when she had the
problem wrapped up; I was learning. She continued, "There are some
things, however, that we can be certain of: one is that they must find
a way to neutralize Sethra, Morrolan, and Aliera, among others whose
names you don't know."

"They have two of them; why haven't they killed them?"

"You know how hard it is to kill the wielder of a Great Weapon."

"I remember a Jhereg who managed it, once."

"So Morrolan told me. Yes, it can be done, by a judicious combination of sorcery, surprise, and more sorcery. But even then, had
Morrolan not been returned to life, Blackwand would have continued
to guard his soul. And it might have done far more than that; the
Jhereg assassin was a fool. By now, Vlad, you should begin to understand something about the Great Weapons."

That shut me up. I remembered some of the tricks those things
can do. Once I had seen Aliera—but never mind.

"But can they continue to hold Morrolan and Aliera captive?"

"It seems they can. I hadn't thought so, and I still don't know
how."

"Probably with help from the Serioli," I suggested.

She actually looked startled. At least, she sat back in her chair
and stared at me. That was twice in the same conversation; I felt
smug.

"Well, well," she said after a moment. "You know more than I
should have thought."

I shrugged.

"Yes, it may be the Serioli," she agreed. She frowned, and seemed
lost in thought. It flashed through my mind that I had never before
seen her lost in thought, and the idea of that powerful mind bending
its energies in some direction made me feel more puny and pathetic
than all the pyrotechnics she had displayed before. What was I doing
here, anyway?

"Don't you remember, Boss? You're going to kill her."

"Oh, right. That."

Verra finished her thought. "It is complex," she announced.

"They are playing a deep game, and there is no way to understand all of it at this stage."

I stared at the ceiling, which was white, and very high over my head. I said, "Isn't it a pain when you have to come up with a plan based on incomplete information?" No one responded. I said, "Goddess, do you have a guess about what killing you has to do with it? I mean did they think I actually could, and would, or was it just a complex piece of subterfuge?"

She said, "Oh, anything they can do to make me uncomfortable is all to the good, as far as they're concerned; it may be nothing more than that. If it is part of something deeper, then I don't know what. Yes, it is very possible that they expected you to march in here and kill me. Or perhaps they hope merely to confuse me, and hinder my efficiency."

" 'The ways of the gods are mysterious,' " I quoted.

"Yes."

"Also annoying, capricious—"

Teldra gave my arm a squeeze, and I shut up.

"Goddess," said Teldra. "Can you tell us what we are to do?"

"What to do?" she said. "In order to accomplish what? In order to serve whom? Me? Aliera? Morrolan? Sethra?"

"I was thinking of the Serioli," I said. "At least, no Serioli has ever annoyed me. That makes them unique on the list."

Verra snapped her head toward me, and I couldn't keep myself from flinching. She noticed it and smiled, and I felt myself flushing.

"If you please, Goddess," said Teldra, "you were telling us what we ought to do."

"Yes," she said. "I was. The problem is not only that we do not know everything; it is also that we do not all have the same interests. This makes the problem complicated."

"Simple things are never problems," I told her. "Unfortunate, maybe, but if it isn't complicated, it isn't really a problem."

The Goddess nodded. "Very good, Vlad; I didn't expect such wisdom from you."

I grunted and didn't tell her I was quoting my grandfather; I'd rather she stayed impressed.

"The Jenoine," said the Goddess, "have achieved access to your world on several occasions, most recently just a few years ago. We have beat off attacks on the Great Sea of Chaos, on the Halls of Judgment, on the Imperial Palace, and, lately, on Dzur Mountain. Their efforts have not been successful. I will share with you some of my thoughts."

I almost said, "Thank you so much," but caught myself.

She continued, "I cannot think why they are making this effort so recently after their last failure. Two possibilities come to mind: the attack on Dzur Mountain was part of something larger, and this is another piece of it; or they have had a sudden and unexpected opportunity."

"If they were looking for an opportunity, why didn't they make their move during the Interregnum?"

"What makes you think they didn't?" said Verra.

"Oh," I said.

We fell silent, then, in the Halls of Verra; and for the first time I wondered where we were. Up in a mountain? Beneath the ground? Floating in the air like Castle Black? On another world?

"First of all," said the Goddess suddenly, "you must free Morrolan and Aliera."

"No," I said. "That's just what they're expecting us to do."

"You are jesting," she said. "But are nevertheless correct."

I shrugged. "All right. How?"

She frowned. "Describe for me how they are held."

I did so, and she said, "Very well. I am familiar with the substance. Here is what you must do," and she told me.

"Oh," I said. "And that will work?"

"I believe so."

"You believe so? What if you're wrong?"

"Then perhaps the Jenoine won't kill you for trying."

"Great. All right. Say it works. What then?"

"If Morrolan cannot reach through to his portal, then it is because the Jenoine are preventing him from doing so. You must force them to stop."

"Force them?"

"Yes."

"And just how do I go about doing that, or are you going to express confidence that I'll come up with something?"

"Come, my little Easterner. Have all your years in the Jhereg been wasted? Do you not even know how to threaten and intimidate?"

Just then, I felt about as intimidating as a norska. I said, "Usually, Goddess, in order to make a threat, one requires the power to carry it out. At least, one requires this in cases where the threat won't be believed."

"Very good, little one. You search for the general law that applies to the specific case. You have become a philosopher."

I hadn't known it was that easy.

She said, "Once Morrolan and Aliera are free, Pathfinder and Blackwand ought to prove a sufficiently intimidating threat, don't you think?"

"Okay," I said. "I mean, they intimidate me."

"Well, there you have it," said the Goddess.

"But don't tell them I said so. What do we do then? I mean, after I've released Morrolan and Aliera, threatened the Jenoine into letting us go, and let Morrolan bring us home. I mean, that's just enough to get us warmed up; you must have a whole plan after that."

"You will then return to Castle Black and await my orders."

I opened my mouth to object, and then shut it. Yes, if there was one place I'd be safe, it was Castle Black—there are reasons for that going back to ancient history, but I won't go into them now.

"All right," I said. "Sure. No problem. Except that the Jenoine will have anticipated this, won't they? And they'll have made plans for it."

"Yes," said the Goddess.

"So you're saying that this will all be a trap."

"Probably."

"But we're not worried about the trap, because we'll have a secret weapon prepared for them."

"What secret weapon is that, little one?"

"I was hoping you'd tell me."

"Your courage, wits, and skill at improvisation, little one. That is our secret weapon."

"Oh, good."

"And, my dear Easterner, do not make the mistake of thinking that I jest; I am quite serious."

"Oh, better."

"There is no question in my mind that you can do it."

"Oh, best."

"Do you doubt me, Taltos Vladimir?"

"Perpetually, Demon Goddess."

She gave a short barking laugh. "Go now. Make trouble for the Jenoine instead of for me, and I, I will do as I have been doing: watching over your family."

That was a low blow—there just wasn't anything I could say to it. I wanted to ask how my grandfather was doing, but I wouldn't give her the satisfaction.

"All right," I said.

"Lady Teldra," said the Goddess. "You may stay here, if you wish."

"Thank you, Goddess, but I will accompany my friend."

There was something so matter-of-fact about the way she called me her friend that it caught me up short.

"As you wish," said Verra. Then she frowned. "Of course, I'm not entirely certain how to get back to Morrolan and Aliera."

I sighed. "I suppose you could return us to Castle Black, and we could do it all over again."

"What exactly did you do, little one?"

So I told her that, and her eyes narrowed. "Let me see this chain," she said, so I let it fall into my hand and held it out to her, but instead of just lying there like it was supposed to, it twisted and curled in my hand until it was hanging in midair, my hand providing a base, coiled like a snake about to strike—in particular, about to strike Verra, who drew back with a sharp intake of breath. I almost let go of the chain, but didn't quite. It had never done that before.

"Goddess," I said. "I didn't—"

"I know," she said.

She gritted her teeth and said, "You have no idea, do you?"

"I—"

"Never mind."

She reached out and made motions in the air with her forefinger, and where her finger had been there was a dark line in the air, roughly the size and shape of a sword. It quickly filled in, and I was staring at the image of Pathfinder, hanging in the air in front of me.

"Go ahead," said the Goddess. "Do it."

I hated to sound like an idiot, but, "Do what?" I said.

"Make contact between your toy and Aliera's."

I swallowed. I wasn't entirely happy with the way my "toy" was behaving, but I couldn't think of any good way to get out of doing what she wanted. I started to take a step forward to bring the chain into contact with the image, but it was ahead of me—it reached out on its own, and seemed to grow longer. No, dammit, it did grow longer. The end of it wrapped around the image of Pathfinder's hilt. I braced myself for something to happen when they made contact, but I felt nothing. I concentrated most of my energy on trying to look as if I wasn't at all disturbed by any of this.

"All right," said the Demon Goddess. "I've found them."

Teldra came up next to me and put her hand on my right arm.

The Goddess gave an aimless gesture with her right hand, and a rectangular shape appeared to my left—like the frame of a door, glowing a sort of dull red, and just sitting in the middle of the room. The other side of it looked exactly like this side of it, just showing more of Verra's pasty-white hall.

"Step through," said the Goddess. "And good luck."

"Thank you so much," I said, and, Loiosh on my shoulder and Teldra at my side, walked through the doorway into nothing.

6

TRADING AT THE MARKET

The worst part of that means of transportation was that nothing happened. When I teleport, even without the waves of nausea, there is still the time-delay, and the twisting sense of movement in some inexplicable direction. And then there's Morrolan's window—however that works: you may not feel anything, but you at least see that you are stepping through something, from one place to another, and if there is no reason for those places to be near each other, well, you can use the window to fool your mind. But with this there wasn't even that: one instant I was standing before the Demon Goddess, in her Halls, wherever they were, and then everything was different—I weighed more, the air smelled funny, and the walls were different— that much I approved of. It's damned lucky I didn't have to do anything as I arrived, because I was in no condition to defend myself from a playful kitten.

And, on top of it, I had an instant of terror before I realized that I was, in fact, back in the same place I'd left Morrolan and Aliera, just in a different part of the room and facing a different direction; but turning around, I saw them, across the room and still attached to their wall. My heart rate returned to normal, leaving only the lingering question of what I'd have done if Verra had misplaced me.

Some questions demand answers; others one prefers to just put away and not think about.

Aliera and Morrolan were looking at me. I gave them a jaunty salute from across the room, and walked up to them.

Aliera said, "Well?"

"Well, what?"

"Vlad—"

"Oh. The Demon Goddess? I killed her, of course."

They both immediately glanced over my shoulder at Teldra, who must have given some sign, because Aliera gave me a disgusted look, while Morrolan said, "Your sense of humor, Vlad, leaves something—"

"Yeah, yeah," I said. "Save it. Have our hosts been back?"

"Not yet."

"Well, we should expect them any time."

Aliera gave Morrolan a glance that I interpreted as, "Look who's the strategist now?"

"And then we'll do what?" asked Morrolan.

"What happened with Verra?" asked Aliera.

I answered the second question. "The Goddess and I discussed politics," I said. "And, in fact, I failed to so much as draw this . . . thing."

It hung at my hip, that thing. I had avoided studying it, or really looking at it, but I did so now. It had a shiny black polished hilt, with a simple silver crosspiece, knobbed on the ends. The pommel was also silver: a round ball that would hurt like a bitch if I cracked it on someone's head. The hilt was a bit smaller than usual with Dragaeran weapons, but that was okay, because my hands are small, too. It was very smooth and cool to the touch, I remembered. The blade, which I hadn't yet seen, would be of that ugly, dull, grey-black metal that Morganti blades always have, and might have a blood-groove in it; I didn't take it out to look. It was long for a knife and short for a sword. Impractical in every way, and was probably not even balanced all that well, most likely being a bit blade-heavy. This, of course, was useful for chopping away in battle—military-issue swords are often blade-heavy—but chopping away in battle was not something I did much of.

And it was very strong. I could feel it, even through the sheath— a sort of presence in the back of my mind, whispering its hunger. It wanted to kill, and couldn't care a copper penny who or what it killed; as vicious as a Dragon in the heat of rage, as heartless as a Dzur on a spree; as cold as an Orca closing a deal.

I hated it.

I had used Morganti weapons before, but I had never liked them, never had any interest in being near them. Once, I had had to stand in a room with more of them than I could count; I still sometimes have bad dreams that I can trace to that experience. And this one really was damned powerful. I had taken it along only because I feared the Jenoine might be observing me, and if I didn't have it along, they might have stopped me from traveling to Verra. I no longer wanted it, but didn't feel comfortable just throwing it into a corner of the room, either. I mentally cursed it, and wished that it and all its siblings would get lost somewhere.

I turned my eyes and my mind away from the weapon at my hip, and back to Morrolan and Aliera, who shared some traits with the thing, but at least had a few redeeming virtues. I stood over them, and, in an effort to think about something else, returned to studying, yet again, the manacles, the chains, the spot where they joined the wall, and all the rest. The slightly sweet, slightly bitter taste of the air reminded me that I had to keep my breathing shallow.

"You're scowling," said Morrolan.

"Yeah," I said. "You do it better, but you've had longer to prac-tice."

I knelt down for yet another, closer look, convinced that if I kept staring I'd see something. Years ago I wore an assassin's cloak with all sorts of goodies in it, including a bit of oil which might have allowed me to slide the manacles off. But I didn't carry those things anymore.

"It probably wouldn't have worked anyway without breaking her hand."

"Aliera," I said, "do you mind if I break your hand?"

"If that is the only way to get me out of these," she said, "no, I don't."

I hadn't expected that answer, although I should have.

"That goes for us both," said Morrolan.

Of course it does, I thought but didn't say.

I had killed people without examining them this closely. The manacles were fairly tight, but there was a bit of room between iron and skin.

"What are you thinking, Vlad?" said Morrolan.

"I'm meditating on helplessness as a way of life, and captivity as an expression of artistic fulfillment."

"What are you thinking, Vlad?" he repeated patiently.

I shrugged. "I'm wondering how much time we have. I assume the Jenoine know I've returned. But they never seem to be in much of a hurry. They don't behave the way I expect captors to behave. That confuses me."

Morrolan shrugged. "Have you ever been held captive?"

"Yes."

"I mean, have you ever been held captive by someone other than the Empire?"

"Yes," I said, and didn't elaborate. To avoid dwelling on a memory that wasn't entirely pleasant, featuring, as it did, far too much potato soup, I considered what the Goddess had told me. She had said I'd be able to . . . Okay, maybe. It's hard to argue with one's Goddess.

During this interval, I had continued to study wall, chains, manacles, and wrists; and, I suppose, I had continued to scowl.

"You have an idea, don't you?" said Aliera.

I grunted. "I don't know how much fun it will be for you."

"Do it," she said.

"It might be painful."

"Do it," said Morrolan.

"It might be dangerous."

"Do it," said Aliera.

"You may not survive."

"Do it," said Morrolan.

"It might mean the end of civilization as we know it."

Aliera gave me a disgusted look.

I shrugged. "Just wondering how far you'd go."

"Do it," he repeated.

I was convinced. I couldn't remember the last time I'd heard Morrolan and Aliera agree on anything; how could I fail to go along?

"If they agree, Boss, it must mean it's a bad idea."

"Probably true."

I pulled off my jerkin. The room was suddenly chilly. Morrolan and Aliera looked away from my bare chest, which seemed a bit funny. I took a knife from my belt, and began cutting strips of leather from what had been a shirt only seconds before, but was now merely a supply of fabric. Funny how quickly things can change, isn't it?

"What are you doing, Vlad?" asked Aliera.

I didn't answer. Not answering Aliera when she asks questions like that is one of the pleasures that I had missed since I'd been away.

When I had four strips cut off, I worked them around Aliera's and Morrolan's wrists, between manacle and skin. Aliera was easy; Morrolan had thicker wrists and it took me a while, but I managed. I probably hurt him a little while I was doing it, but, of course, he wouldn't give me the satisfaction of letting me know if I had.

When I was done, there turned out to be enough of a jerkin left to do some good, so I put the remainder back on; it made my stomach seem even colder than it had been.

I sat down cross-legged in front of and between Morrolan and Aliera. I really wanted this to work. Not only was it necessary to accomplish my mission and save the world or whatever the hell I was trying to save, and very possibly the only way for me to get out of this alive, but, more important, if I managed to rescue Aliera and Morrolan it would be something I would never let them forget; the pleasure would be almost too sweet. On the other hand, if I accidentally amputated both of their hands, I'd feel bad. And that was, in fact, a possibility, even though the Goddess hadn't seemed to doubt that I could pull it off; hence the addition of the strips of leather; for one thing, they were symbolically important as barriers, and symbols are very important in witchcraft. And for another, well, maybe, if all else failed, the leather would give their wrists some protection from what I was about to do to them.

"Morrolan," I said, "give me your right hand. Aliera, your left." They did so, clanking. Crazily, it entered my head to wonder what my friend Aibynn, who was a musician, would have said about the note the chains gave off—I mention this as an example of how one's mind works at such moments. Or maybe as an example of how whacked my friend Aibynn is, I don't know.

Teldra said, "Is there anything useful I can do?"

"No, but thanks for asking. Just stay out of my line of vision so you don't distract me." She obligingly backed up a couple of steps.

"Okay, Loiosh. Help me out."

"Sure you know what you're doing, Boss?"

"Of course not. Now help me out."

"Okay."

I started to get light-headed again, and reminded myself to take shallow breaths; that actually had seemed to help, now that I thought about it. Getting dizzy in the middle of this spell would not be in any of our best interest.

"I'll keep track of your breathing, Boss."

"Good. Let's start, then."

Connecting to them came easily; I knew them well by now.

"Energy" is a term that I can't define, at least as I'm using it now: it is uncomfortably vague, and can be twisted into all sorts of bizarre meanings. I've heard it used by sorcerers in a very precise, no-nonsense way, as something they could measure and portion out in precise increments; they even have a word for an increment, though I can't recall it at the moment. I've also heard "energy" used in casual conversation as a way of making something vague and meaningless sound precise and full of significance: "I knew she was mine when I felt the energy pass between us." I've heard natural philosophers use the word much the way sorcerers do, and fools of various flavors use it the way lovers do.

But, whatever it means, energy lies at the heart of witchcraft.

When you have understood the piece of the world you want to change, and aligned your will with the world as it actually is, then and only then can you begin to change it; not to hit the point too hard, but I suppose this is true even in what one does with one's more mundane abilities. The difference is that, when practicing the art of the witch, one can actually *feel* the alignment, *feel* the changes taking place. I call this feeling energy, because I can't think of a better term for it; inside of myself, it comes with a quickening of the heartbeat, a sense of being, for a while, a little more alive, and a sureness of one's convictions. Outside of myself, well, stuff starts happening.

So, yes, connecting to Morrolan and Aliera came easily, and the energy began to build.

Every skill—certainly every physical skill—really consists of learning which muscles ought to be tense, and which relaxed, and when. Increased skill comes with strengthening certain muscles, and, even more, with achieving finer control of the particular muscles used. In the Eastern science of defense, for example, one must learn to keep the proper amount of tension in the thumb, fingers, and wrist, so that the point of the weapon stays in line: too little tension and the weapon can be knocked out of your hand, which is embarrassing; too much and one responds too slowly, which is equally embarrassing. In fact, to show you how picky it can be, your first step in actually mastering the art is when you get control of your ring finger. Later, one learns the proper amount of tension for the forward knee and the rear foot, and so on. It is a training of mind and of muscle, which in the novice are constantly at odds with each other, and in the expert are so strongly united that it is impossible to separate conscious decisions from those made by trained muscles. This state is what we talk about when we refer to "reflexes," which can tell you a lot about yourself.

I say this to make the obvious point that the art of the witch is very similar, except that the "muscles" in question all exist within the mind of the witch. With the simplest spells, all that is needed is the concentration of power; with the more complex spells, a subtlety and flexibility of mind is required. Typically, a witch will use all sort of tools, herbs, and amulets, because these help to focus the mind onto the required path; but when necessary, the swordsman forgets about proper form and technique, and takes the opening that desperation requires and opportunity presents.

Now that I think about it, most of my life has consisted of taking the opening that desperation required and opportunity presented.

I did without tools, herbs, and amulets; instead I built them as metaphors in my mind. I imagined the manacles as four burning pyres, with visible heat patterns emerging from them that I then turned into strips of cloth—not to be confused with the actual strips of leather, which were metaphorically walls keeping the heat from their arms, which were, oh, never mind. I took hold of the metaphorical cloth, not the real leather, and I pulled, throwing it carelessly to my metaphorical side. Fortunately, there was no one in the metaphorical way.

"*Loiosh, look to their wrists; make sure I don't hurt them.*"

"*Got it, Boss.*"

I pulled, and pulled, and it seemed as if I were pulling fabric from an endless spool. Somewhere far, far away, there was conversation; I imagine Morrolan or Aliera or both were making comments or asking questions, but none of it registered—fortunately for all of us. Morrolan, at least, ought to have understood that conversation was a bad idea; that I needed to concentrate or Bad Things would happen. This was a thought I had later; at the time, I was, well, concentrating.

Eventually it became harder to pull, and the flames from the pyres were almost extinguished. I continued because I didn't know just how far I'd have to go.

"*Boss, I can't keep it all away from them.*"

"*Are they being hurt?*"

"*A little.*"

"A little more, then," I said, and kept going, though it was now pretty tough, and slow, and I realized I was becoming exhausted. It was what they call the point of diminishing returns when they want to sound all fancy and technical; to me it was a signal that I was about done.

"*Boss—*"

"Okay," I said. "*That will have to do,*" and I pulled out of my metaphors and symbols and use of energy as a precise vagueness, and came back to the world; whatever world it was, at any rate.

". . . very cold," Aliera was saying. She and Morrolan looked to be all right, so I just grunted at her, thought about using Spellbreaker, but didn't know if it might have some additional effects, and I didn't want any additional effects just then. I pulled from behind my back a knife with a particularly strong, heavy hilt. I flipped the knife, caught the blade, and raised it over my head, then got a good hold on Aliera's left arm.

"What are you doing, Vlad?" asked Aliera as I brought the knife down as hard as I could on the manacle, being careful not to touch the bitter cold metal with my hand. It shattered with a sound like broken pottery, rather than iron, and her wrist was free. I repeated the process on her other arm and broke the hilt of the knife as well as the manacle, leaving me staring at a blade and a tang, with a bit of bone hilt still clinging to it. Oh, well. I had more knives.

I pulled another and used it on Morrolan's right arm, breaking the knife's hilt and doing nothing to the manacle. I scowled and pulled yet another, wishing I carried as many as I used to, but this one turned out to do the job: there were now four lengths of chain hanging from the wall. Morrolan and Aliera stood up.

Hot damn.

"Good work, Vlad," said Morrolan, alternately rubbing each wrist with the opposite hand. "I'll take over now."

Figured.

I couldn't really object; I didn't have any energy to object with. It wasn't the sort of exhaustion you get when you've just run half a mile; my breathing was easy, and I was even remembering, with occasional nudges from Loiosh, to make my breaths shallow. And it wasn't sleepiness: I wanted to lie down, but I was nowhere near sleep. No, it was its own thing, the aftermath of a spell. A lethargy that I can only compare to the aftermath of sex, and that is too obvious an analogy, and has been used too often in books on witchcraft, for me to want to push it, so let's just say I was too tired to object.

Morrolan rubbed each wrist in turn, as if to warm them up, or to assure himself that they were still there. Then did something quickly with his hands, and he was suddenly holding a thin, black, polished stick in his right hand. It was about five feet long, had rounded ends, a few silver tracings on it, and I'd never seen it before.

"What is that?" I managed to say.

"My wizard's staff," said Morrolan. "I am a wizard. We have staves, you know. They go with the office."

"And I've never seen you use it before because . . . ?"

"In my own world, Blackwand has pretty much replaced it, but here, there are limits to what Blackwand can do, so I revert to my earlier skills and implements."

"I suppose it is immensely powerful and you can do all sorts of amazing things with it."

"Naturally."

"And you've had it with you all along?"

"I always have it with me."

"Then please explain to me why, by Verra's skinny ass, couldn't you have—?"

"While I was fettered," he said, "its power was nullified. The Jenoine are rather skilled in counterspells. Now I am unfettered, and, if there are no objections, I propose to use it. You don't mind, do you, Vlad? Or have you other questions?"

"If that means you intend to get us out of here," I said, "then I'm all for it. If you have some other plan, we'll have to negotiate."

"That's my plan," said Morrolan.

"Not, however, theirs," said Aliera, sweetly. I followed the direction of her gaze, and saw that the two Jenoine were back.

"So," I said to no one in particular. "I guess it comes down to negotiation after all."

I looked at the Jenoine, then glanced back, and saw, heard, and felt Pathfinder and Blackwand being drawn from their sheaths, Morrolan first transferring the staff to his left hand. Then he set the staff spinning; it seemed very light in his hand. I hoped he was doing more than showing off how good he was at making a stick spin.

The wizard's staff was spinning at his side, he held Blackwand in his other hand, and next to him stood Aliera, holding Pathfinder, with its point at the Jenoine's face. In the Jhereg, we call this "negotiating from a position of strength." I suspect the Dragons have a similar term.

I didn't have a position of strength. I didn't draw a weapon, because I wasn't sure what to draw, and because I was in no condition to wield a flyswatter.

Teldra barked, coughed, grumbled, and chattered at them; one of them replied similarly. I strained to guess the tone of the conversation, then gave it up as hopeless.

"Any idea, Loiosh?"

"Sorry, Boss. Not a clue."

"I hate sitting around while other people decide what's going to happen to me."

"Well, you can always do something stupid."

"No, I think I'm over that, for the moment."

"Note down the date."

"Oh, shut up."

Morrolan and Aliera took a step toward the Jenoine; Teldra kept talking.

The big, ugly thing just stood there, not appearing to notice the Great Weapons, much less the wizard's staff, or the cold-blooded, highly skilled Easterner assassin who was bravely cowering next to the Dragonlords.

"Do that thing's eyes remind you of something, Boss?"

"Yes, Loiosh. Fish eyes. Is it important?"

"Probably not."

From my position, I couldn't see Morrolan's face, but I had a partial view of Aliera's: there was a gleam in her eye, and a sort of twisted grin on her lip. Morrolan, I was sure, was scowling. He scowled well. Aliera grinned, Morrolan scowled, and I sneered. There you have it.

They closed with the Jenoine, and I suddenly thought of the Morganti dagger in my belt. Well, I could join them. I mean, it wasn't a Great Weapon, but it was a Pretty Good Weapon. I might do some good. I might be able to help. I might prefer to cower as far back in a corner as I could.

"Good plan, Boss. Let's go with it."

"Sold," I told him. I managed to stand up, then took a step backward, stopped, drew the Morganti dagger, and went up to stand next to Morrolan.

"Boss—"

This had happened to me before—going forward into danger that wasn't at all my type of danger, when I knew I ought to go back, and I hadn't then understood why I did it, and I didn't know this time. Bugger. The Morganti dagger seemed alive in my hand. Yes, it was a dull, grey color. Yes, it did have a blood-groove. It was a narrow blade, very light and useful-feeling in my hand, about eighteen inches long, and not nearly as blade-heavy as I'd suspected it would be. It was also hungry, and, as I'd suspected, it was very powerful; I felt it and hated it.

And worried about it, as well. The Jenoine had given it to me, and now I was going to use it against them. Wouldn't they have thought of that? Was that what they wanted me to do? Could it hurt them, in any case? According to Verra, no it couldn't. But if not, then I didn't have anything that could.

The Jenoine took a step forward, and extended its left hand; I felt the sick tumble in my stomach that accompanies the realization that action, and a sort of action I hate, is now inevitable: The *maybes* had dissolved into the dust, the *I hopes* had taken wing, the alternatives had narrowed to one, which was the same as vanishing to none at all—I've never understood the arithmetic of that.

All right, then. If Morrolan could fight with two weapons at once, so could I; I let Spellbreaker fall into my left hand.

"Tell it," said Morrolan, still spinning his staff, "that it will permit us to leave at once, or we shall destroy it."

Teldra said, "Lord, that's what I've been telling her, though I have perhaps phrased it differently."

"And?"

"She is considering her options."

"How rational," said Aliera.

"Was Aliera being ironic, Boss? Or was that an insult?"

"We'll probably never know, Loiosh."

"Vlad," said Morrolan. "I can feel the gate. Are you ready to go through it?"

"Sure," I said. "But now, what's the plan. Are we trying to escape, or do we want to kill this thing?"

The thing we were talking about kept looking at us; I had the impression it was holding itself ready for action, and that it didn't seem terribly worried.

"Kill it," said Aliera, and, at the same time, Morrolan said, "If we can get out cleanly, we should."

"I'm with you, Morrolan."

Aliera sniffed disdainfully.

Then things happened too fast for me to follow—it was one of those. I can't tell you who attacked first, or what form the attack took. I can't tell if the Jenoine's response was physical, magical, or some combination. I only know that, suddenly, everyone was moving, and I was lost in the combinations of limb, steel, and spell. I know that I was looking for an opening to use the Morganti dagger I held, and I know that I was trying to keep Spellbreaker in between me and anything nasty that it might send at me, and I know that I failed miserably at both efforts.

I can't tell you what Morrolan, Aliera, and Teldra were up to, but my part in the affair was mercifully brief—I lost consciousness within a matter of seconds. And, while I couldn't be sure what their situation was after it was over, at least mine was easily and readily understood when I awoke: I was manacled to the wall in almost exactly the same spot Aliera had occupied before. Teldra was next to me, unconscious, blood trailing down from the corner of her dainty mouth.

Well, Morrolan and Aliera were now free, in exchange for an Issola seneschal and an Easterner ex-assassin. A neat two-for-two swap. I wondered who had come out ahead on the trade. I was pretty sure it wasn't me.

7

ASKING FOR AND RECEIVING ASSISTANCE

"Think you can wake her up, Boss?"

"Don't know, Loiosh. Any reason why I should?"

"Uh . . . I'll get back to you on that. Think you can break these manacles the way you broke the other ones?"

I hefted them . . . they were lighter than they seemed.

"I hate repeating a trick," I told him. *"But I'm willing to make an exception this time."*

"That's big of you, Boss."

"But I'm going to wait, if you don't mind; I don't think I could manage a sleep spell right now."

While I waited and recovered, I did a quick check, and found to my surprise that the Jenoine had left me all my weapons. Why would they do that? The Morganti weapon was lying on the floor, no doubt right where it had fallen; they hadn't even taken it. Why would they capture me, but leave me all my weapons? They weren't supposed to do that. Maybe I should get them a copy of the rules.

Teldra stirred next to me.

"Good morning," I told her.

She squeezed her eyes shut without ever opening them, then did so again, and again. I waited.

"Any idea what that thing did to me, Loiosh? Why I lost consciousness?"

"No, Boss. It happened too fast. I didn't notice it even looking at you—you just went down."

I looked at Teldra again; she was working on becoming conscious, but it was taking a while.

"Okay, let's make a note not to underestimate the Jenoine."

"Right, Boss."

I leaned my head back, started to take a deep breath, and caught myself. I hate it when I need to take a deep breath but I can't—I'd have to find a different psychological crutch.

I caught an echo of my familiar's psychic snicker.

"You aren't helping any."

"What happened?" said Teldra.

"To begin with," I said, "the world was created from the seeds of amorphia spread from the droppings of a giant . . . no, I guess you aren't awake enough to appreciate my wit. I don't know what happened, Teldra. We're right where Morrolan and Aliera were, but I'm assuming our friends got away. Well, I don't know; maybe I shouldn't assume that. I hope they got away. I don't know. Tough bastards, those guys."

She chuckled. "Morrolan and Aliera, or the Jenoine?"

"Well, yeah."

Teldra nodded.

"How do you feel?" I asked her.

She stared at me. I recognized the look; I'd been on the other side of it often enough.

"Sorry," I said. "Stupid question."

She flashed me a Lady Teldra smile.

"It seems she's all right, Boss."

"Guess so."

Teldra seemed about to speak, but I closed my eyes and rested my head against the wall behind me, and she held her peace. The wall was smoother than it looked. I relaxed, prepared myself, and considered what I was about to do. After several minutes, Teldra said, "You're going to do something, aren't you?"

"Eventually."

"Can I help?"

I stirred, opened my eyes, looked at her. "Any training in witch-craft?"

She shook her head.

"Then I'm afraid not," I said.

I closed my eyes again and muttered, "Trágya."

"Legalább," she agreed.

My head snapped around. "You speak Fenarian?"

"Why yes," she said.

I grunted, wondering why I was surprised. "How many languages do you speak, Teldra?"

"Several," she said. "And you, Vlad?"

I shook my head. "None well. A bit of Fenarian. A smattering of a few other Eastern languages. But not enough to actually think in any of them—I always have to translate in my head."

"I see."

"How do you do that? How do you learn to think in another language?"

"Hmmm. It isn't an all or nothing thing, Vlad. You say you don't think in Fenarian, but what would you say if I said, Köszönöm?"

"Szivesen."

"Well?"

"Well, what?"

"Why did you say that?"

"You said, 'Thank you'; I said, 'You're welcome.' "

"But did you make that translation in your head, or was it automatic?"

"Ah. I see." I thought about that. "Okay, you're right. It was automatic."

"That's the beginning of thinking in the language."

"Like whenever I make a comment, Boss, and you say—"

"Shut up, Loiosh."

"Okay," I said. "You make a good point. But if I've got the basics, the rest is awful slow to follow."

"But it will get there if you keep speaking it. It starts with rote responses, such as thank you and you're welcome."

"Basic courtesy," I said. "Maybe all languages have rote responses for those: hello, how are you, that sort of thing. I wonder."

"They do," said Teldra.

"Are you sure?"

"The languages without courtesy built into them didn't survive long enough for us to remember them. Because, of course—"

"Yes," I said. "I see."

I pondered this linguistic profundity for a moment.

I considered what I had just done, and was soon going to do again. "Is witchcraft a language?"

"Hmmm. I don't know. I should imagine it is. I know that sorcery is."

"Witchcraft," I said, "does not have courtesy built into it."

She laughed. "All right. If we're counting, you've scored a point. If we are going to call those languages, and we might as well, they don't have built-in courtesy." She frowned suddenly. "Unless we consider . . . no, that's too far-fetched."

I didn't want to encourage her to go wherever she had been about to go, so I said, "How did you and Morrolan meet, anyway? If you don't mind my asking."

"It was out East," said Teldra. "During the Interregnum, in a village whose name translated to 'Blackchapel.' This was before he knew who he was, and—"

"Before he knew who he was?"

"Before he knew he was human."

I blinked. "I think you're going to have to explain that."

"I didn't realize you didn't know," said Teldra. "Certainly, it is no secret."

"All right."

"The Lord Morrolan was brought to the East, beyond his ancestral homelands, as an infant, just around the time of Adron's Disaster. His parents didn't survive, and so he was raised by Easterners. He grew up thinking he was simply an extraordinarily tall Easterner."

"You're kidding!"

"No, my lord."

"Well I'll be—really? He thought he was human? I mean, Easterner?"

She nodded.

I shook my head. "Amazing."

"Yes."

"Most extraordinarily tall," I reflected. "How did he find out?"

"It couldn't be concealed forever," she said. "In any case, I was also in the East, and of much the same age. We met at about the time he was completing his pact with Verra, in which I was able to be of some service to him, and I was also of some help when he was gathering his Circle of Witches."

I nodded. I knew this circle existed—they occupied the East Tower, but I had never had occasion to go there, and still didn't know exactly what he used them for. But, no doubt, I would never know all there was to know about Morrolan.

I shook my head, trying to get used to the idea of Morrolan being raised as an Easterner.

"Where in the East was he?"

"There are—or, rather, were—a series of small kingdoms near Lake Nivaper, just south of the Hookjaw Mountains."

"Yes, I know them. They speak Fenarian in some of them."

She nodded. "His name at the time was Fenarian: Sötétcsilleg. 'Morrolan' is just the same thing, rendered into the ancient tongue of the Dragon."

"Amazing," I said. "All right, so you helped him sacrifice villages of Easterners to the Demon Goddess. Then what?"

She smiled. "That was later, and they were Dragaeran villages. Eventually, he returned to reclaim his ancestral homeland, and he was gracious enough to give me residence. I was poor, of course, and had nowhere else to go. I remain very grateful to him."

I nodded, wondering what she was leaving out. Most likely, anything that was to her credit or Morrolan's discredit. She was like that. It sometimes made me a little uncomfortable to never know exactly what she was thinking, but, on the other hand, it was nice to know that there was at least one being in the world who wouldn't say anything nasty about me.

"You're awful sensitive for an assassin, Boss."

"You've said that before, Loiosh."

We returned to silence; I waited to recover and hoped I'd have time to do so; in the meantime my mind wandered, starting with the rather remarkable revelations about Morrolan and proceeding from there. I don't remember most of what I thought about—the sort of flitting, random thoughts that can only just barely be called thinking. But then I did eventually have a real, true thought, and it brought me up so sharply that it burst out of my mouth before my brain had entirely finished processing it: "Aw nuts. If Morrolan and Aliera did escape, I'll bet they're going to want to rescue us."

"Of course," said Teldra.

"Ready to start, Loiosh?"

"Boss—"

"I'll be fine."

"Boss—"

"If I'm still chained to this wall when Morrolan and Aliera show up, I'll almost certainly die of shame. The chances of messing up the spell are much less."

I got the impression Loiosh wasn't convinced. I wasn't either.

"Teldra," I said. "I've changed my mind. You can help."

"Yes?"

"You saw what I did with the knives?"

"Yes."

"Good," I said, and reached to hand her some—and only then realized that the Spellbreaker was back around my wrist. I stopped, hand in midair, and looked at Teldra.

"What is it, Vlad?"

"Loiosh," I said, "how did it get back there? Last I remember, it was in my hand, and I was waving it around like an idiot. I can't believe the Jenoine not only let me keep it, but were kind enough to put it back around my wrist for me."

"They didn't, Boss."

"Talk."

"It sort of slithered over to you, and, uh, it kind of crawled up your arm."

"On its own?"

" 'Fraid so, Boss."

Well. Wasn't that interesting?

I handed Teldra my last three daggers, pulling them out of various places. I hoped they would be enough—I used to carry a lot more.

"You know what to do?"

"I know what to do, but not when to do it."

"I'll try to say something. If I seem to lose consciousness, that would be a good time. Oh, give me one back for a second, I need to expose some more skin first."

She didn't ask, and I didn't explain; I just cut away four more strips from my jerkin. The air was even colder with still more of my belly exposed. I handed two of the strips to Teldra, asking her if she knew what to do with them. She nodded. She didn't appear at all nervous, which I attribute to acting ability, probably inherited; stupidity would be the only other possible explanation, and I didn't think she was stupid.

When we had managed to get the leather between the manacles and our wrists, she nodded at me, as if signaling that she was ready. I gave her back the last knife. I was now as close to unarmed as I'd been in some time. My rapier—

"Where is my rapier?" I said.

"Across the room, I think."

"How did that happen?"

"I don't know."

I considered the matter further, saying aloud, "If they know how we got out the last time, they might have done something to prevent this from working."

"I know," said Teldra.

"But they keep not behaving the way captors are supposed to."

"They probably weren't raised on the right sorts of bedtime stories and songs."

"And bad theater," I agreed. "But I'm starting to think they have a whole other plan in mind."

"What sort of plan?"

"I'm not sure," I said, which was not an outright lie, at any rate. "All right, then. Let's try it."

She said, "Vlad, do you think we're doing what they want us to?"

I paused, then sighed. "I wish I knew. Are you willing to go through with it anyway?"

She smiled. "Of course. It would be rude not to," proving that even Issolas are capable of self-directed irony. This, while maybe not an important discovery, was, somehow, a pleasing one.

"Let's do it, then."

She nodded. I held out my hand, and she took it; her hand was dry and cool.

I began.

You don't need to hear about it again, do you? I knew better than to let my fear interfere with what I had to do. Loiosh was his usual steady self, and, to make a long story short, I turned out to be sufficiently rested not to destroy myself.

The big difference between doing it on someone else and doing it on myself was that the coldness from my wrists became more and more insistent, and there was an awareness somewhere deep inside me that I could be seriously hurting myself. I had to trust Loiosh.

I was used to trusting Loiosh; over the years, I've gotten pretty good at it.

I concentrated, and pulled at imaginary skeins of fabric until it rolled over me, covered me, and I felt like I was going to drown in it; the chill on my wrists beginning to feel like heat, and insisting more and more on my attention; but I still had a bit left in me when the whole thing was shattered—quite literally—and I was pulled back to a hazy sort of half consciousness, vaguely pleased that my wrists were now free, noting that Teldra's were as well, and hoping that I wouldn't have to do anything strenuous like moving for at least a year or so.

She said something, but I didn't quite catch it. I tried to ask her to repeat it, but that, too, was beyond me.

In case you've missed it, I was more than a little exhausted. I closed my eyes, leaned against the wall, and concentrated on keeping my breathing even and shallow.

"I imagine," I said after a while, "they ought to be showing up any second."

"The Jenoine?" asked Teldra. "Or our friends?"

"Both, I should imagine. At the same time, presumably. That's how it ought to work out."

"You're just saying that, Boss, because you know if you say it it won't happen that way."

"I'm an Easterner, chum. I can be superstitious if I want to."

I rested, and recovered, and felt hungry. I found some more dried gammon in my pouch and offered some to Teldra, who gratefully accepted; then I watched her attempt to eat it daintily. She succeeded. I'd have been more astonished if I could have spared the energy for astonishment.

"Well," I said, "the longer it takes them—any of them—to show up, the better for us."

She nodded, and continued being dainty with dried gammon.

I wondered why she didn't make me feel rude and uncouth, but I suppose that was part of her talent. Or magic. You can always say it's magic if you don't understand it; and, who knows, you might be right.

While we stayed there—free of the chains but unable to move (in my case, unable to move for a number of reasons)—my imagination took flight. I wondered what Morrolan and Aliera were doing. They must be with Sethra, talking things over, making plans. Had they made contact with Verra? Was she going to take an active role in this? How about the Necromancer?

I pictured the lot of them, sitting in the library at Castle Black, or in one of the sitting rooms at Dzur Mountain, or in Verra's Hall; planning, scheming, debating.

Or maybe they'd all just gone and decided to take a nap, figuring, hey, what's one Issola and one Easterner? Maybe they'd just leave us here.

Or maybe they were eating, the bastards.

Meanwhile, in this structure, or near it, perhaps the Jenoine were coming up with their own schemes, or chuckling about how well this one had worked (did Jenoine chuckle? I couldn't imagine it). Perhaps they, too, had forgotten us. Perhaps, in the grand scheme of things, we didn't matter. Verra had as much as told me that I mattered because she was going to make me matter. I had mixed feelings about this.

Eventually, various needs brought me to my feet; I carried one of the chamber pots into a corner of the place and relieved myself, feeling like a drunk who's just staggered out of Coriaton's Public House. Then I made it back, drank some water, and waited.

Time dragged, and my imagination soared, and I considered my Fate. Teldra remained silent, perhaps aware of my thoughts and not wishing to disturb them, or perhaps she was busy with her own thoughts. Even Loiosh remained still.

But I considered who I was, and whether, when all was said and done, I would make a difference in the world. I had rarely had such thoughts—lately I hadn't had time for them, and before that they had never occurred to me.

But had Fate included me in its plans?

Did I even believe in Fate?

"Teldra, do you believe in Fate?"

My words shattered the stillness, like a sorcerous explosion, but she hardly blinked.

She said, "In a sense."

"Yes?"

"I believe in paths and choices. I don't believe in an inescapable fate, but I believe we are each given several possible directions, and sometimes we choose one without being aware of having made the choice."

I nodded. "I think I understand."

"But at other times, we know. Sometimes you realize you cannot stand still, and to move forward, or move back, or move to the side will set you on a new path."

"Does it matter to you if you make a difference in the world?"

"I do make a difference, Lord Taltos."

"Vlad."

"Very well. Vlad. I make a difference whether I wish to or not. I hope to make a good difference, if only in a small way."

"I wonder," I said. "I wonder whether a small way is enough for me. And I wonder if a big way is too much."

"Hmmm. What brought this up, if I may ask, Vlad?"

"I don't know. Too much time on my hands, boredom, and remembering my conversation with Verra."

"What about your conversation with Verra?"

"What she said about me being a tool."

"Oh," said Lady Teldra. "There is another thing about the Goddess."

"Yes?"

"Sometimes, when she speaks to us, we do not hear the same thing."

"I don't understand."

"It has been said that she speaks in words we can each understand, and that we will each understand her in our own way."

"Isn't that true of everyone?"

"Perhaps. But I didn't hear anything about you being a tool; I heard . . . well, it doesn't matter what I heard."

"Hmmmm," I said wisely, and didn't press the matter, though I wanted to badly. "I think," I said, "that I may be approaching one of those decision points you were talking about."

"Maybe," she said. "But I suspect, my lord, that you made your decision some time ago, and are just now beginning to understand its significance."

I let that one float around for a bit, then felt myself snarling. "All right, there's only so much of this I can take. I need to be doing something."

"You're feeling better, then?"

I considered, then said, "Yes, in fact, I am."

"Well then," said Teldra, "I am ready. But I don't know what we ought to be doing."

"It's not like I have a plan or anything," I said. "But it seems to me that, if we aren't going to just wait for our friends or our enemies, we should see if we can get out of this room."

"But then, will they be able to find us? Our friends, I mean."

"I hope so." I shrugged. "One would think that they could reach us psychically, if they were close enough."

I stood up, moving slowly and carefully, and walked across the room to where my rapier lay, all unnoticed and neglected. I checked it—it was fine. I returned it to my sheath. Then I walked over to the Morganti dagger. I thought for a while, made a decision, then hesitated because I didn't want to, then made myself pick it up and put it into its sheath.

"I don't see any doors," said Teldra.

"Of course not," I told her. "That would make everything too easy."

I stretched a bit—pleased to be up and around and walking. Teldra walked next to me, Loiosh on my shoulder, a rapier at my hip, a very strong Morganti dagger in a sheath next to it, Spellbreaker around my wrist, and my remaining couple of daggers concealed about my person. I felt ready for anything, as long as it wasn't too threatening.

We walked around the big, almost empty room, looking at walls, floor, and ceiling. It took a fair bit of time, but I didn't mind; I was pretty much recovered—though I felt generally sore and rather tired, and Loiosh had to keep reminding me to take shallow breaths. Except for the empty shelves placed here and there, seemingly at random, there wasn't much to see. Everything was very plain, flat, featureless—depressing.

Eventually we made it back to the place where we had been shackled. I said, "There's no way out."

Teldra nodded.

"Which answers the question about whether the Jenoine have sorcery, I imagine."

"Sorcery," agreed Teldra, "or, at any rate, something very much like it. But I thought that had been answered when they first appeared."

"Yeah. Or when they knocked me out. Okay. So, now what?"

"I don't know."

She didn't say, "Coming up with plans is your job," but I had the feeling she was thinking it. I didn't scowl, but she probably had the feeling I wanted to.

I said, "If I felt able to perform a spell, I might test the solidity of the wall." I pushed against the nearest wall, demonstrating, then said, "Hmmmm."

"What?" She pushed against it too. "What is it, Vlad? It feels like a wall."

"Yes, but what if it isn't everywhere?"

"Illusory walls?"

"Maybe," I said. "But I was thinking real walls, but a doorway made to look like a section of wall."

"Oh. Yes, that would be possible."

"You go that way, I'll go this way."

She nodded agreement, and we went around the room, pushing at the walls everywhere. If they were illusion, the illusion included the tactile, and didn't give when pushed.

"So much for that," I said, when we were back to where we had started.

She nodded. "Next idea?"

"You sure it isn't your turn?"

Her smile flicked on and off.

"You know, Boss, they don't actually have to have a doorway at all."

"I know, I know. But that's what they say about the keep of an Athyra wizard. And we know better."

"Just because it wasn't true—"

"I know, Loiosh. Now shut up and let me think."

He refrained from any cracks about that. I have come to appreciate the small blessings in life.

I considered matters for a bit, then said, "All right—if we're going to test it, we're going to test it."

Teldra gave me a look of inquiry. I let Spellbreaker fall into my hand. I could see Teldra wanting to ask what I was up to, but she didn't, and I didn't volunteer the information—if I was going to look ridiculous, at least I didn't have to explain why.

I struck Spellbreaker against the wall above where we had been chained up. It gave off a dull ringing sound.

"Vlad?"

"Get used to that sound, Teldra."

"Very well," she said.

I took a step to the right, and struck the wall again. It sounded just the same. I took another step, and another, and so on.

It was a big room, and it took a while, but I just told myself I was killing time until either the Jenoine reappeared, or Morrolan and Aliera showed up to rescue us, or something else happened.

Move a step—whap. Move a step—whap. Move a step—and then, when I found it, I almost missed it anyway. I was about a third of the way from where I started when I struck the wall, and started to move past it, but noticed that Spellbreaker had changed again. It was shorter, the links smaller. I stopped, looked at it, then at the spot of blank wall I was facing.

I struck the wall again, and a light tingle went up my arm, and I was looking at a doorway. Not even a door: rather a large stonework arch, maybe twelve feet high at its top, and big enough for four of me to walk past arm in arm. It was just there, as if to say, "What took you so long?"

I glanced back at Lady Teldra, who had been walking beside me to keep me company.

"Yes," she said. "I see it, too."

I not only saw it, but I felt the wind through it. Through it, mostly what we could see was darkness, except for the points of light in the sky.

"Stars," said Lady Teldra.

"I know them," I said. "They have them in the East, too."

"I know," she said. "I remember."

"I don't know exactly what they are; some say the homes of the gods."

"Some say each is a world," said Teldra. "That when we go

through a necromantic gate, we are stepping onto one of those points of light, from which we could look back and see our own world as a point of light. I like that notion."

"I'm not entirely certain that I do," I said. "I've never liked stepping into the unknown."

She refrained from any of the obvious observations she could have made to that, merely falling silent and waiting with me. Even as I watched, I realized that it was becoming brighter; it was dawn wherever we were, and I started to be able to make out features of the landscape.

It took several long moments before I was able to bring myself to step through the archway, toward the strange world, the emptiness, and the stars of the heavens.

8

FISHING ETIQUETTE

Here's a quick story for you, before we go any further:

In the earliest days of the World, Darkness mated with Chaos and produced three daughters. The first was Night, the second was Pain, and the third was Magic. Now Chaos went on and mated with the Sky, producing a son who was Evil. One day, Evil, being jealous of his stepsisters, captured Magic and took her away to his secret fortress beyond the World. But Magic called upon her Mother, Darkness, who heard her cries, and, seeing everything, saw what Evil had done.

Darkness then summoned Chaos and said, "Look what your son has done! He has taken Magic from the World."

Chaos then turned on his son, Evil, and cast him out, and rescued Magic, restoring her to the World. Then Evil cried out, saying that he repented his act, and praying that his father not abandon him. Chaos could not turn his heart from his only son, so he relented and permitted Evil into the world as well, but from that moment on, Magic has mistrusted Evil, though Evil still pursues Magic; and Darkness watches over them both, so that wherever you find Evil, you will find Darkness there, watching; and Chaos will sometimes be found in the aid of Magic, and sometimes in the aid of Evil.

Do you like it? It is an old story of my people, and there are some who believe it literally. I myself think there are elements of truth in it, because another name for Magic is Verra, the Demon Goddess, and, who knows, perhaps the Jenoine really are Evil. Beyond that, I don't care to venture; if there is a personification of Darkness, not to mention Chaos, then I don't want to know about it.

So here we were, maybe in the power of Evil; at least on their world, and maybe Magic would help us, and I was very much afraid that, if the Jenoine didn't get me, I'd trip over my own metaphors and break my neck.

These were my thoughts, then, as we stepped out of the door, and I don't know how it was for Teldra, but for me there was a shock: the sudden realization that the entire world was not that one room of that one building.

"Anything or anyone, Loiosh?"

"Not as far as I can tell, Boss."

We walked twenty-five or thirty feet away from it, and looked back; I was half expecting it to have vanished, but it was still there, the outside looking quite a bit like the inside, except that the surface was rougher—it seemed to be just chunks of rock stuck together. A closer look indicated an odd shape to the structure—it was hard to tell from this close, but it seemed that it had an angle to it; that it wasn't quite straight up, and there were bits of projections sticking out. Was this significant of anything? Stupid question. What was significant and what wasn't with these beings?

I turned my attention to the landscape, and eventually thought of Dzur Mountain.

There was nothing there that actually looked like Dzur Mountain, mind you, but—

Okay. A stream, maybe fifty or sixty feet wide, cut across and dominated the landscape, flowing diagonally toward me from my right to my left, about a hundred yards away at its nearest point; a few spindly trees with stubby branches and massive leaves all along their lengths dotted the banks on both sides, and what seemed to be a stonework bridge appeared not far away. To my right were a couple of low hills, all brown and rocky, and to my left the ground was flat but sloping gently down, maybe dipping to meet the stream, maybe not. And above it all (quite literally) was this terrible, bright object burning down on everything. I'm not trying to be mysterious—I had been to the East, and I knew damned well that it was a Furnace, just as we had in the Empire, only here, as out East (and a few places in the far West), it wasn't hidden by a constant overcast. But I had forgotten how painfully bright it was, and how dark were the shadows it caused when it met anything else. It was low in the sky, a little to my left as I stepped out of the door, and, among other things, it highlighted everything else, including the few white puffy bits of over-cast in a sky that was otherwise as blue as the sky above Fenario, giving me a very strange feeling of homesickness that juxtaposed with the harsh certainty that I was in a world that, perhaps, no other human had ever set foot on before.

So Teldra and I studied all of this, and that's when I thought of Dzur Mountain. It was a very nice mix of natural elements, here, and I'd swear someone had crafted it. I don't know why—I'm not sure what the indications were; but it looked for all the world like someone had sat down and said, "Okay, the river runs this way, straight, then we'll put a curve in here. How 'bout a couple of hills?" and like that.

"You're right," said Teldra.

I looked at her. "I beg your pardon?"

"Dzur Mountain," she said.

"Oh. I hadn't realized I'd spoken out loud."

"You muttered it under your breath."

"Hmmm." I wondered where I'd developed the habit of doing that? Probably from being alone so much of the time. I was going to have to watch out for that; it wasn't a good habit.

"Nothing lives," murmured Teldra.

I started to ask what she meant—I mean, there was grass, and there were trees and such. Then realized: I saw no birds in the air, no small animals hopping around, much less big ones; looking at my feet, I didn't even see any insects. "You're right," I said. "We seem to be the only living things here."

"Oh," she said, smiling. "That time I did it."

My hand strayed to my rapier, and I suddenly had the feeling that this entire world—everything that had happened since walking through Morrolan's window—was a massive illusion; was one of those elaborate living dreams, such as I had encountered in the Paths of the Dead.

"It's real enough, Boss."

"Are you sure?"

"I'm sure. If there is a glamour, it's to conceal something, not to alter the appearance of what we're seeing."

"That's sort of a fine distinction, chum."

"I know," he told me.

Well, that was part of Loiosh's job, so I had to trust him. Besides: if he was wrong, and it was all an elaborate dream like the ones in the Paths, well, there had been no way out of those except to treat them as real and work through them.

But the lack of critters was hard to get used to.

"What do you think, Teldra? Was this whole area fabricated?"

"Maybe, Vlad. Maybe the whole world."

"No," I said. "I know it wasn't the whole world."

"Oh?" she said. "How can you tell?"

"Because if they can do that, we don't have a chance against them."

She laughed. "Ah. I see. I'm not familiar with that logic."

I shrugged. "Actually, I'm not kidding. That's one thing I learned in the course of my long and checkered career. If your only chance of living through something is if your enemy isn't a sorcerer, or doesn't have a spare dagger, or can't jump an eleven-foot crevasse, then you assume your enemy isn't a sorcerer, or doesn't have a spare dagger, or can't jump an eleven-foot crevasse."

"Hmmmm," said Teldra. "I see. It makes a very practical sort of sense."

"Yes," I said, involuntarily remembering the guy who could jump an eleven-foot crevasse, much to my disgust—but I survived that one anyway, because he turned out to be wearing the wrong kind of boots. Long story; never mind.

There was a bit of a breeze coming from my left; not too strong, just enough to tickle the back of the neck. It brought no smells except the sort of sweet scent that seemed to be part of the air here. This reminded me, again, to keep my breathing even and shallow.

"Well," I said, "Teldra, you must have studied all the old songs and stories, and you must be better read in history than I am, and since I almost never attend the theater, you must attend more often than I do."

"Perhaps," she said.

"Well then? What does one typically do in a situation like this?"

Teldra looked at me.

"I mean, usually when one finds oneself on an entirely different world, barely able to breathe, surrounded by a bizarre environment, beset with enemies with the strength of gods, and with no way home—what are the usual steps?"

She barely cracked a smile.

"Usually," she said, "one calls for help of one's patron god, who then assigns one an impossible task in exchange for minimal aid, which aid turns out to be ironically fatal. Or else one discovers a powerful artifact of unknown properties, which, upon use, proves to take over one's soul, so that, after the rescue, one kills one's beloved."

"I see. Well, now you know why I almost never attend the theater."

Teldra supplied the obligatory chuckle and I looked out once more at the world around us—suddenly taken by the fear that Morrolan and Aliera would not come, and the Jenoine would not come, and we would find no way out; that we would remain here for the rest of our days. Which days, now that I thought of it, wouldn't be long if we didn't figure out how we were going to eat. But I knew this fear was groundless. Whatever Morrolan had done in the past, I knew that he would never stop trying to rescue us as long as he was alive. And, of course, things being as they were, death might not manage to stop him either.

I sighed.

"You know, Loiosh, if anyone had told me yesterday at this time that thirty hours later I would have rescued Morrolan and Aliera, nearly killed the Demon Goddess, and found myself trapped in a prison the size of the world, unable to decide if I was hoping to be saved or was hoping not to be saved, I'd have said, 'Yeah, sounds about right.' "

"You probably would have, Boss."

"I think this says something about my life choices."

"Uh huh."

I looked around at the world, noticing the perfection of the stream, the hills, the mountains—the general sense that everything had been planned and crafted. I had the sudden irrational (and, I'm sure, wrong) notion that this little part of the world was all there was—that everywhere out of sight was just sort of grey and unfinished; and I was also again reminded of the Paths of the Dead, though I'm not sure why.

Teldra and I began walking. The ground was soft and springy, and we soon reached the banks of the stream, which were only two or three feet above the flow. I leaned over and stared into it, watching it. It hardly seemed to be moving, yet occasionally the crests would break into diminutive whitecaps. It was neither blue nor green nor red, as is most of the water I've seen, but sort of an olive; I could not imagine what accounted for this. I couldn't see the bottom, but it seemed neither shallow nor dirty.

"What is it, Boss?"

"This water."

"What about it?"

"I don't know. It's no more natural than the rest of this place, but . . . it isn't perfect."

He said nothing; I continued studying it. Teldra remained a foot or two behind me, silent, the soul of patience. I stooped, then knelt. I reached out toward the water, then changed my mind, holding my hand motionless. Then I—how shall I put this—extended my senses. It's hard to describe; it's sort of like the difference between hearing something and intensive listening; or between resting your hand on velvet, and closing your eyes and luxuriating in the feel of it; only with a sense that . . . oh, forget it. It's a witch thing.

In any case, I reached out, for the water, and—

"Yes," I said aloud.

"Yes?" echoed Lady Teldra.

"Yes," I agreed.

She waited.

I turned to her. "The water," I said. "It isn't water."

She waited.

"Boss—"

"I don't know, Loiosh; I'm working on it."

Aloud I said, "The water isn't like the rest of the place. Well, it is and it isn't. It's—I don't know. I want to follow it."

"All right, Vlad. Upstream or down?"

"Uh . . . you ask good questions."

The source or the result; the theoretical or the practical; find out what it all means, or go straight for where something can be done about it. A moment of sublime indecision, with a chance to learn something deep and important about myself. Or perhaps not; I know that by inclination I'm a source man; I like to understand things as completely as possible, but if I was to do something before things were done to me, I couldn't take the time.

"Downstream," I said. "Let's see where this goes."

She nodded, Loiosh mumbled an agreement into my mind, and we set off. The stream meandered gently, the ground underfoot was soft and springy if uneven; the air still had that sweetness. I was getting used to taking shallow breaths. The scenery didn't change much, and the water was quieter than the forest streams I'd become used to finding by sound and smell.

After most of a mile, I realized that I was hearing something—a low sort of rumble. It was oddly difficult to localize, but seemed to come from ahead of us.

"Loiosh, you said you couldn't fly, but—"

"No, I can do it, I think."

"Then—"

"I'm on my way, Boss."

He left my shoulder and flew off ahead of me, his flight strong and smooth, mostly gliding, wings flapping now and then, smoothly; quite graceful, actually.

"Gee, thanks, Boss."

"Oh, shut up. Are you all right?"

"Yeah, I can manage. I just have to glide a lot, and I won't be able to keep this up very long."

"You won't have to. What do you see?"

"I'd say water, only you claim it isn't water, so . . . wait a minute. It's getting louder. It's—"

"Yes?"

"Well, it's safe enough. Come ahead."

"All right."

The ground rose a little, leaving the water—or whatever it was— about twenty feet below us in a sort of cleft, like a scale model of a river valley, all green and stuff. Loiosh returned to my shoulder as I took the last few steps. The roaring became louder—like, each step noticeably increased the volume; soon we'd have had to shout to be heard, and at about that time we came over a rise and saw it—a waterfall, or it would have been a waterfall if whatever was falling had been water. Certainly, it behaved like water as it went over the lip and struck the bottom, about a hundred or a hundred and twenty feet below; complete with what seemed to be mist springing up from it. The lip was narrower than the stream, I'd say about thirty-five feet. The "water," for lack of a better word, rushed over it in a tremendous hurry to reach the bottom. I watched, fascinated the way one sometimes is by nature, though I hesitate to call it "nature"—I didn't believe this was any more natural than anything else I'd seen since I got here.

It fell majestically. It foamed and swirled in the pool at the bottom, before heading off downstream; I picked out particles and watched them plummet; I watched the mist rise and curl. I wondered what it was.

On my arm, I felt Spellbreaker stir. Just a little; a sort of twitch that could almost have been my imagination, but no, it wasn't.

And then I knew.

Of course, you—who have heard all of my story to this point, and are now sitting back drinking your favorite wine and listening to my voice pour out—you had it figured a long time ago. And, I suppose, I ought to have too. But it is one thing to hear about it, and quite another to be there with it, watching it, hearing it, and not really wanting to believe that you're looking at what you think you're looking at.

"Amorphia," I said aloud, naming it, making it real. According to some of the beliefs surrounding the practice of witchcraft, to name it was to give it power; according to others, to name it was to give myself power over it. This felt like the former.

"What?" shouted Teldra.

I leaned over until I was talking into her ear. "Amorphia," I repeated, making my voice calm, as if I were announcing nothing of any importance. "The stuff of chaos."

She stared at it, then nodded slowly, leaned over, and spoke into my ear. "Yes," she said. "You're right. It is amorphia. Only controlled. Going where the Jenoine wish it to go, and doing what they wish it to do."

I nodded, and led us back from the brink, just a score or so of paces over the hill so we could speak in normal tones. I said, "I didn't think amorphia occurred anywhere except at home."

"Neither did I," she said.

I grunted. "So, which is scarier—that they have created a river of amorphia, or that they are able to create a river of amorphia? Or, for that matter, the fact that the Jenoine have permitted us to see all of this?"

"I begin to believe," she said, "that the reason we haven't been molested is that, quite simply, we are too insignificant to worry about."

"Insulting," I said, "but it could be true. It would explain why we've been permitted to see this, too—we just don't matter."

Teldra exhaled briefly through her nose and watched the scene. I watched with her. She said, "And we were wondering if there was any magic here."

I listened to chaos splash over the cliff. From where we stood, we could see the rush of the gathered amorphia about to plunge over the falls. Now that I knew—or, perhaps, now that I had admitted to myself what it was—it looked even less like water; the color changed as you tried to focus on it, but now appeared mostly to fluctuate between steely grey and a dark, unhealthy green. And while it almost behaved as water should, it didn't quite do that, either.

"Well, we've certainly learned something," I remarked into the air.

Amorphia. The stuff of chaos. According to some, the stuff of life; according to others, the basic building block of all matter and energy. I didn't know; I wasn't a magical philosopher, and I'd certainly never studied the ancient, illegal, and frightening branch of sorcery devoted to such things.

I'd used amorphia once, and since then had skimmed a couple of Morrolan's books to pick up useful-looking spells, but I'd never studied it.

I *had* used it once.

A long time ago, in the heart of the city, trying to save the life of Morrolan (who was dead at the time; don't ask), faced by several sorceresses of the Bitch Patrol—the Left Hand of the Jhereg—I had called upon abilities I didn't know I had, I had hurled something at them they could not have anticipated any more than they could counter it.

Yes, I had done it once.

I let that memory play around in my head, remembering the feel of a tavern floor against my face, and a sense of desperation; a desire to do something, anything, and the explosive release of a power I had inherited because, once, my soul had been close kin to the soul of some idiots who played around with that power. That day, I had been an idiot, too, and had been rescued by Aliera before I dissolved myself and a section of Adrilankha into the basic component of all matter and energy, or whatever it was.

I remembered that day, years ago, and separated from me by so many experiences that it might as well have happened to a different person.

Only I wasn't, really, a different person. And, try as I might, I couldn't shy away from the implications of that.

"Boss—"

"*Not now, Loiosh. Let me work it through on my own; there are too many angles to this thing.*"

"*All right.*"

If anyone asked me if I knew the Elder Sorcery, I could say no with a clear conscience. I *didn't* know it, in any meaningful way.

But—

The Elder Sorcery is, perhaps, the most difficult branch of magic, at least until you try to throw them all together and tie them up in some object where you also keep your soul so you get to call yourself a "wizard" for whatever satisfaction that will bring you. I had once harbored illusions about learning sorcery as it was practiced before the Empire, before the Orb, before what I'd call civilization. I had a sort of start, owing to an accidental relationship in my past life. I abandoned the study early on, because not only was it difficult, and scary, but I just had too damned much else going on in my life at the time.

But I did have a pretty good memory of step one—that is, the first and easiest spell, the one necessary to continue on to the more difficult spells. And this spell, if I could pull it off, just might prove useful.

My brain raced, and worked at a few of the angles until it ran down, by which time I had already opened up my small pouch of witchcraft supplies, and dug around for a bit. I didn't have a lot of stuff with me, and everything I did have was valuable, but what can you do? I picked out the ceramic bottle of dira juice because it wasn't too hard to come by, and the main use it had was treating a particular jungle fever that I'd so far managed to avoid. I poured the contents on the ground. I noticed Teldra looking a question at me. I shook my head.

I found a loop of leather and hung it around the neck of the bottle; then I walked over to the bank where the amorphia flowed like water.

Teldra cleared her throat. "I was just wondering," she said, "how you're going to keep the bottle from dissolving in the amorphia you're trying to capture."

"Oh," I said. "You've known Morrolan a great deal longer than I have; haven't you read any of his books?"

"Not on the Elder Sorcery. Have you?"

"Yes," I said.

"Oh." She considered. "And you learned how to do whatever it is you're doing?"

The questions were a bit intrusive for Teldra, but I couldn't blame her; hanging around while an incompetent plays around with amorphia is worth at least a couple of innocent questions.

"More or less," I told her.

She bit her lip and didn't ask anything else, for which she ought to have received whatever sorts of medals her House gives out.

I started the bottle spinning in a wide, slow loop, directly in front of me, about a foot over the stream. "It really isn't that difficult," I said, "if all you want to do is capture some of it. It's just a question of speed." As I spoke, I started spinning the bottle a little faster— not much. "Amorphia will take, uh, some measurable fraction of a second before it begins to operate on matter that comes in contact with it. The trick is just to get it before it destroys or alters whatever vessel you're using to capture it." I glanced at her. "Move a couple of steps to the right, please."

She did so, silent.

The other trick is the little matter of the spell.

There isn't a lot to say about it. It's a pretty simple spell, really— well described by the book. You just draw the power through your link to the Orb. . . .

Yeah.

There's the catch. The whole "link to the Orb" problem. I was currently missing one of those.

To the left, however, there were alternatives, if you were willing to risk interaction with unfettered, raw amorphia. I happened to have a supply of that near to hand.

I stared at the stream.

Do you know how hard it is to look at water? To see it, when it's flowing past you? You see foam, or swirls, or crests, or whitewaters, or maybe the streambed, or maybe the reflection off the surface, but it is very hard to actually see the water. It is even harder when it isn't actually water, but amorphia, the quintessence of formlessness; it is hard to see formlessness, because what we see is form. Try it sometime, if you have any raw chaos lying about; it is simultaneously too much and too little to grasp.

But I kept trying, staring at and then past the subtle color shifts, rigorously refusing to believe in the shapes my mind tried to impose on the shapelessness. And at length—I don't know how long it was—I began to seep into it. Those sorcerers who spend a lot of time working with amorphia say that every such experience is a step closer to madness. Judging from Aliera and Morrolan, I think that is probably true. But fortunately, I didn't have to go too far, just enough contact for one little spell.

I felt a response within me; something like and yet unlike the first feelings that a spell is working. To the right, I felt as if I were secure and comfortable and relaxed, and to the left I felt as if I were on the edge of a precipice and one small step, or the loss of my balance, would send me hurtling over into insanity.

The balance issue was a good metaphor, and also quite real, because, as I readied the spell, I leaned over the stream. Should I slip in, it would be a quicker death than many that I've come near, but it isn't how I choose to spend my last measurable fraction of a second.

I changed the angle, so instead of spinning parallel to the stream, it was almost perpendicular. I timed the spin—it was just over a second for a full loop. I wished I remembered just what the measurement on that measurable fraction of a second was; at the time, that hadn't been the sort of detail I was interested in, not being able to imagine being in this situation. Was it around half a second? A little less? I sped up the spin just a trifle, then let my breath out slowly.

"Here we go," I said aloud. "Keep your eye on this thing; there should be something flying out onto the shore behind me." I executed, or perhaps I should say *released* the spell as I lowered my arm so the bottle splashed into the stream.

The first good news was that I didn't fall in; but I hadn't really expected to.

The second good news was that the stream didn't splash on me; I'd been afraid of that, but couldn't think of a good way to avoid it.

The third good news was that the leather suddenly felt lighter in my hand, and a glance told me that there was nothing hanging on the end.

But the real good news was that Teldra cried out, "I saw it! Something flashed. It went off that way."

I followed her pointing finger, dropping the leather just in case there were unpleasant things clinging to the end of it.

The grass here wasn't terribly long; it only took five minutes or so before I found it. I reached down and picked it up, just as if doing so didn't scare me.

It took the form of a small stone, perfectly round and about an inch in diameter; it was very heavy for its size, and had a sort of milky hue somewhere in between blue and purple.

"Got it," I said, holding it up.

She came over and inspected it, Loiosh doing the same from my shoulder.

"Pure amorphia," I said, "but in a form that can be worked with."

"If you say so," said Teldra

"I say so."

I slipped it into my pouch as if it were no big deal.

Teldra nodded as if it were no big deal, and said, "All right, then, Vlad, what next?"

That was a good question. But I now had Spellbreaker, a powerful Morganti dagger, a chunk of amorphia, my training as a witch, and my native wit. Might as well use them for something.

I said aloud, "Patience my ass; I'm going to go out and kill something."

9

How to Break Unwelcome News

Teldra frowned. "Excuse me?"

"Never mind; an old Jhereg joke. Let's go back."

"Back, Vlad?"

"To our prison."

I watched her face, and decided she was struggling between courteously agreeing and rudely asking if I had lost my mind. I politely cut in before she had to choose.

"This place"—I gestured aimlessly—"gives me the creeps. I don't mean just here, I mean this whole area. The Jenoine will be able to find us anywhere on their world, if they want to, so being out here will only make it harder for Morrolan and Aliera to find us."

"Ah," she said. "You've resigned yourself to being rescued, then?"

"Heh. I'm still thinking about it."

"And you have another idea, don't you?"

"Hmmm. Sort of a plan."

She smiled. "That's good enough for me," she said, and we headed back for the building that had been our prison. I should, perhaps, have been surprised that it hadn't vanished while we were out of sight, but it hadn't, and the door was still where we'd left it. We went back inside. The door vanished as we stepped through, but I wouldn't give it the satisfaction of being startled by that.

"What's the plan this time, Boss?"

"If I told you, you'd just laugh."

"Probably."

"You could learn a lot from Teldra."

"*The ocean says the river is wet. The snow says the ice is cold.*"

"*Is that like, the jhereg says the yendi is a reptile?*"

"*Shut up, Boss.*"

I studied the big, empty room on the big empty world, considered my predicament, thought over my idea, and tried to be optimistic. I glanced over to where the shackles still hung on the wall. The Jenoine could put us back in them easier than I'd gotten out of them. But why should they? After all, the whole reason—

"Teldra, do you think I'm paranoid?"

She blinked. "Lord Taltos?"

"I keep seeing devious plots everywhere, and thinking that everyone must have two or three layers of subterfuge behind every action."

"I recall, my lord, your affair with the Sorceress in Green. It seems to me you were correct on that occasion."

"She's a Yendi."

"And these are Jenoine. Much more worrisome. With a Yendi, one at least *knows* everything is subterfuge and misdirection. With the Jenoine, we don't understand them, and we don't know if they understand us."

I nodded. "Okay, a point."

She continued, "I think it reasonable to wonder if we are doing what they want us to—if they have everything planned, and each step we have taken is in accordance with their wishes. Didn't Sethra say as much? Yet it is uncertain, because we behave unpredictably, and we don't yet know to what extent they can anticipate and understand us. I'm working on that," she added.

"You're working on that?"

"Yes."

I wanted to ask her in exactly what way was she working on it, but if she had wanted me to know, she'd have told me. All right, then. I'd go ahead and assume I was right in my surmises until I found out I was wrong—by which time it would probably be too late, and I wouldn't have to worry about it. There are advantages to fatalism.

"Hungry, Teldra?"

"No, thank you."

I grunted and shared a bit of jerky with Loiosh. Teldra went over to the wall and sat down, her knees up, arms around her knees—she managed to make the position look dignified and graceful.

I said, "Teldra, what, exactly, is the soul?"

"I hope you're asking rhetorically, Vlad. I've never studied magical philosophy. I only know the mundane answer—that which is left after the death the physical body—the life essence—the personality, separated from matter."

I nodded. "Yeah. I've never studied magical philosophy either. I guess I should have, at some point."

"Is it important?"

"Yes."

She looked a question.

I touched the Morganti dagger at my belt and said, "These things destroy souls. It would be very useful right now to know exactly what they destroyed, and how they did it, and what it all means. I'm trying to avoid being embarrassed at a critical moment."

"I see. I'm afraid I can't help you."

She had already helped. I leaned against the wall next to her and pondered the soul.

"Boss, why is it you always get philosophical just when—"

"Shut up, Loiosh."

He snickered into my mind; I ignored him.

To think of the soul as a field of sorcerous energy usually anchored to a living body might be incomplete, but also might be close enough to be useful; at least, to the best of my knowledge, that was how a Morganti dagger treated it. It said nothing about how such a nebulous thing as a personality could be contained in a field of sorcerous energy, but Morganti weapons are notoriously unconcerned with personalities.

If it was good enough for a Morganti dagger, it was good enough for me.

Heh.

Teldra was looking at me.

I cleared my throat. "I assume you want to be let in on what my plan is."

"That's up to you, Vlad. If you think I should know, tell me. Otherwise, not."

I stared at her. "You really do trust me, don't you?"

"Yes," she said.

"By the Halls of Judgment, *why?*"

"Because you keep surviving, Vlad."

She said it so matter-of-factly that I was almost convinced. "Heh," I said. "I'm just being saved for some spectacularly awful death."

"If so," she said, "I'm sure you'll comport yourself with dignity."

"Dignity? Me? Not bloody likely. If I go down swinging, it'll be because I think swinging is more likely to get me out of it than running. If I go down running, I won't be surprised."

She gave me a smile as if she didn't believe me and said, "I hadn't meant to turn the conversation morbid."

"Oh, don't worry about that, Teldra. Most of my thoughts are morbid. I think it comes of having spent so long killing people for a living. Strange way to live, when you think about it, so I try not to, but I can't help it. On the other hand, you work for a guy known for sacrificing whole villages, so I guess I'm a bit of a piker by comparison."

"More like hamlets than villages, Vlad. And he *was* at war against them at the time, you know."

"Oh. Actually, I hadn't known that. I just chalked it up to another example of how charming my dear Goddess can be."

"It was while he was consolidating his power and retaking his ancestral homelands. They worshiped Tri'nagore, a God you don't hear from much anymore, and had overrun Blackchapel, killing everyone in it. Morrolan returned the favor, and sent their souls to his Patron Goddess."

"I see. They don't tell that part of the story."

"The Lord Morrolan refuses to be put in the position of defending his actions. He considers it undignified."

"So he'd rather everyone thought him a bloodthirsty butcher?"

"Yes."

"Yeah, I guess he would at that."

To the left, I reflected, he could be bloodthirsty enough, however much Teldra downplayed it. I recalled an incident at Castle Black. I wasn't paying much attention, being involved in some rather nasty squabble with another Jhereg at the time, but I remember him challenging another Dragonlord to a duel, and then doing everything to the guy except making him unrevivifiable—I mean he dismembered the poor bastard, and seemed to take great joy making the fellow's death as slow and painful as he could. This was a memory I didn't care to dwell on; I don't enjoy such scenes. But it was certainly impossible to deny that that side of Morrolan existed. I wondered—

"Teldra," I said suddenly. "Do you recall a certain Lord Vrudric e'Lanya whom Morrolan fought a few years ago?"

She looked at me quizzically and nodded.

"Can you tell me what that was about?"

"You don't know, Vlad? Vrudric was casting aspersion on Adron's character."

"Adron? Adron e'Kieron?"

"Yes."

"That's it? Morrolan did that to him because he was casting aspersions on the character of the guy who was either so greedy, or so incompetent, or, at best, so misguided that he destroyed the whole Verra-be-damned Empire and dissolved Dragaera City into amorphia? *That* guy?"

"Adron is one of Morrolan's heroes. I thought you knew that."

"No," I said. "I hadn't known that. But Adron . . . okay. It's strange, but I guess I can get used to it. Hmmm. Morrolan e'Drien. Who was Drien, anyway?"

"A contemporary of Kieron the Conqueror, perhaps the first Shaman who was a warrior, or the first warrior who was a Shaman. From what I gather, he or she was brilliant, fiery, talented, creative, powerful, and emotionally unstable."

" 'He or she'?"

"As I understand it, Drien was born female but transformed herself into a man around the time of the founding of the Empire. Or it may have been the other way around. I don't know if the man or the woman had offspring, or both; and perhaps the story isn't true, but that is the tradition."

"I see. Hmmm. But then . . . never mind. What about the other story? I mean the one about Morrolan charging up to Dzur Mountain when he found out that there was someone in his domain who hadn't paid him tribute."

"Oh." Teldra smiled. "Yes, that one is true."

I chuckled. "Oh, to have been there to witness that conversation. I don't suppose you went along?"

"Hardly."

"Did he ever say what happened?"

"No. But it can't have been anything too horrid; they've been friends ever since."

"Oh yeah? Does she pay him tribute?"

"I don't know," said Teldra, smiling.

"I'll be sure to ask him. Sometime when we're not in the middle of trying to batter our way out of a trap set by demigods. Which reminds me, I had an idea about that. I'll give you the rough outline of—"

"*Boss!*"

I spun around. Morrolan and Aliera were back, both holding their swords in their hands, and looking like I felt—that is, full of the desire to kill something.

"Welcome," I said, "to our temporary abode. I'm afraid our hospitality may be—"

"Where are they?" said Aliera.

I shrugged. "They forgot to say where they were going when they left. Actually, I forgot to ask them. I was napping at the time, as I recall. Oh, by the way, Morrolan, I'm curious about whether you get any tribute from Dzur Mountain."

"Vlad," said Morrolan, "do you have any idea what we had to do to get back here? To even find the place, much less break through, required the Necromancer to spend twelve hours pulling memories out of Blackwand—memories she didn't know she contained. After that—"

"How long has it been, in your world?"

"Not long. A couple of days. A very busy couple of days, I might add."

I nodded. "A few hours, here. Did you bring any food? Jerky and gammon are getting old."

Morrolan and Aliera looked at each other. "No, sorry," said Morrolan.

"Perhaps it would be best to get going, then."

"Yes," said Aliera. "That's the idea." Morrolan was frowning his frown of concentration—I hoped and believed doing what was necessary to get us out of there.

"That is," I added, "if the Jenoine will let us. Do you think they will?"

"Perhaps not," said the Lord of Castle Black, looking up suddenly. "But we are prepared for them to attempt to stop us. Unfortunately, the gate has shut again. I'm going to try to open it." He did that thing with his hands again, and he was once more holding his thin, black wizard's staff. This time I noticed something: a blue ring that he always wore on his left hand was no longer there, yet I had been certain he had been wearing it an instant before. Okay, it was a nice trick, and it had some flash. I could always respect flash, if it didn't conflict with practicality.

I looked at Morrolan, as if seeing him for the first time, with all that Teldra had told me buzzing around in my head. Adron? He certainly was far more complex than I had ever thought him. It suddenly flashed into my head to wonder if he and Sethra were currently or ever had been lovers. Now *that* was an interesting thought, and one that would probably come back to me on many cold nights— assuming, of course, that I would have the opportunity to have many cold nights.

Which brought me sharply back to the present. I said, "Sethra is in on this, isn't she?"

"Yes," said Morrolan. "And she's at Castle Black, in the Tower, waiting to assist us."

I nodded. "Knowing, I'm sure, that her help is likely to be either insufficient or unnecessary."

"Yes."

I felt myself scowling, and my stomach growled, just to make sure I understood how it felt, too.

"Got it," said Morrolan suddenly. "Over here, quickly."

There was a shimmering waviness in the air, gold colored, about six feet behind Morrolan.

"Very well," said Aliera, walking toward it. "Let's do it; the gate won't remain open forever. Teldra, you first. Hurry, Vlad."

"They're late, Boss."

"Seems like."

Teldra and I took a step toward her.

Sometimes, things are so close—almost this, or just barely that; one thing and another, balanced just so, that there seems to be an instant where they are both happening, and neither happens, and each path is fully realized, like a psiprint, held in place by the strength

of mutual impossibilities. Sometimes lives—your own or another's—
depend on decisions that come within a whisper, a hair, a fraction of
breath, of going one way, or the other. Have you the strength of will
to do what you know—*know*—is the right thing, or will your appetite
rule the moment? Will you allow the anger of an instant to command
your tongue, and make a breach that can never be healed, or will
you manage to hold ire in check for just long enough—a tiny portion
of a second—to escape?

Sometimes it is so close, so very close.

I took a step forward, and—

—as my footstep faded, I could almost hear—

—an infinitely extended moment, nothing happening, taking forever, but much too fast—

—was instantly aware—

—voices whispering in the silence, with the silence, not disturbing it—

—a foot almost descending, simultaneously in one place and another—occupying two places at once, but that's what movement is
all about—

—that Loiosh was no longer with me. Even before—

—leaving perception, without the awareness of whence it sprang
except—

—all life is movement, which is to be here and not here and the
same time, or here and there simultaneously, or to deny time, or to
deny place—

—I realized that my surroundings had changed, that I was uncertain where I was, that—

—that it came from outside of self, if such a distinction is valid
without time or place to hang it from, and the voices—

—is to be, in fact, nowhere, and nowhere is—

—Teldra and Aliera and Morrolan had cross-stepped while I
lunged, I knew—

—came with eyes, and ears, and other things that—

—everywhere is here and there and there ought to be a way—

—that I was out of touch with my familiar and it—

—gave me the feeling that I was being studied, scanned, analyzed,
and ultimately—

—to seize control, or at least to act, or at the very least to make a decision—

—had been years since I had come so—

—discarded, and permitted—

—to be holding a chain of gold light, in my mind if nowhere else, so that in and through the shield of swirling gold which suddenly—

—close to panic—

—to stop, or resume—

—seemed to me to be a *place*, not a thing, that I could—

—but that, like so much else, is self-defeating, so I—

—the interrupted pace, the walk, the step, which in turn permitted—

—enter into and go through and be changed by—

—tried not to think about it, but trust in him and me, and just do—

—a junction of thought and a resonance of experience, so that I managed, or thought I managed, or almost managed—

—spinning corridors of gold that were within and without, and then through once more, leaving me—

—and I guess it worked because what was before me became behind me, and here became there, which was all right, because I—

—to make contact, once more, with my familiar familiar.

—somewhere real at last.

—was back.

"Well," I said or thought, lying against the cold stone floor. "If it isn't one thing, it's another."

"Are you all right, Vlad?" It took me a moment to realize the voice belonged to Teldra, and even longer to understand that the question begged an answer. What the answer ought to be was beyond me.

"Vlad?"

I turned my head and made eye contact with her, looking up at her impossibly tall form, hoping she would see that I was at least somewhat sensible.

"You okay, Boss?"

"Ask something easier, it'll take me some time to figure that out."

"Where did you go?"

"That's what I was going to ask you."

Around then, I realized that we hadn't actually gone anywhere—we were still in the Jenoine's prison.

"Vlad?" This was Morrolan's voice. I managed to turn my head and see that he and Aliera were still there, as well. So nothing had changed, but everything had.

Story of my life.

I found my voice and managed, "How long?" In my own ears, my voice sounded weaker than I actually felt.

"How do you feel?" asked Aliera. Why can't anyone just answer a Verra-be-damned question?

I started to say something snappy, but it was too much work, so I said, "Dry."

Morrolan held a flask to my lips, and I drank some water. Damn, but it was good. I was going to ask him where he found it. Water. Wonderful stuff. Who knew?

"What happened, Vlad?" asked Morrolan. Yeah, like I was the right guy to ask.

"How long has it been?" I repeated. It was easier to talk now. I opened my eyes, not sure when I had closed them. Aliera and Morrolan were directly over me, staring down. Teldra was out of sight. Loiosh stood on the floor next to my left ear. Being the center of so much interest wasn't as pleasant as I would have expected.

"As far as I can tell, you've been unconscious for around nine hours."

"More like ten," said Aliera.

Morrolan said, "My judgment—"

"Doing what in the meantime," I said.

"Failing to reopen the gate," said Aliera, with a look at Morrolan that the latter ignored.

"Okay," I said. "Would someone like to help me up?"

Morrolan reached a hand out. With his help, I was able to stand up, and after a moment I was able to remain standing on my own. The room spun, then settled out, and—

"What the—?"

"What is it, Vlad?"

"Where are we?"

Silence greeted the question, which meant the answer couldn't be anything I wanted to hear.

Aliera said, "Vlad, we're in the same room we've been in all along."

Yeah, that was one of the things I hadn't wanted to hear.

Teldra was now looking at me, too. "What is it?" said Morrolan.

I took a deep breath and blew it out slowly. Where to begin?

"There is more to this place than used to meet the eye," I said. "Either we've all been taken in by an illusion, or I'm being taken in by one now."

Aliera closed her eyes momentarily, then opened them. "I detect no illusion," she said. I shrugged.

"Perhaps," said Morrolan, "you could describe what you are now seeing."

"There is a large rock, or stone, in the middle of the floor—right there." I walked over to it, but didn't touch it. "It's about three feet high, maybe five feet long, and a foot and half wide at its widest point, but very irregular and jagged; it is mostly a dark shiny grey, with pink veins running through it."

I glanced over at them, they were looking at me, not the rock. *"I don't see it, Boss."*

"Figures."

"That way," I said, "against the wall, are four large jugs or vats, pottery of some kind, green with black geometrical patterns near the neck. They're just a bit under five feet high and—" I walked over to them. "One seems to be filled with sand, another with ash, this one with, I don't know, looks like water but I wouldn't count on it, and this last one with something that looks like very tiny seashells."

I turned my head. "Over this way—right here—is the doorway that Teldra and I found earlier; it is now plainly visible."

Morrolan and Aliera looked at her; she shrugged and said, "Yes, we did find a doorway there."

They turned back to me. "What else?" said Morrolan.

"The shelves are all filled."

"With?"

"That one," I said, gesturing, "has weapons. I mean, things that are obviously weapons—that look like weapons even to me. Swords, knives, daggers, lances, pikes. Things like that. There must be a hundred of them, all in all. The one over there has—I wish you could see it—it's full of crystals. Some of them the size of the end of my finger, some of them fist size, a few of them the size of a lormelon. They're a bit scary. And the colors vary from a mild pink to a deep purple, almost black. The big ones are both of the black color. Like I said, they're a bit scary."

I cleared my throat. "The shelf over at the far end has things I don't recognize. Mostly metal, and peculiar shapes—some wheels, some devices made of several pieces riveted together, some partly made of leather or something else. Some that remind me of that strange object Sethra has. I would assume they are sorcerous devices of some kind, but I don't know. I don't feel like touching any of them. And the last shelf, this one, has more odd contraptions, but I recognize manacles among them.

"Okay," I continued. "So much for the shelves. The walls are all painted with designs—black paint against a background that doesn't look like I thought it did—more like a greyish blue. And the designs are, well, probably sorcerous. All geometrical shapes. The walls are covered with them, top to bottom, and there are various symbols scrawled in amongst them. I can draw them for you, if you'd like."

"Yes," said Aliera, at the same time Morrolan said, "Perhaps later."

I grunted. "There is also a table at each end of the room, and chairs around it. All metal, all much larger than any furniture for either you or me. Go figure, huh? Oh, and the ceiling looks the same as it did before, except that there are more lighting devices than I'd thought.

"So, that's about it. It's obvious that they've done something to my head during this last—how long? eight hours?—or I wouldn't be seeing this stuff. I'll leave it up to you clever people whether I'm now being taken in by illusion, or all the rest of you are. If we go by majority, I'd guess it's me that's seeing things. And there's also the fact that Teldra and I never tripped over any of that stuff earlier. And the fact that I can't imagine why they would have messed with my head to allow me to see what's really here. Chances are, while I was gone, they did other things as well, to make sure I'd carry out whatever plan they have. But I do want all of you to admire how calm, cool, and collected I am while discussing the fact that my head has been messed with. Okay, your turns."

Aliera addressed Morrolan. "It's the rock that interests me most."

"Yes," said Morrolan. "Does it sound familiar?"

Aliera nodded. I felt ignored. Loiosh nuzzled my ear. Teldra came over and stood next to me, not saying anything or even looking at me, but it was nice of her.

"I think," I told her quietly after a moment, "that you ought to leave me out of your plans."

"Do you feel as if your mind has been tampered with?"

"No."

"Or probed?"

"No. But it seems likely, doesn't it?"

"It is possible. But it seems more likely that a glamour has been removed from your eyes than one placed there."

"Sure. But why? And how, for that matter?"

She shook her head. Meanwhile, Morrolan and Aliera had finished their conference. Morrolan said, "Vlad, we will not be telling you of our plans until we can ascertain whether your mind has been tampered with."

"Hey," I said. "Good idea. I should have thought of that myself."

He answered me with a Morrolan look. I went over and sat down against the wall; I didn't feel like using the Jenoine's furniture.

"Okay, Loiosh. You know how we do this."

"Right now, Boss?"

"Right now."

Aliera approached. "Vlad, I'm wondering if that rock you describe has any—"

"Not now, Aliera. I'm busy."

She raised an eyebrow, I suppose wondering if I were kidding.

"I'm having my brain examined. It should only take a few minutes."

She glanced quickly at Loiosh, then nodded and walked away to continue her conference with Morrolan. I let my head rest against the wall, closed my eyes, and tried to think of nothing. I've never been good at thinking of nothing.

Loiosh had done this maybe half a dozen times, and he was starting to get good at it; I felt the invasion, but there was less of that rattling, jangling sensation, like being hit on the numbing point of the elbow except in the brain. I sat still and waited it out, thinking of nothing but what was going on inside my head. Thinking about what is going on inside your head is a good way to make yourself miserable, if you haven't any other methods handy, but there was no way around it. As he sniffed and poked through the nooks and crannies of my thinking gear, I'd get flashes, unbidden, of moments of my past. I remembered the descent into Deathgate, the sight of my hands gripping the ropes, their feel against my palms, and sometimes I'd look down and see the top of Morrolan's head below my feet, the roar of the falls in my ears. I remembered the feel of Cawti's breath, fast in my ear, my hand in the small of her back as we explored each other. I remembered the feel of a ship's deck beneath my feet, the creaking of the sails, and the endless blue-green of the sea. I remembered the Necromancer's cold, cold fingers on my soul, the edge of Blackwand against my throat, the voice of the Imperial Inquisitor as the Orb circled my head and the Empress looked on, and the laugh of the Serioli who led me by circuitous routes to the Wall of Baritt's Tomb.

It indicated how much better Loiosh was getting that so few of these memories were unpleasant.

Presently he said, *"All right, Boss."*

"All right?"

"All right."

"What do you mean, 'all right'?"

"I mean 'all right.' "

"All right, as in, all is right?"

"That's the all right I meant, Boss."

"Okay, I think I got that part. Now the tough one: How certain are you?"

He hesitated. *"Pretty sure."*

"Pretty sure?"

"Pretty sure."

"What do you mean, 'pretty sure'?"

"I mean 'pretty sure.' "

That wasn't exactly the answer I wanted. I've found I often don't get exactly the answers I want, but I keep asking questions anyway.

"And, Boss—"

"Yes?"

"Now I'm seeing it, too."

"Well, that's something then. Either I'm not under a glamour, or you are as well."

"Heh. I'm a jhereg, Boss. The being hasn't been spawned that could put a glamour on me."

"Cocky little son-of-a-bitch, aren't you?"

"Damn right."

"I'm back," I announced to the room in general. No one cheered immediately, but I got a smile from Teldra. I said, "Loiosh believes my brain has probably not been tampered with, for whatever that's worth."

"Probably?" said Aliera, frowning.

I shrugged. "Best I can do; take it for what it's worth. And he's now seeing the same thing I am."

"Which means," said Aliera, shrugging, "that perhaps he is under a glamour as well."

I said, "He's a jhereg. The creature hasn't been spawned that could put a glamour on him."

Aliera frowned, looked over at Morrolan as if to see if he was convinced, then shrugged.

Loiosh said, "Thanks, Boss."

"No problem, chum."

I said, "Now, Morrolan, can you tell me what happened?"

"What happened?" asked Morrolan. He was leaning against the wall near where we'd been chained up, arms folded, looking cool and imperturbable.

"The attempt to get us home."

"Oh. Nothing happened. They sealed the gate."

"Then we're stuck here?"

"For the moment, yes."

"I see. Is sealing your gate, uh, easy to do?"

"No."

"Why would they want to keep us here now, when they could have kept us here the first time?"

"I don't know," said Morrolan. "And I should very much like to. Is this all part of a plan of theirs, or are they improvising as much as we are? You perceive it is a rather important question."

"I'm glad I'm not the only paranoid in the room," I said.

"It isn't paranoia, Vlad, if they really are—"

"So I've heard. Okay, so we can spend all our time wondering if they have all this planned and every step we take is according to their wishes, and when they have us good and ready, they'll crush us like bugs. Or, alternately, we can stop worrying about what moves they're going to pull on us, and start thinking about what moves we're going to pull on them."

Morrolan sniffed and said, "Good idea, Vlad. How do you plan to go about it?"

"Nothing fancy," I said. "I had just planned to kill them, and go from there."

Aliera shrugged. "Couldn't hurt," she said.

10

"Tell me about this rock," said Aliera.

"All right," I said. I walked over and stood in front of it. "The edges are all jagged. It looks like a large piece of something that was once even larger, if that gives you any idea. I told you about the colors, but there's also a very thin sort of purplish vein running along one side."

Aliera said, "Does it seem at all crystalline?"

"No, not . . . well, yes, I guess sort of, if you look at it right."

Morrolan nodded. "Well, Aliera?"

She nodded and said, "Trellanstone."

Morrolan nodded.

I said, "If you don't mind—"

"Trellanstone," said Aliera, "is what the Imperial Orb was fashioned from."

"Oh," I said. "Well. And here I thought it might be something interesting."

About then I caught something in Aliera's eyes, and then in Morrolan's, and realized that they were both a lot more excited about this than they were willing to let on.

"I don't suppose," I said, "that either of you have studied Orb-making? I can see where having an Orb might be useful right around now."

"Certainly," said Aliera. "Then all we'd need would be a source of amorphia."

"Oh, we have that," I said, enjoying dropping it into the middle of the conversation, like, "Oh, the Easterner? Yes, he's the Empress's consort."

I certainly got Morrolan and Aliera's attention quickly enough. "What are you talking about?" said Morrolan.

"Lady Teldra and I went for a walk while we were waiting for you. It's a lovely place, really, except for the air and how heavy you feel. There is a river of amorphia just outside of that door."

They both glanced over at Teldra. You could see them thinking, "That's it. Poor Vlad's mind has snapped at last."

But Teldra nodded and said, "He is quite correct."

"A river of amorphia," repeated Morrolan, almost reverently.

"Impossible," said Aliera. She turned to Morrolan. "Isn't it?"

He shook his head. "I can't imagine how such a thing could be. We need to look at this."

"Yes," said Aliera.

"I'll wait here," I told him. "If the Jenoine emerge, shall I ask them to wait, or suggest they return when it is more convenient?"

Aliera snorted. There was a lot of that going around. Having made her statement, she turned and headed toward where I told her the door was, stopped, and turned back.

"Where is the bloody door?" she said.

I managed not to chuckle, started to answer, but Morrolan said, "One thing at a time, please. I, too, wish to observe this thing, but I wish first to address the issue of why Vlad can see what we cannot, and what, if anything, we can do about it."

I could see that Aliera wanted to argue with him, but apparently couldn't find any good pretext, so she clamped her jaw shut, and returned. I found I was enjoying this: two sorcerers, who had to be dying to investigate one of the most remarkable discoveries in the history of magical philosophy, and they were just going to have to wait.

To add some more confusion into the mix, I said, "Excuse me. This rock-that-turns-into-Orbs. Would you mind telling me about it?"

"It's magical," said Aliera dryly.

I glanced over at Teldra, but she was just standing, near the wall, the epitome of patience. I turned back to Aliera and said, "Thanks loads." She started to speak, but I cut her off. "Look, there's too much I don't understand here, and neither do you. If we're going to work this together, I'd like to have some idea of what this stuff is we're talking about. We're paralyzed until we have at least a reasonable guess about what is real and what isn't."

"I have never," said Aliera, "had any particular problem knowing what is real."

"Oh, no? Think about it. Morrolan is right. Why do I see what you don't? Whose mind has been tampered with? What is the illusion? And, more important, *why*? That's the part that really bothers me. I can understand casting an illusion in front of all our eyes, but why then remove it from one of us, or some of us, whichever it is?"

Aliera frowned. "All right," she said. "Granted. I don't know."

Morrolan cleared his throat. "It is possible," he said, "that removing the illusion was an error. We still don't know exactly what happened while you were gone. Did you, for example, use your chain?"

I was suddenly very aware of Spellbreaker, wrapped around my wrist. "Yes," I told him. "As it happens, I did. At least, in my mind. I thought about it. Could just invoking Spellbreaker in my mind have broken the illusion?"

"Perhaps," said Morrolan.

"Perhaps," I agreed. "Then again, perhaps not? How can we tell?"

"Let me think about that," he said.

"Okay," I agreed. "While you're thinking, could you fill me in a little?"

"On what?"

"For starters, just what is that rock?"

"Well," said Morrolan, "you know, basically, how sorcery works, right?"

"I know how to do the simple stuff, if that's what you mean."

"No, I'm talking about how it works. The theory."

"Oh. No, I'm proud to say I haven't a clue."

"Oh," said Morrolan, with a look that indicated he was suddenly stumped. I took a perverse pride in that. I guess I was in a mood.

Aliera came to his rescue. "The basic idea," she said, "is simple enough: Everything is made of matter, or energy, which is the same thing in a less organized form. Amorphia is the opposite of matter. The purple vein in that rock is necrophia. Necrophia is a substance which can control amorphia, and which responds to the human—or

Eastern—brain. Sorcery is the art of learning to manipulate necro-phia, as Elder Sorcery is the art of learning to manipulate amorphia."

She stopped, as if she were done. Heh. I said, "And necromancy?"

"The art of using necrophia, and amorphia, to control the energy levels of different life-states."

Oh, well, now I understood everything. Heh. I said, "And witch-craft?"

She looked at me, blinked, then turned to Morrolan.

"Witchcraft," he explained, "is something else again."

"Ah," I said. "Well, good. That helps." Before they could respond, I remarked, "I've never heard of necrophia before."

"Your education," said Aliera, "is sadly lacking."

Morrolan said, "Witchcraft is a process of understanding and changing—the more you understand a thing, the more you can change it, and the more you work to change it, the more deeply you understand it. Sorcery is a process of correspondence—the minute amounts of energy generated by the mind must be made to correspond to the Orb, which in turn permits the release of the energy contained in the Sea of Amorphia, and this energy thus becomes available to use to manipulate the world."

"You should have been a teacher."

He ignored me. "That rock you describe contains an ore that has the property of resonating with amorphia, and with our minds; that is why the Orb was constructed from it."

"All right, I can see that. Mmmm. I imagine it is rare?"

"It only appears as a gift from the gods."

"Okay, that would be rare. Is it sentient?"

"How could it be sentient?"

"You're right," I said. "Stupid question." I don't know if he caught the irony, but I'm fairly sure Aliera did; she smirked. I continued, "All right, I think I see a bit of how the arts fit together. Now: Why would the Jenoine put us in a room with this in it?"

He didn't have an answer for that one. Morrolan has always been better at understanding how objects work than how other beings are thinking.

Teldra said, "They don't think the way we do." Because it was Teldra, I didn't make any remarks. She continued, "They don't con-sider us enemies in the same way we consider them enemies; nor do they see us as threats. They worry about our escaping the way one might worry about a pet greeterbird making its way out of its cage; and they worry about our damaging their artifacts the way one might worry about a pet kitten getting into the jewelry box. By sealing the area against necromantic gates, and laying a mild glamour on us so that we cannot see the objects in the room, they believe they have done enough."

There was a moment of silence; then Morrolan cleared his throat. "How long have you known this?" he said.

"I suppose, in a way, since I spoke to them. What I have just told you, my lord, only occurred to me this instant. I am still considering the matter and trying to understand, but it seems to me that they spoke to me—insofar as I could perceive tone—in the tone one might use to, well, a greeterbird. They were amused that I could form any sort of coherent thought; they think we're cute."

"Cute," said Aliera e'Kieron.

"Cute," said Morrolan e'Drien.

"*I* am *cute*," said Loiosh.

I said, "And that didn't, uh, annoy you at all?"

"I thought it interesting," said Teldra. "Actually, I didn't put it together in exactly that way; I've been thinking about it since the conversation, and that is my conclusion."

"Hmmmm," I said.

"Cute," repeated Aliera.

"All right," said Morrolan. "I think we can accept that. So, what do we do?"

"Kill them," said Aliera.

Morrolan rolled his eyes. "Of *course* we're going to kill them," he said. "I meant, *how?*"

"I wonder," said Aliera, and her voice trailed off.

Morrolan waited, then said, "Yes?"

Aliera hesitated, then finally said, "Do you suppose, if Vlad were to strike us with Spellbreaker, it would break the glamour on us?"

Morrolan frowned his thoughtful frown. I contemplated giving Morrolan and Aliera a good, hard whack apiece, and tried to refrain from smiling. Morrolan said, "I believe it would be less likely to remove the glamour than to, uh, damage many of the items you and I carry about with us, if you understand what I mean."

Aliera nodded. Oh, well. I wouldn't have enjoyed hitting Teldra anyway.

"But," said Morrolan, "I do want some way to remove the glamour; that stone could be very useful. And, perhaps, some of the other things in here could be useful as well. Have you any ideas, cousin?"

She shook her head. Then Lady Teldra cleared her throat; conversation stopped and we all stared at her. It would have been terribly embarrassing if she'd had nothing more than the need to clear her throat. But, no, she said, "It is just possible that the stone itself could help."

Aliera frowned. "I don't understand. If we can't even see it . . . ?" She was a lot more polite than she'd have been asking that question of Morrolan or me.

Teldra said, "Vlad can see it."

Morrolan scowled. "The air in this place must slow my brain down. You're right, of course."

I cleared my throat; quite a different effect than when Teldra did it. "Uh . . . what exactly does this involve?"

"Nothing you haven't done before," said Morrolan.

"Heh. There are many things I've done before—"

"You must let me see through your eyes," he said. "It is a simple enough spell, as you recall."

"Yeah, I know that. But there's no sorcery here. Can we do it with pure psychic energy?"

"Not reliably enough," he said. "But we have no need to."

"Oh? Without sorcery, what do you use as a link?"

For answer, he drew Blackwand. I recoiled instinctively from the assault on my mind—the feeling, something in between hearing and smell, of a hungry animal; a feeling that has to have been built into me at some level of instinct or below, that made me aware of the sweat in my armpits, and how hard it was to breathe, and made the room, however large it was, seem too close.

Suddenly I wasn't having fun anymore. "I'd rather not touch the blade, if it's all the same to you," I said.

He seemed amused; maybe it was his turn to have fun. He said, "Well, I'm certainly not going to let you hold her."

"I—"

"Don't worry; she doesn't bite."

I stared at the dark, dull grey blade, then back at Morrolan. "Yeah, right."

"Do it, Vlad."

"I—"

"Do it."

I took a deep breath, hesitated, then laid my palm on the blade quickly, before I could think about it too much. It was faintly warm, which metal isn't supposed to be. And it almost seemed as if it were vibrating, or trembling, just a little.

"Okay, dammit, do it before—"

"Keep still, Vlad. I have to concentrate."

I tried to keep my growl inaudible.

Loiosh's feet shifted on my shoulder; he wasn't liking this either. I can't say why, and it doesn't make sense, but that made me feel a little better.

The most terrifying things, in some ways, are those that catch us off guard—a shock out of nowhere, danger unanticipated, all that. And yet, in other ways, to see something coming, know it is about to happen, and be unable to prevent it has its own special terror. But there are times—rare, but they happen—when you see the danger before you, it builds up, you brace yourself—and then it's over, before you had time to really get a good scare going, much less the unpleasantness that you were scared of.

This was like that.

Morrolan said, "Okay, I'm done."

"You're done?"

"Yes."

"That's it?" Even as I questioned him, my hand was free from that blade, jumping off as if of its own volition.

"That's it," said Morrolan.

"Uh . . . did it work?"

He nodded and turned to Aliera. "All right, cousin. Your turn."

"I don't feel any different," I said.

They ignored me. Loiosh said, *"Boss, it would be Morrolan who feels different."*

"Oh," I said. *"Yeah, I knew that."*

Now Aliera drew Pathfinder, but she swung it over toward Morrolan; it no longer had anything to do with me, so I was free to back away. I did so.

Presently, Aliera turned to Lady Teldra. "This will be trickier," she said.

Teldra nodded and came forward; I didn't want to watch, so I walked over to Morrolan. "Well?" I said.

"Well what?"

"Are you now seeing—"

"Yes."

Creep.

"So, how was my description?"

He glanced around the room, and grunted; I imagine so he wouldn't have to tell me how good a job I'd done. Teldra, by this time, was blinking rapidly and looking all about.

"Okay then," I said. "We've gotten this far. What next?"

No one answered me directly, but Aliera looked at the door that she could now, evidently, see quite clearly. Then she looked an inquiry at Morrolan. He winced. It was obvious that he wanted to go exploring, and was damned curious to see our river of amorphia; it was equally obvious that he didn't think it was what he should do just then.

"All right," said Aliera, who could read him as well as I could. "We'll wait on that." She went over to the rock, and began studying it; her hands reached out as if to touch it, stopped, drew back. She frowned.

"Yes," she said. "It is trellanstone." She smiled suddenly, "And a nice, big, juicy one, too." Her eyes were green, and looked alarmingly catlike, and I would have gotten worried if I hadn't been worried already.

"All right," I said. "Let's hear it."

"It's simple enough," said Aliera. "The trellanstone will permit us to break through whatever is blocking—"

"No," said Morrolan.

"What do you mean, no?"

"That isn't how we're going to do it."

"Oh?" said Aliera. "It isn't? Then, pray, how *are* we going to do it?" She let the irony drip from her lips onto the floor and crawl over to rub against Morrolan's leg.

My eyes rolled up of their own accord. I walked to the far side of the room, pretty much out of earshot, because listening to Morrolan and Aliera yell at each other was already getting old; I found it was not one of the things I missed, although it had never bothered me before. I wondered if being away from people had changed me, made me less patient with minor annoyances.

"No, Boss, it's just made you introspective."

"Shut up, Loiosh."

"Impatient, too."

I sent a psychic growl in his direction, then sat down against a wall and leaned my head back. Morrolan and Aliera, after an instant of conversation, walked out of the door Teldra and I had found. I blinked. Well, I suppose they figured if they were going to argue, they might as well investigate our story at the same time.

Teldra came over and sat down next to me.

I said, "Well, whatever happens, it has been a pleasure having the chance to speak with you."

"Thank you, Vlad. I feel the same way."

I wondered if she really did. That's the tricky part about the Issola; you can never be certain how they are feeling. Maybe it doesn't bother Dragaerans, not knowing how someone is actually feeling, but we Easterners aren't like that. I wondered if it bothered Teldra to know that, when she really, actually liked someone, that person would always have to wonder how much was genuine, and how much was show.

After some time, Morrolan and Aliera came back through the door, approached us, and Morrolan said, "All right, we have a plan."

"That's lucky," I told him.

His eyes narrowed, but he must have decided to let it pass. Best for him.

"Worked yourself into a mood, haven't you, Boss?"

I mentally grunted at my familiar. Morrolan said, "We're going to attempt something with the trellanstone. We're going to—"

"Use it to break through whatever is blocking you from opening the gate?"

He closed his eyes, then opened them again. Then he slowly and carefully explained the plan to me. Teldra gave nary a twitch of an eyebrow, and Aliera's eyes had turned blue. When Morrolan was finished, he said, "Are there any questions?"

I hardly knew where to begin. I said, "How did you come up with *that* idea?"

"In part, because of your river of amorphia. The fact that they have it changes everything. And, moreover, this is something that—I believe—lies within our power."

I grunted at him and muttered, "If all you've got's a stick, everything looks like a kneecap."

"Beg pardon?" said Morrolan.

"Never mind; old Jhereg saying."

He graced me with a look of distaste and turned to Lady Teldra. "You are clear on your role?"

"Yes, my lord."

"Aliera?"

She rolled her eyes, which Morrolan and I took as an affirmative.

"Then let's begin."

"He didn't ask if I was ready."

"And I'm not going to either."

Morrolan took a position next to the trellanstone, hovering over it like a goose over her goslings. Aliera stood in front of it, to Morrolan's left, and laid her hands on it, touching and feeling it as if looking for handholds. For this stage, Teldra and I were back and out of the way, watching. Aliera's hands came to rest, and she nodded to Morrolan. He licked his lips. I recognized that gesture—I'd been there often enough myself, just before trying something difficult and a little scary.

Sometimes it almost seemed as if Morrolan were human. He placed his hand on the stone, near Aliera's. Presently he said, "All right, I'm getting something."

"Yes," she said.

I couldn't see her face, but I saw the concentration in the muscles of her back, and in Morrolan's case, in the muscles of his jaw. They were working. It was nice to see for a change. They fell silent, I assume communicating psychically; Teldra and I waited patiently for them to finish. Or, rather, Teldra waited patiently; I waited. Presently my feet started to hurt; standing hurts more than walking. I shifted from foot to foot and tried to catch Teldra's eye, but she was watching the sorcerers work.

Abruptly, and for no reason I could see, the veins in the stone began to glow—not much, you had to be watching closely, but it was there, like a yellow phosphorus, if you can imagine such a thing.

Morrolan said, "Okay, Vlad. Get ready."

"I'm ready," I told him, which wasn't entirely a lie. I let Spellbreaker fall into my hand, and felt a very small, subtle vibration running through it, almost a tremble, as of eagerness.

"Boss—"

"Not now, Loiosh. I don't want to think about it."

Easier said than done, that not thinking about it business; but I really didn't want any distractions just then, because if Morrolan's plan worked, things were just about to get interesting. I touched the rapier at my side, started to check my daggers before remembering that most of them were lying in pieces around the room. My hand accidentally touched the sheath of the Morganti blade I still carried; my hand then returned to the hilt of my sword and remained there, so I looked like I was ready to draw in a hurry—like I was ready for action. Maybe Morrolan would be impressed if he glanced over at me. Maybe if the Jenoine showed up suddenly they'd see how ready for action I was and die of fear.

"I'm getting something," said Aliera. "It's opening." I happened to notice her hands, which now gripped the stone very tightly; her fingers were white. I looked for some change in the stone itself, but didn't see anything.

"All right, Vlad," said Morrolan, in that tone of voice he uses when he's keeping tight control on his emotions—which is usually, now that I think of it.

I nodded, even though he couldn't see me, and, under my breath, I began an invocation to Verra. It was one of the old ones, one of the first I had ever learned, and I shan't repeat it here. At first, I was only going through the motions, but soon enough I felt Morrolan's presence, and, through him, Aliera's, pointing out to me the direction, as it were, in which to, well, direct my efforts. I recited the invocation over and over, trying for some sort of response, or at least the feeling that I was getting through.

It is strange, the things I've done to the inside of my own head.

In one way or another, that is where all magic is; that is *what* all magic is, and that is why it is magic—you treat the contents of your skull as if they were a sort of world that you can walk around in, filled with objects that you can manipulate; creatures with whom you can communicate; landscapes that you can observe. This bit of witch-craft is a narrow stream, and you dip your feet in it and splash. This piece of sorcery is a lever you can move stones with, and you grunt and sweat until it moves and you feel the satisfaction of watching it roll down a hill. And the invocation was a chat with a Demon God-dess who bore only the most passing and coincidental relationship to the being I had met, who had from time to time aided me, and who had used and was using me for purposes I was only beginning to have a glimmering of.

The conversation was strictly one-sided; how could it not be, being a creation of myself with myself. One-sided, yet (and here is the magic) it must have done something, because as I stood upon that world whose air was nearly unbreathable, in that room whose contents were nearly unknowable, doing things to my head that are nearly indescribable, feeling a connection within me in a language almost untranslatable, there appeared before my real eyes a hint of red and golden sparks generated by nothing, that shimmered there for a moment, until they took shape, solidified, and became the God-dess herself, who appeared standing, tall, composed, and with a wry look, and she said, "Well, I'm here. Now you must tell me, are you traitors, or fools?"

11

DISAGREEMENTS WITH DEITIES

All sorts of replies came to mind, but I managed to hold them back. Letting Morrolan and Aliera deal with her would be more fun.

The Goddess stood taller than Morrolan, and glared down at him. He put on his supercilious look and seemed unimpressed with her glare; if it was an act, it was a good one, and if it wasn't he had a remarkable amount of confidence in himself. Or he was a complete fool, which I'd suspected for some years. Or, at any rate, a Dragonlord, which is much the same thing.

He said, "You believe they planned all this, Verra? That they wanted you here? Fine. So what? Sethra believes—"

"Sethra," said the Goddess scornfully.

It had never occurred to me that I might one day hear "Sethra" pronounced scornfully; that would have to count as the big shocker for the day.

Morrolan shrugged. Aliera said, "Sorry if you were inconvenienced, Mother, but we were tired of waiting around."

"It isn't a matter of convenience, my dear. It is a matter of permitting them to bring me to a place where they can destroy me."

Morrolan said, "Most of a day, I believe." I stared at Morrolan for a second, trying to figure out how that made sense in regard to anything, then decided not to try.

"I shan't let them," said Aliera.

Verra said, "You shan't let them?"

"That is correct."

"My darling Aliera—"

Teldra cleared her throat, and instantly had everyone's attention. She said, "Our apologies, Goddess, if we have been precipitate. But may I beg you to tell us, now that we have acted, what we ought to do?"

The Goddess smiled, as one might at a kitten rolling on the floor playing with a piece of string. She said, "Ah, my little Issola. How sweet. Well, I will answer your question. First, we—" She stopped in midsentence, stared at something over Teldra's shoulder, and said something that sounded like, "kyrancteur!"

At first I thought it was an exclamation in some foreign language, or else she'd suddenly recognized a friend who was invisible to the rest of us, but then Morrolan said, "Yes. Or trellanstone, if you prefer; that is the name we have always known it by."

"How could it have come to this place?"

"It is," said Morrolan. "With Vlad's help, using an old invocation," which, in case you didn't notice, made no sense at all.

Verra didn't seem bothered by the non sequitur. "I see," she said slowly. I looked up at her bony face, with its slightly askew forehead, and strange jawline, and deep-set eyes, and the thought suddenly came to me: *She's scared.*

I found myself thinking, *Dear Verra, protect us,* before I caught myself. She glanced at me, and a smile flickered briefly around her lips, then went out. She turned her eyes once more to the trellanstone. Presently she asked, "What was it, exactly, that Sethra said?"

Morrolan cleared his throat, started to answer, stopped, and finally said, "There was a great deal of military theory in it."

"That doesn't astonish me," said the Goddess.

"I might summarize it by saying that complex enemy plans are the easiest to defeat, and we shouldn't be afraid of walking into a trap."

"Uh huh. What else?"

"She reminded me that they can be killed."

"So can we all."

Morrolan shrugged. "I have never liked giving up the initiative."

"Nor I," I muttered under my breath, earning me a quick glance from the Goddess, who evidently had very good hearing.

"And yet, my love," said Verra to Morrolan, "we are here, on their world, and they can appear if and when they wish, so they have the initiative. And if little Sethra is that certain, why isn't she here herself?"

"Mother," said Aliera. "You know the answer to that very well."

Verra gave her an indulgent smile. "Perhaps I do."

"I don't," I remarked, but they all ignored me.

"Moreover," continued Aliera, "you also know, I am certain, that if you hadn't wanted to come, you wouldn't have. You are no demon to be summoned and dismissed, and no one here except perhaps our Easterner could take you for one."

"Could I have refused a plea for help from my daughter?"

Aliera snorted. "Easily."

Verra chuckled. "My darling child, you don't know me as well, perhaps, as you think you do."

Morrolan said, "It is the only means we have of learning," which made no sense whatsoever; I was starting to get used to that though.

Aliera herself didn't deign to respond. The Goddess spread her arms and gave Morrolan an exaggerated bow. "Very well, then," she said. "You have summoned me, and I am here. What, exactly, is your plan?"

Aliera and Morrolan looked at each other.

After an embarrassing moment, Verra said, "You don't have a plan?"

"Not exactly," said Morrolan.

"Plans are overrated," I said. "Let's just start killing things. If there's nothing else around, we can always kill each other."

"Don't tempt me," said Morrolan.

I snorted. Verra said, "Perhaps you should allow the three of us to confer, my dear Easterner."

"Sure," I said. "I'll just amuse myself by exchanging sarcastic comments with Loiosh."

"No doubt you will," she said.

Lady Teldra was standing across the room, as calm and patient as an issola, as if waiting for some call that hadn't come. She had taken herself away from the conversation while no one was watching. I reflected on what a fine skill it would be to know when you weren't wanted at a place you didn't want to be, so you could make everyone happy by going away. I walked over to her. She looked up at me, a slightly quizzical expression on her face. I said, "How do you do that, Teldra?"

She smiled and raised her eyebrows, and came as close to looking smug as I'd ever seen her.

I said, "So, all right, how do the laws of courtesy tell us we should handle this mess?"

"The laws of courtesy," she said, still smiling, "are strangely silent on the subject."

"I'm not surprised."

"In any case," she added, "I think you know them as well as I do."

"Oh, yeah," I said. "If there's anything I know, it's courtliness and good manners. I'm even better at politesse than I am at refining petroleum."

"I know little of petroleum, Vlad, but I do know that you are actually quite skilled in the arts of courtesy."

"Right."

Behind me, Aliera and Morrolan were continuing to speak to the Goddess, but I couldn't make out what they were saying. In the event, this did not displease me.

"It is the simple truth, Lord Taltos. It is how you survived for so long in the world you used to inhabit—or, more precisely, the worlds."

I bit back a smart reply and just waited. After a moment, she said, "The Jhereg has its own rules and customs, you know—codes of appropriate behavior. You couldn't have survived among them without knowing what all of their signals mean. And I've seen you with my Lord Morrolan. That is another different set of codes."

I snorted. "I've almost pushed him far enough to kill me. More than once."

"I know that, too," she said.

"Well then?"

"What stopped him from killing you?"

"His strong sense of self-interest combined with iron self-control."

"I don't believe that is entirely correct, Lord Taltos. I know him rather well, I think, and there are severe limits to his self-control, whereas there are no limits to his pride. Had you pushed him far enough, you would have faced a mortal contest."

Morrolan, Aliera, and the Goddess all turned and walked out the door. I guess if you put a pretty little stream outside your door, people will want to look at it. I hoped the Jenoine would feel gratified.

"Okay," I said to Teldra. "Look. I'll concede that, over the years, I've learned that there's no point in making a bad situation worse, and that it's less work to talk yourself out of a tough spot than to slice your way out, and that words, while potentially deadly, are less deadly than Morganti daggers. But I don't think that is quite the same thing as being courteous."

"I believe, Lord Taltos, that it is very much the same thing. And you know more than those things, if I may say so. You know when a casual insult is, in fact, courteous under the circumstances—and when it is not. You know when to make a friendly gibe, and when the gibe is not quite so friendly, but still called for. You know how to negotiate from a position of weakness but make it appear to be a position of strength. These are the sorts of things I'm talking about. And do you know how many of our folk—and yours—never learn these lessons that appear so simple to you?"

"Maybe, being an Easterner, I have a natural talent."

"You forget how many Easterners I have known, Vlad. Your people have no such natural talent. In fact, the conditions under which your people live tend to promote the opposite: an irritating obsequiousness, or an aggravating combativeness."

After a moment's thought, I said, "That's true."

She nodded. "It is really all a question of taking appropriate action for the circumstances. I'm sure you realize that I could have this conversation with few others—human or Eastern—that I know. Some it would embarrass, others it would merely confuse."

"Yes, I understand."

"You have learned, faster than some of my own House, what actions—and words are only a special case of actions—are appropriate to the moment."

"A survival skill, Teldra."

"Yes, it is."

"Ah. That's your point, isn't it?"

She smiled, making me feel like my grandfather had made me feel when I had managed the correct riposte after parrying a lowline cut.

Morrolan, Aliera, and Verra returned at this point, speaking in low tones. I gestured toward them and said, "And the Goddess?"

"What about her?"

"What need has she of courtesy?"

"Toward her peers, the same as you or I. Toward us? None. Many of the gods, I believe most of them, display a certain degree of courtesy even though none is needed. Those who don't acquire a reputation."

"For being, say, chaotic?"

"Yes."

"So it is all a question of courtesy?"

"It is all a question of doing the appropriate thing. Of acting as the situation calls for."

"Appropriate thing. You keep saying that, Teldra. When someone walks up to me and says, 'Out of the way, whiskers, you're blocking the road,' is it appropriate to bow and say, 'Yes, my lord?' Is it appropriate to suggest his mother was a toothless norska? Or to quietly step out of his way? Or to urinate on his boot? Or to pretend to ignore him? Or to put a knife into his left eye? Just what does appropriate mean, anyway?"

"Any of those things might be appropriate, Vlad, and I daresay there are circumstances where you might do any of them. But you are always, or nearly always, correct in which you choose. And this is not a matter of instinct, but of observation, attention to detail, and experience. Appropriate action means to advance your own goals, without unintentional harm to anyone else."

"Unintentional harm."

"Yes."

"By Verra's tits," I said, forgetting then remembering that the pair of them weren't all that far away, "you're as cold as Morrolan, aren't you?"

"Yes," said Teldra, "I suppose so. Or as cold as you."

"Me? I'm not cold. I'm the soul of compassion, understanding, and courtesy."

"Yes," said Teldra, dimpling. "You are indeed. But only when it is appropriate."

I chuckled. And, "Okay. I'm convinced. All problems are matters of courtesy, and I am the personification of tact. So, to return to the question, what is the appropriate thing for us to do now?"

"I have no idea," said Teldra, still smiling. "I imagine that is what our friends are discussing right now."

I glanced over at them: heads together, deep in conversation.

"Great," I said. "I can hardly wait to see what they'll come up with."

"I have no doubt," said Teldra, "that it will be entertaining."

I nodded. "Entertaining. Good. That's always been high on my list for the kind of plan I need to get out of a fix."

She didn't reply. I shrugged, gave her a hint of a bow, and wandered over to the others. As I approached, they all stopped talking and looked up, like they'd been caught at something.

"Well?" I said. "Have we come up with the ultimate solution to all of our physical and spiritual problems? Have we saved the world, made sure the Empire is secure, and—"

"That will do, little Easterner," said the Goddess, giving me a look that made me question what Teldra had just been telling me. I restrained an insolent shrug, perhaps answering the question.

"What do you think, Loiosh? Am I the very soul of tact, discretion, manners, and courtliness?"

"Am I a three-legged tiassa?"

"Just checking."

"We have decided," said Verra, "that if the Jenoine are not polite enough to appear suddenly and force us into action, we will attack them."

"That took serious discussion?"

"Yes."

"Yeah, okay. I sort of suspected you might come up with that one. Have you worked out the details yet?"

"Some of them."

"Okay. How are you going to try to get me killed this time?"

"This time," said Verra, "we just might succeed."

"Heh. You should be so lucky."

Morrolan said, "We're trying to reach the Necromancer. We're hoping she—"

"The Necromancer!"

"Yes. We're hoping—"

"With you and Aliera and the Goddess and Sethra Lavode we don't have enough of a concentration of power? You need to bring the Necromancer in on this? How 'bout the Empress, for the love of V . . . something or other."

Morrolan waited for me to run down, then spoke again. "We're trying to reach the Necromancer," he said. "We're hoping she can find the Jenoine, and a way to get at them. Our problem at the moment is reaching the Necromancer."

"Why do you need the Necromancer at all? Why not have Aliera do it?"

"What are you talking about, Vlad?" asked Aliera a bit impatiently.

"Pathfinder," I said, and suddenly they were all staring at me.

Then, "Pathfinder," repeated Aliera.

"Damn," said Morrolan.

"How did I manage to not think of that?" said Verra.

"How did *I* manage to not think of it?" said Aliera.

"Pathfinder," said Morrolan.

"All right, all right, I'm a genius," I said. "Now we've thought of it. Can we get on with whatever we're going to do?"

"I've never met anyone so impatient to get himself killed, Boss."

"Shut up, Loiosh."

"Yes," said the Goddess, "I believe we can, as you put it, 'get on with it.' Aliera, your weapon?"

I involuntarily took a step back as Aliera drew, and, as the weapon cleared her sheath, I noticed something odd.

I had been in the presence of Morganti weapons a great deal more than I cared to in my brief life; and the same is true of the Great Weapons. I had become, if not used to, then at least familiar with the ugly and terrifying sensation of their presence—sort of the mental equivalent of finding sour milk in one's pitcher, combined with the feeling of waking up suddenly after a dream of being in a cave with a dzur blocking the exit while anklesnakes slithered around behind. But what was odd was that I suddenly realized that Pathfinder felt different from Blackwand. Not that it was at all pleasant, you understand, but it was as if I were picking up bits of personality from the weapon. I don't know, maybe what is strange is that I'd never noticed it before.

Exactly what the differences were was harder to say, except that Pathfinder didn't seem to be quite as, well, aggressive as Blackwand. Morrolan's weapon gave me the feeling that it would love to have the chance to swallow my soul if I'd just come a little closer; from Aliera's weapon I got the feeling that it would devour me without a second thought if I gave it the chance, but it wouldn't go looking for me, either. Also, Blackwand gave me a strong sense of a female personality, whereas from Pathfinder I got no clear indication of a sex. Aliera's sword, it seemed, was more patient, perhaps more protective, and there was a sense of inquisitiveness; while from Morrolan's blade I picked up feelings of arrogance, of strength, of the desire to get to smashing things. And there were other, more subtle differences, too, that I couldn't exactly identify but was now aware of.

I also became aware that Morrolan had said something. "Excuse me," I said. "I was distracted. What was that?"

"I said that is a good idea, Vlad. You may need it."

I almost said "Need what?" before I realized that I had allowed Spellbreaker to fall into my hand. It was dangling, inert, about a foot long, with tiny little links. For a second I stared at it; then I recovered and grunted something at him, and fingered it.

Aliera held Pathfinder out in front of her, the blade at about a forty-five-degree angle toward the ceiling. Her eyes were almost but not quite closed—reminding me, crazily, of how Aibynn looked when playing his drum. I waited, sort of expecting Pathfinder to start glowing or something, but nothing of the kind happened.

After a while, Morrolan said, "You need to find—"

"Shut up, cousin," said Aliera pleasantly.

Morrolan clamped his mouth shut, and Aliera returned to doing whatever it was she was doing. As I waited, I felt a stirring in my left hand, as if Spellbreaker were trembling a little.

"*Something is happening with that thing, Boss.*"

"*Noticed that, did you?*"

"*I'm not sure I like it.*"

"*I just wish I understood what it meant. Any Serioli around to ask?*"

"*I wouldn't be surprised. We've got everything else.*"

"Okay," said Aliera suddenly. "I'm getting something."

Her eyes were a little more open now, and she was focusing in front of her, in the middle distance—I followed her glance, but there was nothing there, so she was probably seeing things not apparent to a regular pair of unenchanted human eyes. I happened to look at Verra, then, and she had an expression on her face of the sort you'd associate with any mother seeing her daughter pulling off a difficult task. If I'd let myself, I could have gotten very distracted thinking about just how bizarre that was.

Then I noticed that the tip of Pathfinder was trembling, very slightly. I don't know how much you know about the science of defense, or about Aliera's skill as a swordsman, but, believe me, that hint of movement at the tip of her blade bespoke more intensity of magic and power than a roomful of pyrotechnics.

"Here we go," said Loiosh.

I wanted to be holding my rapier, or a dagger, or something, but I didn't know what, so I just waited.

"They aren't far away," said Aliera. "This world, within a few thousand feet, in fact. But . . . barriers. There are barriers of some kind. I don't yet know of what kind, or how strong. Stand closer to me."

We did so. I made sure Teldra was between me and the Goddess, not for any particular reason except that I didn't feel like standing next to her.

I said, "Does anyone know what we're going to do when we get there?"

"We're going to attack them," said Morrolan.

"Oh."

"We should have surprise working for us," he added.

"Do you really think so?"

He didn't answer. Verra said, "The theory, my little Easterner, is that they don't actually want to kill us, or they'd have done so already."

"What if what they wanted is to kill you, Goddess?"

"They may find that difficult."

Aliera was murmuring under her breath—the sort of murmuring one might expect of a rider urging his horse over a difficult jump.

"Can you get through them?" asked Morrolan.

"Of course," snapped Aliera. "Now let me concentrate. Be ready."

Be ready.

They were always saying stuff like that.

Just exactly what does that mean, anyway? Be ready. Like, have your eyes open? Be certain you've had a good meal and used the chamber pot? Now is the wrong time for a nap? Make sure you aren't sneezing when It happens? What, exactly? It means nothing, that's what it means. An empty noise.

"I'm ready," I said.

"As am I," said Morrolan. "Yes," said Teldra. Verra did not deign to speak, and no one expected her to, I suppose because being a goddess means never needing to sneeze.

I was watching the trembling at the end of Pathfinder, so I saw it when it happened: A tiny spark appeared on the very tip of the blade. The trembling caused it to jump around, leaving diminutive golden trails in the air; I couldn't tell if they were really there or were just products of my vision. Not, I suppose, that it mattered. There began to be a sensation of motion—the kind of motion that happens in dreams, where nothing changed, and my feet didn't move, but there was the feeling as if my stomach had suddenly been left behind and needed to catch up—not the wrenching nausea of a teleport, fortunately, but still unsettling.

The sense of motion increased.

"Shallow breaths, Boss."

"Right."

Sometime in there, Morrolan had drawn Blackwand—it tells you how messed up my senses were that I hadn't noticed, still didn't feel it; all I was really aware of was the sensation of motion, as if something had pulled me from the bottom of a hill and I start up up up rolling and spinning and being everywhere at once and no place at all happening at the same time and time again you've been through this before you realize that you'll never forget everything you thought you knew about moving from one place to another flash of light flickering and still moving past and present and future filled with unknown dangers appearing from everywhere nowhere somewhere somehow what when where was I and how did I get here from there we are slowing down down down stop.

There were four of them; maybe two of them were the same ones we'd seen before, but I couldn't tell them apart well enough to say. Two were standing, two sitting on what appeared to be an uncomfortable-looking couch. I'd been among humans, Dragaerans,

Serioli, cat-centaurs, and gods. One way or another, they were people—but these were *things*. They looked like things, and I thought of
them as things, and I really wanted to put them away like things.

The first bit of bad news was, the things didn't seem startled by
our presence. If we were counting on surprise, we could be in real
trouble.

One of the sitting ones was holding something that appeared to
be some sort of tube, with projections that fit nicely into its hand. If
it was a weapon, we could be in real trouble.

It was clear that two of them, including the one with the tube,
were looking at Verra. It was possible that their idea all along was to
kill her, and now that we had brought her, the rest of us could simply
be disposed of. If that was their thinking, we could be in real trouble.

I had no time, just then, to pay attention to surroundings—I
think I noted that we were indoors, and that was about it. Things
happened so quickly that I just had no time to note the sort of details
that can save your life; we might be in the Jenoine equivalent of
someone's parlor, or of a sorcerer's laboratory, or the weapon room of
their Imperial Guard for all I knew. We might be surrounded by
Jenoine food and drink, Jenoine books, or Jenoine death traps. If the
latter, we might be in real trouble.

"*I think we might be in real trouble, Boss.*"

"*It's possible.*"

"Let's do it," said Morrolan.

There was no time for any other remarks, so we all got to work.

12

Exercising Due Care for the Comfort and Safety of Others

It's funny, but it didn't occur to me until much later to think of it in terms of four of them and five of us. None of the ways things could have gone had much to do with numbers. Morrolan and Aliera were the first to move, Great Weapons flashing. The Goddess strode forward, right behind them, leaving Teldra and me standing there for just an instant before I cursed, put my hand on the Morganti dagger, started Spellbreaker swinging in a slow circle, and tried to figure out something useful to do.

Nothing came instantly to mind.

The two who were sitting remained sitting. One of the others turned its hands over as if asking why we might want to disturb it—Morrolan and Aliera began moving at this one. That left the other one for the Demon Goddess, while Teldra and I were, I guess, just along as witnesses.

It seemed like the opening of some sort of dance—Morrolan and Aliera moved toward either side of the one, who stepped forward as if to place itself between them—in the worst possible position except for letting them both stand behind it. There was a strange grace to its movements. Was it an especially athletic one of its kind? Were they all like that? How can you tell when you're seeing something typical of a species, and when you're seeing an interesting individual of that species? Why does my mind always wander like that when I'm frightened and don't know what to do?

Verra, in the meantime, began to circle to her left with the other Jenoine, who obligingly circled to its left, as if it had no qualms about turning its back to me.

"*Careful, Boss. The two sitting ones are watching you.*"

I acknowledged the warning. But, still, I had a Morganti dagger; if the thing were willing to actually show me its back, how could I resist? Offering a Jhereg your back is like offering a Dzur an insult or an Orca a free piece of merchandise: he'll find it hard not to take it even if he has no use for it. I kept my hand on the hilt of my dagger, watched, and waited.

Two things happened, then, so close together they were almost simultaneous—one was the sudden realization on my part that the room was shrinking in all directions; in other words, the walls were collapsing inward, very quickly. The other was that Verra laughed. I know that I flinched, I don't know if any of the others did, and then, just as quickly, the walls stopped collapsing.

"*Illusion,*" said Loiosh. "*Never fooled me for an instant.*"

"Yeah. Me, *either,*" I told him.

Spellbreaker was about a foot and a half long, with rather thick, heavy links; I kept it spinning slowly. Verra and the Jenoine facing her had both stopped. It was, unfortunately, just short of giving me the nice shot at its back I wanted. While both of their eyes faced forward, they were also wide-set—they had, then, better peripheral vision than humans or Dragaerans, and I needed to be aware of that when trying for a back shot.

We trained professionals notice stuff like that.

The Goddess and the Jenoine appeared to have locked gazes; I couldn't tell if they were engaged in some sort of massive, mystical, magical struggle happening on a level beyond my comprehension, or if they were just having a good old-fashioned stare-down.

Teldra came up to my side; perhaps to share in whatever protection Spellbreaker might give, perhaps just to back me up if I was attacked.

I said "Any ideas, Teldra?" and out of the corner of my eye I saw her shake her head.

"*Shallow breaths, Boss.*"

"*Check, Loiosh.*"

My thoughts were still on the Morganti dagger at my side, but I didn't draw it; wouldn't know quite what to do with it. My instincts told me to wait and see what happened, that this was not—yet—my moment.

Then Aliera lunged suddenly with Pathfinder, and Morrolan struck with Blackwand in a downward slanting arc at the same time. Their timing was precise, their coordination perfect. It ought to have been a deadly combination, the more so as the Jenoine made no effort to avoid either attack. It worked perfectly, except for the part where the Great Weapons were supposed to stab or cut the Jenoine; that didn't happen. Both weapons stopped what appeared to be a fraction of an inch away from their respective targets. Offhand, I didn't know anything tough enough to withstand the direct attack of a Great Weapon. Nor, in fact, did I want to know any such thing, or even think about it too hard.

Then I realized that whatever had neatly stopped Pathfinder and Blackwand had stopped Aliera and Morrolan as well—they were standing utterly motionless, as if frozen by their weapons' contact, or near contact, with the Jenoine. That was no good at all.

I get the shakes when I think back on that moment—Aliera e'Kieron and Morrolan e'Drien and Pathfinder and Blackwand held motionless by these things, while Verra, whether she was doing something or not, at least wasn't casually destroying them the way she ought to be, and, on top of it all, there were those two just sitting there, not even getting involved, as if it weren't worth their effort. That's how I feel now. But at the time, all I felt was irritation, especially directed at those two sons of bitches who were sitting on their superhuman godlike asses.

I really wanted to do something to get their attention.

Okay, I know how stupid that is, I should have been giving thanks to Verra—who was, after all, only a couple of feet away—that I *didn't* have their attention; but maybe I was temporarily nuts or something. No, I won't say that. I won't plead the excuse of being off my head. I remember clearly and coldly making the decision, and putting it into action.

My right hand left the vicinity of the Morganti weapon—which, powerful as it no doubt was, was certainly not going to do anything Pathfinder and Blackwand couldn't do—and reached into my pouch. I made my motions small and smooth to avoid attracting premature attention and, almost immediately, my fingers found what I'd sent them after.

"Boss, do you know what you're doing?"

"More or less," I told him.

"Oh, good."

It was, in fact, something that, years before, I had been warned in the strongest possible terms never to do again. But the first time I hadn't had any choice. This time was different: this time I was irritated.

What I was about to do wasn't like witchcraft: a focusing of the will, a concentration on desire; nor was it at all like sorcery: an almost mechanical application of known laws to achieve a precise result. When I'd done it before, years ago, it had been born out of anger, frustration, and desperation, and on top of it I had had my link to the Orb to provide the power to get it started. This time I had none of that—just the idea, which had been in the back of my head since my walk with Teldra, and the vague notion that I ought to do something.

But I did have a few things working for me: For one, the simple knowledge that I'd done it once before, which was by itself of incalculable value. For another, my memory, confused and imprecise, but there, of how that had felt, and where I had reached into myself, and how I had found those innate abilities inherited through the connection of my spirit to ancestors stretching back to when Sethra was young. And, for still another, I had the device in my fingers—a small, purple-blue stone, smooth as a pearl, which would act like the rendered goose fat that provides the basis of a good red pepper sauce.

I held it up.

Verra said, "Vlad!"

I remember her saying it, and maybe I was just concentrating too hard to permit myself to be distracted, or maybe I decided that this was a good time to ignore her. In any case, I reached into the stone, and into myself, and cut loose the moorings that held reality anchored to time that passes and the space that uses time, tried my best to give it some focus, and let it go.

I suddenly had the attention of all four Jenoine.

I smiled at them. "Hi there," I said.

The two who were sitting rose to their feet far quicker than I'd have thought they could. I moved Spellbreaker, which was still spinning, a little to the side so it would be out of the way of whatever I was about to do, if I could do it. Something seized hold of the un-reality between my fingers, and I felt it start to dissolve.

The two Jenoine moved toward me. I concentrated on them, imagined them dissolving into the raw, eternal, basic matter—or non-matter—of the universe, all coherence vanishing in light and shadow and formlessness.

"Vlad!" said Verra. "Don't!"

So far, so good.

Suddenly, Aliera and Morrolan were free again—and I don't know what had been done to them, but they didn't like it much, because they both jerked back suddenly, as if simultaneously kicked in the chest. Morrolan sprawled on his back; Aliera managed to stay on her feet, but, to the extent that I could spare any attention for them, they didn't seem happy.

Verra had stepped back from the one she faced, and was looking at me; Teldra emitted some sounds that I knew to be in the language of the Jenoine—her voice was even and level as it chirped and croaked and squeaked. Verra's hands were up, and she was making gestures in my direction and Aliera and Morrolan were charging in again, and things got even more confused, as one of the Jenoine who had just risen said something in its own language, though it was hard to hear over the roaring sound that I realized had been steadily grow-ing, and was coming from between my fingers, which was also the source of the reddish-golden light that was streaming out toward three of the Jenoine, who held their ground, their hands clasped together in front of them in a gesture of supplication, though no doubt it meant something else to them, and in the confusion, now that my little purple stone was entirely gone, and the light and the sound were fading, I drew the Morganti dagger to give them something else to worry about, but two of them were worrying about Verra, who seemed to have taken all the light into herself, or at least she was glowing, and she seemed taller as one of them lifted its hands toward her, and another, who was still holding that odd tube, lifted it until it was pointed directly at the Demon Goddess, who said, "That was stupid, little Easterner; she couldn't have hurt me with that thing."

"What was stupid?"

"*You okay, Boss?*"

"*What the—?*"

"Welcome back, Vlad," said Aliera.

"Back," I repeated, at which point things came into focus, and I said, "Sethra! What are you—?" Then, "How did I get back to Dzur Mountain?"

"Over my shoulder," said Morrolan.

"Damn," I said. "I missed it, didn't I? And I'll bet it was fun, too."

"It was successful," said Aliera. "That is, we're here."

"How long has it been?"

Aliera said, "About an hour," at the same time as Sethra said, "A week and a day." They looked at each other, both started to speak, then looked at me.

I managed to say, "Never mind. My fault. I—what happened to my arm?"

Sethra hesitated, then said, "We aren't exactly sure."

"My arm doesn't seem to be working," I explained.

"I know," said Sethra.

I felt my heart start to pound. Now was a hell of a time for it to start that. I took a deep breath, reminded myself that I shouldn't, then realized that it was all right after all. I made myself speak evenly. "I don't know if I'm more frightened that my arm doesn't work, or that Sethra isn't sure why."

"I hope to find out," said Sethra.

I nodded. "Well, why don't you tell me about it."

Of course, Aliera and Morrolan started speaking at once, glared at each other, and so on. I waited patiently. Finally, Aliera said, "Do you want the short version, or the long version?"

"Just tell me what happened, all right?"

"We attacked them. There was a skirmish. You unleashed pre-Empire sorcery, which succeeded in freeing Morrolan and me from whatever was holding us, and also, it seems, broke whatever was keeping us from our gate. No one was hurt except you—"

"None of them?"

"No."

"Hmmm," I said. "They're pretty tough, aren't they?"

"Yes," said Morrolan.

"Okay. What happened to me?"

Morrolan and Aliera looked at Lady Teldra, who nodded and

said, "Yes, I saw it. You went forward toward one of them, holding the dagger—"

"—the Morganti dagger."

"Yes."

I nodded. "I don't remember . . . wait . . . yes, I do. I remember drawing it and moving in."

"Yes. Then one of them aimed some sort of weapon at Verra. You interposed yourself, and—"

"I *what?*"

"You interposed yourself between Verra and the weapon of the Jenoine, and were struck by it somewhere high on the left arm or shoulder."

"I didn't really."

"You did, Boss."

"You did, Vlad," said Teldra.

"Why?"

Verra chuckled. Morrolan said, "I'd give my summer palace to know."

"You don't have a summer palace," I said.

"True, but I'd like one."

"I'd like my left arm back. I can't believe I did that."

"None of us can," said Morrolan.

I glanced at the Goddess, who was looking at me with an unreadable expression. I'm tired of unreadable expressions. I said, "Is that what you said was stupid, Goddess? I thought you meant my use of the Elder Sorcery."

"That too," said the Goddess. "You could easily have destroyed us all before I could contain it."

"I have confidence in your Godlike abilities," I said.

"You—"

She didn't finish the thought. I had left a Goddess speechless. I wondered how that would count when I reached the Halls of Judgment. I said, "Spellbreaker didn't help?"

"It isn't that kind of magic," said Verra helpfully.

"Then what kind is it?" I asked, more because I was annoyed than because I wanted an answer; which was just as well because the only answer I got was a slight smile from Verra. I turned to Sethra. "You don't know what happened?"

"Not exactly. Are you in any pain?"

"No."

She nodded. "I suspected you wouldn't be. It probably works di-rectly on the muscle."

Verra said, "They had something like that when I knew them, for use on test subjects. But it was larger and clumsier."

"Test subjects," I repeated.

Aliera said, "Any idea how to effect a cure?"

"Not yet," said Sethra.

"I see."

After an uncomfortable silence, I said, "All right, then what hap-pened?"

Morrolan said, "At about the same moment you went down, Al-iera and I struck at two of them." He glanced at Aliera, then said, "I cannot speak for my cousin, but I put a great deal into that attack."

"Heh," said Aliera.

"They were able to avoid physical contact with our weapons— I'm not certain of the nature of their defense—but our attack that time nevertheless appeared to discommode them."

"Heh," I said.

Aliera shrugged. "At any rate, they were not able to paralyze us as they had the first time. We had both struck them once before, a coordinated attack—"

"I remember that," I said.

"I don't know what happened next," said Morrolan, "except that it was Verra who did it."

The Goddess said, "I did little enough. The Easterner's foolishness destroyed the devices that were keeping us on their world; I merely transported us off it, which you or Aliera could have done. I did take the opportunity to give them a few things to keep them out of the way. They still fear me," she added.

"I imagine they do," I said. "Then what?"

"I picked you up," said Morrolan, "as the gate began to open. That was, perhaps, an hour ago."

"An hour. That's all?"

He nodded.

I rubbed my left arm. There was no sensation in it, but neither did it feel cold or especially warm to my right hand, for whatever that was worth. It is odd touching a lifeless limb. My fingers felt my arm, but my arm couldn't feel my fingers. It's a strange sensation. Try it sometime.

"A very respectable escape," I ventured. "Well done."

"And yourself," said Aliera. "I must disagree with Mother; I believe your attack was worth the risk. At least, I don't know how we'd have gotten away otherwise."

"I do," said Verra, giving Aliera a stern look that made me want to giggle.

Aliera shrugged. "Well, we managed it, and without much harm. That's the important thing."

I glanced at my injured arm, and started to object to the "without much harm" business, but didn't.

"No," said Morrolan. "The important thing is that Vlad, however well intentioned, invoked powers he does not understand, and cannot control, and nearly got us killed."

"Sorry about that," I said. "It seemed like a good idea at the time."

"It was a good idea," said Aliera. "It was also necessary, after my cousin made such a clumsy strike at the Jenoine—"

"It was hardly clumsy," said Morrolan. "It was quite sufficient, or would have been, if the Jenoine had not succeeded in blocking it, as, in fact, he blocked yours. More easily, I suspect."

"Not likely," said Aliera. "In fact, as I recall, you were late in your—"

The worst part was, I was too weak to get up and walk away.

"I was hardly late," said Morrolan. "If anything, you—"

"Oh, stop it," I said.

They ignored me.

"If anything I *what*," said Aliera. "Pathfinder was—"

"*Stop it!*" I said, and for an instant they stopped. I rushed into the void like Sethra rushed her reserves into the breach at the Battle of Ice River Crossing (actually, I know nothing about the Battle of Ice River Crossing except that there was one and Sethra was there; but it sure sounded knowledgeable, didn't it?). I said "Can you two, just one time, give a tired and injured man a little peace? Besides, your arguments, as always, are stupid to begin with. Morrolan goes out of his way to be contentious toward Aliera because he idolizes Adron and therefore believes his daughter ought to not only be his equal in all matters, but ought to do and say everything exactly the way Morrolan imagines Adron would; and Aliera, of course, idolizes her big, powerful, brave cousin Morrolan, and so has a tantrum whenever he fails to live up to the Morrolan she's manufactured in her head. It's infernally stupid, and I've been listening to it for more years than a short-lived Easterner should have to, and I'm heartily sick of it. So shut up, both of you."

I ran down at last.

"*My goodness, Boss.*"

I was a bit surprised myself; I hadn't known I knew most of that stuff until I said it, and wouldn't have believed I'd have said it if I knew it. And now I got to sit there and wonder if, after all of Teldra's remarks about how tactful I was, I had finally stepped over the line.

I risked a look at the pair of them.

Morrolan was looking down, a self-conscious, maybe even embarrassed smile trying to fight its way past his facial control. Aliera was *blushing*. Actually blushing. This was as remarkable as having astonished the Demon Goddess. I don't know, by the way, how the Goddess reacted to my outburst, because I carefully avoided looking at her.

Morrolan cleared his throat, started to speak, then didn't.

Eventually, Sethra filled the silence with, "Well, my friends, it is certainly the case that Vlad could use a little quiet. Or, at least, less volume."

Morrolan grunted something that sounded like agreement; Aliera looked down and nodded. They hadn't even looked at each other. I hoped I hadn't made things uncomfortable for them. Except that part of me hoped I had.

Before anything else could happen, I turned to Teldra and said, "I'm glad you survived."

"I did," she said. "Thank you."

"What was it you were saying to them, right when I was doing whatever I was doing that created such a fuss?"

Teldra chuckled. "I suggested that it would be easier for them to resist the effects of the amorphia if they were to release Morrolan and Aliera."

"Oh. Was that all?"

"Almost."

"Oh?"

Lady Teldra blushed. "I'd rather not say, if you don't mind."

I felt my eyebrows rising. Aliera, and now Teldra. What was the Empire coming to? Morrolan chuckled and said, "A well-timed, properly delivered insult can unsettle anyone. I don't know exactly what she discovered that a Jenoine might find so offensive as to disrupt its concentration, but I am not astonished that Teldra knew."

"Teldra," I said admonishingly. "Was that polite?"

"It was," she explained, "appropriate."

Morrolan snorted.

"In any case, we're alive, and free. It's over," I said hopefully.

The Demon Goddess gave a small laugh. "Over? Do you really think so? Do you imagine that your escape has foiled whatever campaign the Jenoine have begun? Or that I will be satisfied letting them continue their mischief without making any sort of counter?"

I sighed. "No, I suppose not. But I'm injured; whatever you do won't include me, will it?"

I looked at Morrolan, Sethra, and the Demon Goddess, and sighed. "Well, can we at least have a decent meal before we do whatever it is we're going to do?"

Sethra nodded. "I think that is an excellent idea. I'll see to it."

She left to have food prepared, and my stomach growled and rumbled at the idea. I closed my eyes.

I heard the sounds of people sitting, and, wounded arm or no, enjoyed the feeling of being momentarily safe. The muscles in my shoulders and neck relaxed, and I took a big lungful of normal air that I didn't have to think about breathing.

Presently, a rough, high-pitched voice said, "Wine, my lord?"

I opened my eyes, saw Tukko, and closed my eyes again. "Yes," I said. And, "please," I added, because Lady Teldra was nearby. I sat up, discovering that it was harder than I'd have thought without being able to use my left hand, and took a glass of something red and sipped it. My tongue liked it—it was faintly nutty and had a bit of tang to it—but my stomach complained that it wanted something solid before I got too involved in this whole drinking business. I caught Teldra looking at me, and lifted my glass to her. "To survival," I said.

"Yes, indeed," she said.

Sethra returned and said, "Dinner will be ready in an hour." She smiled at me and said, "Will you survive that long?"

"I think so," I said. It suddenly occurred to me that, while Sethra was off giving the order for food to be prepared, Tukko, the only servant I'd ever seen here, was with us. Was there a staff of cooks I'd never met? If so, why, since Sethra's usual diet didn't feature anything that needed cooking? If not, had she gone off to arrange for some culinary ensorcellment? Of all the myriad mysteries surrounding the Dark Lady of Dzur Mountain, I knew that this one was going to bother me. Maybe I could bring myself to ask her. Sometime when Lady Teldra wasn't around.

I drank my wine, and Sethra sat down next to me. "Let's see that arm," she said. I couldn't show it to her because I couldn't move it, so I just shrugged my one good shoulder and looked away. Out of the corner of my eye, I could see her holding it, rolling my sleeve back, touching it; but I felt no sensation.

I said, "Evidently the nerves have been damaged, too; I can't feel your charming, cold, undead fingers."

"Mmmmm," she said. Then, "Yes, it *is* nerve damage, not muscle damage." She continued her inspection. I tried to think about other things without much success.

"Is it repairable?" I asked eventually, trying to keep my voice casual, as if I were asking if a blunted dagger could be resharpened.

"I'm not sure," she said in much the same way. Bitch.

"Good wine," I told her. "Thanks."

She smiled as if sharing a joke with herself and said, "You are most welcome, Lord Taltos."

She set my arm back in my lap and said, "We'll have to see."

I nodded. No one spoke. I cleared my throat and said, "So, all right, what's the plan?"

13

While in the Care of the Physicker

"It's too soon to talk about plans," said Morrolan. "I'm still trying to recover."

"Nonsense," I said. "It's never too soon to talk about plans. Making plans is one of the great joys of my life. Sometimes, on a lazy afternoon, I just sit around and make up plans. I've often said—"

"Be quiet, Vlad."

"Feel better now, Boss?"

"A bit, Loiosh."

"You know, Morrolan," said Aliera. "He has a point. It wouldn't hurt any to start thinking about how we're going to go after them."

"It's too soon to talk about plans," I said. "I'm still trying to recover."

Morrolan favored me with a disgusted look.

Sethra said, "Lady Teldra, I assume you will grace us with your company at table?"

"That is kind of you," said Teldra. "Yes, I should be delighted." For a moment that confused me, until I remembered that she was Morrolan's servant, which fact had somehow gotten lost in the last few days.

"Good," said Sethra.

"Let me see that arm," said Aliera abruptly. She came over and knelt down next to me, picked up my arm, and stared at it. "Nerve damage can sometimes be repaired," she said after a moment.

"Yes," said Sethra. "Sometimes, depending on the nature of the damage. In this case, I can't quite tell what they did." This, of course,

made me feel great. What is it about physickers, or sorcerers acting
as physickers, that makes them talk about the sick guy as if he weren't
in the room?

Aliera turned to Verra and said, "Mother? Do you know how it
works?"

"The one I remember worked on the muscle, not the nerve," she
said.

"Well, can you help?"

"Perhaps," said the Goddess.

Perhaps. I liked that. What's the point of divinity if you can't
help your devoted worshipers? I sat there, my arm hanging limp, and
thought evil thoughts.

Sethra suggested I lie back down and relax until we were called
to table, which seemed like a good idea, so I did, and I believe I
actually dozed off for a while, to be woken by Loiosh, who is quite
accomplished at waking me, explaining that he was used to surviving
on scraps, but if I wanted any more than that it was time for me to
be moving.

I grunted and struggled up to my feet, which, as I've already
observed and now discovered again, is harder than you'd think when
shy an arm, then followed Aliera and Teldra, who were having a
quiet conversation and making their leisurely way to the dining room.
I sat down with Teldra on one side of me, and Sethra, at the head
of the table, on the other; Morrolan and Aliera were across from us.
I said, "Where is the Goddess?"

"Is that a philosophical question, Vlad?" asked Morrolan.

"Yeah, I suppose."

"She has returned to her own domain," said Aliera.

"What, she didn't like the menu?"

Sethra smiled at that, but gave no response; nor was one needed,
because Tukko came in at that moment, carrying a large silver platter
in each hand. He set one of them down between Morrolan and me,
the other between Teldra and Aliera.

"Oh," said Sethra, in a tone I'd never heard from her before.

I looked up, and she was staring at the food with a look of distress
on her face. I tried to remember when I'd seen her distressed before.

"Vlad, I'm sorry," she said. "I didn't realize what was being prepared."

I looked at the food again, frowned, and then figured it out and chuckled. "Oh," I said. "That's funny, in a grim sort of way."

My father had never approved of what he called "half-prepared food," of which this was a sample. I don't have a problem with it, myself—it's sort of fun to put things together yourself, adjusting the quantities, and so on. But my father believed that a good chef made all the decisions about food; if the guest added even a bit of lemon or salt to something my father had built, then, he believed, there must be something wrong—either with the food or with the guest.

I think this says more about my father than about food.

The item before us consisted of treska leaves—fresh, green, and curly. One would spoon a tiny bit of plum sauce onto a leaf, add a minute quantity of dried kethna, a morsel of diced leek, a piece of lime, a slice of bitterwort, a sliver of ginger, and a dusting of dried red pepper. One then rolled the thing up and popped it whole into one's mouth. I'd had versions of this before—most of the islands had something like it, using dried seafood of some kind in place of kethna, as a lovers' snack. Cawti and I had once—but never mind that. The point is, you need two hands to prepare it, and Sethra had just realized that it was exactly the wrong thing to serve just then, and she was mortified. I was amused. Hungry, but amused.

The funniest part was that I caught Sethra glancing at Teldra. Teldra, for her part, said, "Here, I'll wrap one for you."

"That would be great," I said.

She put one together for me, her long, graceful fingers nimble and precise as she measured each ingredient out on the leaf that lay in the palm of her hand; then she rolled it up in a smooth motion, and handed it to me with the least hint of a bow. I smiled at her, took it, and ate it. It was very good; the bitterwort slid through the plum sauce, and then the ginger and the red pepper sort of burst in on your tongue along with . . . well, you get the idea. I had two more of them, making a point of eating slowly to give Teldra time to wrap and eat a couple of her own. Tukko came in with the next course, shuffling about and moving much quicker than it seemed he was. He gave us each what I thought was just a ball of rice, only the rice had been prepared with ginger, and saffron, and I swear a tiny bit of honey; it was quite remarkable.

"My compliments, Sethra," I said.

"Thank you, Vlad," which was just about the only conversation for some time.

The fruit was a selection of local berries, some of which I hadn't run into before, but they were all good, and served with ice and thick cream, after which came thin slices of beef, just barely seared and seasoned with pepper and parsley and calijo, and served with fresh, thick-crusted dark bread. I couldn't cut it with the knife, so I just set the meat on the bread and tore off bites of both.

It was very good.

I ate a great deal.

I noticed that I was sitting with my feet wrapped around the legs of my chair, which is something I've found myself doing when serious about eating. I stopped at once, of course; it's hard to look tough with your feet wrapped around the legs of a chair. Sethra picked at her food, as she had the other times I'd eaten with her. I knew she didn't eat much, for obvious reasons; I wondered if she enjoyed the flavors. Add that to my list of things I'll never ask her, but would like the answer to.

Eventually, I sat back, stretched out, and said, "Okay, Sethra. Give me a couple of hours to digest, and I'll take on every Jenoine you have, all at the same time."

"Careful what you promise," said Sethra Lavode.

"All right," I said. "Let me rephrase that."

Morrolan chuckled. So did Loiosh. I'm quite the jongleur when out of danger and with a meal inside me. Eventually we made our way back to the sitting room, and Tukko brought out a liqueur that was older than Morrolan and much sweeter, featuring the smallest traces of mint and cinnamon—an odd combination, but a successful one, and I'm pretty sure there was some honey in there, too.

I moaned softly. Sethra said, "Is the arm beginning to hurt?"

"No," said Aliera. "That's his moan of contentment after a good meal."

"Now, how would you know that?" I asked her.

She gave me an inscrutable smile that she must have learned from Morrolan. I grunted and drank some more, and enjoyed the transitory sense of contentment I was feeling.

Sethra looked at my arm some more—and when I say she looked at it, that's what I mean. She stared at it so hard I'd say she was looking right through the skin, which is probably what she was doing, at least on some mystical level that I'll never understand.

After several minutes, she said, "I don't know. I'm not sure if I can do anything about it, but it looks like I may not have to."

"How, it'll fix itself?"

"I think so. It seems like it might be a temporary condition. I've been watching the signs of activity in the nerves, and it now seems clear that it is getting better rather than degenerating."

"Degenerating," I said. "Okay. What would that have meant?"

"Paralysis, then death, probably from suffocation when you became unable to breathe, unless your heart became paralyzed first, which would have killed you more quickly. But, as I say, it isn't going that way, it is repairing itself."

"Hmmm. Okay, that's good news. Any idea how long?"

"I can't say."

"Remember, we Easterners don't live more than sixty or seventy years."

"I doubt we're talking about years."

"Good. Then I imagine you're not going to ask me to do anything until I have two good arms, right?"

"I'm not sure we can wait, Vlad."

"Oh? You mean, after two hundred thousand years, or whatever it's been, things suddenly got urgent? When, yesterday?"

"Yes," said Sethra. "I believe things have become urgent. They became urgent when Morrolan and Aliera were taken. Everything is at a new level now, and developments are taking place quickly."

"But—"

"More important," she continued, "I doubt they will give us time to do anything at all."

"They wouldn't attack Dzur Mountain again, would they?"

"I hope so. Anything else they might come up with would be worse, because we haven't any preparations for it."

"Hmmm," I said, because that always sounds wise. "Have you spoken to the Empress?"

"Yes."

"Well then—wait. You have?"

"Yes."

"Oh," I said. "And, uh . . . what does she say?"

"She wants me to deal with it."

"She wants you to . . . with all of her resources, she has no one else to call on except—"

"Me? And Morrolan e'Drien, and Aliera e'Kieron?"

"Uh . . ."

"Go ahead, Boss; talk yourself out of this one."

"Shut up, Loiosh."

"I was referring to myself, Sethra," I said.

"Ah. Well, she is calling on me, and I am calling on you."

"You are—"

"Traditionally, this is exactly the sort of thing the Empress has called upon the Lavodes for; it is what we were created for. Now, as it happens, I am the only Lavode left. Well, there's one other, but he isn't ready yet."

"The Lavodes were created to fight the Jenoine?"

"The Lavodes were created to handle threats or potential threats to the Empire that were fundamentally non-military."

"I see." I thought about it. "But I thought the Lavodes were disbanded before the Interregnum."

"That is true, but I always thought that was a bad idea. The Empress, as it happens, agrees with me."

"Ah. She agrees. Well, how nice. And evidently the Demon Goddess agrees with you, too. And Aliera agrees, and Morrolan agrees. And Teldra, of course, can't help being agreeable. So I guess you've got agreement all the way around except from the Verra-be-damned Easterner who'd really like to have his left arm working again before doing anything stupid."

"You might have a choice," said Sethra. "But most likely you won't."

"Great. So we're going to be in for it, whether we want to or not. What do we do?"

"Do you have any suggestions, Vlad?"

"For handling rampant Jenoine? No, that has never been a specialty of mine."

"Then, perhaps, you'd care to shut up and let us figure something out."

"Ouch," I said. "All right. I'll just sit here like any good weapon, and wait to be pulled from my sheath, blunted edge and all."

"Good," she said. "That's just what I want."

That hadn't been the answer I was looking for, but I decided to be content with it before I encouraged something worse. I fell silent, just sitting there with my left arm hanging limp and useless in my lap.

"I wish," said Aliera abruptly, "that we could find a way to carry the war to them."

Morrolan looked at her. "Since that is such an obvious observation that you could not possibly have any reason for making it, I must assume you have an idea as to the particulars."

She smiled sweetly at him, and suggested where he might put his assumptions, but caught herself, glanced at me, and eventually said, "No, as it happens, I was musing. I can't think of any way to do so."

Morrolan nodded. "If we're speaking of wishes, I wish we understood them better."

"I have a few guesses about them," said Aliera, "based on what we've just been through, and what I've picked up from Sethra and my mother."

"All right," said Morrolan. "Keep talking."

Sethra leaned forward attentively; I pretended to be bored with the whole thing.

"My first guess is that, whatever their long-term plans are, their next objective is Verra. We know that she has been their enemy for her entire existence, and everything that has happened can be seen that way—even the nonsense about trying to convince Vlad to kill her might be second-level deception, or even a straightforward attempt to convince him to do so."

"Yes," said Sethra. "I agree with your reasoning. Go on."

"All right," said Aliera. "My second guess is a little more daring."

Morrolan muttered something under his breath.

"I believe," said Aliera, "that their second target is the Orb."

Sethra stirred. "The trellanstone?"

Aliera nodded. "The best way to attack the Orb would be with a device with similar properties."

"Then why," said Morrolan, "were we allowed to see it?"

"You think you were allowed to?" said Sethra. "I thought you had managed to penetrate their illusions, and see it in spite of them."

"That's what I had thought, too. But if the trellanstone is im-

portant, then why, of all the places in the Universe, would they put
us near it, illusions or no? In fact," he continued, "there's been too
much of that going around with these things. Too many coincidences.
Too many times we have to ask ourselves, 'Why would they do that?'
All the way from asking Vlad to kill Verra, to doing nothing while
Vlad broke us out of the manacles, and doing nothing again while
he broke himself and Teldra out, and then allowing us to see the
trellanstone, and—"

"My Lord Morrolan," said Lady Teldra suddenly.

He stopped, and turned to her. He'd forgotten her, as had the
rest of us. Her eyes were just a trifle wide.

*"I know that look, Boss. She just got something. You get the same
look when you finally figure out the obvious."*

"How would you know what I look like? You're on my shoulder."

"We have ways."

Meanwhile, Teldra was holding up a finger, asking us to wait,
making little nods to herself as pieces fell into place. Then she said,
"If I may be permitted to express an opinion."

Morrolan nodded impatiently.

"I think, perhaps, you do not understand the Jenoine."

He chuckled. "That, my dear Teldra, is hardly news."

Her smile came and went like a straight shot of plum brandy,
and she said, "I learned something of the Jenoine years ago, most
especially their language. I'm sure you are all aware that language
holds the key to the thinking of a culture. And, of course, one cannot
spend time in such illustrious company as my Lord Morrolan, Sethra
Lavode, and such gods as they come in contact with from time to
time, without learning more. And then, I spoke with them."

She paused. I wondered if she got her sense of drama from Morrolan, or if he hired her because of it. "When you speak of place, you
are speaking in terms that would not make sense to them. They have
a concept of 'place,' but it is used in their mathematics, not in their
daily lives."

"All right," said Aliera. "You have our attention."

"I have heard some—including you, Aliera—speak as if the Jenoine had come to our world from another place. This is not entirely
true. I—please bear with me, this isn't easy to describe." She hesitated. "The clearest way to say it is that they do not move as we do,

nor do they remain stationary as we do. That room in which we were held captive is, in an important sense, the only 'place' they have. At least, as we would use the term 'place.' The world that Vlad and I explored was, to them, the same place as the room. When we shattered the enchantment that kept us from seeing some of what was in the room, what we did was the equivalent of breaking out of that room and exploring other places in the structure. When we physically left the room to explore the world outside that room, we were, in their view, spirit-walking. Well, that isn't exactly right—it isn't such a perfect reversal, but it is something like that."

"Well," said Aliera. "That makes everything clear."

Teldra frowned. "Let me try again."

"Take your time," said Morrolan, giving his cousin a dirty look.

"Think of them this way: They are to us as amorphia is to normal matter. To them, our world and the place where we were held captive are the same place, differing only as states of being. I . . ." Her voice trailed off.

"I'm sorry to say," said Morrolan, "that I don't understand."

I was glad I wasn't the only one.

"The Necromancer," said Sethra suddenly.

"Ah," said Teldra. "Yes."

Morrolan said, "Shall I summon her?"

The mere mention of her name explained some of it—it meant we were dealing with the sorts of mind-bending things that are beyond the powers of normal people to understand.

"I'm not certain," said Aliera, "that I could survive that just now."

I thought about making a comment about Aliera's delicate emotions, but good sense prevailed. A lot of my best wit is shared with no one except Loiosh and you, so I hope you appreciate it; he usually doesn't.

Teldra took her comment seriously. "It requires an adjustment in thinking that doesn't come naturally. I began to get glimpses of it when I studied their language, but I didn't actually understand it until speaking with them. Yes, the Necromancer must necessarily understand these things, and I'm certain she could explain it better than I."

Morrolan cleared his throat. "I don't suppose," he said, "that you could explain the, uh, practical ramifications."

"I believe I can," said Sethra Lavode.

Teldra shot her a look full of gratitude. Meanwhile, I was think-ing, "Wait a minute; how is it Teldra knows this stuff and Sethra doesn't?"

She answered the question before I could decide if I wanted to ask it aloud.

"What you are saying, my dear Teldra, makes sense of many things I have almost understood. Yes. It explains why they were able to achieve access to Dzur Mountain just when they did. It was not, as I thought at the time, a failure of my mundane defenses, nor of the magical ones. It was an attack from a direction that was unex-pected, because, if you will, I didn't know the direction existed."

Teldra nodded. "To themselves, they would say they redefined your defenses."

"Yes."

"Okay," I said. "Good. Now I understand everything."

"In practical terms," said Sethra, as if I hadn't spoken, "it explains at least some of the peculiar behavior you witnessed while confined. In particular, the place they kept you is, as you said, the only place they have. The world the only world, the building the only building, the room the only room. They were, in that sense, in there with you the entire time. You didn't see them or hear them when their atten-tion was focused elsewhere. They—"

"Rubbish," I said.

"Excuse me, Vlad?" said Sethra, who I imagine wasn't used to being addressed that way.

I repeated my remark, then amplified. "I don't care if they con-sider it a place, or a state of mind, or, well, or whatever they consider it. They are real beings. They have bodies. They have places those bodies are."

"What is your point, Vlad?" said Sethra, who seemed to be doing me the courtesy of taking me seriously.

"You don't sit a bunch of prisoners down in front of a powerful object, even concealed, unless either you *want* them to find it, or . . ."

I stopped, considering what I had been about to say.

"Yes, Vlad?" said Morrolan. "Or?"

"Or unless you have no choice."

Sethra said, "How could . . . oh. I see. Yes, that makes sense."

Morrolan and Aliera were already there. Morrolan said, "It was the trellanstone that was holding us in place, that was keeping that gate shut. Yes, I can almost see that."

"Almost?"

"Well, it needs something to work with."

"You don't think there is enough amorphia on that world?" I said.

"Oh, right," said Morrolan.

Sethra looked at us. "Amorphia? How could there be amorphia there? It only occurs on our world. They cannot duplicate the conditions that gave rise to it without, in all probability, destroying their entire world."

I said, "I don't suppose there is a quick explanation for that remark, is there Sethra?"

Morrolan and Aliera looked impatient, but Sethra said, "The Catastrophe that created the Great Sea in the first place resulted from several fluke occurrences, as well as some nasty scheming and plotting on the part of Verra and others with her. But the fact that it failed to entirely consume the world is the biggest fluke of all. Amorphia is not something that is containable, by its very nature. To create it is to end everything."

"But Adron's Disaster—"

"Very nearly destroyed the world again," said Sethra, "but the one advantage the gods had in containing it was the existence of the Great Sea. Had the Great Sea not been there, the Lesser Sea might well have destroyed all life in the world." She shook her head. "I simply cannot conceive of the Jenoine finding a way to produce amorphia."

"Well, they did," I said. "Or else found another way to get it, because they've got it."

Morrolan and Aliera told her about the river of amorphia we had found, Teldra and I making the occasional murmur of agreement. When they had finished, Sethra said, "I didn't think they could do that. I still don't understand how they can do that," which was followed by an unpleasant silence, during which we all, I suspect, contemplated the powers of the Jenoine.

"Are they gods?" said Morrolan suddenly.

Sethra shook her head. "I do not believe so. Teldra?"

"Not in any meaningful way, at least as far as how they see themselves."

"Well, that's something," said Morrolan, which was much like what I was thinking. "So, then, how do we approach them? How do we defend ourselves against them, beyond that we've been doing for thousands of years?"

"Don't forget the weapons," I pointed out.

"Weapons?" said Sethra.

"They had whole racks of weapons. Mundane weapons, the sort of thing I think of as weapons. Things that cut, and stab, and make nasty gouges. If those bastards are so bloody magical, what do they need with weapons?"

"Good question," said Morrolan. "He's right, they had quite a collection of them. What are they for?"

"That," said Sethra, "I think I can answer. I believe that, after establishing themselves here, they intend to subvert a portion of our citizens and use them as a mundane army."

"How can they subvert them?" said Aliera.

"If they can, indeed, attack the Orb, then they can, at least potentially, gain access to the minds of those who are linked to it."

That thought made me shudder. For one thing, I was linked to the Orb myself.

"Well, let's see," said Aliera. "Consider what we know about them. They are after my mother, and perhaps others of the gods as well. It is the gods who are protecting our world—I think I now understand a little how they are doing it. But what the Jenoine want is full access to our world. What prevents them from having it are the Lords of Judgment, the Orb, the power of Dzur Mountain. They attacked Dzur Mountain once before, and failed to take it."

"Barely," said Sethra under her breath.

"Therefore, our defense of these things—"

"Defense," said Morrolan like it was something foul. "Why not attack them instead? I've always preferred attacking to defending."

"I know," said Sethra. "But you are still young, and may yet learn."

He glared at her. She ignored it and said, "Go on, Aliera."

Aliera continued, "Our defense of these things has to happen on several levels at once. We require the assistance of the Lords of Judgment, in the first place, and I should think we really ought to consult the Necromancer after all."

"Yes," said Sethra. "But whatever we're going to do, we ought to do it quickly. We don't know how much time they're going to give us. And worse, we don't know where they're going to attack."

"Yes, we do," said Morrolan suddenly, sitting upright, and staring off into space.

We all looked at him.

"Trellanstone," he said. "It all revolves around the trellanstone, or kyrancteur, in the language of the Serioli. They managed to find some, and they are using it. They wanted Aliera and me out of the way to—"

Sethra figured it out first. "Oh," she said. "Yes. I should have seen it at once."

Then Aliera got it, and nodded slowly. "Foolish of me. One of them was able to stop a simultaneous attack from two Great Weapons. It should never have been capable of stopping even one of them. I was so annoyed, I didn't stop to wonder how it managed it. Yes. There is only one way it could have done that. How annoying."

Of course, I could have sat there for the rest of my life and never figured it out, but Sethra realized I was confused and took pity on me.

"Trellanstone," she said. "It is useful for manipulating amorphia— raw chaos. So far as I know, there are two places in the universe where one can find amorphia, and both of them are on this world. The Great Sea of Amorphia is protected by the Orb, which is protected by the Empress, who is protected by the Lords of Judgment, by Dzur Mountain, and by the Orb."

"Ah," I said. "And so now we know, I'm sure, where they got the amorphia from in the first place."

"Yes," said Sethra. "We used the power of the Greater Sea to protect the Orb, and used the Orb to protect the Greater Sea. It never occurred to me that they might tap into the Lesser Sea, because it isn't connected to the Orb. But they have somehow tapped into it. They have been draining it, and learning to control it with the trellanstone, and that could give them what they need to attack the Orb."

"The Lesser Sea," I said. "Well. Can't we just cut it off from them?"

Sethra nodded. "Yes. And we will. I can do so myself. But then what?"

"Then," said Morrolan, "they will use their trellanstone to attempt a permanent link with it, much as the Orb is linked to the Great Sea. If they achieve that, they will, in effect, have the seeds of their own Empire on our world."

I nodded. "Yes. And after that things could get all kinds of difficult, couldn't they?"

"They could indeed," said Sethra. "We must act at once. Every moment that passes, they draw more energy, and become stronger, and it will make it harder to resist them. We must cut off their flow, and then be prepared to make certain they cannot re-establish it. That means facing them down right there, at the Lesser Sea of Chaos."

"Adron's Disaster," said Morrolan.

Aliera nodded. "I was afraid Daddy would cause trouble sooner or later."

14

I was glad Teldra and Loiosh were there, because I didn't want to be alone.

Morrolan, Sethra, and Aliera had left us, continuing their discussions as to who should speak with whom about what—Morrolan to speak with the Empress, Aliera to talk to the Necromancer, and so on, and what they should tell them. Dzur Mountain is a big and lonely place, and some of that feeling rests in each chamber, no matter how small and warm; with little effort I could imagine the nightmares from my childhood creeping out of the corners—especially since this was a place where some of the nightmares were real. And it didn't help that it required very little imagination to see Jenoine appearing out of nowhere; from all evidence, that was a very real possibility.

Teldra and I spoke for a while about the meal, and the furnishings of Dzur Mountain, and other things. I wanted to ask her about Cawti, but I refrained. Instead I said, "Do you think I was out of line, Teldra?"

"My lord?"

"My, uh, blowup at Morrolan and Aliera. Was I out of line?"

"I don't believe it is my place to say, my lord."

"Heh. In other words, yes."

She shook her head. "No, I simply mean it is not my place to say."

"All right."

She hesitated, then said, "I think you, being wounded, had the right to request respect for your injury."

"Mmmmm. But you wish I hadn't said it?"

"I'm not certain, Vlad. Certainly, everything you said is true. Not exhaustive, but true."

"Not exhaustive?"

"I mean your insight was well taken. But, there is still much you don't understand about my Lord Morrolan. For all of his skills and strengths of character, Morrolan is still a young Dragon. He knows this. It is why he wanted me as his seneschal. To know and take steps to counter one's weaknesses is praiseworthy, in my opinion. Also, rare."

"I see. Other than having the desire from time to time to slaughter a few hundred helpless peasants, what does it mean to be a young Dragon?"

"It means seeing the world with one's self as the center."

"Really? I've never considered Morrolan to be self-centered."

"He isn't," said Teldra. "Not as the term is usually meant. There is a subtle but important difference, Vlad, between thinking only of yourself, and seeing the world as it affects you." She smiled suddenly. "And the difference, by the way, is exactly what courtesy is all about."

"You'll have to explain that to me."

"Do I, Vlad? I somehow doubt that."

"Oh?"

"Oh. But, very well. Morrolan is generous, and self-sacrificing, and always glad to be of help to a friend, but sometimes he sees things first from how they affect him. It means he will sometimes go into a situation wondering what he should do, rather than wondering what needs to be done."

"That's pretty subtle, Teldra."

"Not as subtle as you might think. Or, rather, it is a case where subtleties can become very large. Sometimes, for example, you step into a situation where the thing that needs to be done is nothing at all; someone looking at it from his own perspective is unlikely to realize this."

I made a noncommittal sound, trying to work it all out.

"I know of one case late in the Interregnum—because my Lord Morrolan told of it himself—where he was a division commander under Sethra. He was, he says, an effective commander, but he had the bad habit, when given an order, of sending back suggestions to

Sethra about what she should do with the rest of the army to support him, not quite able to realize that she might have thought of these things, and that it was she who had the best view of the entire picture, and was placed to make those decisions. The result was a small increase in friction among the staff, and a series of delays in carrying out her orders. His intentions were good, but he was seeing everything from his own perspective."

"Hmmm," I said. "Okay, I see your point. And, yeah, Morrolan is like that, sometimes. So is Aliera, for that matter."

"Yes, she is also a young Dragon."

"Which, of course, is part of why they keep knocking heads, notwithstanding my juvenile outburst earlier."

"Of course."

I shrugged. "Well, okay, I'm glad we settled that. What are young Issola like?"

Teldra flashed me a smile. "Obsequious to the point of irritating, or else timid to the point of invisibility. What about young Easterners?"

"Brash, cocky, and convinced we can beat anything that walks, flies, or swims, and that we know all the answers to everything."

"Rather like Dzur, then."

"I guess. I'm generalizing from one example, here, but everyone generalizes from one example. At least, I do."

That earned an actual chuckle; I felt very proud.

I added, "Of course, by Dragaeran standards, all Easterners are young Easterners."

"Yes. Which is only one of the reasons Easterners are treated the way they are by humans."

"Morrolan is an exception; he deserves credit for that. As are you, by the way."

"Thank you," said Teldra. "In my case, I can't help it, it's how I was raised." She smiled.

There were footsteps in the hall, and I knew it was Sethra before she appeared, either because I recognized her footsteps, or because of some subtle psychic awareness of her that I was developing. She nodded to us and said, "Have you two solved all of our questions of grand strategy for us?"

"No," I said, "but we've solved a great deal of the mystery of the mysterious Morrolan."

"I'm impressed," said Sethra, sitting down in an oversized chair to my left. "That's much more difficult." It seemed to me, watching her sit, that she was tired. I guess she'd been busy enough while we were away.

I said, "You reached the Necromancer?"

Sethra nodded. "She'll be along directly."

I tried to say, "Good," but couldn't force the word past my lips, so I settled for the old brusque nod. Sethra glanced at my arm and said, "Any change?"

"About five or six minutes ago it twitched a little. Hardly anything; I was talking to Teldra and barely noticed it."

"Very well," she said. "That's probably a good sign. The muscles are coming back to life, which means, among other things, that they aren't entirely dead."

"You thought they might be?"

"It was a possibility."

"Why didn't you tell me?"

"What good would it have done you?"

"It would have given me a good excuse to have a hissy-cow, right when I badly wanted to have one."

"A hissy-cow?"

"Uh . . ."

"No, no, Vlad. Don't explain." She chuckled. "A hissy-cow. I think I like that."

I had gotten a chuckle out of Teldra and Sethra within the same hour, and that after making Teldra and Aliera blush, and before that I'd managed to shock the Demon Goddess. My life was now complete. I decided this was a good time to quit, so I leaned back and closed my eyes, only to be interrupted by the sound of more footsteps. I didn't want to open my eyes, for fear that the Necromancer would be there, so I did and she was.

You must understand, it isn't that I'm afraid of her. I've spoken with her, and, if you can get past the fact that she's undead, and that her mind is perfectly comfortable living in places that would drive me mad, and that for her the distinction between the living and the dead is just a matter of which way she's facing, she's a perfectly decent sort, as Dragaerans go. It's just that her showing up just then meant that things were liable to start moving, and I was very happy sitting on a couch in Dzur Mountain, feeling relatively at peace with the world, and luxuriating in the notion that no one, just at that moment, would be able to kill me.

"The technical term is 'self-pity,' Boss."

"Did I ask for the technical term?"

"Hello, Vlad," said the Necromancer, in that strange, almost hollow-sounding voice of hers, with her eyes looking more through me than at me.

"Hello," I said, resisting the urge to growl.

Aliera was standing next to her, and nodded me a cool hello. "How's the arm?" she said.

"It twitched."

"Good," said Aliera. "I was hoping it would do that."

Bloody great.

Sethra said, "Have you explained what we require of the Necromancer?"

"No," said Aliera. "I thought I'd leave that to you."

"Very well. While I do so, I think you know what your next task is."

"Yes," said Aliera. "I shall attend to it at once."

Sethra nodded, and Aliera took two steps forward, one step to the side, and vanished as if she had stepped through an invisible doorway.

Sethra Lavode turned to the Necromancer, and I suddenly had the feeling that I was present at one of those great historical moments that you read about, wishing you were there. Here was the Enchantress of Dzur Mountain explaining to the Necromancer the plan of campaign against the ancient enemies of the Dragaeran race. This might be one of the great turning points in the history of the Empire. It seemed incumbent on me to say something to undercut to the whole significance of it, but nothing came to mind.

The two pale, black-clad undead women regarded each other— thin faces, ancient eyes; sort of a strange mirror image. Sethra was perhaps a little taller, and her hair was a bit darker and longer; the Necromancer gave the appearance of a little more age, though this was illusory. In addition, though I knew Sethra was a vampire, the

Necromancer looked like one—so pale, wasted, drawn; like someone in the last stages of some horrible disease.

"We are expecting an attack from the Jenoine," said Sethra.

"Where?"

"The site of Adron's Disaster."

The Necromancer's eyebrows went up. "Is it unprotected?"

"Yes. The other has been protected all along, almost by accident, as it were. And it never occurred to me to look for an attack that way."

The Necromancer nodded, closed her eyes for a moment, then opened them. "Nothing yet," she said.

"Are you certain?"

The Necromancer frowned and said, "What do you mean?"

"Look again. Look for anything that doesn't belong."

"Very well," she said. Then, "Oh."

"They are tapping it?"

"Someone is. It will take a while to find out where it is going, but it certainly seems like their workmanship."

Sethra nodded. "I suspected it, from what Vlad told me. They are evidently collecting it in quantity."

"Collecting it? Raw?"

"So it would seem."

"How are they keeping it unstable?"

"They have found a large piece of trellanstone, and use it to keep the amorphia flowing, rather like a stream, from what Vlad and Teldra said."

"I see. Yes, that might work, if you had someone monitoring it at all times, and if it was physically near the trellanstone."

"The stream ran within a few hundred feet of it."

The Necromancer nodded. "This could be a real problem," she said, almost as if she cared. "Have they stirred?"

"They have indeed. Morrolan and Aliera were taken, Verra threatened—yes, they are stirring."

"Then they are ready with their stroke."

"So it would seem. Except that we have freed Morrolan and Aliera; I don't know how that will change their plans. But we have to assume they're still going ahead with it."

"Very well," said the Necromancer. "What do you require? I can cut their access easily enough."

"Insufficient," said Sethra. "Can you keep them out of the area?"

The Necromancer was silent for a moment; then she said, "I don't know. It's so large. Thirty-five or forty square miles, the last time I looked."

"Yes," said Sethra. "The Empress will almost certainly be willing to help."

"Then perhaps," said the Necromancer.

"If you cannot keep them out, do you think you could, perhaps, keep them in?"

The Necromancer frowned. "One of them, certainly. Ten or twelve of them, all with access to the power of the amorphia, impossible. But the same set of enchantments can be used in both directions."

"All right," said Sethra. "Good. You ought to start your preparations at once. In the meantime, I need to be there, along with Morrolan, Aliera, and whoever else we can gather together quickly. How much time will you need?"

"I don't know. I won't know until I start. Certainly, several hours, even with the Orb. Possibly a day or two. I wish you had told me sooner."

"I wish I had realized sooner what they were up to. We cannot wait a day or two before cutting off their link. I'm nervous about waiting even another hour."

"I shall hurry as much as I can."

"Yes. We will move as soon as we can, and, if you aren't ready, then we will endeavor to hold the place until you are."

The Necromancer nodded and said, "I'll get started, then." She turned away without ceremony, took three steps, and sort of faded away in midstride, leaving a trail of golden sparks behind her; possibly for effect, though that didn't seem like the sort of thing she'd do.

She left the room just as Morrolan returned—he coming in by the door—according to some sort of law of conservation of wizards. The Necromancer left in a shower of sparks; Morrolan appeared with a flapping of wings. Jhereg wings, to be exact. Rocza's wings, to be precise. Loiosh left my shoulder and flew toward her, the two of them doing a sort of midair dance of greeting, then flying around the room once together before landing on my shoulders, and continuing the reunion with neck and face rubs behind my head. It was all very cute.

"I told you I was cute."

"I thought you might be missing her," said Morrolan.

"I was, and so was Loiosh. Thank you from both of us."

He nodded to me, then faced Sethra and announced, "The Empress agrees."

"Good," said Sethra. "So does the Necromancer."

"I love it when a plan comes together," I remarked to no one in particular.

Morrolan shrugged and said, "Here, Vlad." He reached into his cloak and emerged with a bag, which he emptied on the table near my elbow. It contained half a dozen daggers of various sizes. "I thought you might like to restock," he said, "so I grabbed these from my armory. I don't know exactly what you like, but one or two of these must be all right."

"Yes," I said. "That was very thoughtful of you." I inspected them, then placed all of them about my person in various ways. It took some work, with only one hand to work with; but this reminded me to make sure they were all accessible to my right hand. That put one behind my back, one between my shoulder blades, one in my right sleeve, well, you get the idea. Having them there made me feel better at once. I stretched my feet out in front of me and leaned back. Sethra said, "You look like a man who isn't going anywhere, Vlad."

"Well, I don't plan on leaving here any time soon. Am I mistaken about something?"

"I had planned to bring us to the site of Adron's Disaster right away. We don't know when they will appear; I'd just as soon anticipate them."

I looked at my left arm, then at Sethra, with what I hoped was an eloquent expression.

She nodded. "I take your point. But Spellbreaker could still be useful, if you can manage to wield it right-handed."

I sighed. "Very well," I said, and made it to my feet. "I assume Aliera will be joining us soon?"

"I should imagine. Morrolan, if you will please reach your cousin when she becomes available, and let her know that we are leaving now, and give her our precise location."

He saluted, with, I think, a touch of irony. I imagine he was still annoyed about her "young Dragon" remark earlier.

I drained off the remainder of my wine and said, "Do you ever get tired being the general-in-chief, Sethra?"

Sethra gave me a wry smile. "This is half of a general's dream, Vlad: a campaign with no need for a quartermaster. The other half, of course, would be a campaign with no subordinates to keep happy. If I ever have both of those at once, I'll consider my existence fulfilled and become part of the rock of Dzur Mountain again."

"*Again?*" said Loiosh.

"Again?" I said.

She shrugged and didn't answer, damn her.

I carefully set down my wineglass and said, "Well, shall we be about it, then?"

"Yes," said the Dark Lady of Dzur Mountain. She turned to Teldra and said, "If we have the chance to negotiate with them, we will take it, but the difficulty will be knowing if they are deceiving us. Do you think you can tell?"

"I don't know," said Teldra. "I hope so. I will certainly try."

Sethra nodded. "All right. Let's make an end to this."

"Do you think," I said, "that this will really be the end?"

"If we're lucky, it will end this gambit on the part of the Jenoine."

"That's good enough for me," I said, trying to sound like I was all kinds of excited to be part of it. My arm hung there, limp and useless, and Spellbreaker unraveled. I took it in my right hand, and managed, after too much effort, to get it around the wrist. It felt funny there. It also felt funny to be carrying a Morganti dagger. And not having a working left arm felt funny as well. I was a walking joke.

"*Shut up, Loiosh.*"

"*I didn't—*"

"*I know. It's what Sethra would call a preemptive strike.*"

Morrolan said, "Is there anything we need?"

Sethra touched the hilt of Iceflame at her side and said, "No, I believe we have what we need."

"Do you have the location?"

"I will in a moment. Bide."

Teldra came up next to me. I said softly, "Do you know what she meant by 'becoming part of the rock of Dzur Mountain again'?"

"No," said Teldra, just as softly. "I was wondering myself."

"She was probably speaking metaphorically."

"Probably."

I wasn't convinced; I'll bet Teldra wasn't either.

Teldra took a moment to construct me a sling out of a dark grey linen towel she procured from somewhere. She set my arm in it carefully, and I grunted a thank-you.

"Let's go," said Sethra, and we gathered around her. I touched my grandfather's amulet, just to reassure myself that it was still there, and it occurred to me suddenly that I'd been wandering about without any of my protections and hadn't even noticed—this could be dangerous habit. On the other hand, if I were killed by the Jenoine, I would have no need to worry about the Jhereg. You take your consolations where you find them.

I had gotten to about this point in my reflections when the walls abruptly collapsed and opened up to the outdoors—or that's what it seemed like. We stood now on a small rock ledge, overlooking the Lesser Sea of Amorphia, where the greatest city of the Empire used to be until Aliera's daddy had a hissy-cow at the Emperor. I must make a point of telling Sethra not to underrate the power of the hissy-cow.

I looked out upon the raw, seething amorphia below us—the quintessence of chaos, crying out to be organized, and defying anyone's ability to do so. Some of those with me knew what it took to create order out of chaos; those we were expecting also knew. Some wanted to use it for one thing, some another, and therefrom sprang conflict mortal. Me, I'd just as soon let the damned stuff be.

The old city of Dragaera had grown up in what once, I'm told, was a fertile plain, fed by several streams and rivers coming down from a range of mountains that has more names than peaks. The mountains, which were west of the city, were now behind my left shoulder, except for bits of them that spread out in the form of sharp, ugly bits of greyish rock, one of which I now stood on. There were no signs of any rivers from where I stood, and what had been the city and most of the plain was a swirling mass of colors— browns, greens, and oranges, mostly—murky in places, sparkling at times, occasionally even pulling back to show what appeared to be brown dirt beneath. It did, indeed, seem very much like an ocean, if you can imagine an ocean with no tides, but instead with random waves that lash out up to two hundred feet from the "shore"— waves with the charming property that the merest touch will not only kill you, but cause you to instantly dissolve into nothing. It was not my favorite place to be; especially here, about fifty feet away from it.

To be fair, I should add that being above it was rather safer. Not safe, but safer.

"Now what?" said Morrolan. "Spread out, or remain together?"

"Remain together," said Sethra. "And settle in; we might be here awhile."

"Should have brought some chairs," I said. Morrolan gave me a Look.

So I squatted down. My arm gave another twitch. Maybe, if I were lucky, it would start working again before I needed it. I massaged the arm through the sling for a bit and couldn't even feel it.

Sethra drew Iceflame and pointed it out toward the middle of the Sea, staring intently after it. Then she sheathed Iceflame and said, "All right. Any time now."

"That was it?"

"That was it. I have broken their link. Now we wait. If the Necromancer can seal this place off from them before they arrive, then we can all go home. If not, then we get to fight them. If we are lucky, they will be unable to re-establish a link right away, so they will be fighting without the advantage of sorcery, and a good strike with a Great Weapon will kill them. If we are not lucky, things could be more difficult."

"Here's to luck," I said.

"There they are," said Sethra, and my heart jumped into my mouth. I stood, and tried to let Spellbreaker fall into my hand, but missed the grab and it slithered onto the ground. As I groped for it, I following Sethra's gaze until I spotted a shimmering in the air not fifty feet away from us, on the same ledge.

"Okay, here we go, Loiosh."

"Boss, it's Aliera and the Demon Goddess."

"Oh. So it is."

"Sethra," I said, "you did that on purpose, didn't you?"

"No," said Sethra, as she took her hand off the hilt of Iceflame.

Getting the chain wrapped around my wrist again gave me something to do while I recovered. Aliera and the Demon Goddess came up to us, and looked out over the sea. There was an expression on Aliera's face that I'd never seen before. Was she actually staring out at *that* and thinking of her father? How could she? Then again, how could she not?

The first words out of Aliera's mouth were "What did the Necromancer say?"

"She's working on it," said Sethra. "But she says it may take a while."

I said, "Well, we have the Goddess here; maybe she can do something."

"Not quicker than the Necromancer," said Verra, in that oddly echoing voice of hers.

"Why not?"

"Because," said the Goddess patiently, "she's better than me."

I stared at her, wanting to say, "But you're a Goddess!," only that would have sounded stupid, so I just swallowed and said, "Okay."

Sethra said, "Very well, then, Verra, I will keep my attention focused the other way." I'd run into people who were hard to understand; the Demon Goddess is the only being I have met who makes those around her incomprehensible. There is something very wrong about having that effect.

Aliera drew Pathfinder; I took an involuntary step back. Aliera pointed her blade out generally toward the Sea, and swung it back and forth a couple of times, then she made some sort of indefinite grunt under her breath. "Nothing yet," she said.

Morrolan said, "I could reach the Necromancer and—"

"Disturb her while she works," finished Sethra.

Morrolan scowled, then chuckled. "Yes," he said. "That was my intention. You don't like the plan?"

"As much as you like waiting," said Sethra.

Morrolan looked at her. "You don't mind waiting, do you, Sethra?"

She laughed. "At my age, one gets used to it, little Dragonlord. I spend more time waiting than doing anything else."

Morrolan shook his head. "I can't imagine getting used to it."

"You see? You have more in common with our friend Vlad than you ever thought."

I opened my mouth to protest, then shut it again. Morrolan had nothing to say, either. We stared out over Adron's Disaster, which did the dance of amorphia: colors shifting, shapes appearing and vanishing, and always something faintly enticing, the way a tall cliff is enticing to someone afraid of heights. I kept my eyes above it as much as I could, because I didn't want to look at it, but didn't want anyone to know I was afraid to actually watch it.

"*You want to look useful, Loiosh?*"

"*You mean just to impress them? Of course.*"

He and Rocza took off from my shoulder and began flying around the area in opposite directions. I said, "*Don't get too close to it.*"

"*We don't intend to, Boss.*"

Sethra said, "Are we going to get any help from the Empress?"

"Yes," said Morrolan. "She's sending the Court Wizard."

"Ah."

That was irony—Morrolan had been Court Wizard for some years, since an unfortunate incident involving Sethra the Younger, who had held the post previously.

The Goddess said, "I believe we will be ready for them."

Aliera said, "If you missed that, she said we will have aid from Barlen, and several of the other Lords of Judgment."

This brought up several questions, such as why in blazes they needed *me* here; but what I said was "Aliera, why is it that whenever the Goddess your mother speaks, everyone hears something different? It seems—"

Sethra broke in suddenly, "The Necromancer says they are coming. She can't stop them, but she hopes to be able to hold them here."

Loiosh and Rocza returned to my shoulder. Aliera, Morrolan, and Sethra all drew their weapons. I managed to unravel Spellbreaker without dropping it.

I was disappointed.

I'd really been hoping Aliera would answer my question.

15

I wondered if Sethra was happy about having guessed right. Myself, I'd just as soon she'd been wrong.

"I see them," said Aliera.

I followed her gaze, and spotted them almost at once, about fifty yards from us, standing right next to the Sea—closer than I'd have gotten to it for any reason, ever.

"They've spotted us," said Morrolan pointlessly, because they were obviously staring at us.

"What are those things they're carrying?" I asked.

"Probably something magical," said Aliera.

"Thanks," I said.

"*Loiosh?*"

"*I can't tell from here. Should I get closer?*"

"*No.*"

In the course of moving away from the rampant Great Weapons, I discovered I was next to Teldra. "Okay," I said to her in low tones. "I've got a plan. First of all, are you secretly Mario?"

"No," she said.

"Oh. All right, so much for that plan."

She laughed more than it was worth; maybe she was scared too.

As far as I could tell, the Jenoine were doing nothing except looking at us; Aliera, Morrolan, Sethra, and Verra spread out a little, leaving Teldra and I just a bit behind them.

I said to her, "Perhaps you should have a weapon."

She shook her head. "I hardly know which end to hold."

I nodded, thinking that I'd still feel better if she were armed. But why? What did I have to offer her that could hurt them? And then, for all I knew, she could be armed; you never know about an Issola. Hell, maybe she was secretly Mario. It would certainly solve a lot of problems if she were. I looked at Spellbreaker. It was long this time—almost three feet—but the links were very, very fine. I set it swinging slowly.

I took a step forward, then, and Sethra said, "Wait, Vlad."

I stopped. Maybe she had a plan. I'd like her to have a plan. I'd like any reason not to get any closer to those things.

"Sethra, are we going to attack?"

"Bide, Vlad. I'm not yet certain."

I bit back more questions, and waited.

"There!" said Sethra, suddenly.

I looked where she was pointing, and saw a dark figure standing, about as far from the Jenoine as we were, but on the opposite side.

"It's Barlen," said Loiosh.

"He should help."

I glanced at Verra, and saw her locking eyes with Barlen briefly. I felt smug, as if I'd caught her at something; supposedly they were ancient enemies and lovers. That's the sort of thing gods do, you know. It's all in the legends. If this thing continued, I was going to have to start believing in legends.

Then the other Lords of Judgment appeared. Four . . . six . . . maybe ten of them, spreading out over the area. Some I might have recognized from the Halls of Judgment if I'd been closer. Some of them appeared to be more or less human from this distance, others not—I recognized one figure that seemed to be nothing more than a burning stick; another took the form of a cat-centaur; there was a thing that reminded me a little of that chunk of trellanstone, only with legs and spindly little arms; yet another seemed like a walking prism, at least, there were a lot of colors, and my eyes couldn't focus on it; and there was even a dragon which, from across a long distance, seemed almost to catch my eye for an instant, as if it knew me. I stared back. Could it be that one from the Paths of the Dead? No, for some reason, it didn't seem like that dragon. Eventually it looked away, leaving me wondering.

"Sethra," I said. "Is this it? I mean, is this going to be the cata-

clysmic battle between the gods and the Jenoine? And, if so, may I
please be excused?"

The Enchantress of Dzur Mountain didn't look at me, but said,
"I sincerely hope not, Vlad. This would be a bad place for such a
battle; the results would be unpredictable. But it might happen. My
hope is just to keep them away from the Sea and unable to use it,
and to inflict enough punishment on them to discourage them from
trying again. And to answer your other question, no, you may not.
We may require that artifact you're carrying, and someone who knows
how to use it."

Wonderful.

The Jenoine were looking around them, and, as far as I could
tell, did not seem unduly disturbed.

"All right," said Sethra. "Let's move in."

Just exactly what I wanted to do. But they all just nodded, so I
did too. They all started closing in on the Jenoine, so I did too. They
all put expressions on their faces like they were ready to conquer or
die, so I did too.

"*Do you do everything they do, Boss?*"

"*Sure.*"

"*If they all jumped into the Sea of Amorphia, would you do that,
too?*"

"*Not again.*"

"*Heh.*"

Rocza shifted on my shoulder, and I caught the psychic whispers
of Loiosh telling her something—she probably didn't like the place
much. Well, who did?

We moved closer to them—so did the gods. If I'd been attuned
to more levels of magic, I have no doubt I would have detected all
sorts of powerful enchantments swirling about above the place that
was itself the most powerful of enchantments. I set Spellbreaker spinning a bit faster.

"*I'd really like to be somewhere else, right about now.*"

"*Oh, c'mon, Boss. Where's your sense of history?*"

"*I like to read about history, not make it.*"

"*You see, Boss? It's because of attitudes like yours that there are so
few human heroes.*"

"*And so many humans.*"

"Heh."

Rocza shifted again on my shoulder.

"*How is she doing, Loiosh?*"

"*She'll be fine, Boss.*"

"*Are you sure? She seems nervous.*"

"*Right, Boss. As opposed to you and me?*"

"*Good point.*"

We continued on, another step, two, three, closer to where the Jenoine stood, on the very edge of the Sea.

"*Boss, does this remind you at all—*"

"*No. It doesn't. Shut up.*"

I realized that I was still avoiding looking at the amorphia—sort of skirting it with my eyes. I didn't want to look at the Jenoine, either, but I made myself. I watched them, and tried to keep an eye on our Divine allies. This really was shaping up to be one of those battles they write songs about. I wondered if I'd get mentioned—the Easterner, Jhereg, outcast, walking around unarmed except for a length of chain that was useful for blocking magic of a kind that I wasn't going to encounter here. Maybe Teldra and I could find a quiet spot and continue our discussion of the philosophy of courtesy. I had enjoyed that. In fact, on reflection, I had enjoyed that more than I had enjoyed anything for several years. Strange, isn't it? I hadn't even realized it at the time, but trapped on a world not my own, perhaps in a universe not my own, held by godlike beings intent on some ineffable evil, Teldra and I had sat back and had the sort of discussion that I most enjoyed, the sort that Cawti and I had once had.

Bugger. This was not precisely the right time to start feeling maudlin. But those were my thoughts as I moved toward destiny or whatever it was I moving toward. Destiny, a spot in a ballad, or a quick death, maybe, if the Jenoine noticed me, or if I slipped a little and fell into *that*.

As deaths go, that one wouldn't be bad.

I mean, dying in pain has never been high on my list of desires. But, on the other hand, I'm not real fond of the death that comes on you out of nowhere, not even giving you time to realize that you're going. When I had thought about it—and, in my line of work, I had found my thoughts often straying toward that most morbid of all subjects—I had often felt that I wanted to go peacefully, while awake, not in pain, but aware that I was going—with time to say goodbye to life, so to speak, even if it were only to be a temporary goodbye until an awakening in the Paths or in a new incarnation. But then, I wondered, what if I got that, and, in the event, proved craven? The last moments of life have always seemed to me to be a good time for a last mental balance sheet—a chance to say to yourself: Okay, how did I do? How terrible to arrive at that point reasonably happy, only to find that in your last extremity you lost your dignity with your life, and that your whole image of yourself was proved to be only a lie! Rather than that, I'd prefer to go in my sleep, which I've always dreaded; or even by the sudden hand of an assassin, as has seemed most likely for the past several years, or perhaps by a wrong step into amorphia.

Sorry to drag you along for all of this, but, as I say, those were my thoughts at that moment, and if I had to live through them, you have to as well. Deal with it.

Ummm . . . would you be mad at me if, after all of this buildup, nothing much happens? Heh. Don't worry about it. Stuff happens.

Distantly, in the back of my head, as it were, I was aware of Loiosh communicating with Rocza, who seemed to settle down a bit.

We were walking directly toward the Jenoine, but the Lords of Judgment weren't—they were instead spreading out, as if to protect against a retreat. Myself, I was all in favor of permitting the Jenoine to retreat if they wanted to. But why did we have to be the group that moved toward them? Two answers popped into my head at once: first, we had the Great Weapons, and, second, I had no doubt that it was Sethra Lavode who was giving the orders.

There was even someone or something above the Jenoine—at least, there seemed to be a hovering sort of darkness about fifty feet up that appeared thick enough either to contain something sentient, or perhaps even to be something sentient, though if it was it was nothing I wanted to get to know personally.

Aliera said, "Sethra, look."

We all stopped and looked, and discovered that we were, in fact, not the only ones moving directly at the Jenoine: the dragon was, too.

"Well, that is hardly surprising," said Sethra.

"Who is it?" asked Aliera.

"You don't know?"

"No, should I?"

"Yes."

"Well then, who—"

"Not now," said Sethra. She frowned, and finally said, "Very well. Leave her alone, we'll adjust."

I wasn't sure I liked the sound of that, but it wasn't my decision. There is a certain relief that goes with knowing that someone else is making the decisions. Maybe if I were to live two or three thousand years I might get to the point of liking that feeling. Watching Sethra, I got the impression that she was in psychic contact with someone or other, maybe with all the gods at once, so she could direct the battle. I don't know.

The closer we got, the bigger they looked. And the scarier. They didn't look so large out here as they had when surrounded by walls; but they were big, and so bloody *alien*. Their arms were awfully thick, and their hands looked capable of crushing a human skull without too much work, and even from this distance their eyes seemed to glitter with intelligence, and with powers beyond my comprehension. I guess the problem was, I just had too much time to think about things. In my own line of work it was different—either it was an unexpected attack, in which case I was too busy to be scared until it was over, or, preferably, it was something I had planned out to begin with. This was just all wrong.

Sethra turned to us suddenly and said, "She did it."

I was about to ask who did what, but Aliera said, "The Necromancer?"

Sethra nodded.

"Good," said Morrolan.

"I don't get it," I said. "They're already here. What's the point of—"

"She has blocked their passage out," said Sethra. "They have no choice now but to flight."

I looked out over the Sea of Amorphia, then looked away. "Good place for it," I said.

"Yes, in some ways it is," said Sethra. "In spite of the unpredictability of the results, if they fail to achieve their link, then they have an additional threat, with no compensating advantage."

I had been being ironic, but I didn't explain that to her.

At that point the Necromancer herself shimmered into existence a few feet away, walked over, and joined us, as if she were taking her constitutional. She nodded to Sethra and ignored the rest of us. Apparently she was the one being in existence who was immune to Teldra's powers.

We continued our stroll toward the Jenoine: Teldra, me, Aliera, Morrolan, Sethra, the Demon Goddess, and the Necromancer. We kept getting closer, and they still didn't act, though now I could hear them jabbering away in their own language, probably deciding which of them got to eat which parts of which of us. There was no indication that they were worried.

"Dammit, Loiosh. I wish they wouldn't just stand there, waiting. I wish they'd do something."

"Sure, Boss. What would you like them to do?"

"Well, jumping in the Sea would be nice."

"Heh."

"Or they could even surrender to us. That would be fine."

I probably shouldn't have said anything, because it was right about then that they went into action. Well, okay, it probably had more to do with the Necromancer, and even more with the fact that we were barely twenty feet away from them, but it seemed that way.

The way things had developed, there's no way I should have been caught by surprise, but I guess that's one of the problems with surrendering the initiative—they moved very fast, and for a second I froze—Spellbreaker flopped there, swinging back and forth a little. From their position, facing out in all four directions, they moved suddenly, and as if they'd trained for the maneuver for years. They seemed to grow larger, and one of them reached out for us, as if to grab and crush us, though more likely he was going to—

"Vlad!" said Sethra sharply, and I started Spellbreaker swinging again.

"Left!" said Loiosh, and I moved to the left, though I'm not sure what I was avoiding. I bumped into Teldra and we both stumbled. Teldra kept her balance, but I ended up on one knee, automatically raising my hand so I could keep Spellbreaker spinning. Spellbreaker obligingly shortened itself—I felt it vibrating in my hand, looked at it, and saw the links become larger. When I looked back up, my view was blocked by Morrolan and I don't know what happened, but Sethra was holding Iceflame up above her head, and there was lightning and flashing and all that sort of stuff going on somewhere in front of me—it was really shaping up into one of those big sorcerous battles they always talk about. What was I doing here?

I wasn't even aware of how loud things had gotten until I saw Aliera shouting but realized I couldn't hear her—not that it mattered, she was probably yelling some sort of Dragon war cry or something. She was also moving Pathfinder around in some sort of pattern—I wanted Pathfinder to be emitting flashes, sparks, lights, but whatever Aliera was doing with it didn't show.

Blackwand, on the other hand, was doing everything I could have wished—he would point it, and it would flash, and he'd point it somewhere else, and it would shoot out something black and scary-looking.

Verra was writhing and gyrating, as if possessed by something that made her arms flail and her body twist from side to side.

The Necromancer stood very still, her arms at her sides.

The noise, I eventually realized, was a sort of constant, rolling thunder; it seemed to come from everywhere. I concentrated on keeping Spellbreaker moving and tried to stay aware of what was going on, and watch for anything that might come at me, though it was hard, because Morrolan was in front of me blocking my view—and he may, of course, have been blocking more than my view.

Then Morrolan stumbled and went down in front of me, and I realized that one of the Jenoine was close. Very close. Too close. Way too bloody close—like maybe ten feet away. I wanted to look at Morrolan, to see if he was bleeding, or showed any apparent signs of injury—but I couldn't take my eyes off the Jenoine.

Well, okay. Score one for their team.

As far as I could tell, the Jenoine wasn't looking at me; it was concentrating on Verra. Frankly, I'd be more concerned with a God than with a one-armed Easterner too. Aliera knelt down next to Morrolan, Sethra turned away, I guess concentrating on one of the others, and there was a tremendous flash of light from directly overhead that left me seeing spots just as I was wondering if I should get involved somehow. I kept seeing flashes out of the corners of my eyes and couldn't tell what was from the Sea and what was caused by our friends and what was caused by our enemies. The air had that queer tang it gets after a heavy thunderstorm.

"*What was that, Loiosh?*"

"*Something from that guy overhead, I think, Boss.*"

"*Good. Did it accomplish anything?*"

"*I don't know. But one of them is down.*"

I saw it, then—one of the Jenoine was down indeed, and wouldn't be getting up again, and there was no mystery about what had taken it out: the dragon was holding it down with two paws and tearing chunks out of the thing with its teeth, and scattering it in all directions, as if to tell us that good, old-fashioned gore did, indeed, belong in a battle of gods, demigods, and wizardry.

Well, okay. Score one for our team.

Aliera turned her back on Morrolan and took two steps, which brought her next to the Demon Goddess her mother—the two of them stood facing one of them—perhaps the one that had laid out Morrolan. I watched, motionless.

The three of them began moving in a circle, and as far as I could tell, not doing anything else. I glanced around, trying to get an idea of what else was going on. Another of the Jenoine stood on what I have to call the shore for lack of a better term, staring out over it with its hands extended—probably, I suppose, doing whatever it was they came here to do in the first place.

I supposed I should do something to stop it. Heh.

Another continued to be dismembered and gutted by the dragon, who wanted to make a thorough job of it, and the remaining one stood with its back to the one on the shore, making sweeping gestures with its arms while the gods stood around it, trying to close but unable to—Barlen, in particular, was scraping his huge reptilian feet in the dirt as if scrabbling for a purchase. It is not every day that one gets to see the gods stymied; I might have even enjoyed it if I weren't part of the whole thing.

Judging from the sparks and flashes that occurred in front of the Jenoine, the gods were throwing all sorts of things at it that didn't get through, and there was that god overhead, dominating everything, making flashes of light that made the daylight seem brighter than bright. It was all very magical and stuff.

I tried to watch everything at once. I was conscious, once more, of how relaxed I was now that the time for action was at hand. My fear was somewhere behind me—I recognized it, but it was as if it were someone else's fear. I don't know, maybe that's how heroes feel. If I ever meet a hero, I'll ask.

Teldra knelt down next to Morrolan and bent over him. The Jenoine facing Aliera and the Demon Goddess moved toward Verra, and she moved toward it, and there was a flurry of activity, and Aliera gave a yell or a scream that I saw more than heard. Sethra turned toward Morrolan and Teldra, as if noticing them for the first time, and yelled something to me that I couldn't hear over the other sounds, which had done nothing except gotten louder—the roaring was almost painful.

Then Sethra pointed Iceflame at the Jenoine that was tussling with Verra and moved into the maelstrom. Aliera took a step in that direction, fell, stood up, took another step, fell again, stood up again, and fell once more. The Jenoine stood over Aliera, both of its hands raised in fists over its head, looking like it wanted to pummel Aliera physically, which couldn't possibly have done her any good. The dragon, which had finished its meal and was now trying to get at the Jenoine who was holding off the Lords of Judgment, turned toward us, then, its mouth open, showing teeth the size of Blackwand, and began to move in our direction.

Then, just as if things weren't weird enough, Morrolan's right arm, still holding Blackwand, raised itself until it was pointed at the Jenoine—apparently without any direction from Morrolan himself, who gave every appearance of lying senseless on the ground, Teldra still kneeling next to him, bent over him. It was downright disconcerting.

Blackwand gave out some sort black flash, and the Jenoine reeled for an instant and took a step backward. Aliera rose to her feet and pointed Pathfinder at its breast. Maybe Morrolan was alive after all. The dragon, for no reason that I could see, stopped as if it had struck a wall, rolled over—something that big does a lot of rolling over when it rolls—and then came to its feet once more, and shook its head in a very human gesture.

I took a step closer to Morrolan, so I could get a clear view of his face.

"He looks dead, Boss."

"I think so, too. I hope it doesn't discommode him."

Then Teldra stood up and looked at me, and if there had been any doubt about Morrolan's condition, Teldra's expression would have removed it.

If you ever feel like torturing yourself, playing the "if only" game is a good way to go about it. If I had heard what Sethra had been yelling at me, or had managed to guess it. If I had known what they were doing. If I had moved a little quicker—or a little slower. If, if, if. You can kill yourself with ifs.

Or you can kill someone else with them, I suppose.

I looked up at the Necromancer, hoping maybe she could do something, but she hadn't even noticed Morrolan fall, and I dared not disturb whatever she was in the middle of.

One thing I know about revivification is that time is critical. I stood there, Spellbreaker spinning, and tried to think of something I could do that would get this over with fast, so Aliera or Verra or Sethra could start working on him. My arm twitched again in its sling, just to let me know that it would probably be useful again when it was too late. I would have liked to have at least dragged him away from the fight, but I couldn't with one arm.

Then Aliera went flying backward, tumbling backward like a seed bag without the seed, landing next to the dragon. I thought she was dead, or at least injured, but she put her hand on the dragon's head, and, using it like a handhold, rose to her feet at once, shook her head in a gesture terribly reminiscent of the dragon's, then turned back toward the battle.

It was terrifying to think that one of those things was entertaining the Demon Goddess, Sethra Lavode, the Necromancer, a dragon, and Aliera e'Kieron—after having killed Morrolan e'Drien. Quite terrifying. And another one was holding its own against the Lords of Judgment, against the gods themselves. I just didn't belong here at all.

Aliera didn't seem too worried—she raised Pathfinder, gave a scream that was so loud I heard it over the roaring, and charged.

The Jenoine noticed her, flung the Demon Goddess away, and faced Aliera.

Pathfinder seemed about to take it in the neck, but it held up a hand and, just as before, Pathfinder was held motionless, as was Aliera.

Evidently, they had succeeded in re-establishing their link with the Sea. I wondered if that meant we could retreat now, call it a lost battle, and go home.

I guess not.

Verra jumped on its back, biting and scratching at it like a tag in a brothel who just discovered that someone has borrowed her favorite gown and gotten a wine stain on it.

The Jenoine spun quickly, striking Aliera with the Demon Goddess's feet—the whole thing suddenly looked more like a tavern brawl or a scene in a farcical play than an apocalyptic battle between the forces of Good and Evil. Aliera was knocked backward again, while the Goddess fell from its back, landing at its feet, leaving its back to us. There was the perfect backshot I'd been looking for before, but I will confess to you that never for an instant did it occur to me to take it.

It did occur to someone else, however.

I felt a pluck at my side, as if a clumsy cutpurse were operating against me. I reached down to grab the wrist, forgetting that that hand didn't work. Before I could do anything else, Teldra was past me, holding the Morganti dagger she had pulled from its sheath at my belt.

Before it could turn around, Lady Teldra struck it, hard and low in the back.

No matter how powerful the Jenoine, a Morganti dagger between the shoulder blades will seriously cramp its style.

I guess it was the surprise, the unexpectedness of the attack that did it, but, of all the sorceries and Great Weapons and gods and dragons and necromancies, it was that attack with that weapon that got through.

The Jenoine jerked and tensed, spun around, and its face, insofar as I could make out an expression on its alien features, seemed twisted into a grimace.

For a moment that, in my memory at least, stretches out forever, I felt hope; could it actually be that after Iceflame, Blackwand, and Pathfinder had failed, that thing had succeeded? Teldra had stuck it deep, that was for sure, and maybe, just maybe.

Time stretched out, and everything took a horribly long time.

The Jenoine reached behind itself, and when its hand came back into view, it was holding the Morganti dagger, which it neatly and smoothly buried in Lady Teldra's breast.

16

Funereal Customs

The Jenoine, having destroyed Teldra, turned away; obviously still in pain, and, it seemed to me, maybe even a bit disoriented. Well, I suppose if you've just had a powerful Morganti dagger plunged into your vitals, you are permitted a little disorientation. Aliera shook herself and started to stand, the Demon Goddess rose to her knees, Sethra lowered Iceflame and turned toward Teldra. The Necromancer stood there, apparently oblivious. Morrolan remained dead, but not as dead as Teldra was or I felt.

I was close to her; I took a step and knelt down beside her, suddenly as oblivious as the Necromancer to both my friends and to the Jenoine. The expression on her face was one of mild astonishment. Her eyes were opened, but sightless, vacant; there was nothing there. It was all gone. Teldra was gone.

The Morganti dagger was deeply buried in her, and still leaking blood—with a blade that long, it must be nearly all the way through her.

I reached for the dagger to draw it out of her, though I knew it was already too late. Maybe I was thinking of saving her, maybe I was planning to attack the Jenoine with it; more likely I was just not thinking.

It was hard to get a grip on it with Spellbreaker still in my hand; I was unwilling to drop the chain, and I had no other hand to use. I managed to wedge the end of the chain between my palm and the hilt of the blade, and got a sort of weak grip.

A tingling began to run up my arm, mild but unmistakable. It was different from the tingling I was used to feeling when Spellbreaker intercepted some nasty that was aimed at me—it was sharper, for one thing, and it didn't stop. I kept hold of the weapon and the chain, and the tingling increased, becoming almost painful.

"Boss, what is it?"

"I don't know. There's something—"

Spellbreaker stirred in my hand, twisting against the smooth hilt of the dagger. I watched, fascinated, as it twisted and curled up and around, doing its snake imitation. I'd seen it before, at odd moments, and never understood why. Nor did I now; I just watched.

The links, already small, were becoming even smaller—they shrunk as I watched, which was creepy. At the same time, the end of the chain touched the blade, and then ran up its length in what was almost a caress. The other end, the end I was holding, was almost moving, though at first I didn't feel it through the tingling that was still running up my arm.

Spellbreaker's links kept getting smaller, almost vanishing entirely as distinct links, and it seemed to be getting longer overall. Was it, somehow, trying to rescue Teldra? If it was trying, did it have a chance?

I watched, fascinated. If the Jenoine had wanted to, it could have crushed my head without really trying, because between the death of Teldra and the strange things Spellbreaker was doing, I had forgotten it was there; but I guess it was distracted by Sethra and Aliera and Verra, the way I was distracted by—

—The links were entirely gone now, leaving Spellbreaker looking almost like a thin golden rope, and as I watched, it began to wrap itself around the hilt—it really was trying to save Teldra. I realized I was holding my breath.

It continued slithering around, more snakelike than ever, covering the hilt as if it were a hangersnake trying to strangle it; I had moved my hand to get out of the way, keeping contact with the blade only through the pommel. The tingling continued, and then I realized that the weapon was actually vibrating in Teldra's breast.

If there was, as I suspected, some sort of battle going on within the Morganti blade, then continuing to hold it was a bad idea.

I should let go.

I really should let go.

"Boss—"

"I can't. I just can't do it."

Well, if I couldn't get away from the fight, maybe I could help.

"Boss, do you know what you're doing?"

"Not a clue, Loiosh. Be ready to pull me out."

"I don't know if I'll be able to."

"I know."

There was a battle raging around me—gods and demigods and wizards and undead battling; but I might just as well have been in my old office, in the quiet space in the basement, where I used to perform witchcraft when I had nothing to worry about except how to find the guy whose leg I wanted to break, or how to get the most out of the new brothel I'd just opened.

I miss the days when I used to be nostalgic.

Lady Teldra was inside the dagger, somewhere, somehow, and I was going to go get her or . . . well, I was going to go get her.

I should have been surprised by how easily my awareness entered the chain, but even the action seemed normal, natural, inevitable— sending my consciousness spinning along inside Spellbreaker was the easiest thing in the world, and I could have done it at any time, if I'd ever thought to try. I was moving, flying even, through corridors of gold; endless corridors, with side paths and trails leading everywhere and nowhere, with a warm, almost hot breeze caressing my face.

I felt Teldra all around me, from everywhere—a sort of friendly reserve, giving the gold a reddish tint, and in that moment, I think I discovered her secret, I learned how she could manage to be so friendly to everyone who entered Morrolan's keep for whatever reason: She liked people. She just plain liked them. It was strange. My grandfather was like that, too, but I couldn't think of many others. Cawti, perhaps, when she let herself. It was strange, knowing someone like that; I guess it was why I had never been able to understand her, and why I always, even to myself, made ironic remarks about her courtesies, and tried to find hidden motives in everything she did; it is hard to be comfortable around someone who just likes you for no reason, when you've always—

No, there wasn't time for that. I needed to find her—find the center of the Teldra-ness amid all the confusion of gold and movement and corridors whipping past.

I called her name, but got no response, and yet I could feel her presence; her personality, which I'd had so much trouble defining, was overwhelming. But it was static, too: that is, she didn't seem to be feeling or doing anything, she just *was*.

As I hunted for her—moving, it seemed, in part because I desired it, and in part pushed along by some power of which I was only dimly aware—I began to notice, here and there, what seemed to be nondescript greyish threads hanging haphazardly among the corridors through which I sped. I grabbed one as I passed; it seemed the right thing to do. The thread came with me easily, and as I held it, Teldra seemed closer—the feeling of her presence stronger. I grabbed another, and another, one of them with my left hand. Okay, here and now, I had two good hands. Why not? Each time I saw a greyish strand hanging from a wall or ceiling, I grabbed it and held it, and if I missed one, I reached back without even looking and got it, too. I pulled the threads in and tied them together, holding them.

I was no longer aware of the tingling sensation that had been running up my arm, but now, instead, it seemed as if that entire tingle was filling my body, leaving me feeling strong, alert, even powerful; it was a heady sensation, but not an unpleasant one. I wondered if I should be worried.

"*Loiosh, should I be worried?*"

There was a long, long moment before he replied, which was unusual, and when the reply came, it was faint and distorted, as if from a distance. "*I don't know, Boss. I don't know where you are, or what you're doing, or . . . everything is heating up here, the Demon Goddess and Sethra and Aliera are . . . I'm scared, Boss.*"

When your familiar is scared, it's a good time for you to be scared, too.

But—

I didn't feel worried. The whole idea of having a familiar is to tell you when to be frightened by something that doesn't appear frightening—a familiar is your other self that watches to make sure nothing is being done to you while your attention is elsewhere, and this was just such a situation, but my instincts were telling me to push on, to keep searching for Teldra, to keep grabbing at whatever those strands of power were.

If Loiosh had told me to pull out, I would have, but he wasn't certain, which left me to make the decision. It was close. But one thought just wouldn't go away: If it were me in there, and Teldra had decided to look for me, she wouldn't have stopped while there was any hope left.

Okay, the decision was made: Press on.

A famous Iorich once said that the difficult part of being a Justicer was sounding one hundred percent when you felt fifty-one percent. I knew what he meant: I tried to put the doubt behind me so I could continue my psychic, or necromantic, or mystical journey through Spellbreaker, but it wasn't easy, because doubt is less easily dispelled than illusion, and with doubt come tentative half-measures—and nothing worthwhile has ever been accomplished by tentative half-measures.

There was a keen sense of traveling along with me, almost an ache for Teldra, but it was a distraction—as were my uncertainties about whether I was controlling or being controlled by the forces I was playing with, and my knowledge that, while I was sending my consciousness through the links of the strange artifact I called Spellbreaker, all the time the battle was going on around my physical body—but then, there wasn't a lot I could do to influence that anyway, was there? I couldn't do them any good, and it was pointless of them to have brought me to this place. If only I had—

If only I had—

Oh.

Maybe you've had it all figured out all along and have been waiting for me to catch on—those of you who have been following my path, walking beside me through sorceries, deaths, pain, betrayal, and wizardries beyond human comprehension—but believe me it is much easier to figure out when you are sitting back watching it unfold before you than when you have your awareness spinning through strange, mystical corridors while outside of you rages a battle in which the very gods are only holding their own. In any case, it was only at that moment that I understood what I was doing, what I was creating.

Half-remembered conversations, half-heard remarks, bits of folklore, years of observations without comprehension—so the Serioli had simply been telling me the simple, unvarnished truth in the most straightforward way it knew how; and that was why the Goddess had been so ambivalent; and that's how Pathfinder had saved Aliera's life—all came together into the explosive epiphany that I had been, all unknowing, doing just exactly what I should be doing.

Yes, now I understood.

And with that understanding came confidence, and with confidence came decision.

Teldra was gone, and yet not gone. She was there, but it was pointless to find her. What mattered were those greyish strands of power. What mattered was completing the transformation, that would save as much of Teldra as could be saved.

Fine, then.

By an act of will I stopped, and I summoned the greyish threads to me until I held all of them in my grasp—an instant it seemed, and I think it was. I wrapped them around my left wrist. The next one, and the next one. I had all the time in the world, so I could be careful and thorough, and I was; as careful as an Issola is of every nuance of tact; as thorough as a jhereg is at extracting every morsel of food from a corpse. I took my time, and did it right: pulling in the tiniest threads and securing them, making sure they were woven so close to me that we could never be separated; there was no longer a Spellbreaker, or a Lady Teldra, or a Morganti dagger, or even a Vlad; we were all something different now. The Jhereg? Heh. Let them come after me with their pathetic Morganti weapons. Just let them.

Almost as an afterthought, I repaired the trivial damage in my left arm, which had been repairing itself anyway. I both knew and felt that what I was wrapping the links around was, in fact, my soul. My conversation with Teldra about the nature of the soul came back to me with a sort of gentle irony; Teldra was like that. My own irony was harsher—maybe she'd exert some influence on me. I didn't think I'd mind. I wasn't seeing anything anymore, nor was I hearing anything, I was just being, and doing, and then I was done.

I came back to myself, to the real world around me, and found that I was still on one knee, next to Teldra's lifeless body. She lay with an arm up over her head, her eyes open, glassy, and sightless, her long hair all scattered about. She'd never have permitted her hair to look that way. Her mouth was open a little, in that moronic way you see from time to time on derelicts who gather in the evenings near Barlen's temple near Malek Circle. It was all wrong on Lady's Teldra's face. I looked away, and at what was in my right hand—a long Morganti dagger, with a hilt like a very fine golden chain. It fit my hand like an additional finger, like it should have been there all along, or maybe it had been there all along and I'd never been aware of it.

It?

Her. It was, after all, Lady Teldra.

I stood up and faced the Jenoine, which was moving at an impossible speed, fending off attacks from Sethra and Aliera and Verra—Aliera had some blood on her, and seemed both dazed and determined; the Goddess had grown larger, and her eyes flashed with hate. Sethra, like the Necromancer, who still hadn't moved, had no expression on her face at all, but moved in and out, looking for openings in the Jenoine's defenses—which were, in fact, rather formidable: there were lines of power flowing from its fingers, which formed glittering patterns in the air that left no room for anything to get past, but through which it could strike at will, lines that I knew must have been there all along, but which I could now see for the first time. Lines keeping Pathfinder and Iceflame, and Verra with the power she embodied just by being who she was, completely absorbed in coping, because to do otherwise would court destruction of those who wielded the Great Weapons, and permitting the wielder to be destroyed was something a Great Weapon would not permit, because beyond any practical considerations—far, far stronger than any practical considerations—there were bonds of love: Pathfinder loved Aliera, Iceflame loved Sethra. Blackwand loved Morrolan.

And Lady Teldra loved me.

The defenses the Jenoine had formed were, as I said, formidable, but the defenses were also, at the same time, laughable. Of course Iceflame and Pathfinder and Blackwand would be stopped by them; powerful as those weapons were, they had not been made for this. As I attacked the Jenoine's defensive spells I felt the same tingling I used to feel when Spellbreaker used to intercept something aimed at me. I cut through them as if they were paper.

The Jenoine felt its defenses fail. It turned around and, quick as a striking Issola, I thrust Lady Teldra up under its chin and into its head.

It roared and spasmed as if every muscle in its body had contracted at once, and then I felt rather than saw Iceflame and Pathfinder join the party, and a sense of power, energy, and well-being flooded through me, and I understood the reason for that now, too.

It collapsed into a heap at my feet; I felt as if I could take on all the Jenoine in the universe with one hand tied behind me. I heard myself laughing as I turned to face the remaining two, but at that moment, the Necromancer gave a cry and fell to her knees, and, just that quickly, they were gone, leaving only half the gods in the world, one very large dragon, and our little group standing on the spot of Adron's Disaster, next to Morrolan, who was dead, and his seneschal, who was more than dead.

Or perhaps less than dead.

The sudden silence was shattering; I basked in it, feeling as if I could emit sparks, and would if I weren't careful for those around me. It was so quiet, I could hear my companions breathing; I realized then that the Sea made no sound, not even ocean-type sounds.

"Doing all right, chum?"

"Grand, Boss. And Rocza is fine, too. And so are you, by the way, though I was worried there for a bit."

"Yeah, me too."

"I think I'm jealous, though."

"Bite me."

He did, but in the nicest possible way.

Sethra knelt next to the Necromancer, who stirred and shook her head as if to clear it—positively the most human thing I had ever seen her do.

"They broke the Necromancer's block, didn't they?"

"Brute force and desperation," said the Demon Goddess in her strange voice, made even stranger by the awful silence. "But for some reason, they released their link to the amorphia."

"So we won?" asked Sethra, sounding surprised.

Verra looked at Morrolan and Teldra lying on the ground, and nodded.

Aliera said, in the strangest voice I'd ever heard from her, "Daddy did it. Daddy took their link from them."

Sethra stared at her.

Aliera nodded and said, "I asked him to, and he did." Well, it was nice to know they were doing something while I was distracted.

Sethra looked out over the Sea and said, "Adron is out there?"

"Yes. I suspected he would be."

"Conscious? Aware?" said Sethra.

Aliera shrugged. I understood that shrug. "Consciousness" and "awareness" aren't always clear-cut concepts, as I had just learned. There were tears in Aliera's eyes. Well, there was plenty to cry about, I suppose, and there'd be more if we didn't get to work on Morrolan soon. I looked over to where the Jenoine had been, but there was no trace they had ever been there; the gods and even the dragon were gone as well. It was only Sethra and Aliera and the Necromancer and the Goddess and me; and Morrolan and what had been Teldra. Morrolan's sword had returned to his side, still gripped by his dead hand; I'm not sure when that happened.

"We need to get to work on Morrolan," said Aliera, her eyes still glistening.

Sethra stood up and nodded to her. "Yes," she said. "And quickly." She looked at Teldra's body, lying on the ground, then at the weapon in my hand, then at me.

"Well done, Vlad," she said.

Aliera, standing dazed and bloody behind her, but with a grim expression on her face, nodded. The Demon Goddess, however, had eyes only for the blade I carried.

Well, who could blame her? "You can put that thing away now," she said at last.

I looked into her eyes and chuckled. "Very well, my Goddess."

Verra scowled.

I cleaned her on the Jenoine's body—some customs must be observed, after all—then sheathed her, with some regret, my hand trailing over the smooth, gold hilt that had once been Spellbreaker. I was delighted to discover that sheathing her did not diminish the sense of her personality.

I watched Verra, who was looking back at me, but she had nothing more to say. With an aimless gesture of farewell, she turned into shimmering sparks and was gone. Sethra, meanwhile, had lifted Morrolan in her arms.

"Come, stand next to me," she said.

Aliera looked out over the Sea, I suppose saying farewell to her father. Then Aliera, the Necromancer, and I took positions next to Sethra, and then we were gone from that place, and we were once more in the heart of Dzur Mountain.

17

Taking One's Leave of Friends

They laid Morrolan on a couch, and Aliera and the Necromancer began working on him. I watched for a while, then turned to Sethra. "So we won."

She nodded. "Yes, I'd call this a victory. They wanted to establish their own link to amorphia. That is, a permanent link, on our world, with which to challenge us. They failed to do so. And we destroyed two of them, which is no small feat."

"Good."

Sethra shook her head and murmured, "Adron."

"Yes."

"It's hard to believe. Sentience is, well, I don't know."

"Yeah, sentience is a strange thing, isn't it?"

She glanced up at me, catching my tone of voice, and said, "I shall miss her."

"Yes," I said. Then, "Did you know?"

Her eyes widened. "You mean, what was going to happen?"

"Yes. Teldra, the weapon—all of it."

"No, Vlad. I had no idea. If I'd had any idea, I should never have—no, I didn't know."

"What was it you yelled to me, in the middle of it all?"

She gave me an ironic smile. "You don't want to know."

"Probably not, Sethra, but tell me anyway."

"I told you to watch out for Teldra. It looked like she was contemplating doing something foolish."

"Yeah, I guess she was."

"But I suppose it is best for all of us that it turned out that way."

"All of us, except for Lady Teldra."

"Yes. Well, you are now a member of a rather exclusive club, Vlad. You are one of those the gods have cause to fear. Congratulations to you, and to Godslayer."

"Lady Teldra," I corrected her gently.

She shrugged. "As you prefer."

I touched the hilt and it was almost as if I could feel her fingers touching mine. I said, "Do you suppose the Jenoine knew?"

"No," said Sethra. "They would never have put the weapon into your hands if they had suspected. They wanted you to kill Verra, just as they said."

"You mean, that was it? They really expected me to just go and kill her?"

"Yes, which would have allowed them access to the Lesser Sea, where they could have established their own link—that is, a permanent one, with, in essence, their own Orb. It would have been a powerful blow against us. Although, knowing that Adron is still, in a sense, in there, I don't know what effect that would have had."

I shook my head. "But Sethra, all kidding aside, I was never going to kill Verra. I mean, I never even thought seriously about it."

"Yes, I know."

"It doesn't make sense."

"It doesn't make sense to us, Vlad."

"If they have so little understanding of us, Sethra, I'm not sure how worried about them we should be."

"Whatever their understanding, they have a great deal of power."

"But still. With such intricate plans, how can they be that far off?"

"They don't understand us, that's all. They never have. Talk to Verra sometime; that's been their flaw from the beginning."

"I don't think the Demon Goddess wants to have a lot to do with me these days. And that's fine with me."

"Yes, I suppose it is. And Vlad—"

"Yes?"

"Should I happen not to be around when Lady Teldra wakes up, you will not forget to give her my regards?"

"Wakes up? What do you mean?"

She smiled. "I think I'd rather not tell you."

Damn her.

Aliera, still bloody and dazed-looking, stumbled over and sat down next to us. I looked over at Morrolan, and saw the gentle rise and fall of his chest.

I nodded to Aliera. "Congratulations," I said.

She nodded and closed her eyes.

Sethra said, "Good. Now let's see to you." Aliera was, evidently, too exhausted to argue; she struggled to her feet, and accompanied Sethra out of the room.

The Necromancer walked over from Morrolan's side and sat down opposite me. We looked at each other for a while, and then she said, "I can bring you wherever you'd like."

"Thanks," I said. I looked over at Morrolan. "Who gets to tell him about Teldra?"

"Sethra, I should imagine."

"Lucky Sethra."

"What are you going to do?"

"Same thing I've been doing."

"You have rather less to fear from the Jhereg now—at least, Morganti weapons shouldn't frighten you as much."

"That's true. But I've recovered a bit from the bravado I was feeling, uh, earlier. I'd just as soon not give them a chance."

She nodded. "Where then?"

"Perhaps I'll visit my grandfather."

"I'm certain he'd like that."

"Or else I'll head East."

"Your ancestral homeland?"

"Yes. I was there once before, and rather liked it. Maybe I'll organize a defense there, in case Sethra the Younger decides to try to conquer it. I beat her once, maybe I can beat her again."

She studied me for a little. "When did this idea come to you?" she said at last.

I shrugged. "I don't know. Just now, I guess, while I was talking to you. Why?"

"It sounds a little public-spirited for you, Vlad."

"Maybe it's Lady Teldra's influence," I said ironically.

"That's what I was thinking," she said, without irony.

"Oh," I said. "Well, maybe I'll do something else."

"Is Lady Teldra's influence that bad a thing?"

I thought about that. "No, I suppose not."

"I shall miss her," said the Necromancer. "And you," she added.

I almost made an ironic remark about that, just out of reflex, but I refrained.

Maybe my reflexes were changing, but I didn't care to examine them too closely to find out.

I said, "Has anything exciting been happening in Adrilankha lately?"

She smiled a little. "I'm afraid I don't keep up on such matters."

I nodded. "All right," I said, deciding suddenly. "Here's what I'm going to do. I'm bloody well going into Adrilankha, and I'm bloody well going to have a meal at Valabar's, and if the Jhereg find me, fine, and if they don't, I'll figure out what I'm going to do next while I eat. If there's one thing I've missed—"

There was a soft moan from the couch. As I looked, Morrolan's eyes fluttered open. His mouth opened and he tried to speak, but couldn't manage.

"We won," I told him. "It wasn't pretty, but we won."

No, I wasn't going to be the one to tell him.

"Boss, your stomach is going to be the death of us all."

"Very probably, chum. But don't complain, you get the scraps."

"Oh, I'm not complaining. Just observing." Rocza shifted on my other shoulder; I imagine Loiosh had given her a hint of what was coming. For a wild jhereg, it hadn't taken her long to develop a taste for civilized food.

"All right," I told the Necromancer. "Let's go, then."

"Now? You don't wish to wait for Sethra and Aliera?"

"Please give them my farewell."

"You sure, Boss? Right now?"

"I don't want to be here anymore."

The Necromancer stood up. I said, "Can you put me right in front of their door?"

"Easily," she said.

"Good, then."

"What are you going to have?"

"I don't know, but it will start and end with klava."

Morrolan cleared his throat, tried to speak, then exhaled loudly and lay back.

"I'm sorry," I told him.

He looked at me, eyebrows raised.

I shook my head. The Necromancer put her hand on my shoulder, I put my hand on Lady Teldra. Loiosh and Rocza took their positions, and Dzur Mountain was gone, and I was outdoors, facing the familiar sight of Valabar's, which, of all things, hadn't changed a bit. I smelled onions and garlic and broiling kethna. There were no assassins waiting to kill me, at least yet.

I removed my amulets from their box and put them back on, just out of reflex, and stepped inside.

BIO

What would you like to know about me, assuming that you care? My full name is Steven Karl Zoltán Brust. I was born in 1955, so I'm forty-two at the time of this writing, and I have a big bald spot which I cover up with a hat, but I was wearing the hat before I developed the bald spot so it doesn't really count. I live in Minneapolis, Minnesota, except that I spent this last winter in Arizona, and if you don't know why, you haven't spent a winter in Minnesota.

I play drums, guitar, banjo, and Middle Eastern percussion, and I've written some songs, and I have produced a solo record called *A Rose for Iconoclastes*; if you want information on the record you can get it by sending E-mail to UncleHugo@aol.com, and if you don't understand the title you need to read more Roger Zelazny.

In addition to the abovementioned Zelazny, my heroes are: Alexandre Dumas, Mark Twain, Leon Trotsky, Dorothy Parker, Mickey Hart, and Mike Caro. If you don't recognize one or more of these names, it doesn't make you a bad person.

I have a Strapping Son named Corwin and three Charming Daughters named Aliera, Carolyn, and Toni. I live with my Lovely Associate, Liz Cooper, in a beautiful house in a crummy neighborhood. I have a dog named Miska and a double-yellow-headed Amazon parrot named John Henry Holliday, and if you don't know his nickname you should see Val Kilmer in *Tombstone*.

Liz has a cat named Rogue and an African Grey parrot named Loiosh, and if you don't know where the name "Loiosh" comes from, why are you even reading this bio?

My favorite games are Texas Hold 'Em and Stud hi-lo/8. If you don't know what those are, I'd be glad to teach you.

Steven Brust
Lake Havasu City, Arizona
February 1998